A VAST, SCALY HEAD SPEARED OUT OF THE GLOOM

The gateman was a reptilian thing, tyrannosaur-sized. The thing subsisted on the flesh of brain donors and Helga's enemies. As a defense against invasion, it was primitive and crude, but devastatingly effective.

Storm had rehearsed this confrontation for years.

While backing toward his goal he set his glove to short in a single burst of power. The great head, the scimitar teeth came down...

Storm hurled himself aside, gloved hand reaching back like an eagle's talons. For an instant his fingers touched the moist soft flesh inside a gargantuan nostril. The glove blew. Charred flesh putrified the air. The beast flung itself back screaming...

SHADOWLINE

THE STARFISHERS TRILOGY
VOLUME 1

Glen Cook

WARNER BOOKS

A Warner Communications Company

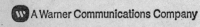

I dedicate this to Richard Wagner.

SHADOWLINE

Book One
ROPE

**Who twists the rope that dangles
from the gibbet?**

One: 3052 AD

Who am I? What am I?

I am the bastard child of the Shadowline. That jagged rift of sun-broiled stone was my third parent.

You cannot begin to understand me, or the Shadowline, without knowing my father. And to know Gneaus Julius Storm you have to know our family, in all its convolute interpersonal relationships and history. To know our family. . . .

There is no end to this. The ripples spread. And the story, which has the Shadowline and myself at one end, is an immensely long river. It received the waters of scores of apparently insignificant tributary events.

Focusing the lens at its narrowest, my father and Cassius (Colonel Walters) were the men who shaped me most. This is their story. It is also the story of the men whose stamp upon *them* ultimately shaped their stamp upon me.

—Masato Igarashi Storm

11

Two: 3031 AD

Deep in the Fortress of Iron, in the iron gloom of his study, Gneaus Storm slouched in a fat, deep chair. His chin rested on his chest. His good eye was closed. Long grey hair cascaded down over his tired face.

The flames in the nearest fireplace leapt and swirled in an endless morisco. Light and shadow played out sinister dramas over priceless carpeting hand-loomed in Old Earth's ancient orient. The shades of might-have-been played tag among the darkwood beams supporting the stone ceiling.

Storm's study was a stronghold within the greater Fortress. It was the citadel of his soul, the bastion of his heart. Its walls were lined with shelves of rare editions. A flotilla of tables bore both his collectibles and papers belonging to his staff. The occasional silent clerk came and went, updating a report before one of the chairs.

Two Shetland-sized mutant Alsatians prowled the room, sniffing shadows. One rumbled softly deep in its throat. The hunt for an enemy never ended.

Nor was it ever successful. Storm's enemies did not hazard his planetoid home.

A black creature of falcon size flapped into the study. It landed clumsily in front of Storm. Papers scattered, frightening it. An aura of shadow surrounded it momentarily, masking its toy pterodactyl body.

It was a ravenshrike, a nocturnal flying lizard from the swamps of The Broken Wings. Its dark umbra was a psionically generated form of protective coloration.

The ravenshrike cocked one red night eye at its mate, nesting in a rock fissure behind Storm. It stared at its master with the other.

12

Storm did not respond.

The ravenshrike waited.

Gneaus Julius Storm pictured himself as a man on the downhill side of life, coasting toward its end. He was nearly two hundred years old. The ultimate in medical and rejuvenation technology kept him physically forty-five, but doctors and machines could do nothing to refresh his spirit.

One finger marked his place in an old holy book. It had fallen shut when he had drifted off. "A time to be born and a time to die. . . ."

A youth wearing Navy blacks slipped into the room. He was short and slight, and stood as stiff as a spear. Though he had visited the study countless times, his oriental inscrutability gave way to an expression of awe.

So many luxuries and treasures, Mouse thought. *Are they anything more than Death, hidden behind a mask of hammered gold?*

And of his father he thought, *He looks so tired. Why can't they leave him alone?*

They could not. Not while Richard Hawksblood lived. They did not dare. So someday, as all mercenaries seemed to do, Gneaus Storm would find his last battlefield and his death-without-resurrection.

Storm's tired face rose. It remained square-jawed and strong. Grey hair stirred in a vagrant current from an air vent.

Mouse left quietly, yielding to a moment of deep sadness. His feelings for his father bordered on reverence. He ached because his father was boxed in and hurting.

He went looking for Colonel Walters.

Storm's good eye opened. Grey as his hair, it surveyed the heart of his stateless kingdom. He did not see a golden death mask. He saw a mirror that reflected the secret Storm.

His study contained more than books. One wall boasted

13

a weapons collection, Sumerian bronze standing beside the latest stressglass multi-purpose infantry small arms. Lighted cabinets contained rare china, cut crystal, and silver services. Others contained ancient Wedgwood. Still more held a fortune in old coins within their velvet-lined drawers.

He was intrigued by the ebb and flow of history. He took comfort in surrounding himself with the wrack it left in passing.

He could not himself escape into yesterday. Time slipped through the fingers like old water.

A gust from the cranky air system riffled papers. The banners overhead stirred with the passage of ghosts. Some were old. One had followed the Black Prince to Navarette. Another had fallen at the high-water mark of the charge up Little Round Top. But most represented milemarks in Storm's own career.

Six were identical titan-cloth squares hanging all in a line. Upon them a golden hawk struck left to right down a fall of scarlet raindrops, all on a field of sable. They were dull, unimaginative things compared to the Plantagenet, yet they celebrated the mountaintop days of Storm's Iron Legion.

He had wrested them from his own Henry of Trastamara, Richard Hawksblood, and each victory had given him as little satisfaction as Edward had extracted from Pedro the Cruel.

Richard Hawksblood was the acknowledged master of the mercenary art.

Hawksblood had five Legion banners in a collection of his own. Three times they had fought to a draw.

Storm and Hawksblood were the best of the mercenary captain-kings, the princes of private war the media called "The Robber Barons of the Thirty-First Century." For a decade they had been fighting one another exclusively.

Only Storm and his talented staff could beat Hawksblood. Only Hawksblood had the genius to withstand the Iron Legion.

Hawksblood had caused Storm's bleak mood. His Intelligence people said Richard was considering a commission on Blackworld.

"Let them roast," he muttered. "I'm tired."

But he would fight again. If not this time, then the next. Richard would accept a commission. His potential victim would know that his only chance of salvation was the Iron Legion. He would be a hard man who had clawed his way to the top among a hard breed. He would be accustomed to using mercenaries and assassins. He would look for ways to twist Storm's arm. And he would find them, and apply them relentlessly.

Storm had been through it all before.

He smelled it coming again.

A personal matter had taken him to Corporation Zone, on Old Earth, last month. He had made the party rounds, refreshing his contacts. A couple of middle-management types had approached him, plying him with tenuous hypotheses.

Blackworlders clearly lacked polish. Those apprentice Machiavellis had been obvious and unimpressive, except in their hardness. But their master? Their employer was Blake Mining and Metals Corporation of Edgeward City on Blackworld, they told him blandly.

Gneaus Julius Storm was a powerful man. His private army was better trained, motivated, and equipped than Confederation's remarkable Marines. But his Iron Legion was not just a band of freebooters. It was a diversified holding company with minority interests in scores of major corporations. It did not just fight and live high for a while on its take. Its investments were the long-term security of its people.

The Fortress of Iron stretched tentacles in a thousand directions, though in the world of business and finance it

15

was not a major power. Its interests could be manipulated by anyone with the money and desire.

That was one lever the giants used to get their way.

In the past they had manipulated his personal conflicts with Richard Hawkblood, playing to his vanity and hatred. But he had outgrown his susceptibility to emotional extortion.

"I'll be something unique this time," he whispered.

Vainly, he strove to think of a way to outmaneuver someone he did not yet know, someone whose intentions were not yet clear.

He ignored the flying lizard. It waited patiently, accustomed to his brooding way.

Storm took an ancient clarinet from a case lying beside his chair. He examined the reed, wet it. He began playing a piece not five men alive could have recognized.

He had come across the sheet music in a junk shop during his Old Earth visit. The title, "Stranger on the Shore," had caught his imagination. It fit so well. He felt like a stranger on the shore of time, born a millennium and a half out of his natural era. He belonged more properly to the age of Knollys and Hawkwood.

The lonely, haunting melody set his spirit free. Even with his family, with friends, or in crowds, Gneaus Storm felt set apart, outside. He was comfortable only when sequestered here in his study, surrounded by the *things* with which he had constructed a stronghold of the soul.

Yet he could not be without people. He had to have them there, in the Fortress, potentially available, or he felt even more alone.

His clarinet never left his side. It was a fetish, an amulet with miraculous powers. He treasured it more than the closest member of his staff. Paired with the other talisman he always bore, an ancient handgun, it held the long night of the soul at bay.

Gloomy. Young-old. Devoted to the ancient, the rare,

the forgotten. Cursed with a power he no longer wanted. That was a first approximation of Gneaus Julius Storm.

The power was like some mythological cloak that could not be shed. The more he tried to slough it, the tighter it clung and the heavier it grew. There were just two ways to shed it forever.

Each required a death. One was his own. The other was Richard Hawksblood's.

Once, Hawksblood's death had been his life's goal. A century of futility had passed. It no longer seemed to matter as much.

Storm's heaven, if ever he attained it, would be a quiet, scholarly place that had an opening for a knowledgeable amateur antiquarian.

The ravenshrike spread its wings momentarily.

Three: 3052 AD

Can we understand a man without knowing his enemies? Can we know yin without knowing yang? My father would say no. He would say if you want to see new vistas of Truth, go question the man who wants to kill you.

A man lives. When he is young he has more friends than he can count. He ages. The circle narrows. It turns inward, becoming more closed. We spend our middle and later years doing the same things with the same few friends. Seldom do we admit new faces to the clique.

But we never stop making enemies.

They are like dragon's teeth flung wildly about us as we trudge along the paths of our lives. They spring up everywhere, unwanted, unexpected, sometimes unseen and unknown. Sometimes we make or inherit them simply by being who or what we are.

My father was an old, old man. He was his father's son.

His enemies were legion. He never knew how many and who they were.

—Masato Igarashi Storm

Four: 2844 AD

The building was high and huge and greenhouse-hot. The humidity and stench were punishing. The polarized glassteel roof had been set to allow the maximum passage of sunlight. The air conditioning was off. The buckets of night earth had not been removed from the breeding stalls.

Norbon w'Deeth leaned on a slick brass rail, scanning the enclosed acres below the observation platform.

Movable partitions divided the floor into hundreds of tiny cubicles rowed back to back and facing narrow passageways. Each cubicle contained an attractive female. There were so many of them that their breathing and little movements kept the air alive with a restless susurrus.

Deeth was frightened but curious. He had not expected the breeding pens to be so huge.

His father's hand touched his shoulder lightly, withdrew to flutter in his interrogation of his breeding master. The elder Norbon carried half a conversation with his hands.

"How can they refuse? Rhafu, they're just animals."

Deeth's thoughts echoed his father's. The Norbon Head could not be wrong. Rhafu had to be mistaken. Breeding and feeding were the only things that interested animals.

"You don't understand, sir." Old Rhafu's tone betrayed stress. Even Deeth sensed his frustration at his inability to impress the Norbon with the gravity of the situation. "It's not entirely that they're refusing, either. They're just not interested. It's the boars, sir. If it were just the sows

18

the boars would take them whether or not they were willing."

Deeth looked up at Rhafu. He was fond of the old man. Rhafu was the kind of man he wished his father were. He was the old adventurer every boy hoped to become.

The responsibilities of a Family Head left little time for close relationships. Deeth's father was a remote, often harried man. He seldom gave his son the attention he craved.

Rhafu was a rogue full of stories about an exciting past. He proudly wore scars won on the human worlds. And he had time to share his stories with a boy.

Deeth was determined to emulate Rhafu. He would have his own adventures before his father passed the family into his hands. His raidships would plunder Terra, Toke, and Ulant. He would return with his own treasury of stories, wealth, and honorable scars.

It was just a daydream. At seven he already knew that heirs-apparent never risked themselves in the field. Adventures were for younger sons seeking an independent fortune, for daughters unable to make beneficial alliances, and for possessionless men like Rhafu. His own inescapable fate was to become a merchant prince like his father, far removed from the more brutal means of accumulating wealth. The only dangers he would face would be those of inter-Family intrigues over markets, resources, and power.

"Did you try drugs?" his father asked. Deeth yanked himself back to the here and now. He was supposed to be learning. His father would smack him a good one if his daydreaming became obvious.

"Of course. Brood sows are always drugged. It makes them receptive and keeps their intellection to a minimum."

Rhafu was exasperated. His employer had not visited Prefactlas Station for years. Moreover, the man confessed that he knew nothing about the practical aspects of slave breeding. Fate had brought him here in the midst of a crisis, and he persisted in asking questions which cast doubt on the competence of the professionals on the scene.

"We experimented with aphrodisiacs. We didn't have much luck. We got more response when we butchered a few boars for not performing, but when we watched them closer we saw they were withdrawing before ejaculation. Sir, you're looking in the wrong place for answers. Go poke around outside the station boundary. The animals wouldn't refuse if they weren't under some external influence."

"Wild ones?" The Norbon shrugged, dismissing the idea. "What about artificial insemination? We don't dare get behind. We've got contracts to meet."

This was why the Norbon was in an unreasonable mood. The crisis threatened the growth of the Norbon profit curve.

Deeth turned back to the pens. Funny. The animals looked so much like Sangaree. But they were filthy. They stank.

Rhafu said some of the wild ones were different, that they cared for themselves as well as did people. And the ones the Family kept at home, at the manor, were clean and efficient and indistinguishable from real people.

He spotted a sow that looked like his cousin Marjo. What would happen if a Sangaree woman got mixed in with the animals? Could anyone pick her out? Aliens like the Toke and Ulantonid were easy, but these humans could pass as people.

"Yes. Of course. But we're not set up to handle it on the necessary scale. We've never had to do it. I've had instruments and equipment on order since the trouble started."

"You haven't got anything you can make do with?" Deeth's father sounded peevish. He became irritable when

20

the business ran rocky. "There's a fortune in the Osirian orders, and barely time to push them through the fast-growth labs. Rhafu, I can't default on a full-spectrum order. I won't. I refuse."

Deeth smiled at a dull-eyed sow who was watching him half-curiously. He made a small, barely understood obscene gesture he had picked up at school.

"Ouch!"

Having disciplined his son, the Norbon turned to Rhafu as though nothing had happened. Deeth rubbed the sting away. His father abhorred the thought of coupling with livestock. To him that was the ultimate perversion, though the practice was common. The Sexon Family maintained a harem of specially bred exotics.

"Thirty units for the first shipment," Rhafu said thoughtfully. "I think I can manage that. I might damage a few head forcing it, though."

"Do what you have to."

"I hate to injure prime stock, sir. But there'll be no production otherwise. We've had to be alert to prevent self-induced abortion."

"That bad? It's really that bad?" Pained surprise flashed across the usually expressionless features of the Norbon. "That does it. You have my complete sanction. Do what's necessary. These contracts are worth the risk. They're going to generate follow-ups. The Osirian market is wide open. Fresh. Untouched. The native princes are total despots. Completely sybaritic and self-indulgent. It's one of the human First Expansion worlds gone feral. They've devolved socially and technologically to a feudal level."

Rhafu nodded. Like most Sangaree with field experience, he had a solid background in human social and cultural history.

The elder Norbon stared into the pens that were the

cornerstone of the Family wealth. "Rhafu, Osiris is the Norbon Wholar. Help me exploit it the way a Great House should."

Wholar. That's the legendary one, Deeth thought. The bonanza. The bottomless pot of gold. The world so big and wild and rich that it took five Families to exploit it, the world that had made the consortium Families first among the Sangaree.

Deeth was not sure he wanted an El Dorado for the Norbon. Too much work for him when he became Head. And he would have to socialize with those snobbish Krimnins and Sexons and Masons. Unless he could devour the dream and make the Norbon the richest Family of all. Then he would be First Family Head, could do as he pleased, and would not have to worry about getting along.

"It's outside trouble, I swear it," Rhafu said. "Sir, there's something coming on. Even the trainees in Isolation are infected. They've been complaining all week. Station master tells me it's the same everywhere. Agriculture caught some boar pickers trying to fire the sithlac fields."

"Omens and signs, Rhafu? You're superstitious? *They* are the ones who need the supernatural. It's got to be their water. Or feed."

"No. I've checked. Complete chemical analysis. Everything is exactly what it should be. I tell you, something's happening and they know it. I've seen it before, remember. On Copper Island."

Deeth became interested again. Rhafu had come to the Norbon from the Dathegon, whose station had been on Copper Island. No one had told him why. "What happened, Rhafu?"

The breeding master glanced at his employer. The Norbon frowned, but nodded.

"Slaves rising, Deeth. Because of sloppy security. The

field animals came in contact with wild ones. Pretty soon they rebelled. Some of us saw it coming. We tried to warn the station master. He wouldn't listen. Those of us who survived work for your father now. The Dathegon never recovered."

"Oh."

"And you think that could happen here?" Deeth's father demanded.

"Not necessarily. Our security is better. Our station master served in human space. He knows what the animals can do when they work together. I'm just telling you what it looks like, hoping you'll take steps. We'll want to hold down our losses."

Rhafu was full of the curious ambivalence of Sangaree who had served in human space. Individuals and small groups he called animals. Larger bodies he elevated to slave status. When he mentioned humanity outside Sangaree dominion he simply called them humans, degrading them very little. His own discriminations reflected those of his species as to the race they exploited.

"If we let it go much longer we'll have to slaughter our best stock to stop it."

"Rhafu," Deeth asked, "what happened to the animals on Copper Island?"

"The Prefactlas Heads voted plagues."

"Oh." Deeth tried not to care about dead animals. Feeling came anyway. He was not old enough to have hardened. If only they did not look so much like real people. . . .

"I'll think about what you've told me, Rhafu." The Norbon's hand settled onto Deeth's shoulder again. "Department Heads meeting in the morning. We'll determine a policy then. Come, Deeth."

They inspected the sithlac in its vast, hermetically sealed greenhouse. The crop was sprouting. In time the virally infected germ plasm of the grain would be refined to produce stardust, the most addictive and deadly narcotic ever to plague humankind.

Stardust addicts did not survive long, but while they did they provided their Sangaree suppliers with a guaranteed income.

Sithlac was the base of wealth for many of the smaller Families. It underpinned the economy of the race. And it was one of the roots of their belief in the essential animalness of humanity. No true sentient would willingly subject itself to such a degrading, slow, painful form of suicide.

Deeth fidgeted, bored, scarcely hearing his father's remarks. He was indifferent to the security that a sound, conservative agricultural program represented. He was too young to comprehend adult needs. He preferred the risk and romance of a Rhafu-like life to the security of drug production.

Rhafu had not been much older than he was now when he had served as a gunner's helper during a raid into the Ulant sphere.

Raiding was the only way possessionless Sangaree had to accumulate the wealth needed to establish a Family. Financially troubled Families sometimes raided when they needed a quick cash flow. Most Sangaree heroes and historical figures came out of the raiding.

A conservative, the Norbon possessed no raidships. His transports were lightly armed so his ships' masters would not be tempted to indulge in free-lance piracy.

The Norbon were a "made" Family. They were solid in pleasure slaves and stardust. That their original fortune had been made raiding was irrelevant. Money, as it aged, always became more conservative and respectable.

Deeth reaffirmed his intention of building raiders when he became Head. Everybody was saying that the human and Ulantonid spheres were going to collide soon. That might mean war. Alien races went to their guns when living space and resources were at stake. The period of adjustment and accommodation would be a raidmaster's godsend.

Norbon w'Deeth, Scourge of the Spaceways, was slammed back to reality by the impact of his father's hand. "Deeth! Wake up, boy! Time to go back to the greathouse. Your mother wants us to get ready."

Deeth took his father's hand and allowed himself to be led from the dome. He was not pleased about going. Even prosaic sithlac fields were preferable to parties.

His mother had one planned for that evening. Everyone who was anyone among the Prefactlas Families would be there—including a few fellow heirs-apparent who could be counted on to start a squabble when their elders were not around. He might have to take a beating in defense of Family honor.

He understood that his mother felt obligated to have these affairs. They helped reduce friction between the Families. But why couldn't he stay in his suite and view his books about the great raiders and sales agents? Or even just study?

He was not going to marry a woman who threw parties. They were boring. The adults got staggering around drunk and bellicose, or syrupy, pulling him onto their laps and telling him what a wonderful little boy he was, repelling him with their alcohol-laden breath.

He would never drink, either. A raidmaster had to keep a clear head.

Five: 3052 AD

My father once said that people are a lot like billiard balls and gas molecules. They collide with one another randomly, imparting unexpected angles of momentum. A secondary impact can cause a tertiary, and so forth. With people it's usually impossible to determine an initiator because human relationships try to ignore the laws of thermodynamics. In the case of the Shadowline, though, we can trace everything to a man called Frog.

My father said Frog was like a screaming cue ball on the break. The people-balls were all on the table. Frog's impact set them flying from bank to bank.

My father never met Frog. It's doubtful that Frog ever heard of my father. So it goes sometimes.

—Masato Igarashi Storm

Six: 3007 AD

BLACKWORLD (Reference: *Morgan's New Revised Catalogue of Stars, Planets, Astrogational Benchmarks, and Spatial Phenomena,* edition of 3007): Sole planet of white dwarf A257-23. Uniface body. Unique in that it is the only such planet colonized by mankind. A small population houses itself in seven domed cities, each essentially a corporate state. Economically important as a transport nexus and rich source of power metals. Major industry, mining. Major export, rare elements. Population, chiefly of negroid stock, of First Expansion origins. The name, however, comes from the fact that life is confined to Darkside. Major tourist attraction, the Thunder Mountains on the western terminator, where slight perturbations in the slow planetary rotation result in tremendous tectonic activity due to heat expansion and contraction.

Blackworld as a reference-book entry was hardly an eyebrow-raiser. Nothing more than a note to make people wonder why anyone would live there.

It was a hell of a world. Even the natives sometimes wondered why anybody lived there.

Or so Frog thought as he cursed heaven and hell and slammed his portside tracks into reverse.

"Goddamned heat erosion in the friggin' Whitlandsund now," he muttered, and with his free hand returned the gesture of the obelisk/landmark he called Big Dick.

He had become lax. He had been daydreaming down a familiar route. He had aligned Big Dick wrong and drifted into terrain not recharted since last the sun had shoved a blazing finger into the pass.

Luckily, he had been in no hurry. The first sliding crunch under the starboard lead track had alerted him. Quick braking and a little rocking pulled the tractor out.

He heaved a sigh of relief.

There wasn't much real danger this side of the Edge of the World. Other tractors could reach him in the darkness.

He was sweating anyway. For him it did not matter where the accident happened. His finances allowed no margin for error. One screw-up and he was as good as dead.

There was no excuse for what had happened, Brightside or Dark. He was angry. "You don't get old making mistakes, idiot," he snarled at the image reflected in the visual plate in front of him.

Frog was old. Nobody knew just how old, and he wasn't telling, but there were men in Edgeward who had heard him spin tavern tales of his father's adventures with the

Devil's Guard, and the Guard had folded a century ago, right after the Ulantonid War. The conservatives figured him for his early seventies. He had been the town character for as long as anyone could remember.

Frog was the last of a breed that had begun disappearing when postwar resumption of commerce had created a huge demand for Blackworld metals. The need for efficiency had made the appearance of big exploitation corporation inevitable. Frog was Edgeward City's only surviving independent prospector.

In the old days, while the Blakes had been on the rise, he had faced more danger in Edgeward itself than he had Brightside. The consolidation of Blake Mining and Metals had not been a gentle process. Now his competition was so insubstantial that the Corporation ignored it. Blake helped keep him rolling, in fact, the way historical societies keep old homes standing. He was a piece of yesterday to show off to out-of-towners.

Frog did not care. He just lived on, cursing everyone in general and Blake in particular, and kept doing what he knew best.

He was the finest tractor hog ever to work the Shadowline. And they damned well knew it.

Still, making it as a loner in a corporate age was difficult and dangerous. Blake had long since squatted on every easily reached pool and deposit Brightside. To make his hauls Frog had to do a long run up the Shadowline, three days or more out, then make little exploratory dashes into sunlight till he found something worthwhile. He would fill his tanks, turn around, and claw his way back home. Usually he brought in just enough to finance maintenance, a little beer, and his next trip out.

If asked he could not have explained why he went on. Life just seemed to pull him along, a ritual of repetitive days and nights that at least afforded him the security of null-change.

Frog eased around the heat erosion on ground that had never been out of shadow, moved a few kilometers forward, then turned into a side canyon where Brightside gases collected and froze into snows. He met an outbound Blake convoy. They greeted him with flashing running lights. He responded, and with no real feeling muttered, "Sons of bitches."

They were just tractor hogs themselves. They did not make policy.

He had to hand load the snow he would ionize in his heat-exchange system. He had to save credit where he could. So what if Corporation tractors used automatic loaders? He had his freedom. He had that little extra credit at boozing time. A loading fee would have creamed it off his narrow profit margin.

When he finished shoveling he decided to power down and sleep. He was not as young as he used to be. He could not do the Thunder Mountains and the sprints to the Shadowline in one haul anymore.

Day was a fiction Blackworlders adjusted to their personal rhythms. Frog's came quickly. He seldom wasted time meeting the demands of his flesh. He wanted that time to meet the demands of his soul, though he could not identify them as such. He knew when he was content. He knew when he was not. Getting things accomplished led to the former. Discontent and impatience arose when he had to waste time sleeping or eating. Or when he had to deal with other people.

He was a born misanthrope. He knew few people that he liked. Most were selfish, rude, and boring. That he might fit a similar mold himself he accepted. He did others the courtesy of not intruding on their lives.

In truth, though he could admit it only in the dark hours, when he could not sleep, he was frightened of people. He simply did not know how to relate.

Women terrified him. He did not comprehend them at

29

all. But no matter. He was what he was, was too old to change, and was content with himself more often than not. To have made an accommodation with the universe, no matter how bizarre, seemed a worthy accomplishment.

His rig was small and antiquated. It was a flat, jointed monstrosity two hundred meters long. Every working arm, sensor housing, antenna, and field-projector grid had a mirror finish. There were scores. They made the machine look like some huge, fantastically complicated alien milli-pede. It was divided into articulated sections, each of which had its own engines. Power and control came from Frog's command section. All but that command unit were transport and working slaves that could be abandoned if necessary.

Once, Frog had been forced to drop a slave. His com-puter had erred. It had not kept the tracks of his tail slave locked into the path of those ahead. He had howled and cursed like a man who had just lost his first-born baby.

The abandoned section was now a slag-heap landmark far out the Shadowline. Blake respected it as the tacit benchmark delineating the frontier between its own and Frog's territory. Frog made a point of looking it over every trip out.

No dropped slave lasted long Brightside. That old devil sun rendered them down quick. He studied his lost child to remind himself what became of the careless.

His rig had been designed to operate in sustained tem-peratures which often exceeded 2000°K. Its cooling sys-tems were the most ingenious ever devised. A thick skin of flexible molybdenum/ceramic sponge mounted on a honeycomb-network radiator frame of molybdenum-base alloy shielded the crawler's guts. High-pressure coolants circulated through the skin sponge.

Over the mirrored surface of the skin, when the crawler hit daylight, would lie the first line of protection, the magnetic screens. Ionized gases would circulate beneath them. A molecular sorter would vent a thin stream of the highest energy particles aft. The solar wind would blow the ions over Darkside where they would freeze out and maybe someday ride a crawler Brightside once again.

A crawler in sunlight, when viewed from sunward through the proper filters, looked like a long, low, coruscating comet. The rig itself remained completely concealed by its gaseous chrysalis.

The magnetic screens not only contained the ion shell, they deflected the gouts of charged particles erupting from Blackworld's pre-nova sun.

All that technology and still a tractor got godawful hot inside. Tractor hogs had to encase themselves in life-support suits as bulky and cumbersome as man's first primitive spacesuits.

Frog's heat-exchange systems were energy-expensive, powerful, and supremely effective—and still inadequate against direct sunlight for any extended time. Blackworld's star-sun was just too close and overpoweringly hot.

Frog warmed his comm laser. Only high-energy beams could punch through the solar static. He tripped switches. His screens and heat evacuators powered up. His companion of decades grumbled and gurgled to itself. It was a soothing mix, a homey vibration, the wakening from sleep of an old friend. He felt better when it surrounded him.

In his crawler he was alive, he was real, as much a man as anyone on Blackworld. More. He had beaten Brightside more often than any five men alive.

A finger stabbed the comm board. His beam caressed a peak in the Shadowline, locked on an automatic transponder. "This here's Frog. I'm at the jump-off. Give me a shade crossing, you plastic bastards." He chuckled.

Signals pulsed along laser beams. Somewhere a machine examined his credit balance, made a transfer in favor of Blake Mining and Metals. A green okay flashed across Frog's comm screen.

"Damned right I be okay," he muttered. "Ain't going to get me that easy."

The little man would not pay Blake to load his ionization charge while his old muscles still worked. But he would not skimp on safety Brightside.

In the old days they had had to make the run from the Edge of the World to the Shadowline in sunlight. Frog had done it a thousand times. Then Blake had come up with a way to beat that strait of devil sun. Frog was not shy about using it. He was cheap and independent, but not foolhardy.

The tractor idled, grumbling to itself. Frog watched the sun-seared plain. Slowly, slowly, it darkened. He fed power to his tracks and cooling systems and eased into the shadow of a dust cloud being thrown kilometers high by blowers at the Blake outstation at the foot of the Shadowline. His computer maintained its communion with the Corporation navigator there, studying everything other rigs had reported since its last crossing, continuously reading back data from its own instruments.

The crossing would be a cakewalk. The regular route, highway hard and smooth with use, was open and safe.

Frog's little eyes darted. Banks of screens and lights and gauges surrounded him. He read them as if he were part of the computer himself.

A few screens showed exterior views in directions away from the low sun, the light of which was almost unfilterable. The rest showed schematics of information retrieved by laser radar and sonic sensors in his track units. The big round screen directly before him represented a view from zenith of his rig and the terrain for a kilometer around. It was a lively, colorful display. Contour lines were blue. Inherent heats showed up in shades of red. Metal deposits came in green, though here, where the deposits were played out, there was little green to be seen.

The instruments advised him of the health of his slave sections, his reactor status, his gas stores level, and kept close watch on his life-support systems.

Frog's rig was old and relatively simple—yet it was immensely complex. Corporation rigs carried crews of two or three, and backup personnel on longer journeys. But there was not a man alive with whom Frog would have, or could have, stood being sealed in a crawler.

Once certain his rig would take Brightside this one more time, Frog indulged in a grumble. "Should have tacked on to a convoy," he muttered. "Could have prorated the damned shade. Only who the hell has time to wait around till Blake decides to send his suckies out?"

His jointed leviathan grumbled like an earthquake in childbirth. He put on speed till he reached his maximum twelve kilometers per hour. The sonics reached out, listening for the return of ground-sound generated by the crawler's clawing tracks, giving the computer a detailed portrait of nearby terrain conditions. The crossing to the Shadowline was a minimum three-hour run, and with no atmosphere to hold the shadowing dust aloft every second of shade cost. He did not dawdle.

It was another eventless crossing. He hit the end of the Shadowline and instantly messaged Blake to secure shade, then idled down to rest. "Got away with it again, you old sumbitch," he muttered at himself as he leaned back and closed his eyes.

He had to do some hard thinking about this run.

Storm placed the clarinet in its case. He faced the creature on his desk, slowly leaned till its forehead touched his own.

His movement was cautious. A ravenshrike could be as worshipful as a puppy one moment, all talons and temper the next. They were terribly sensitive to moods.

Storm never had been attacked by his "pets." Nor had his followers ever betrayed him—though sometimes they stretched their loyalties in their devotion.

Storm had weighed the usefulness of ravenshrikes against their unpredictability with care. He had opted for the risk.

Their brains were eidetically retentive for an hour. He could tap that memory telepathically by touching foreheads. Memorization and telepathy seemed to be part of the creatures' shadow adaption.

The ravenshrikes prowled the Fortress constantly. Unaware of their abilities, Storm's people hid nothing from them. The creatures kept him informed more effectively than any system of bugs.

He had acquired them during his meeting with Richard Hawksblood on The Broken Wings. Since, his people had viewed his awareness with almost superstitious awe. He encouraged the reaction. The Legion was an extension of himself, his will in action. He wanted it to move like a part of him.

Aware though he might be, some of his people refused to stop doing the things that made the lizards necessary.

He never feared outright betrayal. His followers owed him their lives. They served with a loyalty so absolute it bordered on the fanatic. But they were wont to do things for his own good.

In two hundred years he had come to an armistice with the perversities of human nature. Every man considered himself the final authority on universe management. It was an inalterable consequence of anthropoid evolution.

Storm corrected them quietly. He was not a man of sound and fury. A hint of disapproval, he had found, achieved better results than the most bitter recrimination.

Images and dialogue flooded his mind as he discharged the ravenshrike's brain-store. From the maelstrom he selected the bits that interested him.

"Oh, damn! They're at it again."

He had suspected as much. He had recognized the signs. His sons Benjamin, Homer, and Lucifer, were forever conspiring to save the old man from his follies. Why couldn't they learn? Why couldn't they be like Thurston, his oldest? Thurston was not bright, but he stuck with the paternal program.

Better, why couldn't they be like Masato, his youngest? Mouse was not just bright, he understood. Probably better than anyone else in the family.

Today his boys were protecting him from what they believed was his biggest weakness. In his more bitter moments he was inclined to agree. His life would be safer, smoother, and richer if he were to assume a more pragmatic attitude toward Michael Dee.

"Michael, Michael, I've had enemies who were better brothers than you are."

He opened a desk drawer and stabbed a button. The summons traveled throughout the Fortress of Iron. While awaiting Cassius's response he returned to his clarinet and "Stranger on the Shore."

35

Mouse stepped into Colonel Walters's office. "The Colonel in?" he asked the orderly.

"Yes, sir. You wanted to see him?"

"If he isn't busy."

The orderly spoke into a comm. "Masato Storm to see you, Colonel." To Mouse, "Go on in, sir."

Mouse stepped into the spartan room that served Thaddeus Immanuel Walters as office and refuge. It was almost as barren as his father's study was cluttered.

The Colonel was down on his knees with his back to the door, eyes at tabletop level, watching a little plastic dump truck scoot around a plastic track. The toy would dump a load of marbles, then scoot back and, through a complicated series of steps, reload the marbles and start over. The Colonel used a tiny screwdriver to probe the device that lifted the marbles for reloading. Two of the marbles had not gone up. "Mouse?"

"In the flesh."

"When did you get in?"

"Last night. Late.".

"Seen your father yet?" Walters shimmed the lifted with the screwdriver blade. It did no good.

"I was just down there. Looked like he was in one of his moods. I didn't bother him."

"He is. Something's up. He smells it."

"What's that?"

"Not sure yet. Damn! You'd think they'd have built these things so you could fix them." He dropped the screwdriver and rose.

Walters was decades older than Gneaus Storm. He was thin, dark, cold of expression, aquiline, narrow of eye. He had been born Thaddeus Immanuel Walters, but his friends called him Cassius. He had received the nickname in his plebe year at Academy, for his supposed "lean and hungry look."

He was a disturbing man. He had an intense, snakelike stare. Mouse had known him all his life and still was not comfortable with him. A strange one, he thought. His profession is death. He's seen it all. Yet he takes pleasure in restoring these old-time toys.

Cassius had only one hand, his left. The other he had lost long ago, to Fearchild Dee, the son of Michael Dee, when he and Gneaus had been involved in an operation on a world otherwise unmemorable. Like Storm, he refused to have his handicaps surgically rectified. He claimed they reminded him to be careful.

Cassius had been with the Legion since its inception, before Gneaus's birth, on a world called Prefactlas.

"Why did you want me to come home?" Mouse asked. "Your message scared the hell out of me. Then I get here and find out everything's almost normal."

"Normalcy is an illusion. Especially here. Especially now."

Mouse shuddered. Cassius spoke without inflection. He had lost his natural larynx to a Ulantonid bullet on Sierra. His prosthesis had just the one deep, burring tone, like that of a primitive talking computer.

"We feel the forces gathering. When you get as old as we are you can smell it in the ether."

Cassius did something with his toy, then turned to Mouse. His hand shot out.

The blow could have killed. Mouse slid away, crouched, prepared to defend himself.

Cassius's smile was a thin thing that looked alien on his narrow, pale lips. "You're good."

Mouse smiled back. "I keep in practice. I've put in for Intelligence. What do you think?"

"You'll do. You're your father's son. I'm sorry I missed you last time I was in Luna Command. I wanted to introduce you to some people."

"I was in the Crab Nebula. A sunjammer race. My partner and I won it. Even beat a Starfisher crew. And they know the starwinds like fish know their rivers. They'd won four regattas running." Mouse was justifiably proud of his accomplishment. Starfishers were all but invincible at their own games.

"I heard the talk. Congratulations."

Cassius was the Legion's theoretical tactician as well as its second in command and its master's confidant. Some said he knew more about the art of war than anyone living, Gneaus Storm and Richard Hawksblood notwithstanding. War College in Luna Command employed him occasionally, on a fee lecture basis, to chair seminars. Storm's weakest campaigns had been fought when Cassius had been unable to assist him. Hawksblood had beaten their combined talents only once.

A buzzer sounded. Cassius glanced at a winking light. "That's your father. Let's go."

Ten: 3020 AD

The Shadowline was Blackworld's best-known natural feature. It was a four-thousand-kilometer-long fault in the planet's Brightside crust, the sunward side of which had heaved itself up an average of two hundred meters above the burning plain. The rift wandered in a northwesterly direction. It cast a permanent wide band of shadow that Edgeward's miners used as a sun-free highway to the riches of Brightside. By extending its miners' scope of operations the Shadowline gave Edgeward a tremendous advantage over competitors.

No one had ever tried reaching the Shadowline's end. There was no need. Sufficient deposits lay within reach of the first few hundred kilometers of shade. The pragmatic miners shunned a risk that promised no reward but a sense of accomplishment.

On Blackworld a man did not break trail unless forced by a pressing survival need.

But that rickety little man called Frog, this time, was bound for the Shadowline's end.

Every tractor hog considered it. Every man at some time, off-handedly, contemplates suicide. Frog was no different. This was a way to make it into the histories. There were not many firsts to be claimed on Blackworld.

Frog had been thinking about it for a long time. He usually sniggered at himself when he did. Only a fool would try it, and old Frog was no fool.

Lately he had become all too aware of his age and mortality. He had begun to dwell on the fact that he had done nothing to scratch his immortality on the future. His passing would go virtually unnoticed. Few would mourn him.

He knew only one way of life, hogging, and there was only one way for a tractor hog to achieve immortality. By ending the Shadowline.

He still had not made up his mind. Not absolutely. The rational, experienced hog in him was fighting a vigorous rearguard action.

Though Torquemada himself could not have pried the truth loose, Frog wanted to impress someone.

Humanity in the whole meant nothing to Frog. He had been the butt of jests and cruelties and, worse, indifference all his life. People were irrelevant. There was only one person about whom he cared.

He had an adopted daughter named Moira. She was a white girl-child he had found wandering Edgeward's rudimentary spaceport. She had been abandoned by Sangaree slavers passing through hurriedly, hotly pursued by Navy and dumping evidence wherever they could. She had been about six, starving, and unable to cope with a non-slave environment. No one had cared. Not till the hard-shelled, bullheaded, misanthropic dwarf, Edgeward's involuntary clown laureate, had happened along and been touched.

Moira was not his first project. He was a sucker for strays.

He had cut up a candyman pervert, then had taken her home, as frightened as a newly weaned kitten, to his tiny apartment-lair behind the water plant down in Edgeward's Service Underground.

The child complicated his life no end, but he had invested his secret self in her. Now, obsessed with his own mortality, he wanted to leave her with memories of a man who had amounted to more than megaliters of suit-sweat and a stubborn pride five times too big for his retarded growth.

Frog wakened still unsure what he would do. The deepest route controls that he himself had set on previous penetrations ran only a thousand kilometers up the Shadowline.

That first quarter of the way would be the easy part. The markers would guide his computers and leave him free to work or loaf for the four full days needed to reach the last transponder. Then he would have to go on manual and begin breaking new ground, planting markers to guide his return. He would have to stop to sleep. He would use up time backing down to experiment with various routes. Three thousand kilometers might take forever.

They took him thirty-one days and a few hours. During that time Frog committed every sin known to the tractor hog but that of getting himself killed. And Death was back there in the shadows, grinning, playing a little waiting

40

game, keeping him wondering when the meathook would lash out and yank him off the stage of life.

Frog knew he was not going to make it back.

No rig, not even the Corporation's newest, had been designed to stay out this long. His antique could not survive another four thousand clicks of punishment.

Even if he had perfect mechanical luck he would come up short on oxygen. His systems were not renewing properly.

He had paused when his tanks had dropped to half, and had thought hard. And then he had gone on, betting his life that he could get far enough back to be rescued with proof of his accomplishment.

Frog was a poker player. He made the big bets without batting an eye.

He celebrated success by breaking his own most inflexible rule. He shed his hotsuit.

A man out of suit stood zero chance of surviving even minor tractor damage. But he had been trapped in that damned thing, smelling himself, for what seemed half a lifetime. He had to get out or start screaming.

He reveled in the perilous, delicious freedom. He even wasted water scouring himself and the suit's interior. Then he went to work on the case of beer some damn fool part of him had compelled him to stash in his tool locker.

Halfway through the case he commed Blake and crowed his victory. He gave the boys at the shade station several choruses of his finest shower-rattlers. They did not have much to say. He fell asleep before he could finish the case.

Sanity returned with his awakening.

"Goddamn, you stupid old man. What the hell you doing, hey? Nine kinds of fool in one, that what you are." He scrambled into his suit. "Oh, Frog, Frog. You don't got to prove you crazy. Man, they already know."

He settled into his control couch. It was time to resume

his daily argument, via the transponder-markers, with the controller at the Blake outstation. "Sumbitch," he muttered. "Bastard going to eat crow today. Made a liar of him, you did, Frog."

Was anybody else listening? Anybody in Edgeward? It seemed likely. The whole town would know by now. The old man had finally gone and proved that he was as crazy as they always thought.

It would be a big vicarious adventure for them, especially while he was clawing his way back with his telemtry reporting his sinking oxygen levels. How much would get bet on his making it? How much more would be put down the other way?

"Yeah," he murmured. "They be watching." That made him feel taller, handsomer, richer, more macho. For once he was a little more than the town character.

But Moira. . . . His spirits sank. The poor girl would be going through hell.

He did not open comm right away. Instead, he stared at displays for which he had had no time the night before. He had become trapped in a spider's web of fantasy come true.

From the root of the Shadowline hither he had seen little but ebony cliffs on his left and flaming Brightside on his right. Every kilometer had been exactly like the last and next. He had not found the El Dorado they had all believed in back in the old days, when they had all been entrepreneur prospectors racing one another to the better deposits. After the first thousand virgin kilometers he had stopped watching for the mother lode.

Even here the immediate perception remained the same, except that the contour lines of the rift spread out till they became lost in those of the hell plain beyond the Shadowline's end. But there was one eye-catcher on his main display, a yellowness that grew more intense as the eye moved to examine the feedback on the territory ahead.

42

Near his equipment's reliable sensory limits it became a flaming intense orange.

Yellow. Radioactivity. Shading to orange meant there was so much of it that it was generating heat. He glared at the big screen. He was over the edge of the stain, taking an exposure through the floor of his rig.

He started pounding on his computer terminal, demanding answers.

The idiot box had had hours to play with the data. It had a hypothesis ready.

"What the hell?" Frog did not like it. "Try again."

The machine refused. It knew it was right.

The computer said there was a thin place in the planetary mantle here. A finger of magma reached toward the surface. Convection currents from the deep interior had carried warmer radioactives into the pocket. Over the ages a fabulous lode had formed.

Frog fought it, but believed. He wanted to believe. He had to believe. This was what he had given his life to find. He was rich. . . .

The practicalities began to occur to him when the euphoria wore off. Radioactivity would have to be overcome. Six kilometers of mantle would have to be penetrated. A way to beat the sun would have to be found because the lode was centered beyond the Shadowline's end. . . . Mining it would require nuclear explosives, masses of equipment, legions of shadow generators, logistics on a military scale. Whole divisions of men would have to be assembled and trained. New technologies would have to be invented to draw the molten magma from the earth. . . .

His dreams, like smoke, wafted away along the long, still corridors of eternity. He was Frog. He was one little man. Even Blake did not have the resources to handle this. It would take a decade of outrageous capitalization, with no return, just to develop the needed technologies.

"Damn!" he snarled. Then he laughed. "Well, you was rich for one minute there, Frog. And it felt goddamned good while it lasted." He had a thought. "File a claim anyway. Maybe someday somebody'll want to buy an exploitation franchise."

No, he thought. No way. Blake was the only plausible franchisee. He was not going to make those people any richer. He would keep the whole damned thing behind his chin.

But it was something to think about. It really was.

Piqued by the futility of it all, he ordered his computer to lock out any memories relating to the lode.

Eleven: 3031 AD

Cassius stepped into the study. Mouse remained behind him.

"You wanted me?"

Storm cased the clarinet, adjusted his eyepatch, nodded. "Yes. My sons are protecting me again, Cassius."

"Uhm?" Cassius was a curiosity in the family. Not only was he second in command, he was both Storm's father-in-law and son-in-law. Storm had married his daughter Frieda. Cassius's second wife was Storm's oldest daughter, by a woman long dead. The Storms and their captains were bound together by convolute, almost incestuous relationships.

"There's a yacht coming in," Storm said. "A cruiser is chasing her. Both ships show Richard's IFF. The boys have activated the mine fields against them."

Cassius's cold face turned colder still. He met Storm's gaze, frowned, rose on his toes, said, "Michael Dee. Again."

"And my boys are determined to keep him away from me."

Cassius kept his counsel as to the wisdom of their effort. He asked, "He's coming back? After kidnapping Pollyanna? He has more gall than I thought."

Storm chuckled. He killed it when Cassius frowned. "Right. It's no laughing matter."

Pollyanna Eight was the wife of his son Lucifer. They had not been married long. The match was a disaster. To understate, the girl was not Lucifer's type.

Lucifer was one of Storm's favorite children, despite his efforts to complicate his father's life. Lucifer's talents were musical and poetic. He did not have the good sense to pursue them. He wanted to be a soldier.

Storm did not want his children to follow in his footsteps. His profession was a dead end, an historical/social anomaly that would soon correct itself. He saw no future or glamour in his trade. But he could not deny the boys if they chose to remain with the Legion.

Several had become key members of his staff.

Of the men who had created the Legion only a handful survived. Grim old Cassius. The spooky brothers Wulf and Helmut Darksword. A few sergeants. His father, Boris, and his father's brothers and brothers of his own—William, Howard, Verge, and so many more—all had found their deaths-without-resurrection.

The family aged and grew weaker. And the enemy behind the night grew stronger. . . . Storm grunted. Enough of this. He was becoming the plaything of his own obsession with fate.

"He's bringing her back, Cassius." Storm smiled secretively.

Pollyanna was an adventuress. She had married Lucifer more to get close to men like Storm than out of any affection for the poet. Michael had had no trouble manipulating her unsatisfied lust for action.

"But, you see, when he added it all up he was more scared of me than he thought. I caught up with him on

The Big Rock Candy Mountain three weeks ago. We had a long talk, just him and me. I think the knife did the trick. He's vain about his face. And he still worries about Fearchild."

Mouse did his best to remain small. His father's gaze had passed over him several times, a little frown clicking on and off each time. There would be an explosion eventually.

"You? Tortured? Dee?" Cassius could not express his incredulity as a sentence. "You're sure this isn't something he's cooked up to boost his ratings?"

Storm smiled. His smile was a cruel thing. Mouse did not like it. It reminded him that his father had a side that was almost inhuman.

"Centuries together, Cassius. And still you don't understand me. Of course Michael has an angle. That's his nature. And why do you think torture is out of character for me? I promised Michael I would protect him. All that means, and he knows it, is that I won't kill him myself. And I won't let him be killed with my knowledge."

"But. . . ."

"When he crosses me I still have options. I showed him that on The Mountain."

Mouse shuddered as a narrow, wicked smile of understanding captured Cassius's lips. Cassius could not fathom the bond between the half-brothers. It pleased him that Storm had circumvented its limitations.

Cassius was amused whenever a Dee came to grief. He had his grievances. Fearchild was still paying for the hand.

These are truly cruel men, Mouse thought, half-surprised. My own people. I never really realized. . . .

He had been gone too long. He had forgotten their dark sides.

"To business," Cassius said. "If Michael has Pollyanna, and Richard is after him, there'll be shooting. We belong down in Combat."

"I was about to suggest that we go there." Storm rose. "Before my idiot sons rid me of this plague called Michael Dee." He laughed. He had paraphrased Lucifer, who had stolen the line from Henry II, speaking of Becket. "And poor pretty Pollyanna along with him."

Poor Lucifer, Mouse thought. He'll be the only real loser if he manages to keep Michael from docking.

Storm whistled. "Geri! Freki! Here!" The dogs ceased their restless pacing, crowded him expectantly. They were free to range the Fortress, but did so only in the company of their master.

Storm donned the long grey uniform cloak he affected, took a ravenshrike on one arm, strode off. Cassius trailed him by a half-step. Mouse hurried along behind them. The dogs ranged ahead, searching for the trouble they would never find.

"Mouse," Storm growled, stopping suddenly. "What the hell are you doing here?"

"I sent for him," Cassius replied in that cold metallic voice. Mouse shuddered. He was imagining it, of course, but Cassius sounded so deadly unemotional and lifeless. . . . "I contacted my friends in Luna Command. They arranged it. The situation. . . ."

"The situation is such that I don't want him here, Cassius. He has a chance to go his own direction. For God's sake, let him grab it. Too many of my children are caught in this trap already."

Cassius turned as Storm resumed walking. "Wait in my office, Mouse. I'll bring him around."

"Yes, sir."

Mouse began to feel what his father felt. An air of doom permeated the Fortress. A sense that great things were about to happen hung over them all. His father did not want him involved. Cassius thought he belonged. Mouse was shaken. A clash of wills between the two was inconceivable, yet his presence might precipitate one.

How could the Fortress be in danger? Combat simulation models suggested that only Confederation Navy had the strength to crack it. His father and Cassius got along well with the distant government.

Alone in the Colonel's inner office he began to brood. He realized he was mimicking his father. And he could not stop.

Was it Michael Dee?

The foreboding was almost palpable.

Twelve: 2844 AD

Costumed to the ears, wearing the heavy, silly square felt hat of a Family heir, Deeth stood beside his mother. Guests filed past the receiving line. The men touched his hands. The women bowed slightly. Pugh, the twelve-year-old heir of the Dharvon, honored him with a look that promised trouble later. In response Deeth intimidated the ten-year-old sickly heir of the Sexon. The boy burst into tears. His parents became stiff with embarrassment.

The Sexon were the only First Family with a presence on Prefactlas. They had the most image to uphold.

Deeth recognized his error as his father gave him a look more promising than that of Dharvon w'Pugh.

He was not contrite. Hanged for a penny, hanged for a pound. The Sexon kid would have a miserable visit.

The evening followed a predictable course. The adults began drinking immediately. By suppertime they would be too far gone to appreciate the subtleties of his mother's kitchen.

The children were herded into an isolated wing of the greathouse where they could be kept out of the way and closely supervised. As always, the supervision broke down.

The children shed their chaperones and got busy establishing a pecking order. Deeth was the youngest. He could intimidate no one but the Sexon heir.

Sexon fortunes would decline when the boy assumed his patrimony.

The Dharvon boy had a special hatred for Deeth. Pugh was strong but not bright. Only by malign perseverance did he corner his prey.

Deeth refused to show it, but he was terrified. Pugh was not smart enough to know when to quit. He might do something that would force the adults to take official notice. Relations between the Dharvon and Norbon were strained enough. Further provocation could escalate into vendetta.

The call to supper, like a god out of a machine, saved the situation.

Why did his mother invite people with grudges against the Family? Why was a social slight less easily forgiven than a business beating?

He decided to become the richest Sangaree of all time. Wealth made its own rules. He would change things around so they became sensible.

Deeth found the meal unbearably formal and ritualistic.

It was a dismal affair. The alcohol had had its effect. Instead of raising spirits and stirring camaraderie, it had eased restraints on the envy, jealousy, and tempers of the Families the Norbon were excluding from the Osirian market.

Deeth struggled to keep smiling down that long table of sullen faces. The meal progressed lugubriously. The faces grew more antagonistic.

During the desserts the senior Dharvon, sotto voce, expressed his animosity in words. His voice grew louder. Deeth became frightened.

The man was falling-down drunk, and had a reputation for verbal incontinence even when sober. He might say

49

something that would push the Norbon into a corner of honor whence there was no exit save a duel.

The Dharvon was little brighter than his son. He did not have sense enough to avoid offending a better man. And the stupid pride of his heir would, of course, lead the Dharvon into vendetta. The Norbon Family would strike like a lion at a kitten and swallow the Dharvon whole.

But the mouth of a fool knows no restraint. The Dharvon kept pressing.

His neighbors edged away, dissociating themselves from his remarks. They shared his jealousies without sharing his stupidity. Sullenly neutral, they hovered like eager vultures.

Sangaree found feuds entertaining when they were not themselves involved.

Fate interceded just seconds before challenge became inescapable.

Rhafu burst into the hall. His face was red, frightened, and sweaty. He ignored the proprieties as he interrupted his employer.

"Sir," he said, puffing into the Norbon's face, "it's started. The field hands and breeders are attacking their overseers. Some of them are armed. With weapons from the wild ones. We're trying to get them under control in case there's an attack from the forest."

Guests buzzed excitedly. Heads and station masters shouted requests for permission to contact their own establishments. A general rising could not have been better timed. Prefactlas's decision-makers were far from their respective territories.

A few mumbled apologies for leaving ran from the table. What began as a babble of uncertainty escalated into a frightened clamor.

An officer of the Norbon Family forces compounded it. He galloped in, shouted over the uproar, "Sir! Everyone! A signal from *Norbon Spear*." *Spear* was the Head's personal yacht and the Family flagship. "A flotilla-scale naval force just dropped hyper inside lunar radius." A single sneeze broke the sudden silence. A hundred pale faces turned toward the soldier. "No IFF response. The ship types are those of the human navy. *Spear*'s signal was interrupted. We haven't been able to raise her again. Monitors show a sudden increase in gamma radiation at her position. Computer says she was hit in her drive sector and blew her generators."

The silence died. Everybody tried to leave at once, to escape, to flee to his own station. The great terror of the Sangaree had befallen Prefactlas. The humans had located their tormentors.

A gleeful wild devil spun circles of terror around the hall. Children wept. Women screamed and wailed. Men cursed and shoved, trying to be first to escape.

There had been other station raids. The humans had been merciless. They never settled for less than total obliteration.

Prefactlas was an entire world, of course, and a world cannot be attacked and occupied like some pitiful little island in an ocean. Not without overpoweringly vast numbers of ships and men. And, though sparsely settled, Prefactlas had a well-developed defense net. Sangaree guarded their assets. Normally a flotilla could have done little but blockade the world.

But conditions were not normal. The decision-makers were concentrated far from the forces responsible for turning attacks. No one had yet found a way around Family pride and stubbornness and formed a centralized command structure. The various Family forces, because their masters were far away, would be loafing far from their battle stations. Or, if the slave rising were general, they would be preoccupied. Attacking quickly, the humans could be down before defenses could be manned and effective interception barrages launched.

Even Deeth saw it. And he saw what most of the adults

did not. Attack and uprising were coordinated, and timed for the height of this party.

The humans were working with someone on Prefactlas.

Their commander need only take the Norbon station to seize control of the planet. Having eliminated the decision-makers and gotten their ships inside the defensive umbrella, they could deal with the other holdings piecemeal. They could conquer an entire world with an inferior force.

The whole thing smacked of raider daring. Nurtured by treachery, of course.

Some laughing human commander, smarter than most animals, was about to make himself a fortune.

Over the years since their discovery of the Sangaree, and the fact that they were considered animals, the humans had created scores of laws designed to encourage one another to respond savagely. Billions in bounties and prize moneys would go to the conquerors of a world. Even the meanest shipboard rating would be able to retire and live on his interest. A developed world was a prize with a value almost beyond calculation.

The fighting would be grim. Human hatred would be reinforced by greed.

Deeth's father was as quick as his son. Defeat and destruction, he saw, were inevitable. He told his wife, "Take the boy and dress him in slave garb. Rhafu, go with her. See that he's turned loose in the training area. They don't know each other. He'll pass."

Deeth's mother and the old breeding master understood. The Head was grasping at his only chance to save his line.

"Deeth," his father said, kneeling, "you understand what's happening, don't you?"

Deeth nodded. He did not trust himself to speak. Once he had examined and thought out the possibilities he had become afraid. He did not want to shame himself.

"You know what to do? Hide with the animals. It shouldn't be hard. You're a smart boy. They won't be expecting you. Stay out of trouble. When you get the chance, go back to Homeworld. Reclaim the Family and undertake a vendetta against those who betrayed us. For your mother and me. And all our people who will die here. Understand? You'll do that?"

Again Deeth dared only nod. His gaze flicked around the hall. Who were the guilty? Which few would see the sun rise?

"All right." His father enfolded him in a hug that hurt. He had never done that before. The Norbon was not a demonstrative man. "Before you go."

The Norbon took a small knife from his pocket. He opened a blade and scraped the skin on Deeth's left wrist till a mist of blood droplets oozed up. Then he used a pen to ink a long series of numbers. "That's where you'll find your Wholar, Deeth. That's Osiris. The only place those numbers exist is in my head and on your wrist. Take care. You'll need that wealth to make your return."

Deeth forced a weak smile. His father was brilliant, disguising the most valuable secret of the day as a field hand's serial.

The Norbon hugged him again. "You'd better go. And hurry. They'll come down fast once they're into their run."

A raggedy string of roars sounded out front. Deeth smiled. Someone had activated the station defenses. Missiles were launching.

Answering explosions killed his pleasure. He hurried after his mother and Rhafu. White glare poured through the windows. The atmosphere above the station protested its torment. Guests kept shrieking.

The preparatory barrages had begun. The station's defenders were trying to fend them off.

The slave pens were utter chaos. Deeth heard the fighting and screaming long before he and Rhafu arrived on the observation balcony.

Household troops were helping the slave handlers, and still the animals were not under control. Corpses littered the breeding dome. Most were field hands, but a sickening number wore Norbon blue. The troops and handlers were handicapped. They had to avoid damaging valuable property.

"I don't see any wild ones, Rhafu."

"That is curious. Why provide weapons without support?"

"Tell them not to worry about saving the stock. They won't matter if the human ships break through."

"Of course." After an introspective moment, Rhafu said, "It's time you went." He gave Deeth a hug as powerful as his father's had been. "Be careful, Deeth. Always think before you do anything. Always take the long view. Don't ever forget that you're the Family now." He ran the back of a wrist across his eyes. "Now, then. I've enjoyed having you here, young master. Don't forget old Rhafu. Kill one for me when you get back to Homeworld."

Deeth saw death in Rhafu's watery eyes. The old adventurer did not expect to survive the night. "I will, Rhafu. I promise."

Deeth gripped one leathery old hand. Rhafu was still a fighter. He would not run. He would die rather than let animals shatter his courage and the confidence of his own superiority.

Deeth started to ask why he had to run away when everyone else was going to stand. Rhafu forestalled him.

"Listen closely, Deeth. Go down the stairs at the end of the balcony. All the way down. There'll be two doors at the bottom. Use the one on your right. It opens into the corridor that passes the training area. There shouldn't be anyone in it. Go to the end of the hall. You'll find two more doors. Use the one marked Exit. It'll put you outside in one of the vegetable fields. Go to the sithlac dome and follow its long side. Keep going in a straight line out from its end. You should reach the forest in an hour. Keep on going and you'll run into an animal village. Stay with them till you find a way off planet. And for Sant's sake make sure you pretend you're one of them and they're equals. If you don't, you're dead. Never trust one of them, and never get close to any of them. Understand?"

Deeth nodded. He knew what had to be done. But he did not want to go.

"Go on. Scoot," Rhafu said, swatting him on the behind and pushing him toward the stair. "And be careful."

Deeth walked to the stairwell slowly. He glanced back several times. Rhafu waved a last farewell, then turned away, hiding tears.

"He'll die well," Deeth whispered.

He reached the emergency exit. Cautiously, he peeped outside. The fields were not as dark as he had expected. Someone had left the lights on in the sithlac dome. And the slave barracks were burning. Had the animals fired them? Or had the bombardment done it?

Little short-lived suns kept flaring between the stars overhead. A long, rolling thunder of chemical explosions came from the far side of the station. The launch pits had been hit. The shriek of rising missiles was replaced by secondary explosions.

The humans were getting close. Deeth looked up into the heart of the constellation Rhafu had dubbed the Krath, after a rapacious bird of Homeworld. The human birthstar lay there somewhere.

He could not distinguish the constellation. There were scores of new stars up there, all of them too bright, and visibly brightening.

The humans were on the downward leg of their penetration run. He would have to hurry to clear the perimeter they would establish with their assault craft.

He sprinted for the side of the sithlac dome.

By the time he reached the dome's far end the new stars had swollen into small, bright suns. Missile exhausts rayed from them in angry swarms. He could hear the craft rumbling over the explosions stalking through the station.

They were just a few thousand feet up now, and braking in. His escape would be close. If he made it at all.

A flight of missiles darted toward the bright target of the dome. Deeth ran again, sprinting straight out into the darkness. Explosions tattooed behind him. Blasts hurled him forward, tumbled him over and over. The dome lights died. He rose, stumbled ahead, fell, rose, and went on. His nose was bleeding. He could not hear.

He could not see where he was going. The flashing of explosions kept his eyes from adapting as quickly as they should.

The assault craft touched down.

The nearest landed so close Deeth was singed by the hot wash spreading beneath it. He kept shambling toward the forest, ignoring the treacherous ground. When he was safe he paused to watch the humans tumble off their boat and link up with the craft that had landed to either side. The burning station splashed them with eerie light.

Deeth recognized them. They were Force Recon, the cream of the Confederation Marines, the humans' best and meanest. Nothing would escape their circle.

He cried for his parents, and Rhafu, then wiped the tears away with the backs of his fists. He trudged toward the forest, indifferent to the fact that the humans might spot him on anti-personnel radar. Each hundred steps he paused to look back.

Dawn was near when he passed the first trees. They rose like a sudden palisade, crowding a straight line decreed by the station's planners. He felt as though he had stepped behind a bulwark against doom.

56

Once his ears had recovered he had heard stealthy movements around him. He was not alone in his flight. He avoided contact. He was too shaken, and had too poor a command of the slave tongue, to handle questions from animals. The wild ones used a different language. He expected to have less trouble passing with them. If he could find them.

One found him.

He was a quarter-mile into the forest when a raggedy, smelly old man with a crippled leg pounced on him. The attack was so sudden and unexpected that Deeth had no chance. His struggles earned him nothing but a fist in the face. The blow calmed him. He bit down on a tongue that had been damning the old man in High Sangaree.

"What are you doing, please?" he ventured in the animal language.

The old man hit him again. Before he could do more than groan, a sack had been flung over his head, skinned down to his ankles, and tied shut. A moment later, head downward and miserable, he was hoisted onto a bony shoulder.

He had become booty.

Thirteen: 3052 AD

My father had an unusual philosophy. It was oblique, pessimistic, fatalistic. Judge its tenor by the fact that he read Ecclesiastes every day.

He believed all existence was a rigged game. Good strove with Evil in vain. Good could achieve occasional localized tactical victories, but only because Evil was toying with it, certain of final victory. Evil knew no limits. In the end, when the scores were tallied, Evil would be the big winner. All a man could do was face it with courage, fight though defeat was inevitable, and delay the hour of defeat as long as possible.

He did not see Good and Evil in standard terms. The Good and Evil most of us see he simply considered matters of viewpoint. The "I" is always on the side of the angels. The "They" are always wicked. He thought an absolute Islamic-Judeo-Christian Evil a weak, irrational joke.

Entropy is an approximate cognate for what Gneaus Julius Storm called Evil. An anthropomorphic, diabolic sort of entropy with a malign lust for devouring love and creativity, which, I think, he considered to be the main constituents of Good.

It was an unusual outlook, but you have to accept that it was valid for him before you can follow him through the maze called the Shadowline.

—Masato Igarashi Storm

Fourteen: 3031 AD

Storm, Cassius, and the dogs crowded into an elevator. It dropped away toward the Traffic Control and Combat Information Center at the planetoid's heart.

Benjamin, Homer, and Lucifer whirled when their father entered the Center. Storm surveyed their faces grimly. The glow of the spatial display globes, overplayed by the changing light keys of the tactical computer's situation boards, splashed them with ever-changing color. No one spoke.

Storm's sons stared at their feet like shamed boys caught playing with matches. Storm half turned to Cassius, eye on the senior watchstander. Cassius inclined his head. The officer would have to explain his failure to report ships in detection. He would be reminded of his debt to Gneaus Storm. It would be a tempestuous admonition.

The officer's failure was beyond Cassius's comprehension. *He* never let his hatred of the Dees impair his trust. The Dees were a raggedy-assed gaggle of hypocritical thieves, boosters, and news managers. They were a waste of life-energy. But . . . . Cassius suppressed his feelings because he had faith in Storm's judgment. This watch officer had not been with the Legion long enough to have developed that faith.

Should Storm ever fail, openly and dramatically . . . Cassius did not know what he would do. He had been with Storm so long that, chances were, he would bull right along in the official line.

Storm surveyed his sons again. He awarded Lucifer one of his rare smiles. The fool had been trying to kill his own wife.

Storm thought of Pollyanna, shuddered.

He had to let them off easy. This pocket revolt was his own fault. He should have passed the word about the woman.

He did not think much of himself just then. He had done his usual trick, not letting anyone know what he was doing or why. He was screwing up too much lately. Maybe he was getting old. In this business survivors eliminated the margin of error.

He locked gazes with Lucifer. His son stepped back as if physically shoved.

Lucifer was just six years older than Mouse. He was large and well-built, like his father, but his mind had his mother's bent.

Lady Prudence of Gales had been a High Seiner poetess and musician in the days when her people, the mysterious Starfishers, had not completely retreated into the interstellar deeps. She had come to the Fortress as an emissary, recalling Prefactlas, begging for help to save her sparsely populated, remote homeworld from Sangaree domination.

She had touched Storm with naked trust. No man knew where to find the elusive Seiners. She had given him that secret in the naive hope that that would move him to help. She had cast the dice, betting everything on a single roll. . . . And she had won.

And Storm had had no cause for regrets.

He remembered Prudie better than most of his women. A hot, hungry little morsel in private. Cool, competent, and occasionally imperious in public, and daring. Bedazzlingly daring. Never before or since had anyone cozened the Iron Legion into fighting on spec.

He had pulped the Sangaree on her world. She had given him a son. And they had gone their separate ways.

Storm had known countless women, had fathered dozens of children. His parents had had no concept of fidelity either. Three of his brothers had had different mothers. Michael Dee had had a different and mysterious father.

Frieda Storm was guilty of her indiscretions, too. She did not press Storm about his.

So Lucifer had been an artist born. And he was good. His poetry had appeared with that of giants like Moreau and Czyzewski. The visualist Boroba Thring had done a kaleidoshow based on Lucifer's Legion epic, *Soldaten*, using one of Lucifer's Wagnerian scores as background music. But Lucifer considered writing and composing mere hobbies.

He was determined to prove himself a soldier. It was a vain ambition. He did not, as they say, have the killer instinct.

The free soldier had to act without thought or remorse. His antagonists were professionals. They were quick and deadly. They would permit him no time for regrets or reflection on the barbarity of it all.

Storm forgave Lucifer's shortcomings more readily than

he did those of sons with no talents. He had hopes for the boy. Lucifer might someday find and become true to himself.

Benjamin and Homer were twins. Storm's only children by Frieda, they were, in theory and their own estimation, his favorites. They were rebels. Their mother defended them like an old bitch cat her kittens.

Probably my fault they're delinquents, Storm thought. They've been men for decades and still I treat them like boys. Hell, they're grandfathers.

This extended life leached a man's perspective.

The twins were as unalike as night and day. Storm sometimes wondered if he had fathered both.

Benjamin was a blond Apollo. He was the darling of the younger Legionnaires, who considered his father a historical relic. But did they turn to Benjamin in the tight places? They did not. Benjamin Storm tended to fold under pressure.

His mother and friends believed he was the Legion's Crown Prince. His father thought not. If the Iron Legion survived Gneaus Storm, none of his children but Cassius's favorite had what it took to rule and fight a freecorps.

Benjamin could win loyalties with a word, with a gesture. He had that knack for making each individual feel he was the only human being in the universe Benjamin cared about. But could he inspire faith?

Benjamin might command the Legion one day if his father did not appoint a successor. For one commission. Storm could see his son taking over on force of personality. He could not see him succeeding in the field.

Benjamin could play Piper of Hamlin to his own, but those hard cases across the battlefields, the Hawksbloods and van Breda Kolffs, would cut up his charisma and spread it on their breakfast toast.

Homer was Benjamin's antithesis. He was dark of mind and body, ugly, malformed, and congenitally blind. He repelled everyone but his twin. Benjamin was his only friend. He followed his brother everywhere, as if only Benjamin could neutralize the blackness in his soul.

In compensation for her cruelties Nature had given Homer a weak psionic ability that never did him any good. He was bitter, and not without just cause. He was as sharp as anyone in the family, yet was trapped in a body little better than a corpse.

Storm's men saw the twins as living examples of the dualities in their father. Benjamin had received the looks and charm, Homer the hurt and rage and darkness of spirit.

Benjamin met his father's eye and smiled his winningest smile. Homer started sightlessly, unrepentant. He was unafraid. There was no way to punish him more than life had punished him already.

He expected nothing but evil. He accepted it.

Storm hurt for him. He knew the shadow that ruled Homer. It was an old, intimate companion.

At least once a day Storm turned to the book that time had forgotten, rereading and contemplating the message of a Storm dead four thousand years.

> Vanity of vanities, says the Preacher,
>   vanity of vanities! All is vanity.
> What does a man gain by all the toil
>   at which he toils under the sun?

Gneaus Storm, even more than had Homer, had watched the rivers run into the seas, and knew the seas would never fill. Rather, they grew shallower with the ages, and someday would disappear. What did a man profit if, in the end, all his deeds were illusion? The Enemy could not be overthrown. Its resources were infinite and eternal and Storm knew he would only lose the long struggle.

Unlike the Preacher in Jerusalem, Storm refused to surrender. In spite of everything, there could be victory in the spirit. If he kept his courage he could scratch his memory on the cruel visage of defeat. Either to surrender, or to go to his fate with laughter on his lips. This was the only real choice he, or any man, was ever given in this life.

"There's a ship coming in," he growled at last. He jerked his arm upward. The ravenshrike fluttered into the shadows. No one paid it any heed.

No one argued. The truth was evident in the display globes.

"Michael Dee's ship, I believe. Contact him. Clear him a path through the mine fields."

The soldiers did not "yes sir" before returning to work. They would try to impress him with their efficiency now. Trouble lurked beyond the end of their watch.

"Traffic, contact the cruiser too. I want to speak to her master. All defense systems, move to standby alert."

"I have contact with Dee," said the man on Traffic Comm. "Clear channel, visual."

"Thank you." Storm seated himself at a visual pickup. Cassius moved in behind him. Michael Dee's fox face formed on screen. Worry lines faded away. A pearly-toothed smile broke through.

"Gneaus! Am I glad to see you. I was beginning to think you wouldn't answer."

"I had to think about it." Dee's smile faded. His was a con man's face, blandly honest, as reassuring as a priest's. But little folds uplifting the corners of his eyes gave him a sly look. "I could still change my mind. Did you bring my cargo?"

Dee was wearing his natural face. No makeup. No disguise. His dark eyes, narrow face, pointy nose, and prominent, sharp teeth gave him a definite vulpine look. This is the true Michael, Storm thought.

Dee was a man of countless faces. Seldom was he out of disguise, and his talent for shifting identities was preternatural. Given study time, he could adopt the speech habits and physical mannerisms of almost anyone. He found the talent useful in his trade. He was, supposedly, a free-lance newsman.

"Of course. I said I would, didn't I?" Dee sneered as if to say he knew his brother would not throw him to Hawksblood's wolves.

"Show me, Michael."

Exasperated, Dee backed off pickup. Pollyanna Eight showed her pretty face. A little sigh ran through the Center.

"All right. You're clear in. Out." Storm nudged the comm man. He took the hint. He secured the channel before Dee could come back on.

Lucifer sputtered behind his father and Cassius. Storm turned. He forbore any remark but, "Lucifer, go take charge of the ingress locks. Don't let Michael wander. Get him out of his ship and search it."

Dee was treacherous. From childhood he had thrived on sparking strife. The feud between Richard Hawksblood and his brother was his masterwork.

He could not help himself. Meddling and deceit were compulsions. One day his weakness would kill him.

Michael would be involved in more than just bringing Pollyanna home. He was not a one-track man. He always kept several balls in the air.

Storm thought he knew what Dee was up to. Richard's being interested in Blackworld was the giveaway.

Michael would try to involve the Legion. Merc wars made great holo entertainment. He had grown rich covering them. He had engineered a few to have something to tape.

Knowing what Michael wanted was inadequate forewarning. He was devious. His manipulations might not be recognizable.

The Traffic Comm man established contact with Dee's pursuer.

"Cassius. Who is he?"

"Lawrence Abhoussi. One of Richard's best."

"Richard must have sent him out blind. He's surprised to see me."

"Characteristic." Hawksblood was a demon for secrecy.

Storm keyed for sound. "Commander Abhoussi, you're entering restricted space."

The Ship's Commander replied, "We did note the automatic warnings, Colonel. But we were given explicit orders. We have to capture the yacht."

"Polite, any way," Storm whispered.

"And scared."

The Legion had burned respect into Hawksblood's men. And vice versa.

"I know the ship, Commander. My daughter-in-law is aboard. I have to extend her my protection. Why don't you pursue your quarrel with her master after he leaves? If the ship is stolen, I'll let you send in a skeleton crew to collect her."

Abhoussi grew pale. Storm's defenses were formidable. "My orders are explicit, Colonel Storm. I'm to recover the vessel and everyone aboard her."

"This is getting dangerous, Gneaus," Cassius burred.

Storm nodded. "I know your employer, Commander. He's a disciplinarian, but he'll make allowances when you explain why you lost the yacht." Storm killed the sound. "I'm trying to give him an out, Cassius."

"He knows."

The Ship's Commander paused before replying. He kept glancing off screen. Finally, he keyed for sound and said, "I'm storry, Colonel Storm. I have no option."

"Damn," Cassius said.

"I'm sorry too, then. Good-bye, Commander." Storm broke the link. "Fire Control, activate the passive defenses. Don't take the cruiser under fire unless she looks like she'll catch Dee." He rose, started toward the elevators. The dogs rose as he approached.

"Father!" Benjamin called. "Hold on. They've gone Norm." Storm turned. "Abhoussi's inherent velocity is aligned with Dee's and he's closing fast. He's accelerating. Catch point about nine hundred thousand kilometers out."

"Computer?" Storm asked the air.

"Active," a Cassius-like voice replied.

"You following the current situation?"

"Affirmative."

"Analysis please."

The machine confirmed Benjamin's assessment. It added, "Smaller target is decelerating on a line of approach to the ingress locks. Traffic Comm has docking control. Larger target still accelerating in line of approach. Probability nine-zero plus: Intent is to take hyper with the smaller vessel within its influential sphere."

"Free missiles," Storm ordered. "This Abhoussi is damned smart," he told Cassius.

"He jumped on the only chance he's got."

By snagging Dee with his more powerful influential field Abhoussi could neutralize the yacht's drive and drag her beyond the range of Storm's superior weaponry. He could then drop hyper and deal with Michael at his leisure.

It was a tactic as old as spatial warfare, though a dangerous one. Both ships could be destroyed if either's drives were far out of synch.

"That man was a McGraw," Cassius guessed. "Only a pirate would have the nerve to try it."

"Free guns on the outstations," Storm ordered. "Commence action. You're right, Cassius. He's got guts. Pity he's wasting them."

"Some people fear Richard Hawksblood more than they fear Gneaus Storm," Cassius observed laconically. "Then again, he could know something you don't. You haven't analyzed his chances. He comped them while he was talking to you."

"Right. Computer. Analyze success probabilities for the assumed mission of the larger target, henceforth desig Enemy, Bogey One."

Practically trampling Storm's final words, the computer replied, "With Traffic control of Friendly, probability six five plus. Without Traffic control, probability four seven plus. Analysis of random minetracks incomplete."

"Pretty good," Cassius observed. "I'd buy those odds myself."

"And win. He's got the jump on us. Traffic, put Dee on his own hooks. Cassius, take the gun-control master."

Storm himself assumed control of the master board commanding the mines and missiles protecting the platetoid. "Computer. Probability of Enemy success with new board control." The machine was a cryocyborg unit. It could enter the skills of known human operators into its probability equations.

"With Friendly free of Traffic control and analysis of random minetracks complete, probability three one plus."

Storm was pleased. He and Cassius made a difference. He did not like the ever-present plus. The computer was weighting the probability shift in Abhoussi's favor.

Storm examined his board. None of his active mines or hunter-killer missiles would pass close enough to Abhoussi to detonate. The weapons in line of approach were inactive for Michael's sake.

He blew several nearby mines. Maybe he could rattle Abhoussi.

He suspected the plus was being awarded because

Abhoussi was performing better than the average Ship's Commander profiled in the computer. Richard did not hire average men. No merc captain did.

Storm punched more fire buttons. He did no good. Abhoussi was crawling into Michael's safety shadow. The only sure way to stop him was to activate weaponry in the approach path.

"Bogey One, probability of success, four two plus," the computer announced, and almost immediately raised its ante to four three, four four, and four five. Storm cursed softly and continuously.

"Time to jump?" he demanded.

"Twenty-three seconds optimum." Then the computer added, "Hit, beam, remote station twelve. Field anomalies indicate a temporary reduction of efficiency in Bogey One drives. Probability of Enemy success, three one steady."

Storm smiled. "Good shooting, Cassius."

Cassius was too busy to acknowledge the applause. He bent over his master console with the intensity of a virtuoso pianist, totally immersed in his art, webbing Abhoussi with beams of destruction.

Storm turned to his own master, secured it. He had not rattled Abhoussi at all.

He leaned back and watched Cassius while fighting off visions of Pollyanna being crisped by Abhoussi's weaponry. Hawksblood's man was firing only in self-defense, but might have orders to kill if he could not capture.

The odds against Abhoussi lengthened. Storm fidgeted. He placed little faith in computer analyses. He had beaten their odds when they had been five-to-one against him. The best games machines, with brains cyborged in, could not take into account all the human factors of a battle situation.

"Hit, beam," the computer announced. "Drive anomalies. Bogey One no longer accelerating. Probability of generator damage seven zero plus."

"Catch time," Storm asked. It had been telescoping, but Abhoussi had been hand-over-handing it up the scope.

"Eleven seconds."

Storm smiled. Abhoussi was climbing an ever-steepening slope. One more perfect shot from Cassius would do it.

Again he paid his chief of staff his due. The man was not just trying for hits, he was sharpshooting Abhoussi's facility for dragging Michael off to neutral space. And that at a time when he could have eased up and allowed his most hated enemy to perish.

Storm grabbed a mike, called the ingress locks. "Get a boat ready for rescue work. Have it crewed and standing by for astrogational instruction. Is Lucifer there yet?" He cut off before he received a reply. The computer was chattering again.

"Hit, beam. Major drive anomalies. Probability of generator damage nine zero plus. Probability of Enemy success, one three minus."

Storm moved to Traffic. "Contact the cruiser," he told the watchstander.

"Bogey One commencing evasive maneuvering," the computer continued. "Probability that Enemy is attempting to disengage, nine five plus." Abhoussi had accepted defeat.

Establishing the comm link took longer than the action had. Abhoussi was more interested in survival than in chitchat.

When the pale-faced Ship's Commander finally responded, Storm asked, "Can you manage your generators yourselves, Commander? Any casualties you can't handle? I have a rescue boat standing by."

Abhoussi gulped air, replied, "We'll manage, Colonel. We took no casualties."

"All right." Storm blanked off. "Cease firing," he ordered.

The order was unnecessary. Cassius had secured his gun board.

Was Abhoussi telling the truth? He had the feel of a man who would let his people die the death-without-resurrection before putting them into the hands of an enemy capable of using them against his employer later.

Storm called the ingress locks again. "Cancel the boat alert. We won't need it." Then, "Cassius, let's go meet Michael. He'll have an interesting story. Might even tell the truth."

"Good show, gentlemen," Cassius told the watch-standers. "Run a full systems check before you go off duty. See that Supply and Weapons know which mines and missiles to replace." His hard gaze darted from face to face. No one met it.

Storm peered into the shadows. The ravenshrike had concealed itself. It was alert.

"I think we did all right," he told Cassius as they followed the dogs into an elevator. "It was my kind of battle. Nobody got hurt."

"They should all be so chesslike."

A shadow moved in the shadows of a corner of Combat. The eyes of Storm's ravenshrike burned as they watched Homer and Benjamin. Homer slipped into the still warm seat before the mines and missiles board. The blind man caressed trigger switches and status boards with his sensitive fingers. He listened for his sporadic psi. He depressed an activation key, paused, tripped a fire switch.

Daggers of flame scarred the deep space night two light seconds from the Fortress. A swarm of hyper-capable seeker missiles went looking for Commander Abhoussi's cruiser.

The vessel had not traveled far.

Alarms screamed aboard the warship. Automatic weapons responded.

Constellations vanished behind a veil of fire. Abhoussi's engineers seized their only chance. They kicked in the damaged generators. The cruiser twisted away into hyperspace, leaving fragments of itself behind. The seekers, unaware of the cruiser's destination, began cutting lazy search patterns over half-light-year quadrants.

Homer's faint and seldom reliable psi touched upon a remote, short-lived scream. He leaned back and smiled at an aghast Benjamin. "It's done."

"Ah, Homer...." Benjamin could not think of anything to say. He could not meet the eyes of the watch-standers.

Their faces were long and grey. Storm was going to cut their hearts out for not stopping this.

The ravenshrike shuddered as it sensed the psionic scream and the pure disgust of the Center watch. It wrapped itself in wings and shadow, closed its eyes, and awaited its master's return.

Fifteen: 3020 AD

Frog's rescue became high drama. Blake's crews reached him only after he had idled down and gone on intravenous and drugs in an extended, deep sleep free of the distress and pain of radiation sickness. He had emptied his oxygen tanks.

His rescuers had to tunnel under his crawler to reach his belly hatch. They found it fouled with splash scale. They stung a heated hose through his tractor skin into his oxy main. A couple of Blake hogs chipped the scale off his hatch. Others sprayed the tunnel walls with a quick-setting epoxy. They scabbed a pumper trunk over the tunnel mouth and flooded it with breathables.

They *had* to do it the hard way. Near the end, too pained to think straight, Frog had shed his hotsuit again. His stupidity came near costing him his life.

The expenses of the rescue came out of Blake's PR

budget. The holonetnews snoops were on the scene, their cameras purring. The head office saw itself picking up a lot of cheap advertising. The name Blake Mining and Metals would get exposure all over Confederation.

Old Frog had gotten more than he had bargained for. He had not impressed just a little girl and the people of his home town. He was a seven-day news wonder Confederation-wide. His adventure was being broadcast live from Edgeward. Taping crews braved the Shadowline to get his rescue recorded for later broadcast.

He would have been amused and disgusted had he known about it. It was not quite the notoriety he had been seeking.

Sixteen: 3031 AD

Mouse hovered on the fringes of Pollyanna's welcome-home party, attracted by the gaiety, repelled by Benjamin and Homer and what they had tried to do. Academy was all grey discipline and the absence of humor. He needed a little singing and dancing. The younger people were doing both, and building some mighty hangovers while they were at it.

Their elders frowned around the party's edges like thunderheads grumbling on grey horizons. Their faces were marked by an uneasiness bordering on dread. They're standing there like brooding guardian idols in some Bronze Age temple, Mouse thought. Like the tongueless crows of doom.

He tried to laugh at his own gloomy perception. His father's moods must be catching.

Storm, Cassius, and the other old ones had just come from a staff meeting. Mouse had not been permitted to attend. He guessed they had discussed the twins first.

There had been one hell of a traffic load through Instel Communications. Hawksblood had, apparently, been consulted. He could not guess what had been decided. Cassius had had only enough time to whisper the news that the cruiser had survived. Barely.

Then the Vice President for Procurement of Blake Mining and Metals, of Edgeward City on Blackworld, had made a contract presentation.

Mouse could guess the drift. Everyone had come from the meeting damp with apprehension. He could smell their anger and distress. Richard had not been understanding. Blake's man had tried a little arm-twisting.

A squeaky Dee-giggle rippled across the room. Good old Uncle Michael was the life of the party.

His loud, flashy presence was doing nothing for anybody's nerves. Amid the dour, ascetically clad soldiers he was a focus of peacock brightness, raucous as a macaw. At the moment he was a clown vainly trying for a laugh from his brother's staff. The sour, sullen, sometimes hateful, sometimes suspicious stares of Storm, Cassius, and Wulf and Helmut Darksword intimidated him not at all. Storm's sons he ignored completely, except for the occasional puzzled glance at Lucifer or Mouse.

Lucifer was more sour than his father. He moved with a stiff tension that bespoke rage under incomplete control. He watched Michael with deadly eyes. He snapped and snarled, threatening to go off like some unpredictable bomb. He should have been overjoyed to have his wife home.

Mouse's presence was a puzzling anomaly to everyone. He was enjoying their baffled reactions. They knew he was supposed to be at Academy. They knew that even midshipmen who were the sons of men as well-known and respected as Gneaus Storm did not receive leave time without strings being pulled at stratospheric levels. Michael's nervous gaze returned to him again and again.

Dee was sharply observant behind his clown mask. His eyes never stopped roving. And Mouse seldom let his attention stray far from Dee.

Michael was worried.

Mouse sensed his uncle's nervousness. He felt a hundred other emotional eddies. He was enveloped by an oppressive sense of descending fate, as heavy as age itself.

Hatred for Michael Dee. Distrust of the Blake Vice President. Worry about Richard. Benjamin almost obsessive in his dread of what his father would do about his part in the attack on the Hawksblood cruiser. Lucifer, marginally psychotic, confusing his feelings about his wife, his father, Dee, Hawksblood, Benjamin, and distracted by suspicion, jealousy, and self-loathing. Homer . . . . Homer was being Homer.

Mouse wondered if his father was making a mistake by letting Benjamin stew. Ben was not as well-balanced as he liked to pretend. He had nightmares constantly. Now he seemed to be sliding into a daytime obsession with the dream.

Benjamin dreamed about his own death. For years he had laughed the dreams off. The attack on Hawksblood's ship seemed to have made a believer of him. He was running scared.

Mouse glanced at his brother. Benjamin never had taken him in. Ben was nothing but flashy façade. Mouse felt nothing but pity.

The brothers Darksword also had the disease of the moment. They were mad at everybody. Like Storm, they had expected The Broken Wings to be their last campaign. They had expected to live out their lives as gentlemen farmers on a remote, pastoral world far from the cares of the Iron Legion. They were overdue to leave the Fortress already, but ties two centuries deep had proven difficult to break.

Mouse looked at his father.

Storm had been motionless, brooding, for almost an hour. Now he was shaking like a big dog coming out of the water. He skewered the mining executive with a deadly glance. Mouse moved along the wall behind his father, the better to hear.

"We can buy a little time on this thing. Helmut. Wulf. Cassius."

Michael Dee appeared to lean slightly, to stretch an ear.

Storm said, "Kill the Blackworlder. Neatly. See that the corpse reaches Helga Dee. Without her knowing the source."

The condemned man was too stunned to protest.

"You did say Helga's World was mentioned in those papers Richard said he found, didn't you, Cassius?"

"Yes."

"And again on Michael's ship." Storm stared down at Michael Dee. One droplet of sweat rolled down Dee's temple. He looked a little pale.

Michael Dee was the financial power behind his daughter Helga, who managed that cold clerical principality called Festung Todesangst on Helga's World. He and his daughter had just been assigned a potentially embarrassing piece of property.

Mouse stared at his father's back. Not even he could so cold-bloodedly order a death!

"Blow Michael's ship, too," Storm ordered. "Make it look like Abhoussi got close enough for their fields to brush. Have Benjamin and Lucifer take care of it. It's time they paid their dues."

The brothers Darksword seized the executive's arms. They remained impassive as they marched the Blackworlder to his doom. They might have been two old gentlemen off for an afternoon stroll with a friend.

Mouse's guts twisted into a painful little knot.

Storm turned his back on Dee. He whispered, "Cassius,

just confine him on one of the manned outstations. Officially, he never arrived. Pass the word."

"This won't buy more than a month," Cassius replied. "Richard is damned mad. And the Blake outfit is touchy about its people."

Mouse sighed. His father was not a monster after all.

"They'll be realistic. They want us bad. Let's stall and up their ante. I want a seat on their board and a percentage of their take on the Shadowline thing."

"You trying to price us out of the market?"

"I don't think I can. Keep an eye on the twins. We don't need any more of their crap."

"Uhn." Cassius followed the Darkswords and their victim.

Storm departed a moment later. He left his son Thurston, the warhounds, and the ravenshrikes to watch Michael Dee.

His eye narrowed in anger as he brushed by Mouse. He took a hitch-step, as if considering leaving his son with a few choice words about obedience. He changed his mind, resumed his angry stalk. Mouse's failure to return to Academy was the least of his problems.

Mouse sighed. There would be time for the idea to grow on his father. Time for Cassius to argue his case.

He watched his father leave, frowning. What now? Pollyanna had fled along that corridor a moment ago. Why would his father be following her?

Seventeen: 2844 AD

The old man's name was Jackson, but Deeth had to call him master. He was an outcast even among the descendants of escaped and discarded slaves. He lived in a fetid cave three miles from the animal village. He had parlayed a few sleight-of-hand tricks and a sketchy medical knowledge into a witch-doctor's career. His insane temper and magic were held in awe by his client-victims, who were an utterly mean, degenerate people themselves.

In less than a week Deeth knew that Jackson was a thorough fraud, that he was nothing but a lonely old man enraged by a world he believed had used him ill. His career was an attempt to get back. He was a sad, weak, pathetic creature, incontestably mad, and in his madness was utterly ruthless. Hardly a day passed when he did not torture Deeth for some fancied insult.

He brewed a foul grain beer in the rear of his cave. There were hundreds of gallons in storage or process. Deeth had to keep a full mug ready at all times. Inevitably, Jackson was partially drunk. That did nothing to dampen his free-wheeling temper. But what Deeth found most repulsive were Jackson's hygienic standards.

He came near wretching often that first week. The old man refused to do more than stand and aim aside when he voided his bladder. He never bathed. The cave was more fetid than any animal's den.

He kept Deeth on a ten-foot leash knotted to choke at a tug. The boy soon learned that chokings had nothing to do with his efforts to please or displease. The old man yanked when he felt a need for amusement.

For him the sight of a small boy strangling was the height of entertainment.

Having identified a breakdown between cause and effect, Deeth abandoned efforts to satisfy Jackson. He did what he had to, and spent the rest of his time in sullen thought or quick theft.

Jackson made no effort to feed him. Indeed, he flew into a rage whenever he caught the boy pilfering from their meager larder. Nearly every meal cost Deeth a choking or beating.

He learned to endure in Jackson's cruel school. He began to learn the meaning of his father's and Rhafu's admonitions about taking the long view, about thinking before acting.

His initial lesson was the most painful, degrading, and effective. It came as the result of his first ill-considered attempt at flight, undertaken in sheer animal need to escape an intolerable situation.

His third night in the cave, after he had recovered from the immediate trauma of the station's destruction, but before he had become accustomed to maltreatment by the old man, he remained awake long after Jackson sent him whining to the moldy leaf pile designated as his bed. Jackson, seated in a rude homemade chair, drank and drank and eventually appeared to slip away into drunken sleep.

And Deeth waited, forcing himself to lie still despite a heart-pounding eagerness to be away. Hours trooped by in regiments. The last tiny flames of the cookfire died, leaving a small mound of nervously glowing embers.

He rose quickly, quietly, tried to untie the knot at his neck. His shaking fingers would not cooperate. He could not work a single loop of the tangle free. He crept softly to the old man's chair. The nether end of his leash was knotted around its leg.

The smaller knot, though only a simple clove hitch, defied him for several minutes. Jackson's proximity petrified him. His fingers became rigid, shaking prods.

He kept reminding himself that Rhafu had gone raiding at his age, that he was the first-born son of a Head, that he was heir-apparent to one of the oldest and greatest Families. He should have more courage than a common, possessionless Sangaree hireman. He made a litany of it, running it over and over in his mind.

On Homeworld he had been taught to give fear a concrete character, to make it an object to be fought. His choice of object was obvious. The old man was such a malign presence, so filled with evil promise. . . .

The knot came free. He sprinted for the cave mouth. The rope trailed. . . .

The loop around his throat jerked tight, cut off his wind, and snapped him to a halt. He went down, clawing wildly at his neck.

Jackson, good foot firm on the line, cackled madly. He seized a cane and began beating Deeth, pausing to jerk the neck loop tight whenever Deeth worked it loose enough to gasp.

Jackson's amusement and strength finally faded. He tied Deeth's wrists together and passed the rope through a natural grommet in the cave roof. Up the boy went.

He hung like a punching bag for two long days. Jackson subjected him to every torment his dim mind could imagine, including a foul wanting-to-be-loved, ineffectual homosexual pederasty. And through all those endless hours he whined, "Thought you'd leave poor old Jackson here alone, eh? You Sangaree whelp, don't you know you can't outwit a real man?"

Deeth was petrified. How could the old man know?

Eventually he would learn that Jackson was a reject slave who had understood his frightened outburst the night of his capture.

Through the pain and despair came the knowledge that he would have to degrade himself further to survive. He had to ingratiate himself lest the old man reveal his origins in the village.

When Jackson performed a kindness it was for profit or by oversight. Whichever applied, he never mentioned Deeth's background.

Hanging, aching, despairing, Deeth had time to reflect on the teachings of his elders. He began to understand the meaning of patience.

The old man did not break him. Maybe Deeth did not

crack because the idea was too alien. He could not do what he did not know how to do.

On Homeworld they had a saying, "He's Sangaree." It meant, "He's a real man," only more so. It had overtones of unyielding determination and absolute inflexibility.

Deeth was Sangaree.

The old man tired of abusing him. He left Deeth down, seized him by the hair, hurled him into his pile of leaves. After an admonitory cane whack he bound Deeth's hands behind him and secured the nether end of the rope to the grommet, above Deeth's reach. Then he resumed his residence in his chair, chuckling into his filthy beard.

Deeth lay awake night after night, nursing his hatred and wounded ego. He nurtured his patience and determination to have his revenge.

Eighteen: 3031 AD

"Gneaus!" Pollyanna spoke his name breathily. "You've been avoiding me."

"Not really. I've had work to do."

Every curve of the woman, every patch of soft, smooth skin, bespoke sexual craving. She had that look of constant need seen only in young women in love and the most polished of prostitutes. Like the hookers', her eyes become vacant, cool, and snakelike when she was off stage. She posed, one hip thrown out model fashion. Her breath came in quick little gasps.

He was not playing the game today. "I want to hear all about your travels, little lady." He opened the door to her apartment. She tried the close, casual brush-past going in. He answered it with deliberate chill. A ghost of apprehension crossed her too beautiful face.

She pushed herself at him as soon as he shut the door.

Her pelvis moved against him. "I missed you. All of you. And the Fortress. But especially you, Gneaus. Nobody makes me feel the way you do."

"Sit down," he ordered. She backed away, more apprehensive. "Let's hear the story."

There were few men Pollyanna could not bedazzle and manipulate. Hawksblood. Cassius, who made her blood run chill. The Darkswords. And, she had learned the hard way, Michael Dee. But Storm. . . . He had always been so amenable. He must have been using her when she thought she was using him. Her ego was bruised and aching from traveling with Dee. It was not ready for another blow.

Storm was positively grim.

These invulnerables were all old, old men from whom time and experience had leached all innocence, had abraded all boyish vulnerability. There was a darkness in them, a capital wickedness. It called out to the darknesses in her own soul. Their black flames reached out and pulled her like a candle pulled a moth. She was afraid.

"I didn't mean for anybody to get hurt, Gneaus! Honest. I just wanted to meet Richard Hawksblood."

"This is no nursery school, Pollyanna. This isn't polite society. We play by the rough rules. We had trouble enough without your meddling. Your actions can't be separated from ours. You're family. Richard won't grant you absolution because you're a nitwit. You've caused deaths that can't be recalled. Death breeds death. God only knows how many men are going to die because of you."

It was his fault too, he knew. He should have written her off. He should not have tracked Michael to The Big Rock Candy Mountain. But similar logic could be used to assign blame to Michael, Richard, and Lucifer. No, primary responsibility had to remain Pollyanna's. Hers had been the initiating decision.

"Tell me everything, Pollyanna. I don't want anything

added. I don't want anything left out. I don't want you adjusting anything to make yourself look a little better. I just want straight facts. I want, verbatim, including descriptions of tones of voice and expressions, everything you heard discussed. Especially between Richard and Michael, and anybody they talked with. About anything. There's just a ghost of a chance we can still get out of this, or at least tone it down."

"That would take hours." She turned on the tears. Storm ignored them. Pollyanna interacted with reality through a studied repertoire of poses and roles. The real Miss Eight hid out somewhere way off stage, directing the play, pushing the buttons for whatever response seemed appropriate.

"I've bought time." The stricken face of the Blackworlder ghosted through his thoughts. The man had not doubted his fate for one instant. "I need to buy more."

She turned the tears off as quickly as she had switched them on. She began talking in a small, soft voice devoid of editorialization and emotion. She began at the beginning and told nothing but the bitter truth about everything except her motives.

She had seduced Dee and talked him into taking her to Old Earth with him. She now believed he had acquiesced for his own reasons. Their stay on the motherworld had been dull. The one thing that had impressed her had been the poverty of that gutted, overcrowded planet. Michael had been upset because the holonets had not been interested in his coverage of the action on The Broken Wings.

"From Old Earth we went to Blackworld. He kept me locked in the ship while we were there. The only reason I found out was he talked in his sleep. He wouldn't say squat when he was awake. He was worried and scared. Things weren't going right, somehow. He was a little

82

paranoid, like he was afraid somebody might be after him but he wasn't really sure. After Blackworld we went to see Richard Hawksblood. He isn't such a big deal in person, is he?"

She had not been allowed to approach Dee and Hawksblood most of the time. She did know they were talking about Blackworld. What little she knew she had learned from Richard's underlings.

Then Michael had vanished. No one knew where he had gone. Some thought Tregorgarth, some thought The Big Rock Candy Mountain.

"It was The Mountain, Polly. Go ahead. You're doing great so far."

"I had to hang around and wait. It was boring. I hardly ever saw Hawksblood. He was working on the Blackworld project. I never realized how complicated your work is. You don't just jump in the ring like a boxer, do you?"

Storm smiled the weakest of smiles. If nothing else, Pollyanna had confirmed his intelligence about Richard. Hawksblood was in on Blackworld for sure.

"It was two months before Michael came back. That was a couple of weeks ago. He was really happy. Before, when his tapes were turned down and he thought somebody was after him, you couldn't hardly live with him. All he said was that he saw the man and everything was all right. He wouldn't even talk in his sleep."

Who? Storm wondered. Not him. Who else had been on The Big Rock Candy Mountain? Why had Michael been there, anyway?

"He was back about a week when he grabbed me and that yacht and took off for here. Every couple of days he locked me out of Command. Whenever he let me back in the instel set was warm. I don't know who he was talking to. Then we got here. And the rest you know."

And the rest he knew.

He checked the time. Her tale had taken an hour to tell. He had a few questions. He doubted she could answer them.

Pollyanna, he thought, was one hell of a puzzle. She was all surface and no depth. Even when you bedded a stranger she took on some kind of shape as bits and pieces of bed talk jigsawed together. But not pretty Pollyanna. She remained strictly one-dimensional. Her only real attributes seemed to be her beauty and her vagina, and her devotion to both. She had rebuilt her makeup while she talked.

She was a damned android built for modeling and screwing! You could penetrate her body, but not her façade.

Even Lucifer was baffled by her. She seemed to exist solely to be appreciated for her beauty, like a classic painting or cherished poem. Curious.

He had not thought much about Pollyanna before. She was like that painting. There to be enjoyed and otherwise ignored. It was time to start poking around, back in the silly shadows.

He would have to unravel her by reversing the usual process, by what he did not know.

Pollyanna had made a second point clear. The Blackworld affair was deeper than he had suspected. A potential mercantile war over trillions worth of radioactives did not excite Michael. Pollyanna said he seemed indifferent to the opportunity to tape the conflict. It was important to him for some other reason.

It had to be the Game.

That was Dee's label for the feud he had been engineering between Hawksblood and Storm. He did not know Storm knew that. The Game's goal appeared to be mutual annihilation. It had been going on since the founding of the two freecorps.

Storm still could not understand why.

He bullied Pollyanna. "Who did Michael see on The Big Rock Candy Mountain? Why?" The answer had to be important.

Pollyanna did not have it.

"Ah, damn. Damn." He let her kiss him once, then gently disengaged and departed. He returned to his study, put Cassius on call, and turned to Ecclesiastes. He found no solace there. The frenetic, helter-skelter flitting of his mind kept him from following the printed words. He tried the clarinet.

The soul-trying days had come.

Cassius listened without being noticed. "I've never heard you play so mournfully, Gneaus," he said.

Startled, Storm replied, "It's a dirge. I think we've reached the end. I grilled Pollyanna. She's a good observer. You wouldn't figure it considering how vacuum-brained she acts."

"I've sometimes wondered about that."

"You too? Then it's not my imagination. Could anybody be that shallow without working at it?"

"Possibly. Then again, a preoccupation with sexual encounter would make a mask few men, being egoists, would care to lift. You wanted me?"

Storm made a mental note to ask Frieda and his daughter for the woman's view of Miss Eight. "We're getting old, you and I. We're in our sundown days. Things are slipping past us. It's like we're caught in some backwater of time."

Cassius raised an eyebrow. Storm had difficulty expressing his feelings.

"We're on the verge of the nightfall of the Legion. Maybe of all the freecorps. I think we'll be both cause and effect of our own destruction, and I can't see any way out."

85

"As long as there are corporations and rich men who need us, and who won't be intimidated by the government, there'll be work for us."

"Time's catching up with us. Confederation is starting to flex its muscles. It's a historical process. It's inevitable. Democratic control and government regulation are coming on faster than the frontiers are moving out. They're about to catch up with us."

"You're too much the pessimist."

"Consider the past, Cassius. The block vote of pestholes like Old Earth will devour the capital approach. It's an old story. Goes all the way back to Rome. Why do something for yourself if all you have to do is vote for a guy who'll rob somebody else and do it for you?"

Storm's bitterness surprised him. He had not been aware of the strength of his own feelings.

He told Cassius what he had learned from Pollyanna.

"What do you suggest we do?"

"First, secure Dee here. Things will move slower if he's tied down. Have Thurston handle that. He doesn't have the imagination to be taken in by Michael. You go to The Mountain. Take Mouse. You won't send him back to Academy, and you tell me he's interested in intelligence work. The two of you, find out who Michael met there. Keep an eye out for Seth-Infinite."

"You're softer than you pretend, my friend."

Storm shrugged. "Ship him home if he gets in the way. Tell Wulf and Helmut to start getting ready for Blackworld."

"Why?"

"Looks like we'll end up there, like it or not. We ought to be in shape. Oh. Have the older sergeants think up jobs for Benjamin and Homer. We've got to keep them out of trouble. Lucifer I want to backtrack his damned bubble-brained wife. All the way to the place where she was born. Got it?"

"Got it. I take it you won't be here yourself."

"No. I'll rendezvous with you on your way back from The Mountain." He glanced around, half expecting to see Michael crouching in a shadow. "Where we keep Fearchild. I want to ask him a question."

"Where're you going?"

"Festung Todesangst," Storm murmured. "It was the only clue in Michael's papers. Pollyanna mentioned it. So did Richard."

By the raising of an eyebrow Cassius registered as much emotion as he ever did. "To the lion's den. To see Valerie? Or Helga herself?"

"Valerie. Michael will be using the facilities for all they're worth. And *she* will make sure Valerie handles the work. Valerie might know what's going on."

"I shouldn't presume.... Nevertheless.... Gneaus, it's too damned dangerous. If *she* lays hands on you...."

"I'm aware of the danger. But I have my edge. She doesn't expect me. There's an unmonitored landing pad near an out-of-the-way entry lock. I have her recognition codes. I spent a fortune arranging this way in back when they were building the place."

"Gneaus, I don't think...."

"You can't talk me out of it, Cassius. It's got to be done. Let's get on with it. Let's both go and get back before anybody misses us. We can't control Michael forever even if we chain him to a wall."

"I'm on my way."

Storm sequestered himself with the things he loved, strolling around his study, gently touching this or that, remembering, reaching out after timeworn feelings he had almost forgotten. He and Cassius, they were not emotionally normal. Too many hard decisions, too many cruel losses, had turned them into calloused, indifferent men.

He worried about the young ones. Mouse especially. Would they follow the same doomed path? He hoped not.

His study tour was not a habitual practice. It reflected his appreciation of the dangers of Helga's World, and his uncertainty about his ability to get out again. "The risk has to be taken," he growled. "The thing has to be tried. The key is there somewhere. If it's anywhere."

He spent a few minutes with his wife, then collected equipment he had kept ready since the construction of Festung Todesangst. He said no good-byes.

Cassius would know what to do if he did not come back.

Nineteen: 3020 AD

Frog wakened in the Corporation hospital. Three faces hovered over him. One belonged to a Blake medic with whom he had dealt before. Smythe wasn't bad for a Corporation flunky. Another was a small white face with vulpine features and hungry eyes. He did not know the man. The third was Moira. Pretty little Moira. He tried to smile.

There were no officials around. He was surprised when his sluggish mind noted their absence.

He came up cussing like a stuttering Arab. He got his tongue under control, snarled, "Get the hell out of here, Smythe. I been getting away with it fifty years. Blake ain't going to break me with no phony medical bill."

"On the house, Frog."

"On the house, my ruddy red rectum. Blake don't give away no fourth-hand condom." He glanced at Moira, prim and blondly angelic, trying not to squirm worriedly on a hard chair. He misinterpreted her concern as embarrassment. He flashed her a weak grin. "We argue about it later."

He glared at Foxface. The man had perched on a low

dresser, one foot on the floor. "Who the hell you be, guy?"

"August Plainfield. *Stimpson-Hrabosky News.* Pool man assigned to cover you here."

"Uhn?" He got a bad odor from the newshawk. Vulture-reek, maybe. His breed wallowed in it wherever there was human carrion.

He looked at Moira again. She looked anxious, frightened, and tired. Just the worry? Or the holonet people giving her hell?

He was no fan but he had watched enough HV to know the netmen pursued their stories ruthlessly, with a singleminded inhumanity.

He had half feared he would stir them up with his stunt, but had not foreseen that they would go after Moira. He had rehearsed a few choice lines for them. But Moira. . . . She was a baby. She could not handle the pressure.

What did a child's comfort matter to a vulture like Plainfield? His kind saw everyone and everything as fodder for the camera-cannon they used to down the prey they fed their monster audience.

"Moira, you go outside a minute. I got a word to say to this critter." Pain was not making him feel reasonable. He was sure that Smythe, who had gone next door to check his metabolic monitors, was in a dither. The Doc was all right, but he took things too serious.

Hell, let him stew.

Moira crawled off her chair and left without a word. In her public reticence, and other ways, she was aping him. It was her way of showing affection. Frog found it disconcerting. Like so many men who maintain a tight rein on emotion, Frog longed for its expression in others. It provided him an excuse for opening a little himself. And it terrified him. He might get trapped into exposing an Achilles' heel of self.

He used some of his choice words on the newsman.

Then a few more, bloody-minded, colorful, and threatening. Plainfield endured them like a mountain weathering another of countless storms fated to lash its slopes.

"What did you find out there?" he asked when Frog ran down.

"Huh? Find? Nothing. More Shadowline. More Brightside. And if I did find something, I wouldn't tell no creepo like you."

"Thought so. You rambled a lot while you were under. About the yellow, the orange. Dreaming, Doctor Smythe thinks. I've got a notion you weren't. Dreams don't leave men radiation sick. Yellow has meant radioactivity for a thousand years."

Frog's face wrinkled in a frown so deep that for a moment he resembled a dark-eyed prune. "I don't remember so good. Oxygen starvation do things to your brain. Check my log." He smirked. Plainfield was not going to get near his rig till Blake's people checked it out. They might not bring it in for years.

"I did. I didn't find anything. In fact, I found so much nothing that it made me curious. Made me wonder why a man would tell his computer to forget a place that left him half dead of radiation poisoning. Made me wonder why a man would take the trouble to register a formal claim on the shade at the end of the Shadowline when he thinks he's dying. When he's never filed a claim before. And it made me wonder why he revised his will the minute the claim was notarized."

"I want to be buried out there," Frog improvised. "Somebody's going to do it again someday. I want him to bury my ashes on the only claim I ever had."

"Your diction and syntax are improving." Plainfield smiled a smile that made him appear more wolf than fox. "You may be telling the truth. Corporation people who think they know 'that crazy dwarf' figure it something like that. Or think you're rigging a scheme to get them to throw money down a rathole in some cockamamie revenge. I don't suffer their preconceptions. I don't know you. I just know people. I think you found something."

"Just a place to be buried," Frog insisted nervously. This interrogation was not his idea of an interview.

Plainfield's smile broadened. "You might get there quicker than you want. El Dorados, dreams that come true, they have a way of devouring their dreamers."

"What the hell kind of newsman are you, anyway?" Frog was so nervous his customary act was slipping.

"Call me a dream shaper. I make fantasies come true. Mostly my own, but sometimes other people's, too. Those sometimes turn out to be nightmares."

Frog stopped being nervous and started being scared. He looked around for a weapon.

He was in over his head. Bluster was useless, and his condition denied him his customary alternative, attack.

Frustration kindled anger. Hadn't his flesh always betrayed his spirit? Hadn't he always been just a little too short, too small, or too weak? Why wasn't somebody from Blake doing the questioning?

"Why'd you do it, anyway? I mean, make the run. Reasons after the fact could be supplied, I suppose, but I want to know what makes a man try something impossible in the first place. I've studied everything known about Brightside and the Shadowline. There's no way you could have known that you'd find anything out there."

What does make a man throw himself into something for which there is neither a reasonable nor rational justification? Frog had done a lot of thinking during his run. Not once, even remotely, had he been able to make his motives add up. Most of the time he had told himself that he was doing it for Moira, but there had been times when he had suspected that he was doing it for Frog, to salve a scarred ego by showing humanity it was wrong about his being a clown. Yet that had not taken into account the probability of failure, which would have done nothing but underscore his foolishness.

Why, then? A badfinger for Blake? Because he had had some crazy, deep-down conviction that he would find something? No. Not one of those reasons was good enough in itself.

All that time alone and still he had not figured himself out.

The man who hides from himself hides best of all.

"What did you find?"

Frog strove to focus on Plainfield. And realized that his earlier assessments were incorrect. The man was neither vulture, fox, nor wolf. He was a snake. Cold-blooded, emotionless, deadly. Predatory, and unacquainted with mercy. Nor was he owned. This news business was cover. He was a dagger in his own hand.

Plainfield moved toward him. A slap hypo appeared in his palm. Frog struggled weakly. The hypo hit his arm.

Wrong again, he thought. He's worse than a snake. He's a human.

"What did you find?"

Frog knew he would not make it this time. This man, this thing that called itself August Plainfield and pretended to be a newsman, was going to strip him of his victory, then kill him. Even God in heaven could not stop him from talking once the drug took hold, and then what value would he have alive?

Frog talked. And talked. And, as he knew he must, he died. But before he did, and while he was still sufficiently in possession of his senses to understand, another man entered the dark door before him.

Smythe burst into the room, alerted by his monitors. Moira trailed him as if attached by a short chain. The doctor charged Plainfield, opening his mouth to shout.

A small, silent palm weapon ruined Smythe's heart before any sound left his lips. Moira, as if on a puppeteer's strings, jerked back out of the room. Plainfield cursed but did not pursue her.

A sadness overwhelmed Frog, both for himself and for Smythe.

On Blackworld, as on all but a few worlds, the dead never saw resurrection. Even the Blakes remained dead when they died. Resurrection was too expensive, too difficult, and too complex in social implication. And why bother? Human numbers made life a cheap commodity.

Plainfield finished with Frog, then disappeared. The murders went on record as unsolved. Corporation police hunted the newsman, but no trace turned up.

They wanted him for theft. They wanted him for destruction of municipal and Corporate property. They wanted him for suborning municipal and Corporate employees. They wanted him for a list of crimes. But most of all they wanted him because of Frog and Smythe.

Blake had a long, long memory.

Stimpson-Hrabosky News denied ever having heard of Plainfield. How, then, had Blake's cops demanded, had the man reached Blackworld in a *Stimpson-Hrabosky* charter? How, if he was an unknown, had he managed to get himself elected pool man?

Stimpson-Hrabosky responded with almost contemptuous silence.

Their reticence was itself informative. Plainfield obviously carried a lot of weight outside.

In the furor of pursuit the killer's motives became obscured. Only a handful of men knew about Frog's claim and will, and they were the men Plainfield had bribed. They were on trial and no one was listening to them. They were sent into exile, which meant that they were given outsuits and put out of the city locks to survive as best they could.

Blake reasserted its contention that it never left a debt

outstanding, though it might take a generation to repay.

Frog's original will left Moira more than anyone had anticipated. It set up a trust that assured her a place in Edgeward's life.

And life went on.

Twenty: 3052 AD

We were not a cuddly, loving family, but we had our moments. Most of them were a little bizarre.

—Masato Igarashi Storm

Twenty-One: 3031 AD

The Faceless Man smiled and reached out to Benjamin. He wore nothing. He had no hair, no sex. Benjamin cowered, whimpering. The Faceless Man came toward him with a steady, confident step.

Benjamin whirled with a weak wail, ran. The gooey street grabbed at his feet. He pumped his legs with everything he had, yet they barely moved, pistoning in slowed motion.

The streets and walls of the city were a uniform, blinding white. The buildings had no windows. The doors were almost imperceptible. He flitted from one to another, pounding, crying, "Help me!"

No one answered.

He looked back. The Faceless Man followed him with that smile and confident stride, hand outreaching, his pace no greater than before.

Benjamin fled again, along the molasses street.

Now they opened their little peepholes when he pounded. They looked out and laughed. He flung himself from door to door. The laughter built into a chorus.

His tears flowed. Sweat poured off him. He shuddered constantly. His body ached with his exertion.

He looked back. The Faceless Man was at exactly the same distance, walking steadily, hand outstretched.

He ran in a straight line, trying to gain ground. They laughed at him from the rooftops. They called his name, "Benjamin! Benjamin!" in a feral chant. "Run, little Benjamin, run."

He gasped around a corner into a cul-de-sac. He moaned in terror, whirled, and. . . . The Faceless Man was coming to him, reaching.

He threw himself against the walls. He tried to find a foothold, a way to scale their ivory slickness. "Please! Please don't!"

A hand touched his shoulder. The palm and fingers were icy. Thumb and forefinger squeezed together. Fire lanced through his muscles.

He spun and flung himself at the Faceless Man, clamping his fingers around the throat beneath the unyielding smile.

An unseen hand slapped his face, back and forth, back and forth. He did not relax his grip. A tiny fist began pounding his nose and cheeks.

The real pain reached through his terror. He shook all over, like an epileptic in the first second of seizure.

His eyelids rose. He stared into Pollyanna's terrified face. His hands were at her throat. Her bed was a sweat-soaked disaster. She had scratches on her face and marks on her throat that would become bruises. She kept punching weakly.

He yanked the offending hands away. "Oh, Christ!" he murmured. "Oh, Holy Christ!" He slithered back out of the bed, stood over her for a moment. The shaking would

95

not stop. The layer of sweat covering him was chilling him. He seized a robe. It did nothing to warm him.

"Polly, Honey. Polly. I'm sorry. Are you all right? It was the nightmare. . . . It was worse than I ever had it. He caught me this time. I'm sorry. I thought I was fighting him. Are you all right? Can I get you anything?" He could not stop talking.

His heart hammered. The fear would not go away. He almost expected the Faceless Man to step into the apartment.

Pollyanna nodded. "Water," she croaked.

He crossed to her bathroom, found a glass, tried to fill it. He dropped it twice before getting it to her half full.

She had hitched herself up in bed. She was rubbing her throat with one hand while staring at him timorously. She accepted the glass. "You need help," she whispered. "No! Stay away."

"That's the dream. . . . I run through these streets yelling for help and they all laugh at me. And he keeps on coming. . . . He caught me this time. Polly, I don't know what it means. I'm scared. Honey, please don't pull away. I'm all right now. I didn't mean to hurt you. I thought I was fighting *him*."

Pollyanna relaxed, but not much. She edged away whenever he eased nearer, trying to draw comfort from her proximity and warmth.

"Polly, please. . . ."

The apartment door opened.

It was night in the Fortress of Iron. The hall lights had been dimmed. They saw only the silhouette of a man standing with feet widespread and arms crossed. Anger radiated from him.

Lucifer, voice pitched an octave high, squealed, "You slut! You unholy slut! With my own goddamned brother!"

He flung himself into the room. The light of the bedside

lamp caught his face. It was the face of a killer. He seized Pollyanna's arm and jerked her to her feet, hit her once in the gut, doubled her over. He planted another on her chin. He was swinging hard. Benjamin oofed when his brother's fist cracked the second time. He thought Lucifer had broken her jaw.

Lucifer broke his hand. He let out a little mewl of surprise and pain and looked at the fist, puzzled.

Benjamin reached Lucifer, hurled him away from Pollyanna. Lucifer stumbled over a chair and went down. He came up cursing. "You bastard. You leave my wife alone. I'll kill you." He charged Benjamin. His good hand clutched a knife.

Someone looked in the door, stared momentarily, then ran away.

Baffled and frightened, Benjamin crouched, waited. He blocked the knife stroke, punched Lucifer, tried for a grip on Lucifer's wrist above the blade. Lucifer danced back, crouched himself.

They had been taught in their father's schools. They were proficient killers. An uninvolved observer would have considered it an interesting match.

Lucifer feinted, feinted, stabbed. Benjamin slid aside, chopped down at the blade. It was not where he expected it to be. It drew a fine line of blood from the skin of his thigh as it withdrew.

"I'll take care of that," Lucifer snarled, nodding at his brother's groin. "You won't be bedding anyone's wife. Not even your own, you arrogant, pretty bastard." He circled. Sweating, Benjamin waited.

He kicked a pillow at his brother's face. Lucifer leaned out of the way, moved in.

A blast of icy water hit him, hurled him across the room. Benjamin turned. The water hit like the pummeling of a hundred fists. It drove him against a wall. "Stop it, goddamnit!" he raged.

97

The water stopped.

Two Legionnaires stood in the doorway, holding a fire hose. Frieda Storm pushed past them, her face aquiver with anger. She looked every bit as daunting as her father, Cassius. "Benjamin. Get your clothes on. Woman. You too. Lucifer. On your feet. Now!" She kicked him. It was no delicate female toe tap.

She did not ask what had happened. That was obvious.

"What the hell is the matter with you?" she demanded of Benjamin. "There a suicidal streak in you? First that crap with Richard's cruiser, now this."

"Mother, I. . . ."

"Homer did it. Yes. And who's responsible for Homer? Who let him do it? Heinrich, take Lucifer to Medical. There's something wrong with his hand." She moved toward Pollyanna. The girl was getting dressed so fast she kept getting snaps lined up wrong. Frieda grabbed her chin, turned her head one way, then the other. Pollyanna avoided her eyes. "What happened to your throat?"

"I did it," Benjamin murmured.

"What did you say?"

"I did it, Mother. I had the dream. . . . This time he caught me. I was fighting him."

Frieda's face changed slightly. It was not a softening, just a momentary shadow of fear. "I'll have to talk to Madame Endor. Get a new reading. She was afraid this would happen."

"Mother. . . ."

"Benjamin, don't you have any decency? Don't you have any common sense? This is your brother's wife. This is your brother's home. Shut up! I know she's a damned public utility. I know that anybody who asks gets. You should have brains enough not to ask. You should, for Christ's sake, have brains enough to realize that he'd want to see her tonight. He's leaving the Fortress tomorrow."

"Leaving? I didn't know. . . ."

"My father wants him to do something. If you paid attention to anything but your own precious self. . . ." She turned to Pollyanna. "Get this place cleaned up. I'll send someone to help. And be warned. I'm taking this up with my husband when he gets back. Benjamin." She took his hand. "Come on."

Once in the citadel of her own apartment Frieda clutched him close, and whispered, exasperated, "Ben, darling boy, why do you do these things? I just can't keep getting you out of trouble. Your father is going to throw a bearing when he hears about this."

"Mother. . . ."

"He'll hear about it. It'll be all over the Fortress tomorrow, for God's sake. Ben, stay away from her. She's like a cat in heat. She doesn't care."

"Mother. . . ."

"Sit down. There. Good. I want you to think now, Ben. Really think. About you. About that woman. About Lucifer. About what all is happening here. The problems your father and grandfather have. And most of all, about Michael Dee. Michael Dee is *here,* Ben. Did you bother to wonder why? There's a reason. He doesn't do anything without a sneaky reason. And your father and grandfather made the mistake of leaving while he's here."

"Mother. . . ."

"Don't move. Don't talk. Just think. I'll make you a drink."

She did, and while he nursed it she made comm calls. First she spoke with Madame Endor, the occultist she had imported from New Earth. It was a long conversation. She ended it wearing a pale face.

She placed the second call to the armory, waking the chief armorer. She ordered him to provide Benjamin with one of the lightweight weapon-proof "undersuits" Interstellar Technics had been trying to peddle to her husband for wear under ordinary garments.

"I don't care if we haven't bought them, Captain. I'll pay for it myself if the Legion won't. And *make* the modifications. He'll be down for his fitting in the morning." She ended the call angrily.

She went over and sat opposite her son, stared at him till he looked up and asked, "You called Madame Endor, didn't you?"

She nodded.

"About the dream? What did she say?" Frieda did not respond. "Was it bad?"

"Ben, first thing tomorrow I want you to go to the armory. Captain Fergus will fit you with one of the ITI personal suits."

"Mother. . . ."

"Do it, Benjamin."

"Mother. . . ."

"I mean it, Benjamin."

He sighed.

The fear hit him. It was the first time it had come while he was awake. Involuntarily, he looked back to see how close the Faceless Man had come.

Twenty-Two: 2844-5 AD

The Sangaree facility for bearing hatred like a torch against the night sustained Deeth throughout the grim months of his captivity. Jackson sometimes came close to crushing him, and assumed he had, but always, way back behind the meek exterior he adopted as protective coloration, Deeth nurtured his hatred. He thought, planned, and schooled his patience.

A week after his attempted escape Jackson took him

to the village. The visit shook him more than had the old man's knowledge of his racial identity.

The village itself met his expectations. It consisted of a dozen filthy, primitive huts. The villagers were semi-nomadic hunters and gatherers. There were a hundred of them, ranging from numerous children to a handful of old folks.

The chieftain was about thirty Prefactlas years of age. That was barely adult by civilized standards. Here he was an elder. Life in the forest was brief and brutal.

About thirty Norbon workers and breeder fugitives had reached the village. Their condition astounded Deeth.

The wild animals were using their cousins as slaves, and far more cruelly than had the Norbon. The villagers were still exchanging jests about their gullibility.

Deeth followed Jackson as he went from house to house in search of patients. He saw Norbon animals being mistreated everywhere. There was a girl, no older than he, who had been confined in a storage pit for spurning the chieftain. There was a field hand nailed to a rude cross, moaning and coughing up blood. He had fought back. There was a corpse in the square, rotting away. Insects masked it. The man had been roasted alive.

Deeth's stomach churned all day. How could these beasts use their own kind so cruelly? They had no reason.

Was this why his elders held the human species in such contempt?

Jackson had done him an accidental kindness by frustrating his escape. He could have stumbled into something worse.

Jackson used steaming, fetid poultices to treat a growth on the chieftain's neck. Deeth squatted in the dust outside, beside the pit holding the girl. She hid in shadows and tangled, blood-caked, once-blonde hair. Her shoulders were scabby ruins. A cloud of insects surrounded her. She

101

looked like one of the Nordic pleasure girls, a cheap, mass-market product.

There was a steady demand for Nordics. The Norbon raised them real-time. The Family had a good strain.

The Norbon claimed several excellent pleasure strains. Coffee Mulatto Number Three regularly placed in the shows.

Deeth shrugged. That was another reality, a billion light-years away and a thousand years ago. It was another Deeth who had learned pride in Family achievement.

"You," he grunted.

She did not respond. He kept squatting there. The sun crept across the sky, sliding his shadow across her. He felt her growing curiosity.

She glanced up, saw the rope around his throat. Fear and hope crossed her battered face.

Deeth did not recognize her. Clearly, she knew him. He smiled reassuringly.

He felt the caress of compassion, a gnarly, knobbly sort that had its roots more in classroom training than genuine emotion. He had been taught to cherish and maintain Family property. Abuse and waste were sins. Homeworld was a sometimes harsh, always poor planet. Its values and institutions were geared to conservation.

He could order a thousand slaves killed without a touch of conscience if there was a compelling need. He could not waste one, or destroy it out of malice. He could not abide waste or malice in others.

That was fitting in a Head.

He was the senior Norbon on Prefactlas now. The welfare and conservation of Norbon properties were his responsibility.

"Be patient, girl," he whispered. "Endure. We'll create our own good luck."

He felt foolish. His promise was meaningless. He was

powerless to hurt or help. What would his father have done? Or Rhafu?

The same. Endure. Take care of their own.

An animal came howling into the village. He pointed behind him. The empty square filled. Animals hustled their valuables, especially the new slaves, into places of hiding. Bows and spears appeared.

Jackson grabbed Deeth's rope and fled. The old man cursed softly and continuously.

A pair of Marine personnel carriers clanked into the village from the far side. A support ship whickered over, hovered above the square. There were shouts and explosions. They faded as the old man kept putting distance behind them.

Were they looking for him? Deeth wondered. Did they know about his escape? He hoped not. Sant spare him, they would hunt till they got him. Humans were single-minded that way.

They reached the cave. Jackson beat him as though he were responsible for the raid.

He endured.

Months groaned by. Each staggered on like a wounded levitathan.

Deeth spent three-quarters of a Prefactlas year as Jackson's slave. They made weekly trips to the village. The animals had stayed put since the raid. They were afraid to migrate. Stronger tribes might prey upon them.

The slave girl Emily was the only Norbon animal not recovered by the Marines. Deeth visited with her whenever he had a chance. He kept repeating his promise of rescue.

He added the obligation to his hatred. Together they sustained him.

Twenty-Three: 3031 AD

In 3031 the dead did not always stay down.

Human brains were in demand in an exploding cryocyborgic data-processing industry. Personality-scrubbed and inplugged to computation and data-storage systems, a few kilos of human nervous tissue could replace tons of specialized control and volitional systems.

No remedy for degradation in nervous tissue had yet been found. The cryocyborgic environment sometimes accelerated decay.

Nerve life had become the practical span limit for men like Gneaus Storm, who had power, money, and access to the finest rejuvenation and resurrection technology.

The number of brains available for cryocyborging never filled demand. The shortfall was filled in a variety of ways. Old Earth sold the brains of criminals in exchange for hard outworlds currency. A few were available through underworld channels. The bulk came of involuntary salvage.

There were a dozen entrepreneurs who jackaled around the edges of disasters and armed conflicts, snapping up loose bodies to resell organs. Confederation's armed forces often left their lower grade enlisted men where they fell. The soldiers themselves were indifferent to the fate of their corpses. Most were desperate men willing to risk anything to earn a long retirement outside the slums of their birth.

Gneaus Storm's agents dogged the service battlegrounds too, selecting men who had died well. Cryonically preserved, they were revived later and asked to join the Legion.

Most accepted with a childlike gratitude. A rise from a slum to the imaginary glory and high life of the Iron Legion, after having escaped the Reaper by Storm's grace, seemed an elevation to paradise. The holonets called them the Legion of the Dead.

Helga Dee used hundreds of scavenged brains in her business. Only the Dees themselves knew the capacity of her Helga's World "information warehouse." Publicly, Helga admitted only to capabilities in keeping with brain acquisitions that were a matter of public record.

Storm was sure she controlled a capacity twice what she admitted.

Helga's World was a dead planet. The human contagion had touched it only once, to create and occupy the vast installation called Festung Todesangst. The heart of Helga's far-reaching Corporation lay there, deep beneath the surface of that remote rock cold in the claws of entropy, orbiting a dying star. No one went in but family, the dead, and that occasional person the Dees wanted to disappear. No one came out but Dees.

The defenses at Festung Todesangst were legend. They were as quirky and perverse as Helga herself.

Men who went down to Helga's World were like last year's mayflies: gone forever. And Gneaus Storm meant to penetrate that ice-masked hell hole.

He did not expect Helga to welcome him. She hated him with a hatred archetypal in its depth and fury. Michael's children all hated Storm. Each had compelled him to recognize his or her existence and respond. His crime was that he had come out on top every time.

The Dee offspring were worse than their father.

Fearchild had raised his fuss, costing Cassius a hand. Storm and Cassius now kept him confined in a place only they knew. He was a hostage guaranteeing restraint by the others. The Dees were, unfortunately, all irrational, passionate people, apt to forget in heated moments.

Helga had tried to avenge Fearchild by capturing Storm's daughter Valerie and using her as part of Festung Todesangst.

Storm's response had been to capture Helga and deliver her to her own fortress so badly mauled that she had been able to survive only by cyborging in to her own machines. Forever damned to a mechanical half-life, she calculated and brooded and awaited a day when she could requite his cruelties.

Seth-Infinite, too, had given frequent offense. He seemed to be everywhere and nowhere, appearing openly some place like Luna Command, then disappearing before the swiftest hunters closed in. Half the things he did were nose-thumbings at the Storms. Like his father, he was slippery, and he always had several schemes in the air. Like Michael, he did nothing for a simple, linear reason.

It would be a fine, serendipitous thing, Storm reflected, if Cassius surprised Seth-Infinite on The Mountain.

Twenty-Four: 2854-3031 AD

Michael Dee's moments of happiness were tiny islands scattered in a vast sea. His life was a swift one. He had so much in the air that, when he found time to look around, he seemed to have surfaced in an alien universe. In the year of the Shadowline he had nothing but his schemes.

He always had been a little outside. His earliest memory was of a fight with Gneaus over his being different.

Gneaus eventually accepted him. He had less luck accepting himself.

Down on the bottom line Michael Dee did not like Michael Dee very much. There was something wrong with him.

That he was different he first inferred from his mother's attitude. She was too protective, too fearful.

Boris Storm, the man he thought was his father, was seldom around. Boris was preoccupied with his work. He had few chances to be with his family. Michael developed no bond with the paterfamilias.

Emily Storm hovered over her firstborn. She corrected and protected, corrected and protected, till Michael was convinced that there was an evil in him that scared her silly.

What was this dark thing? He agonized over it by the hour and could find nothing.

Other children sensed it. They withdrew. He studied people, seeking his reflection. He found ways to manipulate others, but the real secret eluded him.

Only Gneaus accepted him. Poor bullheaded Gneaus, who would take a beating rather than admit that his brother was strange.

Poor health complicated Michael's childhood. Boris spent fortunes on doctors. Bad genes, they would hazard, after finding nothing specifically wrong.

He was weak, pale, and sickly into his teens. His brother fought his battles. Gneaus was so strong, so stubborn, and so feared that the other children ignored Michael rather than risk a fight.

So Michael began spinning tall tales as an attention-getting device. He was amazed. His stories were believed! He had a talent. When he recognized the power he had to shape the truth, he used it.

In time he came to weigh every word, every gesture, before revealing it. He calculated its effect on his audience carefully. He reached the point where he could not be direct. In time even the simplest end had to be accomplished by complex means.

He never found his way out of that self-made trap.

He was blessed, or cursed, with brilliance and an almost

eidetic memory. He used those tools to keep his webs of deceit taut and strong. He became a master liar, deceiver, and schemer. He lived at the eye of a hurricane of falsehood and discord.

In those days Academy's minimum-age requirement was fourteen standard years. As Gneaus's eligibility year approached, Boris Storm maneuvered to obtain favorable consideration for his son and stepson.

Boris was the scion of an old military family. His ancestors had been career people with the Palisarian Directorate, one of the founder-states of Confederation. He had departed service himself, but could conceive of no higher goal toward which to direct his offspring. He aimed them at commissions all their lives. Their early education took place in a private, militarily oriented special school he set up for the children of Prefactlas Corporation's officers.

Michael and Gneaus first encountered Richard Hawksblood there. He was Richard Woracek at the time. He took the name Hawksblood when he became a mercenary.

Richard was the son of a management consultant Boris brought in to improve his profit margin. The family had no service background. Richard was an outsider among children who saw civilians as a lower life form. Richard was, at the outset, smaller and more sickly than Michael. He was Dee's favorite victim.

Richard accepted slings and arrows with calm dignity and a refusal to be aroused. His imperturbability infuriated his classmates. He fought back by being better than anyone at everything. Only Gneaus was able, on occasion, to rise to the rarefied airs where Woracek soared.

His excellence only compounded his troubles with his peers. Gneaus, who was his closest acquaintance, often became exasperated because Richard would not fight back.

"The scores will even themselves," Woracek promised.

They did.

Eligibility time arrived, and with it Academy's grueling competitive exams. The youths flashed like spearpoints toward the target at which their parents had aimed their young lives. They streaked toward their chances to become card-carrying members of the established elite.

The battery lasted six exhausting days. Part was physical and psychological. A substantial fraction sampled general knowledge and tested problem-solving abilities. The candidates knew Richard would ace those forms. They were surprised to see Michael finish them almost as quickly.

Richard turned in his final test sheet and calmly announced that he had been deliberately answering incorrectly. The monitor asked why. Richard told him that someone had copied some of his answers. Could he retest in isolation?

Computer analysis indicated an unnatural relationship between Woracek's answers and those of Michael Dee. Richard was allowed his retest. He came in with the highest scores ever recorded.

Michael tried it the lazy way. The snake turned on him. He watched his dreams collapse like the topless towers.

He knew it was his own fault. Still, he had a perverse streak. Richard shared the blame. It was Woracek's fault, if you saw it from the right angle.

That was Michael Dee's watershed point. He had begun deceiving himself. His last bulwark of reality gone, he went adrift. He became a one-man universe whose ties to the larger existence were bonds of falsehood and hatred founded on untruth. He had chained himself in fetters so intangible and cunningly forged that even he could not define them.

He did bounce back from rejection. He found a new direction, in a field which valued men with his ability to restructure reality. He became a journalist.

109

The holonets, ratings foremost in the moguls' minds, had abandoned all pretense to objective reporting long ago. When Michael entered the trade drama was the bait that got the audiences to switch on. The bloodier the report the better.

Michael wanted to make it as an independent. He struggled hard for years. Then the Ulantonid War broke.

He showed a knack for being in the right place at the right time. He produced the best coverage repeatedly. His colleagues made tape after tape of disaster after disaster as the Ulantonid blitz smashed toward the Inner Worlds. Michael found the bright spots, the little victories and heroic stands. His coverage elbowed to the top.

While Boris, Gneaus, Cassius, and Richard fought for their lives in what looked a foredoomed effort to stall Ulant, Michael had fun making tapes. The Storms were impoverished by Ulant's occupation of Prefactlas. He grew rich. He set his own price for his material. In the wartime confusion he evaded taxation deftly and invested brilliantly. He bought huge chunks of instel stocks when commercial faster-than-light communication seemed nothing but wishful thinking. He got into interstellar data warehousing, a sideline that would lead to the creation of Festung Todesangst.

Everything he touched turned to gold.

He never forgave Richard. Though his fortunes soared, he was always the outsider at the party. Without that Academy diploma he could not rise above the second social rank. Service officers were the aristocrats of the age.

The war ended. Its chaos continued. Grand Admiral McGraw went rogue. Sangaree raiders continued to harry the spaceways. There were people to blame. Michael got into piracy.

He was careful. Hardly anyone ever suspected. He creamed information from his instel and data corporations to parlay a pair of broken-down destroyers into another fortune.

His extralegal adventures led him into another life-trap.

Twenty-Five: 3031 AD

Helga's World orbited far from its primary. Raging methane winds screamed across its surface. They were as cold as its mistress's heart, as unremitting in their savagery. Storm searched for the telltale heat concentration. Festung Todesangst was dug in deep, tapping the core's remaining heat.

He sent the stolen recognition codes, then injected his singleship into a low polar orbit. He went around three times before detecting the thermal anomaly. He took a fix and hit methane in a penetration run.

Spy-eyes above and below ignored him. No missiles rose to greet him.

He had the right codes.

He smiled tightly, already worrying about the harder task of getting out.

He regretted spending an advantage that could be used but once. He hoarded those with a miser's touch. This one could be saved no longer, and could not be used again. Helga would eliminate the gaps in her protection following his visit.

He touched down. Already in EVA gear, he plunged into a violent methane wind. There was one instant of incredible cold while his suit heaters lagged in their effort to warm him.

"Poor navigation," he muttered. The doorway he wanted lay a kilometer away. The wind-chill might kill him before he got there.

It was too late to cry. Moving ship would tempt fate too much. Hobson's choice.

He started walking.

This lock had been an access portal during construction, a workmen's convenience that had not been sealed. One of Helga's weird guardians would be stationed inside, but she should be a half-century unwary. He thought he could surprise her.

He leaned into the gale, ignoring the bitter cold. Each few hundred steps he examined the glove covering his suit's left hand. He was not sure it would withstand the chill.

His odyssey went on and on. The wind and oxygen snow were gleefully malicious conspirators trying to contrive a disaster. Then there was a slackening of the gale's force. He glanced up. He had entered the lee of the lock housing.

The outer lock door stood slightly ajar. He forced himself through the gap and initiated the lock cycle.

Would the carelessness that had left the door open have allowed icing in the mechanism? The door shuddered, groaned, protesting. It whined shrilly. It broke loose and sealed. Frost formed on his suit and faceplate as breathable air flooded the chamber.

He batted the haze from his faceplate and found himself facing one of the more grotesque products of genetic engineering.

Helga's guardian was an amazon of skeletal thinness, with translucent skin, completely hairless and breathless. She was human and female only by virtue of her navel and the virgin slit between her sticklike thighs. And in her confusion at this unexpected apparition stepping from the lock.

Face-plate frosting made Storm briefly vulnerable but she wasted those seconds. She finally responded by switching on subsonics that caused an increasing dread as he approached her.

112

There was no humanity in her death's-head face. The little muscles under that deathlike skin never twitched in expression. Storm fought the mesmeric assault of the sonics, forced his fear to work for him. "Dead," he told himself.

He felt an instant of compassion, and knew it a waste. This thing was less alive than his most often resurrected soldier.

Storm approached the guardian, left hand reaching.

She looked frail and powerless. The impression was false. No man living could best her without special equipment. Pain, injury, and the normal limits of human strength meant nothing to her. She had been bred to one purpose, to attack till victorious or destroyed.

Storm's glove touched her arm lightly, discharged. The shock was supposed to scramble her neural signals and make her amenable.

It worked, but not as well as he hoped. She became less truculent, but far from docile. He took control, stripped her of her sonics, force-marched her down stairs and inclines. Every ten minutes he gave her another shock, expending more of the glove's power.

He worried. He was squandering his best weapon. If the charge went too soon he would have to kill her. He needed live bait to pass the next obstacle.

His path, as did all corridors from the surface, debouched in a dark, stadium-vast chamber, the ceiling of which was natural cavern. The floor had been machined smooth and covered with a half-meter of sand.

This, Storm thought as he crouched at the tunnel's end, is the real gateway to Festung Todesangst. This is the real guardhouse. Here the most powerful weapons were all but useless. The watchman was of a size in keeping with that of his kiosk.

Helga Dee had a bizarre sense of humor, a cockeyed way of looking at the universe. Her gateman was a reptil-

113

ian thing, tyrannosaur-sized, from a world so massive that here it was as agile as a kitten. Only Helga herself, who had raised it from an egg and lovingly called it her "puppy," could control it. Through its love for her, she claimed. Storm believed she used implanted controls.

The thing subsisted on the flesh of brain donors and Helga's enemies.

As a defense it was primitive, crude, and devastatingly effective. And it was a glass-clear illustration of a facet of Helga Dee. Using it to back her sophisticated surface defenses was her idea of a joke.

The thing's bellow smashed at Storm. His ears ached. He saw nothing but a suggestion of shifting immensity inside the poorly illuminated cavern.

He was not here to ooh and ah at the animals in the zoo. The thing was an obstacle, not a spectacle. It required moving or removing. He took a kilo-weight packet from his tool belt, limpeted it to the amazon's back. He tossed a flare into the monster's chamber to get its attention. He hurled the guardian after it.

A vast, scaly head speared out of the gloom. The skeleton woman vanished into a fangy mouth. A huge yellow eye considered Storm.

The head rose. From the darkness came the sound of a vast bulk moving and of bones cracking.

Storm shuddered. The woman had gone to her death without a sound.

For an instant he wondered why he had not killed Helga when he had had the chance.

He waited. The munching faded. She *would* choose a monster that chewed its food.

The beast rumbled. Storm waited. Soon it was snoring like a healthy volcano. He waited some more, fretting at the delay.

It seemed he had been there half his life, and still he

114

had not started. He still had to penetrate the fortress proper.

The drug was supposed to be fast, but it was old. And the poison with it was slow. He had to wait to be sure.

He wanted the monster asleep while he was below, and dead only after he made his escape. Helga might monitor its vital signs.

He made it three quarters of the way across the arena before the monster abandoned pretense. Its immensity bore down on him like some anachronistic blood-and-bone dreadnought.

It was not moving as lithely as earlier. The drug had had some effect. Storm did not panic, though fear raked him with claws of steel. He faced the charge.

He had rehearsed this confrontation for years. Rote reaction carried him through.

While backing toward his goal he set his glove to short in a single burst of power. The great head, the scimitar teeth, came down, slowly for the beast but incredibly fast in Storm's subjective perception.

He hurled himself aside, gloved hand reaching back like an eagle's talons. For an instant his fingers touched the moist soft flesh inside a gargantuan nostril. The glove blew. Charred flesh putrified the air. The beast flung back, screaming, falling over its tangled legs, tearing at its snout with its foreclaws.

Storm went sprawling. Up on adrenalin to a perilous level, he rose with a bounce astounding in a man of his age. He crouched, ready to dodge the next attack, hoping he could cat and mouse long enough to reach an exit.

The thing was preoccupied. Like a hound stung by a bee it had been snuffling; it kept pawing its nose. It tore its own flesh. When it ground its scaly snout into the sand, Storm laughed hysterically. He fled for the entrance.

The unbreachable gate had been broken. He had penetrated Festung Todesangst.

It took time to get hold of himself, to get his bearings. He wished he could quit. He wanted nothing so much as the peace and security of his study.

Giving in would not matter. He could not win anyway. Not in the long run. Why fight? Why not steal a little peace before the inevitable closed in?

That part of him which could not yield asserted itself. He resumed moving, downward, deep into Festung Todesangst.

The deeps of Helga's World were sterile and lifeless. He walked long corridors with featureless metal floors and wall, under blue-white lights. The only odor was a mild taint of ozone, the only sound a barely discernible hum. It was like walking the halls of an abandoned but perfectly maintained hospital.

The life of Festung Todesangst lay hidden behind those featureless walls. Thousands of human brains. Cubic kilometers of microchips and magnetic bubbles shuffling mega-googols of information bits. Helga's World had become the data warehouse of the human universe.

What unsuspected secrets lay hidden there? How much power for someone able to possess or dispossess Helga Dee?

Immense power. But no force, not even that of Confederation, could plunder Helga's empire. Her father had promised the universe that she would bring on the Götterdämmerung rather than surrender her position. Any conqueror would have to surreptitiously deactivate a dozen thermonuclear destruct charges and disconnect all the poison stores set to kill the brains in their support tanks. He would have to deactivate Helga herself, from whom all control flowed.

It was a setup characteristic of the Dees. What was theirs was theirs forever. Only what was yours was negotiable. No one, especially an avaricious government, was going to rob the family.

Storm meant to steal from a Dee. From the coldest, most hateful, and jealous one of them all. And he would accomplish it with the help of something stolen from himself. The great prize of the queen of the dead was going to become her most severe liability.

He was going to hurt her, and he was going to enjoy doing it.

Kilometers beneath the surface, beneath even the vast main fortress, so deep that his suit had to cool instead of heat, he found the terminal he sought.

It was the master for one small, semi-independent system. It existed for one limited, cruel purpose. It was the focus from which Helga meant to engineer her revenge upon Gneaus Julius Storm. Within it lay everything known about Storm and the Iron Legion. He suspected that it contained things he did not know himself. To it came every stray wisp of information, every gossamer strand of rumor, vaguely relating to himself.

To it, also, Michael Dee came when he had some scheme afoot.

Once upon a time Helga had been a wild-eyed wanton, rushing from thrill to ever more bizarre thrill with the frenzy of a woman condemned. Being locked into the endless boredom of Festung Todesangst was the cruelest fate she could imagine. She extracted compensatory bites from his soul every minute this bottom-most system ran.

The corebrain here, the overbrain that controlled the others, was that of his daughter Valerie. She had not been ego-scrubbed before being cyborged in. Every second that passed, in a vastly telescoped subjective time, was one in which she was aware of her identity and plight.

For this cruelty he would kill Helga Dee. When the time came. When the moment was ripe.

All things in their season.

He stared at the terminal for a long time, trying to disremember that the soul of the machine was a daughter he had loved too much.

Age, Storm would declare when the subject arose, did not confer wisdom, only experience from which the wise could draw inferences. And even the wisest man had blind spots, and could behave like a fool, and remain so adamant in his folly that it would strangle him with a garrote of his own devising.

Storm's blind spots were Richard Hawksblood and Michael Dee. He was overly ready to attribute evil to Richard, and too trusting and forgiving with his brother.

A long time ago, much as Pollyanna had recently, Valerie had vanished from the Fortress of Iron. Storm still was not sure, but suspected the machinations of Michael Dee. Nor did he know Valerie's motives for leaving, though beforehand she had spoken often of making peace with Richard.

His memories of Valerie's case colored his behavior in Pollyanna's. He went haring off to the rescue—perhaps unwisely.

Valerie fell in love with Hawksblood.

Word of their affair filtered back. Storm flew into a rage. He accused Richard of every crime a father ever laid on a daughter's lover. Michael arranged a meeting. Fool that he was, Storm disowned her when she refused to come home.

He was sorry the instant he spoke, but was too stubborn to recall words once flown. And he became sorrier still when Helga, after gulling her own father, snatched Valerie and hustled her off to Festung Todesangst.

Poor Valerie. She went into mechanical/cerebral bondage believing her father had abandoned her, that he had used her cruelly.

Storm had been working on Helga ever since. His vengeance thus far he deemed only token repayment for the destruction of a daughter's love.

They were hard, cruel, anachronistic men and women, the Storms and Dees, and Hawksbloods, and those who served them.

Enough, he told himself. He had crucified himself on this cross too often already. Hand trembling, he jacked his comm plug into a direct verbal input.

"Valerie?"

Came a sense of stirring into wakefulness. An electronic rustling. Then a return his equipment interpreted as "Who's there?" It contained overtones of surprise.

There was just one answer he dared give, just one that would not spark an explosion of bitterness. "Richard Hawksblood."

"Richard? What are you doing here?"

He felt her uncertainty, her hope, her fear. It hit him hard. He had an instant of nausea. Some foul worm was trying to gnaw its way out of his gut.

If he and Richard agreed on anything, it was that Helga should be punished for this.

Richard had loved Valerie. That love was one more unbridgeable gap between them.

"I came to see you. To free you. And to find out what Helga is doing to your father and me."

There was a long, long silence. He began to fear that he had lost her. Finally, "Who calls? I've slept here so long. So peacefully."

He could taste the agony of her lie. There was no peace for Valerie Storm. Helga made sure of that.

Storm replied, "Richard Hawksblood." He wished he knew their love talk, the pet names they had called one another in the night, or the all-important trivia that pass between a man and woman in love. "Valerie, what was that new complex I saw on my way down?" Between

119

Helga's puppy and Valerie's pit he had encountered little but endless sterility and silence, except on the last few levels, where he had to slip through a construction zone as softly as a prowling kitten.

He wondered if Helga's zombie workers would have noticed if he had strutted through their midst. Personality-scrubbed, they were little more than robots. But they might be robots programed to report anomalies.

"Cryocrypts for the sons of my father, whose deaths will be the first step of my mistress's revenge."

Storm subdued his anger response. "How? Why?"

"Helga and her father have decided that my father will fight on Blackworld. They intend to capture some of my brothers and hold them here till the fighting is done."

"Helga would never release them."

"No. Her father doesn't know that."

"How?"

"Michael Dee will capture them."

Storm recalled Benjamin's nightmares. Were they a valid precognition? Could both twins have the psi touch? Could the Faceless Man be Michael Dee? "How will they kill Benjamin?" he blurted.

He grimaced as he spoke Benjamin's name. Richard Hawksblood could not have known that anything of the sort was planned. He could not have done the sums.

"You! You didn't sound like Richard. So cold. He would've. . . . Storm. My father. Here. Only he could suspect. . . ."

She seemed too stunned to give an alarm—or did not want to sound one. Perhaps she had forgiven him just a little.

"Valerie, I'm sorry. I was a fool." The words came hard. He did not admit error easily.

He had to move fast. Helga would have made sure Valerie could keep no secrets. "Honeyhair. . . . Forgive me." He had to do the thing that, when first they had learned of Valerie's enslavement, he and Richard had agreed had to be done.

There could be but one escape for Valerie Storm. He could free her no other way.

Flesh of his flesh, blood of his blood. . . . He had trouble seeing. There was water in his eye.

Shaking, he reached for the large red lever prominent in the center of the terminal. The worm within his gut metamorphosed, became an angry, clawing dragon.

He had thought himself too old, too calloused to feel such pain.

He hesitated for just an instant. Then he pulled the safety pin and yanked the lever.

His helmet filled with a sound not unlike that of someone slowly strangling. His hand strayed toward the comm jack. He forced it away. He had to listen, to remember. This dread moment would never have been were he not a bullheaded idiot.

One must savor the bitter taste of folly as well as the sweetness of wisdom, for wisdom is born of folly well remembered.

She was going. Faintly, she murmured, "Peace. Father, tell Richard. . . . Please. Tell Richard I . . . I . . . ."

"I will, Valerie. Honeyhair. I will."

"Father . . . Play something . . . the way you used to."

A tear forced itself from his eye as he remembered a tune he used to tootle for her when she was a child. He unslung the case on his back, praying the cold and encounter with Helga's guardian had not ruined his instrument. He wet the reed, closed his eye, began to play. It squealed a little, but yielded its child-memory. "That one, Honeyhair?"

Silence. The voiceless, bellowing silence of death.

He indulged in a frenzy of rage that masked a deeper, more painful emotion. For one long minute he let his grief take him. His music became an agonized howl.

Valerie was not the first of his blood he had slain. She might not be the last. Practice did not ease the agony. He could not do it without crying in the night forever afterward.

This Storm, the Storm of tears and grief and fury, was the Storm no one ever saw, the Storm unknown to anyone but Frieda, who held him while the sobs racked him.

He took hold. There were things to do. He had learned something. He had to move fast.

He used the dead face of Helga Dee as a will-o'-the-wisp to follow from Festung Todesangst's deeps. He stalked it with the intensity of a fanatic assassin.

He had thought that he hated Richard Hawksblood. That odium was a child's fleeting passion compared to what he felt now. His feelings toward Helga had become a torch he would follow through the darkness all the rest of his days.

He had not asked the questions that had brought him to Helga's World. But their answers were implicit in what he *had* learned.

They had come to the end of Michael's game. Dee was pulling out the stops, laying everything on the line, risking it all to get whatever he wanted. The Legion and Hawksblood were being pushed into Blackworld like cocks into the pit, to fight and this time die the death-without-resurrection.

Whatever obsession compelled Michael, it was about to be satisfied. Michael was about to attain his El Dorado. There would be war, and there would be feeling in it. The hatreds were being pumped up. The Götterdämmerung could not be averted.

The twilight of the Legion lay just beyond a near horizon. It might mean the end of all mercenary armies. . . .

Storm made a vow. He and Richard might fight, and

both lose, but they would go to the shadows with one victory to light their paths to Hell.

The Dees would go down with them. Every last one.

Twenty-Six: 2845 AD

The last snow was melting in the forest shade when Deeth made his second bid for freedom. He had prepared for months. First he concentrated on convincing Jackson that he had resigned himself to his fate. He faithfully did all he was told, and cared for the old man beyond what was demanded. He made no effort to flee when apparent opportunities arose. Nor did he struggle much against perversions or the incessant maltreatment. He suffered in silence, stoically waiting.

He began decorating the stage of his revenge in the fall, under the guise of caring for Jackson. During autumn he carpeted the cavern floor with leaves. When the chills moved in and it became necessary to keep a fire burning, he gathered piles of firewood. While foraging wood he collected small, sharp stones that he concealed around the cave.

On the night he chose he cut his neck rope with an edged rock. Hours passed while he sawed, painstakingly avoiding rustling the leaves of his bed. When he was done he did not immediately flee.

Holding the parted rope round his neck, he rose and stoked up the fire. The old man wakened, as he always did when Deeth stirred. He cursed Deeth for disturbing him. Deeth bowed his head and went on with his work. Jackson settled back into a grumbling snore.

Deeth built the fire higher and higher. It began to roar, and pull a breeze into the cave.

Concealed near the fire were the things he wanted to

take: a hide blanket, steel for fire-starting, a package of dried fruit. He tossed them out the cave mouth.

Jackson snapped to awareness, suspicious and crabby. He jerked the rope. It flew into his face. He stared at the frayed end in dull-witted surprise.

Deeth seized a forked stick and shoveled fire onto the dry, powdery leaves. He skipped back and toppled the huge kindling stack, carefully prepared for the moment. It slid into the flames. The fire gnawed at it, leaping higher and crackling louder by the second.

Deeth dumped piles of larger wood.

The old man, cursing, terrified, staggered out of his chair and tried to charge through before the barrier became impassable.

Deeth floored him with a thrown stone.

The power of hatred was in his arm. He whistled that rock into Jackson's chest with such force that he heard brittle old ribs crack.

Jackson rose for another try. The trap had closed. He retreated instead.

Deeth watched in fascination as Jackson screamed and danced in the fire. Eventually, crazed with pain, the old man flung himself at the barrier again. He crashed through and collapsed outside, twitching all over, feebly crawling toward his tormentor.

Deeth backed a step when necessary, and collected his supplies, but did not leave till Jackson died.

He felt no real emotion afterward. It had not been an execution, even, just an ending of misery.

He started toward the village.

The boy had been scarred. Something had been carved out of him in that cave. Never again would he feel true, whole, mortal emotion. He had become that fearful, wholly pragmatic monster which has no conscience, and no comprehension of emotion. Henceforth he would fake it, when necessary, as protective coloration, and would believe that everyone else was doing the same. The only things with meaning, most of the time, would be his own whims, fancies, and hatreds. Everyone else he would see as objects to be moved and used.

Deeth had acted now because the village chieftain had condemned the girl Emily to another week in the punishment pit. He could spirit her away without having to sneak her out of the chieftain's house.

He had to enter and leave the village past a guard watching for a night raid by neighboring tribes. Going in, the sentry was asleep at his post. Deeth crept past. Keeping to the deepest darkness, he moved to the chieftain's hut.

The pit had been covered with a lid made of hide on a wooden frame. Rocks weighted it down. Deeth removed it.

He lay on his stomach and whispered, "Emily! It's time." He could see nothing below, but knew she was awake. He heard her frightened breathing.

One of the village's domesticated beasts snorted nearby. It sensed his presence, but was neither noisy nor excitable. It did not give him away.

"Emily! Come on. It's Deeth."

She did not respond.

"Come on!" Time was passing. He dared not waste much on a frightened slave. He reached down, tried to get hold of her hair. His arm was not long enough. "Come on, girl. Give me your hand. We've got to get moving."

She whimpered.

He knew she had suffered, but hardly more than he. What was the matter with her? Was the spirit of these animals that easily broken?

"Your hand!" he snapped. He reached again.

And felt her touch and grab him. He braced himself and pulled. Wriggling and whimpering, naked, she slithered out of the pit.

"Now what?" he asked himself. She could not face the cold unclad, nor could she run through the woods naked. The underbrush would flay her. "Get something to wear," he ordered, indicating the chieftain's hut.

She shook her head.

"Move!" Deeth snarled.

Still she shook her head.

"Dammit, go!" He snapped fingertips against her cold bare buttocks. She yipped softly, then vanished into the house.

Deeth chewed his lip, crouched beside the hovel, watched the hills for the ghost of dawn. They had made noise. Had anyone heard?

The animal made more curiosity sounds, a kind of continuous questioning grunt. It could not leave its pen to investigate. The night creatures of the woods hooted and chattered and whistled.

What about those? He had heard of no large predators. That did not mean that they did not exist. He knew Prefactlas only by what he had seen. Jackson had not let him see much.

The girl returned. She had clothed herself in furs. "Yuloa's things," she whispered. She had stolen them from the chieftain's son.

Deeth chuckled softly, nervously. "We'd better get started. It'll be sunrise pretty soon."

"Where're we going?"

He did not know. He had not planned beyond getting her out of the pit. He just did not know enough about this world.

"Back to the station," he told her. He set off before she could protest. They had to go somewhere, if only to get away from here. She followed after a moment's hesitation.

The sentry had moved, but was asleep again. They passed him carefully.

Deeth stopped after another hundred yards. He did not know the way. The direction, yes, but not the paths.

Pride would not permit him to confess ignorance to an animal. He resumed walking before Emily asked questions.

An hour later, while they were struggling through underbrush on a steep hillside, she asked, "Why don't we use the trail? It's just over there." Panting, she added, "Doing it this way takes a lot of time. They'll be after us pretty soon."

Deeth frowned. Was she going to be a talker, all the time questioning and nagging?

She had a point. And had presented it without questioning his reasons for doing things his way. "You could be right."

He went in the direction she indicated. He encountered a narrow track. The going became easier. They reached the forest's edge as dawn began painting bold strokes of crimson and gold on a canvas of indigo clouds.

"We'll rest here," Deeth said. He settled down with his back against the trunk of a huge tree. Two giant roots made arms for his momentary throne.

Before him lay the plain the Norbon had cleared when first they had come to Prefactlas. It was lifeless now, except for a few feral grazers and the morning birds dipping and weaving after insects. Nothing but ruins remained where the Norbon complex had stood. Even the greathouse, which had been constructed as a fortress, had been smashed level with the plain. Grass and moss colored its fire-blackened remains.

Of the other structures there was even less evidence. The human Marines had done a thorough job.

And then they had gone. Not even a watch unit had been left behind. The baked landing sites of their assault craft had disappeared under new growth.

He stared and thought. There would be little here for

him. Nothing lay behind but torture or death. He had to go on.

Where to? Any animals they encountered would treat them no better than those they had known. And if they reached an area controlled by Confederation humans? The girl would give him away.

Tomorrow and tomorrow. This was today. He had to meet the problems as they arose. Right now he had to keep moving.

"Deeth? Maybe we shouldn't stay here too long. They know I'm gone by now."

Deeth rose and walked toward the ruins. Maybe he could find something useful.

The lower limb of the sun cleared the horizon before they reached the site. Their path led them past scores of skeletons. Some had been scattered by scavengers. Shreds of Sangaree clothing clung to most. Deeth found one small one wearing Dharvon w'Pugh's bright party pantaloons. His skull had been crushed.

Deeth stood over his old enemy. That was no way for an heir to die.

He looked for the kitchens. They seemed the most likely source for something useful.

He poked around for an hour. It was useless. The ruins had been picked as clean as the Sangaree bones. Emily said all the nearby villagers had appeared once the Marines departed.

He came up with a battered aluminum cup and a butcher knife without a handle. He gave them to Emily. He scrounged a pointed, foot-long shard of glassteel for himself. He might be able to mount it on a handle or shaft.

He moved to the armory, hoping to find a weapon. The raiders and scavengers had been thorough. He came up with nothing but a bottle of lasegun coolant he could drain for use as a canteen.

128

He was empting the bottle when the girl shouted. She waved at the sky. A faint chuga-chuga-chuga came from hight overhead.

A Confederation support ship was moving south. Deeth scrambled across the rubble, knocked Emily down. She kicked and screamed and. . . .

The patrol dwindled into the distance. They watched it go. Deeth helped Emily up.

"Why?" she demanded. "They would've helped us. Oh. Well, *I* could've gone with them."

"You're Norbon." Deeth turned his back. He started kicking rubble around, remembering.

He had been on Prefactlas just one week when the raiders came. Not long, but long enough to have fallen in love with the station and staff. It had been his first trip off Homeworld. Everything had seemed romantic. Especially old Rhafu.

What had become of the breeding master? He had been a real man. Probably took several of the animals with him.

"Time to go, Emily," he said. "We should be off the plain before they track us here." He started after the copter. South was the only direction to go.

He was not ready to confront Prefactlas's conquerors, but had to be near their main base when he was. Their headquarters, he guessed, would be the Sexon holding. It was the biggest on the planet, most easily defended, and had the best communications facilities. It would make an ideal bridgehead for human occupation. It lay near the planet's main spaceport, a facility capable of handling the heaviest lighters.

That would have to be their destination. Only there could he get off planet.

There was one small problem. The Sexon holding lay more than a thousand miles away.

The journey took the youngsters three years. It was

punctuated by interims of slavery as grim as their first. Adversity forged nickel-hard transethnic bonds between them. They became a survival unit.

Emily lost any desire to be away from or to betray him.

Years passed after their arrival. They begged. They were forced into schools or orphanages. They did odd jobs. Emily got work as a cleaning girl in the offices of Prefactlas Corporation. They survived. And Deeth almost forgot his father's parting charge.

They were sixteen when the wildly improbable happened. Emily became pregnant.

Deeth's world shifted its axis. He woke up. He began looking in new directions. He could not raise a child himself. He was Sangaree. He had a duty to the infant, wanted or not.

Emily's job had brought her into contact with the President of the Corporation. He was bemused by the girl. He kept plying her with little gifts.

Deeth went off by himself. He did a lot of thinking. And hurting. Emily's suitor was the man who had led the attack on his family. His orders had caused all the deaths at the Norbon station. The man was his dearest enemy. And the one real hope for his unborn child.

Sangaree prided themselves on their pragmatism.

"Go to him," Deeth told Emily. "Make him your man. Don't argue. He has what you need. Yesterday is done. Tomorrow we begin new lives."

She refused. She fought. She cried.

He put her out of their shanty and held the door till she went away. He sat with his back to it and wept.

Twenty-Seven: 3031 AD

The brothers Darksword looked like regimental file clerks. They wore that look of perpetual bewilderment of the innocent repeatedly slapped in the face by reality. Wizards of the data banks. Easy prey for the monsters in the human jungle.

They were short, slim, thin-faced, and watery-eyed. They had pallid skin and stringy brown hair so sparse it belonged on an endangered species list. Helmut affected a pair of pince-nez. The more bold Wulf had had his vision surgically corrected.

They were antsy little men who could not stand still. Outsiders pegged them as chronic hand-wringers, nervous little people who faced even petty troubles with the trepidation of an old maid bound for an orgy.

It was an act they had lived so long they almost believed it themselves.

There was as much ice and iron in them as in Cassius or Storm. Had Storm meant it, they would have killed the mining official without qualm or second thought. Disobedience was an alien concept.

A matched set of stringy old assassins.

Their lives, emotions, and loyalties had been narrowly focused for two hundred forty years. They had followed Boris Storm as boys, in the old Palisarian Directorate. They had attended military school with him, joined Confederation Navy with him, and became part of Prefactlas Corporation with him. When Ulant struck they returned to service with him, and afterward helped him create the Iron Legion. Following Boris's death they had transferred their devotion to his son.

They had been born on Old Earth and taken to the

Directorate young. They had learned the motherworld's harsh lessons in Europe's worst slums.

Two things matter. Sign on with the gang with the most guns. Serve it with absolute devotion as long as it serves faithfully in return.

The centuries had garbled those truths a tad. They could not abandon the Legion now, biggest guns or no. One occasionally reminded the other that it looked like time to get out. Neither moved. They continued serving Gneaus Storm with the implacability of natural law.

Storm had left them in command of the Fortress. The simple fact of his absence presented them with enough problems, Wulf claimed, to frustrate a saint into a deal with the devil.

The Darkswords were curious in yet another way. They were that rare animal, the true believer in an age of infidels. Only they understood how they squared their actions with the moral demands of a Christian faith.

Michael Dee was human quicksilver. Pollyanna, without Lucifer there to compel discretion, seemed to have set herself the task of engulfing every functional penis in the Fortress. She had become a crude joke.

Lucifer had been gone only two days when she lured Benjamin back to her bed, with such indiscretion that everyone in the Fortress knew. Frieda became a volcano constantly on the edge of erupting.

The traditional morality had little weight in the Fortress of Iron, but one tried to avoid needless friction.

Pollyanna did not seem to care. Her behavior was almost consciously self-destructive.

Bets were being made. Would Lucifer return so incensed as to repeat the blood-spill he had attempted earlier? Would Benjamin's wife finally decide that she had taken enough and cut off his balls? It was a crackling tense situation made to order for a Michael Dee.

The preparations for Blackworld lagged. The Legion

had no heavy equipment designed for use in an airless environment. For use in poisonous atmospheres, yes, but not for no atmosphere at all.

At least Richard Hawksblood faced the same problem.

Frieda's passion for the occult had become obsession. She spent hour upon hour closeted with her Madame Endor. She was convinced of the precognitive validity of Benjamin's nightmares. She was making herself obnoxious in her efforts to protect him. A dozen times a day she ran him down to make sure he was wearing the protective suit she had forced the armorers to prepare.

His dalliance with Pollyanna became his sole escape from, and defiance of, her insufferable mothering.

Among the troops there were dissensions explicable only in terms of the presence of Michael Dee. Rumors stalked the barracks levels. There were fist fights. There was a stabbing. The companies and battalions feuded in a manner unrelated to healthy, edge-honing competition.

Storm had been gone ten days. His stabilizing influence was severely missed.

Desperate, Wulf and Helmut decreed that any man not on duty had to report to the gymnasium for intensified physical fitness training. They established a round-the-clock roster of instructors. Exhausted Legionnaires had less energy for squabbling.

Wulf trailed Helmut by a step. They entered the gym. He growled, "The bastard don't have to do anything but be here to muck things up." He glared at Michael Dee. "Look at the damned trouble-monger. Sitting there smug as Solomon on his throne."

Helmut grunted affirmatively. "Would anybody yell if we shoved him out a lock?"

"Not till the Colonel got home. Ah. Look. There's Pollyanna. Want to help me with her?"

Pollyanna stood in a corridor mouth, watching the group around Dee. Her doe eyes were fixed on Michael.

They were filled with a surprising animation. It seemed to be hatred.

Homer and Frieda hovered over Benjamin, Frieda silently daring Pollyanna to come closer. Benjamin was directing the physical drill. The soldiers were not enthusiastic.

Michael watched in silence, unaware of Pollyanna's stare. He wore a contemplative smile.

"You handle her," Helmut said. "I'll take Benjamin and Dee." His voice carried overtones of distaste. Wulf might have asked if he wanted to share a swim in a sewer.

Pollyanna flushed when she saw Wulf approaching. He was pleased. He hoped she saw the thunderheads dancing on his brow.

Cassius, with his computerlike voice and metallic absence of emotion, was the one man Pollyanna normally feared. She seemed unable to remain afraid of a man who had been to her bed.

She had made advances to both Darkswords. They had not responded. She could fear them too. Wulf tried to look as grim as a suicide singleshipper. What he wanted to do took the same intense determination. Her amorality baffled and intimidated him.

"We walk!" he snapped, seizing her arm. She winced. He was stronger than he looked, and wanted to impress her with the fact. "You've got a lot to learn," he growled, propelling her along the corridor. "Only Michael Dee plays Dee games here. He can get away with them. He has Storm's safe-conduct. You've got nothing. You're just another daughter-in-law."

She sputtered. His anger hit her like crashing breakers, drowning what she wanted to say.

"I could put you into detention. I will if you don't start making like a nun. Stay away from Benjamin. And Homer. I've seen you sizing him up. Your pants come down again, it'd better be for Lucifer. Understand? You

134

want to play games, get a deck of cards. This one the rest of us were playing before your grandma crapped her first diaper." They reached her apartment. Wulf pushed her inside.

"One more trick, girl, and you go in the can till the Colonel gets back. That's as plain as I can make it."

She relaxed. He sensed it. "Think you know him, eh? Count your beads. With him it's always the Legion first. A man who's had to kill his own children wouldn't hesitate to send an amateur Dee to Helga's World the way he did with that metal grubber."

His belief in his commander was so apparent that she had to accept its truth. He left her shaking and, he hoped, wondering why she had gotten involved with such terrible men.

Helmut approached the group observing the physical drills. He was only slightly less forbidding than his brother. Dee's smile became uncertain. Benjamin's charm aura faltered. Homer's sightless eyes turned his way, grim as the eyes of death. Frieda glared suspiciously.

She was a raw-boned, stringy-haired blonde, reminiscent of her father, without Cassius's self-confidence. She was alarmed by the purpose evident in Helmut's stride. Storm she could read and handle. Her father she could manipulate. The Darkswords, though, were beyond reach.

That was the impression they liked to give. Helmut threw himself into an empty chair with apparent violence. He glared at them in turn. "Captain Ceislak. Take over here. Benjamin, I've got a job for you. Directing vacuum drills. You start after morning muster tomorrow. Check with Wong. He'll fill you in on what you'll be doing."

Understanding passed between them. Benjamin was about to be moved out of temptation's reach. Putting the Legion through vacuum drills required weeks.

135

A man could do a lot of thinking if he was alone with himself in a spacesuit, Helmut reflected.

"But he could. . . ." Frieda began.

"Get hurt?" Helmut snapped, bludgeoning her line. "Crap. He'll be safer outside. He's not suicidal, is he?" He glanced at Michael Dee, smiling a thin, bitter smile.

Benjamin reddened.

"Accidents happen!" Frieda had become neurotic about her son's safety.

"Relax, Mother," Homer said with heavy sarcasm. "You'd still have me to dote on."

Frieda winced. She forced a smile while coloring guiltily.

Homer's dead eyes glared at the floor. He knew. Even from his mother affection had to be forced.

"Accidents, yes," Helmut mused, smiling at Dee again. "I've been giving accidents a certain amount of thought. They're like mutations. Once in a while one can be beneficial. Wulf and I were discussing the possibilities a bit ago."

Dee's smile vanished. He had gotten the message. And he had noted the marks strain had left on Helmut. It was time he became more circumspect. Helmut had declared, albeit obliquely, that he no longer considered the interests of Gneaus Julius Storm and those of the Legion to be congruent. The hint that he and his brother were ready to eliminate Dee indicated a revolution in thought that could spread throughout the organization. When the old lap dogs stood on their hind legs and growled. . . .

Helmut sat there and smiled as if reading Michael's every thought.

Frieda went on nagging. Helmut finally exploded. "You question my orders, madam? Complain to the colonel when he returns. Meantime, hold your tongue."

It was as harsh an admonition as ever he had given a

woman. She shut up. Storm always supported those upon whom he bestowed the proconsular power.

Having delivered his messages, Helmut went to waken Thurston Storm. Thurston was his relief. Initially, Thurston's sole task had been to birddog Michael. With tension mounting, the Darkswords had been forced to saddle him with part of their burden. They worked staggered sixteen-hour shifts, one sleeping while the other two held chaos at bay.

"Friendly today, isn't he?" Michael observed as Helmut stalked away. "He'd turn on the gloom at a wedding. Put the groom to work before the party started."

Ah, his words were subtle. Benjamin was blind to their snare. "A party. That's an idea, Michael. We need to liven this place up. I'll put me on a going-outside party."

Michael smiled and nodded.

The party, through Benjamin's efforts, shed some of its early artificiality and turned fun. With the help of a few drinks the younger people forgot the pressures that had been building so swiftly and mysteriously. The occasional tentative spurt of laughter erupted from their midst.

Benjamin's mother hovered in the background, as grim as an old raven. She had opposed the party from its inception, purely on feeling. She had been unable to sway Benjamin. Madame Endor had failed. He was in revolt against mothering. He would not let them save him.

He could be as stubborn as his father.

Where were her husband and father? Frieda wondered. The Fortress was going to hell and they were off God knew where chasing women or something.

Dee watched the partyers with a disdainful, mocking smile.

Thurston Storm observed from a doorway. He was a huge, sullen, muscular redhead who looked too simple for even the most obvious subtleties. His appearance was an illusion. He was a dangerous man.

He resented having been left off the guest list. They thought him too boisterous. It did not occur to him that he could simply abandon his duties and invite himself in. He just stood there with his arms folded across his chest. His right hand clutched a needlegun made tiny by the size of his fist. It tracked Michael Dee as if computer-aimed.

Thurston puzzled everyone. He seemed almost a hollow man, entirely an appearance. He had the disquieting vacuity of a Pollyanna Eight. The appearances he presented sometimes conflicted. Occasionally he was a reflection of his father. Most of the time he appeared to be what people took him for, a big, dull, happy fellow who drank as if there were no future, ate for a company, brawled, bragged, and bullied his way through life. A mass of strength without a brain to guide it.

Wulf had absented himself from the party, pleading his work load. Pollyanna was sulking in her apartment. Helmut was asleep. Everyone else was there.

Benjamin looked splendid in a uniform of his own design. It was too ruffled and gaudy for the Legion. His father would not have approved. He was not pleased with it himself. His protective armor softened its effect.

That armor was the finest available. Energy weapons would feed its shields. Anything moving at high velocity would pillow out in its fields. Those fields would seize and wrench aside the metal of an assassin's blade. In a truly hostile environment he could button up and survive on his own air, water, and nutrient soup. He could not be touched. His mother bragged about his invulnerability when she was not being afraid he would find a way to get himself killed despite his protection.

Benjamin invented a game. He had his friends take turns shooting, hacking, and stabbing him. They ruined his uniform without harming him. He laughed a lot.

The point was to aggravate his mother.

Homer, alone in his blindness, shunned for his ugliness, sat and brooded. Another party, strong with the laughter of the beautiful women who gravitated to the Legion. Were they mocking him again? Women always laughed at him. Even that madwoman Pollyanna. Her real purpose for tempting him, surely, had been to mock him. And Frieda, that bitch who claimed to be his mother. . . . She would like nothing better than to have him put away somewhere where she would not be embarrassed by him. She tried hard to pretend, but she could not hide from his flashes of psi.

No one cared. No one understood. Except Ben, his father, and sometimes that young, strange one, Mouse. And his father he could never forgive for having given him life. Surely, with all his power and money, he could have done something. Sight. Corrective surgery for his physical defects. . . .

He knew his father had tried. The human mind in despair seldom responds to the soft persuasion of reason.

In fits, Homer hated Gneaus Julius Storm.

"Homer. You're unhappy," said a voice nearby. He was startled. It contained more compassion than he had ever before heard. He was primed to take advantage of someone's pity.

Odd that he had not sensed the speaker's approach. His eyes were dead, but his other senses were strong. This man was a ghost.

"Who is it?" He did not recognize the voice.

"Michael."

Of course. The sneaking and voice-changing should have cued him. "What do you want?"

"Only to cheer you up. The Fortress is becoming so terribly grim."

Homer nodded. He did not believe a word, of course. Dee was the Prince of Liars, and always oblique. He might indeed do some cheering up, but only as a means to an end.

Homer's suspicion was solidly grounded. His handicap betrayed him. Without vision he could not detect the evil Michael planned. Only on Dee's face was the wickedness obvious, and that for but an instant.

Dee had discovered Benjamin's Achilles' heel. He had gotten the information from the man's staunchest defender, his mother, simply by listening to her brag and worry.

"Would you like to get into the game, Homer? Benjamin is dueling. Maybe he'd give you a go."

"Duel a blind man? You're a fool, Dee."

"Oh, I'll help you. Here. Benjamin. Homer wants a try." Dee glanced over his shoulder. A droplet of sweat dribbled down one temple. Thurston's weapon still tracked him with deadly precision.

"Hell, why not?" Benjamin replied. "Come on, Homer. You'll probably do better than these clowns."

As was customary, the healthy stepped aside, condescending to allow the cripple his moment.

Glibly, smoothly, Dee talked Homer to his feet, placed a dueling knife in his hand, positioned him facing his twin. The gallery watched with amused smiles. Homer sensed their amusement. His temper soared.

"Count of three," Michael said, easing back, trying to place someone between himself and Thurston. "One. . . ."

Benjamin, playing to his audience, presented his chest to Homer's blade. He could not be hurt. No known hand weapon could penetrate the protection of his armor.

"Two. . . ."

Guided by Benjamin's breathing, Homer lunged. He wanted to knock Ben onto his showoff ass.

For a long moment after the drugged tip of the wooden blade slipped through armor proof against any metal there was absolute silence. The tableau became a freeze frame from an old-time movie. Then Benjamin and Homer screamed with one voice. Their psi forces locked. Their rage and pain reached out to envelop the Fortress. Benjamin folded slowly. Homer fainted, toppled onto Benjamin. His mind could not withstand the psi backwash from his twin. Women shrieked. Men shouted.

And as quietly as he had come to the blind brother, while even Thurston's attention was diverted, Michael Dee slipped away.

Pandemonium invaded the hall.

When Wulf arrived he found Thurston raging among a group of young officers trying to avenge Benjamin on Homer. The big man laid them out left and right while screaming for somebody to for God's sake get the twins down to Medical.

A man slipped around Thurston and, with the guilty wooden blade, as Homer recovered consciousness, exacted vengeance. Thurston whirled and cracked the man's skull.

Homer welcomed death with a smile. That dark lady was the only woman who could love him.

Wulf ignored the drama. With Medical a minute away nobody needed die the death-without-resurrection. He was looking for people notable for their absence.

Helmut roared in clad in nothing but underwear. He had a gun in each hand. "What happened?"

"Find Lee!" Wulf ordered. "Kill him. Cut him up and shove the pieces out different locks. The Colonel can't stop it this time."

Helmut looked at the bodies. He needed no more clues.

They separated, seeking a trail. They were hounds who would not be satisfied till the blood of their quarry stained their muzzles.

Wulf was too angry. He missed the most outstanding absence. Frieda. She should have been in the middle of things, screaming and weeping over her poor baby, preventing anything sensible from getting done.

Within minutes the entire Fortress was mobilized for the sole purpose of locating Michael Dee. But somehow, despite the planetoid's limitations, he managed to evade capture.

The brothers Darksword conquered their emotions, repaired to Combat, directed the search from there.

They arrived as the man on instel communications ripped off a printout. It was a frantic message from Storm. Wulf read it first, bowed his head in despair. "Twenty minutes, that's all it would have taken."

"Signal too late. Twenty minutes too late. Sign my name," Helmut said.

"I want Dee," Wulf grumbled.

"Set the hounds on him."

"Yes."

In minutes they had Storm's Sirian warhounds seeking a trail. They found it on Residential Level. It led to the ingress locks. Their questions baffled the duty section. They had seen no one but the Colonel's wife in hours. She and two corpsmen had loaded a pair of medical-support cradles aboard an old singleship. . . .

"Oh, hell!" Wulf swore. "You think . . . ?"

Helmut nodded. He grabbed a comm.

It took two calls to confirm the worst. Dee, following Homer's killing thrust, had seized Frieda and dragged her to her apartment. He had stripped and bound and gagged her, and had assumed her clothing and identity. From there he had gone to Medical and, playing on Frieda's neurotic concern from Benjamin, had convinced the duty corpsmen to transfer the dead to a hospital with planetary resources backing it. Dee had played his part to such perfection that the unsuspecting corpsmen had helped move and load the cryo coffins.

Even those who had known the Darkswords for decades were awed by the rage they displayed.

"He isn't away yet," Helmut remarked after regaining his composure. "He didn't know where the Colonel went when he pulled this. Let's see what they say in Combat. We might have a shot at him yet."

They commenced the counter game backed by Combat's resources.

"He's headed straight out," Wulf said, indicating the Dee blip in the main global display. "Putting on a lot of inherent velocity while he's getting up influence to go hyper." He picked up a pointer and indicated each of a half-dozen blips chasing Dee. "They scrambled fast."

The senior watchstander said, "I sent everybody who was on maneuvers when IL heard what the situation was, sir." He happened to be the man who had disappointed Storm and Cassius in the Abhoussi and Dee incident.

"Very good," Helmut replied. "That's thinking on your feet."

"I scrambled everything in dock, too, sir. I assumed. . . ."

"You assumed correctly," Wulf said. "Anything that will space. They're starting to come on display, Helmut."

A wild spray of diverging tracks began to spread behind the Dee blip. Wulf glanced to one side. "Tactical computer have control?"

"Yes, sir. You can input whatever the situation seems to call for."

"Basal strategy?"

"Build a plane of no return behind Dee, sir. Put the fastest ships on the rim and move them forward to make a pocket."

"Very good. Helmut, looks like we've got him. It might take a while, though."

"We're going to have to get a command ship out. We won't be able to direct it from here for long."

143

The senior watchstander said, "I held the *Robert Knollys*, sir. I've given them a direct feed. They're running a parallel program. You can board and shift control."

"Good. That's a good start," Wulf said.

"I believe we have him," Helmut said, peering into the display tank. "Unless he's headed somewhere damned close. That's a damned slow boat he's running."

"What's the nearest planetfall that direction?" Wulf asked. If Dee made planetfall before the jaws of pursuit closed he would become impossible to find. He would vanish amid the population and marshal his own resources in the time it took to track him down. His resources were not inconsiderable.

"Helga's World, sir."

"Ah!" Wulf began to smile. He and the Colonel definitely had aces up their sleeves.

Helmut said, "Communications are the problem. The control. There's a lot of space out there."

"And?"

"So it's time to call in old debts. See if there's a Starfisher who can relay for us. They don't love Michael either."

Wulf turned to his instel operator. "Go on the thirty-seven band with a loop. 'Storm for Gales.' "

"They'll answer if they're out there," Helmut said.

Wulf shrugged. "Maybe. People can be damned ungrateful." He told the tech, "Let us know if there's a response."

Twenty-Eight: 3052 AD

I said my father had enemies of whom he was unaware. The same was true of friends. He was a hard man, but had a strong sense of justice. It did not move him as often as it might have, but when it did, it made him friends who remained loyal forever. Such friends were the High Seiners, the Starfishers, whom he saved from enslavement on Gales.

Masato Igarashi Storm

Twenty-Nine: 2973 AD

It was pure one-in-a-quadrillion chance. *Glowworm* and her sister raiders had jumped into the gulf and gone doggo, hoping they could lose Navy, which had destroyed one of their band already. It had been a long, hard chase. The three ship's commanders were scared and desperate. On *Glowworm* the group leader nearly panicked when detection picked up approaching ships.

Almost, but not quite. Powered-down vessels are hard to spot unless a hunter gets close. He decided to see what Navy did.

His detection operator soon said, "That's not them, sir. Too big. I mean, we're getting them from too far out, and they're moving too slow."

The group leader studied the patterns. He had seen nothing like this before. In time, he murmured, "Holy Christ! There ain't nothing that big. Nothing but...."

Nothing but Starfisher harvestships.

Navy was forgotten. "Track. Get a fix on their course. And nobody does anything to show them we're here. Understood?" He took his own advice. Ship to ship messages were hand carried by suited couriers till the harvest-fleet left detection.

Eight great vessels shouldering along at minuscule

velocities. . . . The group leader was tempted to abandon his employer then and there. A man could name his price for what he had found.

The Starfishers controlled production of an element critical to interstellar communications systems. There was no other source, and the source was terribly limited. He who won control of a harvest fleet won control of fabulous wealth and power.

In the end, fear drove the group leader to his master.

Michael Dee did the obvious. He gathered ships and went after the harvestfleet. The operation remained his secret alone. He saw not only the obvious profit but a chance to make himself master of his own destiny.

He gambled on a surprise attack. His forces were insufficient for a plain face-to-face showdown with eight harvestships. He gambled, and he lost. He squandered his raiders and barely escaped with his life. In his fury at being thwarted he left three harvestships broken, derelict —and a nation which would do him evil gleefully whenever the opportunity arose.

Poor Michael's life was a trail of bitter enemies made. And some day the pigeons would come home to roost.

Thirty: 2878-3031 AD

The world wore the name Bronwen. It was far from the mainstream. Its claim to fame was that it had been the first human world occupied by Ulant. It would be the last reabsorbed by Confederation. In the interim it resembled one of those gaudy, chaotic eighteenth-century pirate havens on the north coast of Africa. Sangaree, McGraws, and free-lance pirates made planetfall and auctioned their booty. The barons of commerce came looking for bargains in goods worth the cost of interstellar shipment. Freehaulers came looking for cargo to fill their tramp freighter holds. Lonely Starfishers came down from their rivers of night for their rare intercourse with the worlds of men. Millions changed hands daily. The state was not there to watchdog and steal a cut. Those were brawling, violent days, but Bronwen's rulers were not displeased. Fortunes stuck.

Michael Dee should not have visited the world. He should not have risked having his name connected with the rogues he employed. Success had made him overconfident. He did not believe anything could break his run of luck.

The Sangaree came to his flagship, the old *Glowworm,* that Michael had acquired through straw parties when war's end had thrown scores of obsolete ships onto the salvage market. The man did not pretend to be anything but what he was. Michael found him vaguely familiar. Where had he seen the man? In the background in press rooms during the war, he thought. And, possibly, once when he was a child.

Dee did not like puzzles. He did not like not being able to remember clearly. Memory was his best weapon. But the man had never impinged directly upon his reality. . . .

The Sangaree initially claimed to be a buyer. Michael watched the man pass through his security screens, wondering. He did not look the type. Too fat, too self-confident in that intangible way powerful men have. Fencing stolen goods would be a chore for fourth-level underlings.

Dee secured his observation screen and waited.

The man entered his cabin, extended a hand, said, "Norbon w'Deeth. The Norbon."

Michael's underworld connections now extended into the Sangaree sphere. He had dealt with the race directly on occasion. They were sharp, cautious, and carefully honest in their business arrangements. They were paranoiac in their efforts to protect the secrets of Homeworld, Family, and Head.

This was a Head! And his Family's name was turning up everywhere these days. The Norbon had exploded into prominence wherever Sangaree operated.

He took the proferred hand. "An honor. How can I be of service?"

Michael masked his thinking well. He did not betray his consternation and curiosity. The Norbon was just another businessman for all the reaction he showed.

The man was damned young for a Head, he reflected. But you could never be sure in these days of rejuvenation and resurrection. He had the hard lines in his forehead and at the corners of his eyes. The man inside was old in thought if not in his flesh.

The Norbon eyed him. "How's your mother?"

The question took Michael by surprise. It came at him from the least expected angle. "Well enough, I suppose. I've been out of touch with the family."

"Yes. The war did disrupt things, didn't it? And helped some of us profit."

The slightest of frowns crossed Michael's vulpine face. He felt a case of nerves coming on.

"And the rest of your family?"

"Good enough. We Storms are hard to kill."

"I've discovered that."

Michael used a toe to caress an alarm button. In seconds a needlegun, in the hand of a reliable man, began tracking Dee's visitor from behind an apparently solid bulkhead.

"None harder than I, sir. You make me uncomfortable. Can you get to your point?" Michael was surprised at himself. He was never this direct. The Sangaree had him shaking.

"We have *Family* business. With the big F. Your Family and mine. There's an unsettled matter between the Norbon and Storms. No doubt you know the tale. I came to find out where you'll stand."

"You've lost me." The man had Dee totally baffled. It broke through to his face.

"It see I'll have to go back to the beginning. All right. Twenty-Eight Forty-Four. Acting on information received from Sangaree renegades, Commodore Boris Storm and Colonel of Marines Thaddeus Immanuel Walters invaded Prefactlas. They destroyed the Family stations and slaughtered any Sangaree they found. My mother, my father, and hundreds of Norbon dependents were among the dead. Only a handful of people escaped. Norbon w'Deeth was one of the survivors."

Michael shrugged as if to say, "So what?" and did say, "Those are the breaks of the business."

"Yes. That's the human attitude toward risk and reward. Not that much different from our own except that those men felt compelled to make it a slaughter instead of a raid. It stopped being business when they took that attitude. It became vendetta. I survived. It's my duty to exact retribution."

Michael had begun to get the feel of it. His nerves were steadier. "There's a needlegun on you."

His visitor smiled. "I never doubted it. You're a reasonably cautious man."

"Then you're not here to kill me?"

"Far from it. I'm here to sign you up for my side."

Michael's jaw dropped.

The Norbon laughed. "That's the first time I've actually seen anybody do that."

"What?"

The Norbon shook a hand in a gesture meaning never mind. "You're in the middle, Michael. You've got one foot on each side. I want to get them both on mine."

"You confuse me. I don't have any special love for my family. That's common knowledge. But I don't have reason one to want them destroyed, either. In fact, it's a valuable connection sometimes."

"I understand. Yes. The problem is that I've been too obscure. I assumed you knew. Let's go back to your mother. She was slave-born, as humans say. You know that much?"

"Yes. So?"

"She was born and trained at the Norbon facility on Prefactlas. She was its only female survivor. For ten years she and I fought barbarians, Confies, Corporation beekies, sickness, and plain old bad luck together. And we made it through. Our relationship became as deep as one can between a man and a woman. We even parented a child."

Michael began to glimpse the shaggy edges of it. And it was a monster indeed. Yet. . . . Yet it would explain so much that had puzzled him.

It was almost too simple an answer.

"You expect me to believe that crap?"

"It's happened before. It's genetically certain that human and Sangaree spring from the same ur-stock, sometime deep in proto-history. That both races are repelled by the idea doesn't alter the facts. There were races here before ours, Michael. Who knows what experiments they performed, or why, before they faded from history's stage?"

"And who cares?"

Deeth ignored his remark. "There's a curious thing about Homeworld, Michael. It's perfect for human habitation. A lot like Old Earth was before the Industrial Revolution. We Sangaree fill the human ecological niche there. But, and it's a curious big but, there's no archaeological or anthropological evidence of our presence before about the time Cro-Magnon appeared on Old Earth. There's no evolutionary chain. Nothing to connect with. No other primates at all. And we sometimes crossbreed with humans. What conclusion has to be drawn?"

150

That conclusion was irrelevant in an essentially emotional context. And Michael was responding to feelings, not reason.

He had grown up with an absolute presumption that the Sangaree were racial enemies. They were to be exterminated—unless momentary intercourse offered profit or advantage.

I can't be my own enemy, Michael thought.

"That's all I'll say about it now," his visitor said. "Think about it. It's a big bit to chew on. And don't forget. I'll help you as much as you help me. Oh. For what it's worth, you're technically my heir. You're my only child."

Numb, Michael pressed a button. It released the lock on the cabin door. The Sangaree departed.

Michael did not encounter the Norbon again for years. He had ample time to forget. He could not. His character took over. He began to scheme, to find ways he could use the Sangaree.

What he could not see, till it was too late, was that he was the one being used. Norbon w'Deeth was a gentle, subtle spider. He spun his natural son into webs of intrigue so soft that Michael did not recognize the chrysalis of doom enveloping him. In the time of the Shadowline some of the cobwebs were lifted from his eyes. And he wept. By then he could do nothing but follow instructions and try to deceive himself as to who was the real spinner.

Even his best-laid schemes betrayed him now.

Old Frog laughed in his grave. Michael had risked everything to kill the dwarf and suppress his secret till he could exploit it himself. The riches at the Shadowline's end would have gotten him out from under. They would have bought him a comfortable and anonymous new life free of the Sangaree and his family alike.

The Norbon found out. Somehow. And fed him orders that could encompass the destruction of the family Storm.

Dee squirmed. He writhed and tried to get away. The Norbon kept the pressure on, often through Michael's children by a marriage he had arranged, often economically. Michael could not wriggle loose. Perhaps his final defeat came when Deeth compelled him to drop the name Storm and adopt the subtle mockery of Dee.

Michael did not overlook the obvious. He did think of going to his brother for help. He rejected the notion. He knew how his brother would respond. If he believed at all. Gneaus would tell him to stand on his hind legs and act like a man. He simply would not understand.

And by staying in line he could even scores with Richard. That damned Richard. His little moment of spite had started this whole damned thing.

Michael had spun the anchor silk himself, then had lost control of his web to a bigger, nastier spider. In the year of the Shadowline he was caught on the back of a galloping nightmare. His only hope was that she would not deal him too brutal a fall when she reached the end of her run.

He denied hope. In his way he was as convinced of his imminent doom as was Gneaus of his.

Thirty-One: 3031 AD

It was a very exclusive toy shop. It even served tiny cups of coffee or tea with cutesy little cookies. Cassius was in hog's heaven.

"Not very exciting, is it?" he asked.

Mouse squeezed his eyes shut in a fierce squint. "No, it's not." He could not stay awake. They had been on The Big Rock Candy Mountain four days. Cassius had not given him much chance to sleep. "All we do is hunk around asking the same old questions."

"That's what intelligence work is, Mouse. You knock on doors and ask the same old questions till you get the right answers. Or you sit at headquarters and feed the computer the same old answers till it gives you the right question." He wound the music box again. It played a tune neither of them knew. A tiny porcelain mouse twirled and danced to the music. "Isn't that cute?"

"It doesn't seem worth the trouble."

"Mr. Russell. I'll take the music box. Can you have it shipped?"

They did have a few leads. Cassius had good, highly placed contacts on The Mountain, on both sides of the law. He had them asking questions too.

Michael had not worked hard to conceal his presence. They had unearthed a dozen people who had seen him here, there, or somewhere else, usually with Gneaus Storm. A few had seen him with one or two other men not locally known. They had had a hard look.

Dee had stopped being evident after Storm's departure, though he had not himself departed for several days.

"It's worth it. There's a pattern shaping up."

"What pattern?" Mouse signaled the sales clerk/waiter. "May I have another coffee?"

"That I don't know yet. I can see just a little of the edge. We've spread out plenty of money and eyes. Something will shake loose pretty soon."

"Speaking of eyes. Your friend the Captain has been watching us. Through the window and from next door. He doesn't look happy."

A hint of frown wrinkled Cassius's brow. He turned, gazed into the crystal shop connected with the toy store. His gaze met the policeman's. The officer took a deep breath, shrugged, and came through the connecting doorway. He seemed both angry and defensive.

"You might as well join us," Cassius said. "Easier to stay with us. What's the problem, Karl? Why do I suddenly need shadowing?" Cassius squatted, pushed a knobby plastic disk into the back of a caricature of a railroad train engine. The toy began chugging around the floor, tooting an old-time children's tune. The only thing wrong with collecting these things is, if you want to do anything but sit and look at them, you have to special order the energy cells from an outfit on Old Earth. They're not even remotely like anything we use today. Russell! You sure this isn't a reproduction? Do you have a certificate?"

The waiter/clerk brought Mouse's coffee. He brought a cup for the policeman, who turned it slowly between his fingers before saying, "Maybe I'm watching you for your own protection. What're you up to, Cassius? A favor for a friend, that's what you told me. I owed you one. I didn't figure on getting caught in a crossfire."

"Something has happened."

"Something has happened, he says. You're so goddamned right. You've stirred up something I didn't count on."

"What's wrong, Karl?"

"We picked up five bodies this morning, my friend. Five. That's what's wrong. And I don't like it. The Mountain is a quiet place. People come here to get away from it all. They lease little houses in the outback, guaranteed to be fifty klicks from the nearest neighbor. Once a month they fly maybe halfway around the world to come in and pick up groceries or meet a buddy for a beer. If they wanted gang wars they could stay home."

"Karl, you'd better back it up. I missed something."

Mouse shook his head vigorously. Sleep had snuck up on him again.

"The word in the street is, you asked Clementine to do some poking around for you to. Somebody took exception. Violent exception. Four of his boys went down this morning. We don't know who the hell the other guy is. An offworlder. No ID. Took a slug behind the ear. Clementine's old-time autograph."

"Curious," Cassius said.

"Curious, my ass. We've got a little unofficial kind of deal here, friend. We don't bother Clementine. He behaves himself and doesn't scare the tourists. We pick up enough hookers and gamers to pacify the straight-lacers, and the judges release them on their own recognizance. Clementine pays their fines. They're part of what brings the tourists in, so everybody comes up happy. He stays away from the stardust and windowpane and other heavy stuff and we stay away from him."

"A civilized arrangement." Cassius puttered with a toy steam shovel. "Don't you think so, Mouse?"

Mouse shrugged.

"Cassius," the officer said, "it's been four years since we've had a gang killing. There's no competition. Clementine keeps his people satisfied. So I get a friend come in doing a favor for a friend, and all of a sudden I've got bodies all over town."

"I'm sorry, Karl. Honestly. I didn't expect it. I don't understand it. You're sure it's because of me?"

"That's the feedback I get. Some high-powered outworlders don't like questions being asked. They're sending Clementine a message."

"Who?"

"We don't know. Somebody important, I'd guess. From the Big Outfit. Maybe there's a meet on neutral ground. Nobody local would have the balls to push Clementine. He don't push."

"Yeah. I see what you mean. Russell? How much for the shovel?"

"I'm scared, friend," said the policeman. "Clementine is a peaceful guy. But when he gets riled he doesn't have sense enough to keep his head down. He'll fight. If it's the Big Outfit. . . . Well, let's just say I like our arrange-

155

ment. We get along. We don't have any trouble. We all know where we stand. If *they* move in. . . ."

Something buzzed. The officer removed a handcomm from his pocket. "Heller." He pressed the device to his ear. His face became grave.

He put the comm away, considered Cassius momentarily. "That's three more down, friend. Two of theirs and one of Clementine's. It's got to be the Big Outfit. One looked Sangaree."

Cassius frowned. Mouse lost all interest in sleep. Baffled, he asked, "Sangaree? Cassius? Did we walk into something?"

"Sure as hell starting to look like it. Karl, I don't know what the hell is coming down. This isn't what we expected. We came looking for one thing and found something else. I'll talk to Clementine. I'll try to calm him down."

"You do that. And keep in touch. I don't like this. I don't want those people in here." Heller downed his coffee in a single gulp, started away. "Look out for yourself, friend. I don't want to scrape you up, too."

Mouse and Cassius watched him go. "What do you think?" Mouse asked. The boredom was gone. Sleepiness was forgotten. He was extremely uneasy.

"I think we'd better get back to the hotel and lay low. This doesn't look good."

Cassius paused at the hotel desk. "Suite Twelve," he said, requesting the key. "Any messages?"

Mouse leaned against the desk, watching the clerk hopefully. There might be something from his father. There wasn't. Nothing but a brief instelgram from the Fortress of Iron. Cassius read it aloud.

Mouse watched a lean old man come off the street. He had seen the man outside, watching them come in. There had been something strange about his eyes. . . . "Cassius! Down!"

He dove toward the nearest furniture, drawing a tiny, illegal weapon as he flew. Cassius tumbled the other way.

Calmly, the old man opened fire.

A hotel patron screamed, fell, writhed on the plush lobby carpeting. A bolt hit Mouse's protective couch. Smoke billowed.

Cassius hit their attacker with his second shot. The old man did not go down. Wearing a mildly surprised expression, he kept hosing the lobby with beam fire from a military-type weapon. People screamed. Furniture burned. Alarms wailed. Diffused beams skipping off the mirrored walls made it impossible to see.

Mouse gagged in the smoke, snapped a shot at the old man. His bolt singed the assassin's hair. He did not seem to notice.

Cassius hit him again. He turned and walked out the door as if unharmed. . . .

"Mouse," Cassius shouted, "call Heller. I'm going after him."

Mouse placed the call and was outside in seconds.

The old man lay on the sidewalk, curled in a fetal position, his weapon clutched to his chest. Cassius stood over him. He wore a puzzled look. Heller arrived almost before the crowds started gathering.

"What the hell, hey?" the policeman demanded.

"This man tried to kill us," Mouse babbled. "Just walked in the hotel and started shooting."

Cassius was kneeling now, studying the man's eyes. "Karl. Look. I think it's one of them."

Someone in the crowd said, "Hey. That's Cassius. The merc."

"Crap," a companion replied.

The word spread.

Heller snarled at a uniformed officer, "Get this cleaned up before the news snoops show. Take the body down to the plant. Cassius, I've got to take you and your friend down. I can't take any more of this."

Ten minutes later they were inside the police fortress. The street outside had filled with news people. The name Cassius had that effect.

"Just plan on sitting tight till we get this straighened out," Heller said, responding to Cassius's request that he be allowed to visit the man named Clementine. "He can come here if you've got to talk."

The shooting was all the news that evening. The netfolk were trying to establish a connection between the various murders. The editorialists were working the Legion over, insisting that The Mountain did not need its kind. Mouse listened halfheartedly while watching Cassius work.

Walters pulled out the stops. He used all his connections. He drew on the Legion's considerable credit to have the old shooter resurrected. The attempt failed because the man had been too old. He shifted his thrust to the instel nets, where he spent fortunes.

"Karl, you got that stuff ready to go out? I've got a connect with my man in Luna Command."

Heller was impressed despite himself. "Push the red button. It'll squirt when you do."

Cassius punched. "On its way. If there's anything on record about the old guy, Beckhart has it. He runs their Sangaree section. Good man. Taught him myself, years ago."

"I've heard of him," Heller replied. The last few hours had dazed the policeman. He was in over his head. Cassius had turned a local affair into an interstellar incident. He did not like it and did not know how to stop it.

Mouse watched with mild amusement till he fell asleep.

158

The sun was up when Cassius wakened him. "Come on, Mouse. We're heading home."

"Where?"

"Home."

"But. . . ."

'We got what we came for. You do the flying. I need some sleep."

Heller escorted them to the port, which the police had closed till they got the crisis in hand. His okay was necessary before any vessel could lift off.

"Cassius?" Heller said as Walters was about to board. "Do me a favor, eh? Don't hurry back."

Cassius grinned. For a moment he looked like a boy again, instead of a tired, old, old man. "Karl, if you make me apologize one more time I'll puke. All right? I owe you one. A big one."

"Okay. Okay. You didn't bring them here. Go on. Get out of here before I forget I forgot to charge you with carrying illegal weapons."

Mouse glanced over as Cassius settled into the acceleration couch beside him. Walters said, "Set a base curve for Helga's World."

Mouse began the programing. "Why there?" He was baffled. By everything. "Cassius? What happened last night?"

Cassius answered with a snore.

He slept nine hours. Mouse grew ever more impatient. Cassius seldom slept more than five, and resented that, as if it were time stolen from his alloted span.

Mouse took the ship offworld, aligned the Helga's World curve, put her into a power fly while getting up influence to go hyper.

"Keep putting on inherent," Cassius said by way of announcing his return. "On this base you lose about a thousand klick-seconds on your inherent when you drop and we may want to make a fast pass when we get there."

"Now will you tell me what happened while I was asleep?"

"We got an ID on that old shooter. From my friend Beckhart. Turned out nobody else could have filled us in. The guy was supposed to have been dead for two hundred years."

"What?"

"Beckhart's got a computer that remembers everything. When he fed it the guy's personals it dug all the way back to personnel records we captured on Prefactlas. That's where it found him. His name was Rhafu. He worked for the Norbon Family. The Norbon station was where we caught them with their fingers up their butts."

Mouse examined the idea more closely than it seemed to deserve. Cassius's attitude implied that the information was especially significant. "What's the kicker?"

"Beckhart didn't just answer the question I asked. He went looking for the meaning. He instelled us an abstract of his printouts. This Rhafu wasn't the only survivor. The Family heir, a sort of crown prince, made it through too. They managed to get off Prefactlas and somehow reclaim their Family prerogatives. Very mysterious people. Their own kind don't know any more about them than we do, but they're mucho respected and feared. Sort of the Sangaree's Sangaree. They've turned the Norbon into one of the top Sangaree Families. Their economic base is an otherwise unknown First Expansion world."

"What's the connection with us? That old man didn't try to kill us because we had the wrong color eyes. He meant it personal."

"Very personal. You'd have to have Sangaree eyes to see it, though."

"Well?"

"They'd figure a personal involvement got started the night your grandfather and I spaced in on Prefactlas. Nobody has ever quite figured out how they distinguish what's business, what's the fortunes of war, and what's personal. It's a violent and volatile culture with its own unique rules. The Norbon seem to have decided the Prefactlas raid wasn't just war."

"You don't mean they've picked us for the other half of one of those Family vendettas?".

"I do. It's the only answer that makes sense. And our burning this Rhafu will only make them madder. Don't ask me to tell you why. They don't understand us, either. They can't figure out what makes us want to destroy them."

"I'm lost, Cassius. What's the connection with Michael Dee? Or is there one? Wouldn't there have to be? To have brought the old man out?"

"There may be one. I want to think about it before I say anything. You've got a red and yellow on your comm board. You might better see who wants to get hold of us."

Mouse did so. After listening a moment, "Cassius, it's a Starfisher with a relay from Wulf and Helmut."

"Shut up and listen to the man."

In fifteen minutes they knew the worst.

"Push your influence factor to the red line," Cassius told him. "Keep putting on inherent. I want to be going like the proverbial bat out of hell when we go norm again." He remained calm and businesslike while studying the displays the computer brought up on the main astrogational screen. He fed in everything the Darkswords had given them. He plotted alternate hyper arcs for Helga's World.

"But. . . ."

"She'll take it. More if she has to. Check the register. I need the c-relative on the boat Dee swiped."

Mouse punched it up. "Old Mister Smart, my uncle Michael. He grabbed the slowest damned ship we had.

Almost, anyway. Here're a couple of trainers she can outrun."

"One break for the good guys. About time we got one. Well. Look here. We're going to get him. About an hour before he sneaks under Helga's missile umbrella. Sooner if he has to maneuver to get around your father. Start a check down on the weapons systems."

Mouse fidgeted.

"What's the matter?"

"Uh. . . . You think there'll be any shooting?"

Cassius smiled a broad, wicked smile. "Goddamned right, boy. There's going to be beaucoup shooting. First time for you, right? You just hang on and do what I tell you. We'll be all right."

The waiting bothered Mouse. He was not afraid, much. The hours piled up, and the hours piled up, and they seemed no closer than before. . . .

"Here we go," Cassius said, almost cheerfully. "Got your father on screen. And there's your idiot uncle, hopping around like a barefoot man in a sandbrier patch. Give your guns a burst."

The hours became minutes. Cassius kept boring in. "Ah, damn!" he swore suddenly. "Gneaus, what the hell did you have to go and do that for?"

"What?" Mouse demanded. He shed his harness and leaned over. "What did he do?"

"Sit down, shithead. It's going to get rough."

It got rougher than Mouse could imagine.

Thirty-Two: 3052 AD

My father was not a religious man. Nevertheless, he did have an unshakable faith in predestination. Till the very end he thought he was battling the invincible forces of Fate. You could sense that he expected no victory, but you never despaired. You knew that Gneaus Storm would never surrender.

—Masato Igarashi Storm

Thirty-Three: 3031 AD

The Seiner got through just after Storm left the atmosphere of Helga's World.

"He's gone? Already?" The tension he had been riding like a nightmare suddenly dissipated. He found himself emotionally limp, hanging out to dry. His right hand snaked out, secured the instel receiver.

The limpness did not last. Rage and sorrow smashed down on him. It was a crushing emotional avalanche. The feelings were so powerful that a small, stunned part of him recoiled in amazement.

There in the privacy of his ship, locked away from all human eyes, he could safely open the flood gates. He did so, venting not only emotions engendered by his failure to save Benjamin and Homer, but his responses to all the frustrations that had been building since first he had heard of Blackworld and the Shadowline. He wept, cursed, asked the gods what justice there was in a universe where a man could not control his own fate.

The universe and gods, of course, did not reply.

There was no justice in that momentary eddy in chaos. There never had been or would be. A man made his own justice if he wanted any at all.

Storm knew that. But sometimes even the most strongly anchored mind slips its cables and refuses to accept reality. Once in a while, at least, it seemed the gods or universe *ought* to care.

163

Storm vowed, "I'll get a bit of justice of my own." He had been making a lot of vows lately, he realized. Would he survive long enough to see any of them fulfilled?

The shakes were going. The tears had dried. His voice was losing its tightness. He opened instel communications again. "Starfisher? Are you there? Why are you nosing into this?" Those people did not get involved in the troubles of outsiders.

There was a long delay. "Lady Prudence of Gales, Colonel. And other reasons involving the man you're chasing. Not subject to discussion. Do you wish a relay?"

"Yes. Fortress of Iron."

"Ready when you are, Colonel."

"Wulf? Are you there?"

In time, "Here, Colonel."

"Recall Cassius."

"He's finished already. He's on his way. I've inserted him into the pursuit pattern."

"Good. Anything new?"

"Dee is running for Helga's World. The Seiners have given us a projected course. He'll be coming right down your throat. I'm using box and plane and I'm tightening it up to keep him headed your way. I've got Cassius on an intercept that should catch Dee just after he spots you and sheers off Helga's World. The trap should close before he recognizes it."

The trap's mouth closed slowly. Even at velocities many times that of light it took a long ledger of days before the scale of action tightened enough to warrant Storm's taking his ship off auto control. For a while he lay motionless in relation to the nearest stars, listening to the Seiner's reports. He kept influence up so he could make a quick snake-strike at Dee as he came up. Essentially, he was pretending to be a singularity.

Michael did not fall for it. He could not know who was waiting to ambush him, but he did know that there were no singularities near his daughter's world. He shifted course into the one gap apparently open to him.

And there was Cassius, playing a trick not unlike Storm's but remaining in normspace with an inherent velocity approaching that of light.

Dee's nose swung toward the tiniest of cracks in the closing walls of the trap. He attacked it with every erg his ship could give.

Storm put way on. Cassius skipped into hyper. The quiet dance, that might but likely would not end in a blaze of weaponry, began. Storm wondered if his brother were desperate enough to fight. It was not Michael's style, but he might panic, not knowing who had blocked his flight.

Maneuver. Counter-maneuver. Feint and lunge. Dee tried to fake Storm out of position for the vital few seconds he needed to whip past and streak for the safety of Helga's World.

Wulf's pursuing box closed in while Dee surrendered straight-line velocity for maneuver.

Cassius arrowed in on a spear of a course, riding the fastest ship involved. His sprint would put him across Dee's bows if Michael took too long getting past Storm. Even separated by light-hours and without direct communication, Cassius and Storm worked as a team.

Storm became satisfied that his singleship would outperform his brother's. He could commit one narrow error and still not lose his man. In dealing with Michael a second was a treasure to be hoarded against the unpredictable, but Gneaus no longer felt like playing safe. He wanted Dee, and wanted him quick. He decided to risk his advantage.

Pushing as hard as his ship would endure without breaking up under hyper stress, he darted toward where he expected Michael to be next. He fed max power to his influential field. Dee's ship had the stronger generator and would take his under control, but then it would take Michael precious minutes in norm to disentangle the fields. Cassius would arrive. He would mesh his field with the others long enough for Wulf to slam the lid on the box.

Michael recognized his intention. He sheered off. Too late. The tracks of the singleships continued to converge.

Storm pulled closer and closer, at a steadily decreasing relative velocity, till his influential sphere just brushed his brother's.

His singleship screamed. Alarms hooted. An effect that could only be described as fifth-dimensional precession took place as both ships tried to twist away in a direction that did not exist. Storm's shipboard computer calmly murmured portents of disaster.

Swift as lightning and as jagged, hairline cracks scurried across his control-room walls. Even before he heard a sound Storm knew that his engine room's stressteel frame members were snapping, that his generators were crawling free of their mounts. His hand darted toward the manual override, to cancel his approach program, but he knew it was too late. Either his drive or Michael's was badly out of synch.

Dee had won again.

This might be the death-without-resurrection, his hope no more than a chance at a clone. It was no solace that Michael might share his fate.

His hand changed course and shot toward the disaster escape release.

Crystals and fog formed before his vision went. His skin protested the nibbling of a thousand hot little needles as vacuum gulped the contents of his control room. The locked vessels had precessed into norm space. Their conflicting inherent velocities were tearing them apart.

Before the darkness came there was a moment in which he wished he had been a better father and husband. And had had the sense to wear a combat suit going into a combat situation.

Thirty-Four: 2853-2860 AD

Deeth had thought he was immune to pain. Hell, the girl wasn't even Sangaree.... He walked. And walked, without paying any attention to where he was going. His feet responded to some instinct for the debts he owed. They carried him to the spaceport.

It had grown during the human occupation. Prefactlas Corporation involved itself in far more shipping than ever the Sangaree had. The port was furiously busy. The Corporation was gutting the world.

He paused to watch the stevedores unloading a big Star Line freight lighter. The Corporation employed natives and former slaves because human muscle power was less expensive than imported lading machinery.

A familiar face turned his way.

"Holy Sant!" he whispered, spinning away. "It can't be." He looked again. Rhafu's weathered face seemed to swell till it occupied his whole field of vision. The breeding master had aged terribly, but Deeth did not doubt his identity for an instant.

The old man did not seem to notice one curious boy. Back-country kids came in to stare at the wondrous port all the time.

It took all Deeth's will power not to run and hug Rhafu, to seize this one scrap that had survived a devastated past.

He fled instead, his mind a riot. The possibilities!

Rhafu's very existence set off the alarm bells. Was

he a human agent, either human himself or someone who had made an accommodation to the animals? Someone had betrayed Prefactlas. The perfect timing of the attack on the Norbon station reflected possession of solid inside information.

If Rhafu were guilty why was he now a laborer, mildewing on the ass of the social scale? The humans would have killed their traitor the instant he was no longer useful. Or would have rewarded him better.

Deeth locked himself into the crude shack where he and Emily lived. Where he lived. Emily was no longer a part of his poverty. He would never see her again.

He wrestled with his fears and suspicions.

Someone knocked. He had few acquaintances. Police? Emily?

Expecting a blow from the hammer of fate, he opened the door.

Rhafu pushed through, seized his left wrist, glared at the tattoo still visible there. The stony hardness left his face. He slammed the door, enveloped Deeth in a ferocious hug. "Sant be praised, Sant be praised," he murmured.

Deeth wriggled free and stepped back. There were tears in the old man's eyes.

"Deeth. I couldn't believe my eyes when I saw you at the pits. Thought my mind was playing tricks. I gave up years ago. Lad, what's been keeping you? Where've you been?"

Deeth babbled his own questions.

They hugged again.

The past had come home. He was Norbon w'Deeth again. He was Sangaree. He was a Head. . . . Of a one-man Family?

"Hold it. Hold it," Rhafu said. "Let's get organized. You tell me your story, then I'll tell you mine."

"You make me green with anticipation," Deeth complained.

"And compel you to be brief if you want your questions answered," Rhafu countered.

Deeth wasted few words. When he mentioned finding the remains of the Dharvon heir, Rhafu chuckled but withheld comment.

"The girl," he asked when Deeth finished. "You're sure you can trust her? We can reach her."

"She'll keep her mouth shut." He saw murder in Rhafu's eyes.

"It's wisest to take no chances."

"She won't say anything."

"You're the Norbon." Rhafu shrugged as if to say he was acceding to Deeth against his better judgment.

"Tell me your damned story, you old scoundrel. How the hell did you manage to live through the raid?"

"Your father's orders. He had second thoughts about sending you off alone. Said he wanted you to have a bodyguard and adviser during the hard times after the raid."

"*How* you survived is what stumps me."

"It was grim. By then the Marines were dropping their perimeter. We killed all the breeders and field hands who knew me. I dressed up as a wild one. The first Marines in found me leading an attack on one of the guest cottages, howling and screaming and throwing spears around like a rabid caveman."

Deeth frowned.

"It was the Dharvon cottage, Deeth. By then your father had determined that they were behind the raid. They were supposed to get ten points in the Prefactlas Corporation, and all the Norbon holdings. They thought they could get Osiris that way. The animals might have gone through with the deal, too. Boris Storm is an honorable man. I suppose I saved him a lot of soul-searching by killing his Sangaree partners."

"All this because my father couldn't bring himself to share Osiris."

"Who sows the wind reaps the whirlwind. Your father was too jealous of his wealth, in hand or in prospect. Though he did judge the Dharvon correctly when he foresaw that a Wholar would be wasted on them."

"Where do we stand? As a Family."

"In vendetta with the Dharvon. I've resumed communication with your House on Homeworld. The Dharvon have recovered under a cadet line. The Norbon remain a House divided. There is a dwindling Deeth faction still hoping you'll return and lead them to Osiris. The other faction, naturally getting stronger by the month, want a new Head declared so they can control what the House has now. The human and Ulantonid spheres will collide before long. They want to develop a strong raid force and cash in."

"I see." As he remembered talk overheard during childhood, it sounded like typical in-House politics. Neither faction would be overjoyed by his reappearance. "But back to your escape. It couldn't have been that simple. These animals aren't fools."

"It did take some doing. They tried to double check every captive to make sure none of us got away by hiding with the slaves. I mostly outran them. I had a hard few years, then I got settled in here. Except for the occasional agent from off planet, you're the first of our people I've seen in nine years."

"We're the only survivors?" Prefactlas was irrevocably lost, then.

He had known that for a long time. The planet had been lost the moment a Dharvon had approached a human. He had been ducking the final admission. The denial was one brick in the wall he had raised to hide himself from the charge his father had set upon him. "How have you been keeping yourself, Rhafu? And do we have anything to build on?" His duty could be shirked no more.

Rhafu smiled. "I haven't been remiss. Once a field man,

always a field man. Don't let my job fool you. I've become a very rich man. Being the only one of our people here has certain advantages. I've become *the* underworld here. I control it all. Without bragging, I can say the only man on Prefactlas with more power is Boris Storm. Nobody knows who I am, but everybody has heard of me."

"You're the Serpent?"

"In the scaly flesh."

"I'll be damned." Deeth laughed uncontrollably. "Why didn't we run into each other sooner? Years have gone to waste, Rhafu." The laughter evaporated. Rhafu had an empire of his own now. He might consider old obligations a liability.

"Were that true," Rhafu replied to Deeth's direct question, "I wouldn't be here today. I would've gotten off Prefactlas as soon as I had the machinery running smooth. I'd have gone somewhere safe and collected my cut and shown my strength just often enough to keep the would-be independents in line. No. I stayed because I still haven't fulfilled my contract with the Norbon."

Deeth grinned. Rhafu was as sentimental as a Sangaree could be. "What should we do now, Rhafu?"

The old man grinned right back. "That's easy. We just reclaim the Family and its Homeworld power base."

"Really? That's going to take money and muscle, my friend. Do you have it?"

"No. Not enough. We'll have to liquidate here and use the cash to pick up a ship and some good men. We'll have to work Osiris till we're strong enough. We'll have to stay away from Homeworld but keep the Family informed so you don't get frozen out of your patrimony. Osiris will be our leverage. It'll bring them into line. Let's see. Maybe two years? Then at least another two to consolidate and fatten the Family on Osiris? Another five to settle with the Dharvon, defend ourselves in court and accommodate ourselves with any new enemies the feud stirs up, and to thoroughly develop the Osirian operation? Another year or two just for margin? Say plan on at least ten before we're solid, strong, and in any position to get down to the real work your father left us, the destruction of the animals who killed him and your mother."

"That's a lot of years, Rhafu."

"You had something else to do with them? Perhaps you went through all that business in that cave just so you could retire?"

The years rolled away into the dusty corners of time. Deeth and Rhafu made dream after dream come real. They recaptured the Homeworld Norbon. They went to Osiris. They built a Norbon Family as strong and feared as any among the Sangaree. By cunning and guile they devoured several small Houses whom the Dharvon, aware of their Family's complicity in the Prefactlas disaster, tried to frame with forged evidence. When the Norbon rapacity had been sated and they were ready to settle with the Dharvon for all time, Deeth had a friend bring in damning documents lifted directly from Prefactlas Corporation files.

Emily stayed one day after her appearance before the assembled Heads of the First Families. She had become a stunning woman. Deeth felt the yearnings of their earlier life together. As did she. But. . . .

Her years with Boris Storm had chipped the rough edges off her. She was no longer Emily the fugitive pleasure girl. She had become a lady, and one even a Sangaree must respect. She was a completely different person. She merely shared a few memories with Norbon w'Deeth's little Emily.

And Deeth was no longer an orphan boy surviving in a shack in a slum on an enemy world.

They spent a quiet afternoon walking the perfectly

landscaped gardens of the Norbon Family holding, remembering when and trying to get to know the people they had become.

It was a ritual of ending, a final emotional endorsement of the separation that had taken place while they were still those other people. In their respective ways they agreed that there were no debts between them now, no enmities, and no tomorrows.

Deeth shed a tear for her when she left him. And never saw her again.

But the children that she brought with her, the sons, would cross his path again and again.

Book Two
HANGMEN

Who springs the trap when the
hangman dies?

Thirty-Five: 3052 AD

Some of the most unpleasant moments in life come when we have to face the fact that our parents are human and mortal. For me the revelations came in quick succession. They really rocked me, though I think I concealed my shock at the time.

I grew up believing my father a demigod. In an offhand way I knew he was mortal, but it simply never occurred to me that he could be killed. I suppose I should thank my uncle for removing those scales from my eyes.

I have only my father to thank, or blame, for making me realize that even the wise and noble Gneaus Julius Storm could be petty, arrogant, blind, unnecessarily cruel, and maybe even a little stupid. This latter revelation touched me far more deeply than did the other. After all, we all begin life under sentence of death. But nowhere is it written that our time on death row is to be spent compounding the idiocies and miseries of our fellow condemned.

Though I did not love him less afterward, I lost my awe of my father after witnessing his brush with my uncle. For a time just his presence made me suffer.

The loss of an illusion is a painful thing.

—Masato Igarashi Storm

Thirty-Six: 3031 AD

Gneaus Storm gradually drifted up into a universe of gnawing pain.

Where was he? What had happened?

His dying hand had reached the switch in time. Or the automatics had asserted themselves. Somehow, he had been enveloped by the escape balloon before vacuum could take a fatal bite.

He knew that he had not died. There was very little pain in a resurrection. When you died the docs gave you a complete overhaul before they brought you around again. You came out with the vivacity, spirit, and lack of internal pain characteristic of youth. If you did not die, and you came back by more mundane medical processes, you had to play it by Nature's old rules. You took the pain along with the repairs.

More than once Storm wished they had let him go. Or that Cassius had had the decency to return him to the Fortress for proper medical care.

Storm once returned to consciousness to find a worry-faced, exhausted Mouse hovering over his medicare cradle. "Mouse," he croaked, "what are you doing here?"

"Cassius told me to stay," the boy replied. "It's part of my training." He forced a smile.

"He begged me." Cassius's voice, through the additional filter of the intercom speaker, sounded doubly mechanical and remote.

"Son, you've got to go back to Academy," Storm insisted, forgetting that he had lost this argument once before.

"It's arranged," Cassius said.

Perhaps it was, Storm reflected. He was not remembering clearly. The past month was all a jumble. Maybe Cassius had used his clout with the War College.

He tried to laugh. His reward was a shot of excruciating pain. Vacuum had done a job on his lungs.

"He needed somebody to watch you and Michael," Mouse told him, unaware that his father did not quite realize what was going on. "That's not a one-man job even with Michael sedated."

Storm remembered some of it. He smiled. Michael really impressed Cassius. Dee was only a man. He had been bested as often as not. His greatest talent was that of weaver of his own legend.

"He survived too, eh?" He remembered most of it now.

"He came through in better shape than you did," Cassius said. "He took some elementary precautions."

"It was his boat that was off tune," Mouse added. "He jiggered it on purpose. A trick he learned from Hawksblood. Hawksblood sets all his drives so they're off tune with everything but each other."

"His first intelligence coup," Cassius droned. "Though anybody with computer time and a little inspiration could have figured it out. Give him credit for the inspiration."

Mouse reddened slightly.

"We're headed for the asteroid?" Storm asked.

Mouse nodded. Cassius replied, "Yes. There're still questions we might put to Michael and Fearchild." Then, "We won't be able to reach Michael by the usual methods. He's been conditioned to resist drugs and polygraphs. Primitive methods may prove more efficacious."

"Uhm." Storm doubted that they would, though Michael, for all his bravado and daring, was a coward at heart.

How had Dee obtained an immunization course against the subtler forms of truth research? The process was complicated, expensive, and highly secret. Confederation restricted it to its most favored and highly ranked operatives and leaders in the most sensitive positions. Mouse, if he could stay alive for forty years and achieve flag grade, was the only man he knew who had a hope of attaining that signal honor. "Curious, that," he murmured.

"How curious you can't imagine."

Inflections in Cassius's speech were necessarily hard to grasp. This time Storm caught it. "You found something?"

"I think we learned most of it. It will be interesting watching the Dees while we discuss it."

"You can't tell me now?"

"We're fifty-one hours from the asteroid. Take time to recuperate. You're still disoriented. The discussion will be a strain."

"No doubt."

For two days Storm slept or endured his son's vague, intriguing hints about what he and Cassius had discovered on The Big Rock Candy Mountain. He tried to make the best of it by retreating to his clarinet and Bible. One of his sergeants had risked his life to salvage them from the phase-disrupted wreck of his singleship.

His eye was too weak for the book, his fingers insufficiently coordinated for the instrument. Mouse read some for him. Time did not drag. He slept a lot.

Mouse wakened him once, so he could watch while Cassius blurred their influential backtrail in the field around a star. Walters meant to make a complete orbit, take hyper briefly while masked by the star's own field, then drift for a day at a velocity slightly below that of light. The asteroid lay in the cometary belt of the chosen star.

The maneuver was intended to shed any unnoticed tail. Perforce, any such shadow would be operating at the limits of detection and would quickly lose contact.

Storm had Mouse move him to the control room for the stellar orbit.

"Cassius, roll her so the sun'll be topside during orbit," he said.

"You've got it." The star wobbled slightly as Cassius adjusted the ship's attitude. It swelled to the size of a sun. Cassius dove in, sliding around so close that the horizon curves vanished and they seemed to be drifting below an endless ceiling of fire. It was an Armageddon sky from which flames reached down with stately grace, as if to capture them and drag them into all that fury. Even smaller sunspots appeared as vast, dark continents surrounded by vaster oceans of flame. Cassius put all his filters up and let Storm stare, brooding, into that furnace that was the ultimate source of all other energies.

Storm said, "How like life itself a star is. It pulses. It struggles to maintain itself in a boundless ocean of cold despair. Every atom vibrates its little nucleus out, fighting the vampire night sucking its life. And the star fights knowing the struggle is hopeless, knowing that all it can do is die defiantly, going nova as its last grand gesture."

Mouse leaned forward, listening intently. His father seemed to be trying to create some order out of his own nebulous philosophy.

"Entropy and Chaos, death and evil, they can't be beaten by star or man, but in defeat there's always the victory of defiance. This sun is telling me, Gneaus, the mortal flesh can be destroyed, but the spirit, the courage within, is eternal. It need not yield. And that's all the victory you'll ever get."

Mouse watched with watery eyes as his father fell asleep, exhausted by the effort it had taken to put his feelings into words. The youth stared up at the fire, trying to see what Gneaus Storm had seen. He could not find it. He rose and took the old man back to his medicare cradle.

Being moved brought Storm back to a twilight awareness.

All his adult life Storm had been anticipating a fierce and final conflict from which he could win no mundane victory. With almost religious faith he believed that the manipulators would someday push him into a corner from which there would be no escape but death. He had always believed that Richard would be the instrument of his destruction, and that he and Richard, by destroying one another, would spell the doom of their kind.

The fires of the Ulantonid War had ignited a blaze of panhumanism of which Confederation was still taking full advantage. It was bulling its way into broad reaches of relatively ungovernmented space in apparent response to a set of laws similar to those defining the growth of organisms and species. Mercenary armies were among those institutions facing increasingly limited futures.

No government willingly tolerates private competition, and especially not competition which can challenge its decrees. The most benign government ever imagined has as its root assumption its right to apply force to the individual. From inception every government continuously strives to broaden the parameters of that right.

Storm believed he and Richard, if lured into a truly bloody Armageddon, would fight the last merc war tolerated by Confederation. The Services now had the strength and organization to disarm the freecorps. All they needed was an excuse.

Cassius's ship reached the chunk of celestial debris that Storm had long ago developed as a prison for Fearchild Dee. It was a living hell, Fearchild's reward for his perfidy on the world where Cassius had lost his hand.

That had not been a matter of the hazards of war.

Fearchild had been a dilettante merc captain commanding forces his father had hoped to turn into a Family army. The Legion had humiliated him in his field debut. He had tried using Dee tactics to recoup.

Merc wars were ritualized and ceremonial. Their ends were celebrated with a formalized signing of Articles of Surrender and the yielding up of banners by the defeated captain. Fearchild had smuggled in a bomb, hoping to obliterate the Legion staff prior to a surprise resumption of hostilities.

Appalled, his officers had turned on him and warned their opposites. Cassius had been the only Legionnaire injured. He had refused to have the hand replaced.

It reminded him that there were dishonorable men in the universe. He could consider its absence and remember just how much he hated the Dees.

It took Cassius and Mouse two hours to transfer Storm and Michael and their medicare cradles to the asteroid's single habitable room. They wakened the injured men only after completing the task.

Michael awoke with a whimper. The instant he discovered Storm's presence, he wailed, "Gneaus, that man is going to kill me."

Cassius chuckled. His prosthetic larynx made it a weird sound. "I will, yes. If I can."

"You promised, Gneaus. You gave me your word."

"You're right, Michael. But Cassius never promised you anything. Neither did Masato, and I've got the feeling he's mad about what you did to his brothers."

Mouse's attempt to look fierce fell flat. Dee did not notice. He was too involved with himself and Fearchild, whom he had just noticed.

"My God! My God!" he moaned. "What are you doing?"

"Thought he'd be up to his neck in houris, eh?" Cassius asked.

Michael stared, aghast. He was not inhuman. He loved his children. His parental concern overcame his tredpidation. "Fear. Fear. What're they doing to you?"

"Plug him in, Cassius," Storm ordered. "It should make him more amenable."

Mouse and Cassius lifted a passive Michael onto an automated operating table.

Fearchild's situation did not seem cruel at first glance. He was chained to a wall. He wore a helmet that enveloped his head. A thick bundle of wires attached the helmet to a nearby machine.

That machine restricted Fearchild to limits that kept him barely among the living. Like Valerie in Festung Todesangst, he was permitted no lapses in self-awareness. Nor was he free to slide off into insanity. The machine enforced rationality with a battery of psychiatric drugs. At random intervals it stimulated his pain center with an equally random selection of unpleasant sensations.

They were all cruel men.

Mouse worked in a daze, not quite able to believe this place was real, not quite able to accept that his father had created it.

Cassius adjusted Fearchild's machine so the younger Dee could take an interest in what was being done to his father.

Mouse and Cassius strapped Michael to the table, rotated it till it stood upright. Storm watched impassively. Cassius positioned and adjusted surgical machinery which included a system similar to that which kept Fearchild sane. He added an anaesthesia system programmed to heighten rather than dampen pain.

"Do we have to do this?" Mouse whispered.

Cassius nodded. He was enjoying himself.

All cruel men.

"I keep my word, Michael," Storm said. His voice was soft, weak, and tired. "No matter what, I'll never kill you. I tried to make a point on The Mountain. You refused to understand it. I'm going to make it again here, a little more strongly. Maybe you'll get the message this time."

He paused for a minute, gathering strength. "Michael, I'm going to make you beg me to kill you. And I'm going to keep my promise and make sure you stay alive. You ready, Cassius?"

Cassius nodded.

"Give him a taste."

The machine whined. A tiny scalpel flayed a few square millimeters of skin off Dee's nose. A second waldo bathed the exposed flesh with iodine. A third applied a small dressing. The anaesthesia program intensified the fire of the antiseptic. Dee shrieked.

"Enough. You see, Michael? That rig is a little toy I put in when we slapped this place together. I had a feeling you'd make me use it someday. What it will do is skin you a few square millimeters at a time, here and there. You'll get plenty of time to heal so the skinning won't ever end. Think about that. Pain for the rest of your life."

Dee whimpered. His eyes seemed glazed.

Mouse turned his back. He kept jerking from the stomach upward as he fought to keep his breakfast down. Cassius laid a gentle hand on his shoulder. "Easy," he whispered.

Storm snarled, "Michael, Michael, you've just got to play your games. You can't claim you weren't warned. You can't say you didn't know the risks." He waved a weak hand at Cassius. "Do an eyelid now."

Dee flushed a pale shade of death. "My face. . . ."

Cruel men. Cassius laughed. The sound was so malignant it seemed no artificial voice box could have produced it.

"There'll be scars," Storm promised. His voice was soft, musing. "Yes. That will hurt more than the skinning, won't it? Cassius, make sure there are plenty of scars in the program. Do something artistic."

Dee cried, "Damn it, Gneaus. . . ."

"This isn't a pleasure spa, Michael. This is hell. Your own private hell. You brought it on yourself. Then you expect the rest of us to feel sorry for you. It doesn't work that way. We aren't kids now. You can't fool us the way you used to. We're on to all of your tricks."

"Gneaus, not my face."

"You want to tell us why Blackworld means so much to you?"

"It's my way out. . . ." Dee shut up. He refused to speak again.

"Cassius, before we leave I want you to position them so they have to look at each other. Put a sound baffle between them so they can't talk. Now, before we tackle my questions again, tell me what you found on The Mountain."

Cassius sketched the story. Storm occasionally interrupted with a question or to make a point. When Cassius mentioned the elderly assassin, he asked, "Sangaree?"

Cassius nodded.

Storm turned to an attractive and frightened Michael Dee. "So that rumor is true. You have been dealing with them. That won't make you any friends, Michael." He shook an admonitory finger. "Go on, Cassius. This is getting interestinger and interestinger."

A minute later Storm muttered, "I've got a feeling I'll be eligible for Social Insurance after I pay your instel bill."

"Possibly. The man's name was Rhafu."

Storm sent a puzzled glance Michael's way. Dee seemed both disappointed and relieved. "It doesn't make sense, Cassius."

"It does. Keep listening." He explained what he had learned from his friend in Luna Command.

"Why would this mystery Sangaree wait till now to get even?"

"I take it he's really a low-key sort. Tries to get everything lined up perfect before he makes his move. He's probably been chipping away at us for a long time."

Storm looked at Dee. "That could explain a lot of things. But not too clearly."

"I've been doing some thinking. It was a long trip out, watch and watch. Not much chance to talk. Mainly, I tried to figure out why a man would want to destroy his brother so bad he would cut a deal with Sangaree. I didn't come up with anything. Each time I thought I had it, I came back to the same thing. The only things you've ever done were in reply to something a Dee did first. Our friend here is a son-of-a-bitch, but in the past he usually took his lumps when he deserved them. And until just lately he was always pretty impersonal about his crap.

"So I went back and thought it through from the beginning. There had to be a clue somewhere.

"I think it started because he wanted to get even with Richard Hawksblood. Including you was a sop for this Deeth creature. In others words, it's not really personal. It's an arrangement. Deeth helps him get Richard. He helps Deeth get you and the Legion."

Storm stared at his brother. Michael looked terribly uncomfortable. "Why the hell would he take up with this Deeth?"

"That's where I had to strain the old logic box. We have to go back to your father and mother to put it together. You know the family stories. He met her on Prefactlas. She was pregnant when they got married. Boris never found out who Michael's father was. Emily wouldn't say. Like that.

"Check my reasoning. Emily was born a Sangaree pleasure girl. Her genetic tagging was distinctly Norbon. We know she spent several years traveling and living with a boy who may have fathered Michael. He vanished completely once your mother moved in with Boris.

"There was a more notorious disappearance at the same time. The grand master of the Prefactlas underworld, a man we called the Serpent. My friend Beckhart tells me the Serpent and this Rhafu are the same guy. Starting to get a picture?"

"I've got one." Storm laid a finger alongside his nose. "And I don't like it. He's not just dealing with them, he is one of them. The son of this Deeth. Implausible on its face, but you found a few crossbreeds on Prefactlas, didn't you?"

"Too many. And from Michael's expression, I'd say we've hit it square."

"Ah, yes. So we have."

"Gneaus, I. . . ." Dee shut up. It was too late for truth or lies.

The silence stretched out. Mouse began to move around nervously, glancing from man to man.

Storm murmured, "The thing takes shape. We know some whos and whys, and even a few hows. Enough to have upset them by recapturing Benjamin and Homer. But that doesn't really change anything. Probably too late to wriggle out."

"We can kill us a few Dees," Cassius suggested. "I grilled Beckhart on this Deeth. There's no way we can get to him. He's moved off Homeworld. His whole outfit is on his First Expansion planet. He's the only bastard in the universe who knows where it is. So how the hell do you bribe some fool Sangaree to go cut his throat? If we want him, we have to make him come to us."

"Michael stays alive. I gave him my word. He may not be as guilty as he looks, anyway."

"Stop making excuses for him, Gneaus."

Storm overlooked Cassius's remark. "He and Fearchild will be safe here. Remember Trojan Hearse? I'll order a go on it, and start hunting Seth-Infinite. If we nail him down too, this Deeth will have to come out if he wants to keep us running. He won't have any cats-paws left."

"Helga," Mouse suggested.

"She doesn't get around so good anymore," Storm replied. "Warm your instel, Mouse. I've got to talk to Richard."

"We don't have one. We had our wave guides sheered off by friend Michael there," Cassius said. "And we've lost relay contact with your Seiner friend. It'll have to wait till we get back to the Fortress."

"Why are we fooling around here, then? Take me home."

Mouse turned his father's medicare cradle and pushed it into the passage to the ship dock. Michael started screaming behind him.

Cassius had energized the torture machinery.

Cruel men. All cruel men.

A small yacht drifted in normspace. Its pilot patiently watched her hyper scan. She had lost her quarry, but hoped to find it again.

Cassius went hyper. His vessel left a momentarily detectable ripple.

The yacht turned like a questing needle. In a moment it began to accelerate.

Thirty-Seven: 3028 AD

Moira was seventeen when she received the summons. It terrified her. She had heard stories. . . . Not even Blake would *force* her. Would he?

She had no protector. She had had to do her own fighting since Frog's death. She was tough even for an Edgeward girl. But Blake? Fight a demigod?

Frog had, in his stubborn way.

She looked around the tiny room that had been the

dwarf's home, that he had made home for a girl-child abandoned and unwanted by so many better able to provide. She turned an ear to listen for a ghost voice. "Frog, what should I do?"

"Go on, girl. And crank the bastard's nose up his butt if he tries anything."

She really had no choice. Blake was the great bull gorilla boss of Edgeward. They would come and get her if she did not go on her own.

As she prepared, making herself as unattractive as she could, she surveyed the room again. A cool tickle of irrational fear said it might be her last look around.

She had turned it into a museum. Almost a shrine, of and to the crazy dwarf called Frog, whose real name she had never known. There had been no way to show she cared while she lived. She had sensed that he would have been embarrassed by affection. Now, in her most romantic years, with her memories growing ever more vague and rose-lensed, she was, progressively, elevating him to godhead.

Moira did not fit. Edgeward was a black community. She was a curiosity and "old Frog's stray brat." The latter, with the ghost of the mad dwarf always peering over her shoulder, put people off more than did the former.

Old Frog had become a city legend. Edgewarders boasted about him to outsiders. The Man Who Ended the Shadowline. They had brought in his tractor and made a memorial of it. But he still made them nervous.

Dead and canonized was where madmen belonged. His mind had been diseased. . . . They feared Moira might be a carrier.

They did not know what to say or do around her, so they did nothing. She was an outcast without justification, lonely, given far too much time to brood. The pressures of her fellow citizens' trepidations and expectations were creating the thing they feared.

Frog pictures on the walls. Frog things around the

room. The ragged remnants of his hotsuit. A model of his crawler. Brightside charts which bore Frog's stamp, his openings of *terra incognita*. A diary in which Moira jotted what she felt were her most important thoughts, many of which orbited around her namesake, Edgeward's first woman tractor hog, The Girl Who Saw the Sun, a character saint of the same weird canon as Frog. Frog had claimed a relationship. Moira never had learned what it was. It was a mystery she was afraid to delve into. She had started in on the city records several times, and always stopped before she traced the link. She had a niggling little fear that she might find out her patron had had feet of clay.

She dithered. "At your earliest convenience," from Blake meant yesterday, and was that much more intimidating.

"Might as well get it over." She sighed, mussed her hair, and went.

Main offices for Blake Mining and Metals were in a huge old building at Edgeward's center, beneath the strongest part of the meteor screen shielding the dome. Years ago it had been City Hall and had housed city administrators' offices exclusively. Blake controlled that now. Edgeward was a company town. He might as well be in City Hall.

Moira arrived as the afternoon's programed rain began falling. A light breeze drove mist into her face. Scents on the air brought back vague images of herself running across a grassy, wild-flowered plain under a friendly yellow sun, playing with the other children on the breeding farm. It had been a gentle, realtime operation run by a paternalistic station master. The youngsters had not known they were property to be trained and sold. She would not have cared had she known. She had been happy.

She paused on the steps of City Hall and stared upward, trying to glimpse the star-speckled black enemy besieging the city. She saw nothing but sunlights and the piping from which the rain was falling. Edgeward worked hard to deny the night.

The rain fell harder. She hurried through an iris door that would become an airlock should the dome fall.

She entered a small, comfortable reception room. Its sole occupant was a thin, elderly gentleman who reminded her of a grown Frog. He had the leathery look of a life-long tractor hog forced to retire from outservice. He made her nervous. Retired hogs sometimes became antsy and unpleasant.

This man had not. He glanced up and noticed her biting her lip in front of his desk. His whole face broke into smiles. He made it look as if he had been waiting years just for her.

"Miss Eight? Moira Eight? So glad you could come." He thrust a dark, wrinkled hand at her. She took it in a bit of a daze. It felt warm and soft. She relaxed a little. She judged people by the way they felt. Soft and warm meant nice and no harm planned. Cold, damp, hard, meant unpleasant intentions. She knew body temperatures were nearly the same in everyone, yet she depended on the difference in hands—and later, lips—and trusted that part of her unconscious which interpreted them.

It proved right most of the time.

"What. . . . What's it about?" she asked.

"Don't know. I'm just the old man's legs. So you're Frog's little girl. All growed up. You should get out more. Pretty thing like you shouldn't hide herself." As he talked and she blushed, he guided her toward an elevator. "Mr. Blake is in the penthouse. We'll go straight up. He said to bring you right to him."

Moira bit her lip and tried for a brave face.

"Now then, no need to be scared. He's no ogre. We haven't let him devour a maiden in, oh, three or four years."

That's the way Frog used to baby me, she thought. There was something about Brightside that made tractor men more sensitive. *Everybody thought Frog was a crusty old grouch—maybe even Frog thought he was—but that was just people who didn't know him.*

Nobody bothered to get to know tractor hogs well. Their life expectancies were too short. It did not pay to get close to an enemy of the Demon Sun. Men like this one and Frog, who got old running the Thunder Mountains and Shadowline, were rare. Human beings simply could not indefinitely endure the rigid discipline and narrow attention/alertness it took to survive beyond the Edge of the World. Frog had broken down in the end, but he had been lucky. They had brought him out—to be murdered. Maybe this man had had his failure and been lucky too.

She began to grow angry. They had not done a thing about Frog's murder. Oh, they had exiled those people, but the murderer hadn't been caught. She planned to do it herself. She would be of age in less than a year. With Frog's bequest, and the credit from the sale of the salvageable parts of his rig after Blake had deducted recovery costs, she would buy passage offworld and find August Plainfield.

The obsession had been growing from the moment she had looked through that hospital door and realized what Plainfield had done. The practicalities did not intimidate her. She was still young enough to believe in magic and justice.

Her plan was her one rebellion against the dwarf's philosophy. Sour and grumbly as he had been, he would not have wanted her to hold a grudge so deeply it would shape her life.

"Here we are. Top of the tower. Be sure to ask if you can see the observation platform. Not many people get the chance. The view is worth it."

Moira's escort led her into an antechamber almost exactly reflecting her preconception of Blake's headquarters. It *smelled* of wealth. Such spendthrift use of space!

A domed city like Edgeward used every cubic centimeter to some critical purpose. Even open areas were part of a grand design intended to provide relief from the cramped limits of living quarters.

Here space existed without function beyond announcing the wealth and power of its occupant.

"He'll be in his private office, I believe," Moira's companion told her. "Follow me."

"There's so much room. . . ."

"A big man with big responsibilities needs room to wrestle them."

"Thank you. Uh. . . . I don't know your name."

"It's not important. Why?"

"Because you've been kind, I guess. And it is important. I like to know who's been nice so I can think nice things about them." She could not think of a better way to put it.

"Albin Korando, then."

"That's odd."

"For Blackworld, I suppose. My people didn't come here till after the war."

"No, I mean Frog used to talk about you. I was trying to remember your name just yesterday."

"I'll bet he told some stories," Korando said, and laughed softly. He wore a faraway look. Then he saddened. "Some stories, yes. We're here. And Miss?"

"Yes?"

"Don't be frightened. He's just a man. And a pretty good man at that. Very few of the street stories are true."

"All right." But as they paused before the door that would open on a man almost omnipotent, she became terrified of the sheer power she faced.

Korando pushed through. "Miss Eight is here, sir."

Timorously, Moira followed.

The man who swiveled a chair to greet her was not the fang-toothed cyclops she expected. Nor was he old. She guessed thirty-five. Maybe even younger. He had a slight frame which, nevertheless, had about it a suggestion of the restrained power of the professional fighter. His smile was broad and dazzling, revealing perfect teeth. For an instant she noticed nothing else.

"Forgive me for not rising," he said, offering a hand. With the other he gestured at legs that ended in stumps where he should have had knees. "An accident at the shade station in the Shadowline a few years ago. I haven't had time to grow new ones."

"Oh! I'm sorry."

"For what? I earned it. I should know better than to go crawling around under a rogue slave. I've got people who get paid for doing that sort of thing. Albin, bring the lady something. Something mixed, Moira? No, better not. Wouldn't do to have it get around that I'm getting young women drunk. Will coffee do?"

Korando departed when she nodded.

"Well, have a seat. Have a seat. And why this look of perplexity?"

"Uh. . . ." Moira reddened. She had been staring. "I thought you were old."

Blake laughed. His laugh was a pleasant, almost feminine tinkle. She wished she had taken his briefly offered hand to see if it was warm. That hand gestured toward oil portraits hanging on a distant wall. "There they are. The real old ones. My father. His father. And the old pirate who started it all. Obadiah Blake." Three dark, hard faces fixed her with that look which is traditional in ancestral portraiture, a sort of angry calculation or cunning rapacity, as if each had been considering selling the artist into slavery. "They're old enough to suit anybody. I call them the Ancient Marinators. They took everything so serious. They soaked in their own juices." He smiled as if at an old joke. "Greedy grabbers, they were. Had to have it all."

"I guess when you've got it all you can point fingers and say shamey-shamey." Moira was astounded at her own temerity.

Blake laughed. "You're Frog's brat, all right. Hardly knew him myself, but Dad had a few things to say about him."

"None of them kind, I hope." She smiled at Korando as he arrived with a silver carafe and china teacup on a silver tray. Silver and gold were by-products of Blake's mining operations. Both were common around Edgeward. Korando wore one large gold loop earring.

"Not a one. Not a one. And none of them fit for your pretty ears, either. No, Albin, stay. I think my guest would feel more comfortable with a chaperon, though God alone knows how I'd run her down if the fancy hit me."

"As you wish, sir."

Moira smiled gratefully, including both men.

"Well, then," said Blake, "pretty as you are, and much as I'd like to chat and look and wishful think, it's business that made me ask you here, so to business we must. How do you feel about the man who killed Frog?"

She did not have to answer. Her feelings burned on her face.

"That strongly? Albin, rummage through that stuff on the table there and hand Miss Eight the solidos we were talking about last night." Blake's office was a vast clutter. He seemed to be a man without time to keep order.

"Plainfield," she said, handling two cubes about ten centimeters to a side. There were little differences in appearances, but she felt no doubt.

"Those came in yesterday, from Twilight Town. I've got a man up there who watches out for things. Made these of a fellow who's been hanging around their brass. Thought he recognized him from back when. He was one of the ones we exiled when Frog was killed. He was lucky. Got picked up by one of their crawlers. But he wants to come home. Has family here. He's trying to earn his way back in."

"What about Plainfield?" Her voice was hard, her throat tight. Her stomach felt as though she were about to throw up.

"He's using the name Diebold Amelung now, but that's not his real one either."

"What're you going to do?"

"For now, nothing." He raised a hand to silence her protest. "For now. In time, what needs doing. I could have him killed, but then I wouldn't find out what he's up to. I wouldn't find out why he killed Frog. I wouldn't find out if he's connected with some strange phenomena we've observed Brightside. Albin, is that projector ready? Good. Moira, the man's real name is Michael Dee. We've known that for some time."

"And you haven't done anything?" She began to get mad.

"My dear young lady, Blake has done everything possible, consistent with its own interests. Which isn't much, I'll grant. This man, whatever name he uses, is no Old Earth shooter, no crackdome cutthroat. He could buy and sell Edgeward City. He's a very old, rich, and powerful man. He's got a lot of connections."

"So?"

"For you it's simple. You could burn him. You've got nothing to lose. I've got an industrial empire and a hundred thousand people to consider."

"He can't be that important."

"No? He owns a planet. He almost controls the private instel trade. He has interests in all the shipping lines that carry our exports. His brother is Gneaus Julius Storm, the mercenary, who has a personal army of twenty thousand men and the ships to move it. He's associated with Richard Hawksblood, another mercenary. And he has friends in Luna Command who would put Blackworld under embargo simply on his say-so."

"I see. If he's such a big man, how come he's in Twilight?"

"Exactly. Now we're in tune, little lady. Let's watch some clips. Albin."

Korando lowered the lighting and started the holo projector.

"This is the shade cloud we send up from the outstation to cover the run from the Whitlandsund to the Shadowline," Blake said. The holo cube portrayed a tower of darkness, which, she realized after a moment, was dark only due to a lessening of an almost unbearable glare. "We've filtered it down to the limits of resolution."

The hologram changed. Another pillar of dust appeared, viewed from a slightly sunward angle, making a portion look like a tower of fiery motes. "A charter running fourteen hours north of the Shadowline caught this two years ago. We couldn't make anything of it then. Too far to investigate, and in Twilight territory. Somebody thought it might be dust blowing out of a volcano."

The third clip was a still of crawler tracks under artificial lighting. "This one's only about a month old. It was taken a little over two thousand kilometers out the Shadowline by another charter. He thought he'd stumbled across some side trip of Frog's. They didn't look right. Too wide. We checked against Frog's log. He didn't make them.

"Something was wrong. Obviously. It bothered me. Curiosities always do. I had Albin check the records. I had him talk to drivers. And he found out what I thought he'd find out. The only Edgeward man who ever went that far was Frog. So I had Albin make the rounds again. He found several charters who had gotten readings on, or sightings of, dust pillars in the north, especially way out west, where they could be seen from the Shadowline itself. Albin."

The holo changed to a small-scale chart of the northern hemisphere west of the Edge of the World. "Nobody thought they were worth reporting. Just another Brightside curiosity. Once we got interested, we plotted them. They all seem to have appeared along the black line there."

Moira understood. "A shade route to the Shadowline from Twilight territory. That would be expensive."

"She's quick, Albin. And the crawler track confirms it. It was made by a Meacham long-range charter. Twilight is in the Shadowline, at considerable expense in money and man-hours. More than they'd have available for a speculative venture. Putting a line of shadow generators across two thousand kilometers of Brightside is an awesome feat. The cost in equipment and lives must have been phenomenal. I checked with the engineers. They said it could be done, but somebody would have to be crazy to try it. So why did somebody?"

Korando changed clips twice while Blake was talking. The first showed an artist's concept of a peculiar tractor, the second an action sequence of the real thing, slightly different in its lines. The camera angle left no doubt that it had been shot in the Shadowline. Fine lines of intense light ran along the lip of towering cliffs in the background. "This was shot earlier in the week, not far from where we found the mysterious crawler track," Blake explained.

"This doesn't make sense," Moira told him. "There's no profit in it."

"Are you sure? There's got to be. Huge profits. Those Meachams are worse pirates than old Obadiah ever was. I was hoping you could shed some light."

"Me? All I know about the Shadowline is what Frog told me."

"Exactly. The only man who ever went all the way to the end."

199

"You mean he found something?"

"That's what I want to know. Did he?"

"He never said anything. But I only got to see him for a minute before he shooed me out. And then. . . . Then. . . ."

"Yes." Blake swept a hand around to include most of the room. "I've gone over every record we've got, trying to find something. Even those dreadful hours of broadcasts that went out before he made it back. I haven't found a thing. In fact, I've found too much nothing. It's like making a fly-by of a black hole. You know there's something there, but all you can tell is that it isn't. If you see what I mean. A lot of records were tampered with. You can't tell what Plainfield wanted to cover up. And more records seem to have been 'rectified' since. Like that black hole, there's so much nothing that you can tell it's something big and dangerous. And my only recourse is to some very fallible human memories of something that happened a long time ago."

"What about your spy?"

"I'd have to bring him home to question him properly. I'm trying, but I don't think I'll make it. The past few years the Meachams have gotten more paranoid than usual. Like maybe they've got something to hide. Getting the solidos of Dee was damned near impossible."

"You could put someone in, sir," Korando suggested. "Someone with a legitimate reason to come and go. Do the interview there."

"Easier than bringing someone out, I agree. But I'm afraid of how much trouble I might have getting my someone back out, legitimate business or not. My man there gives the impression that outsiders are watched pretty damned close."

"Then stage an ambush in the Shadowline," Moira said. "Use guns instead of cameras. Grab some of their people."

"I don't want them to know we know. That would bring on the war before we're ready."

"War?" Moira and Korando asked. The girl's voice squeaked.

"Of course. If there's something out there worth the trouble they've invested in stealing it, then it's worth our fighting for it to get it back."

Korando said, "Boss, you've got one hell of a subjective way of looking at things. On the map. . . ."

"The Shadowline starts in Edgeward territory. As far as I'm concerned, the whole damned thing is ours. Doesn't matter that it wanders up above Twilight's south parallel."

So there's a little pirate in this Blake, too, Moira thought. She smiled. It took claim-jumper types to make money on Blackworld. "What's my part in this?" she asked. "You knew I couldn't help with what Frog found. So why drag me in?"

"You're right. You're right. Smart girl. I've got something in mind, something complicated. Do you think you could kill Dee?"

"Plainfield? Yes. I've thought about it. I could. I don't know how reliable I'd be afterward."

"Could you *not* kill him?"

"I don't understand."

"Could you be around him, exposed to him, and not do something to get even?"

"I don't know. Maybe. If there was a good reason. What are you driving at?"

"You think you could be friendly? Or more?"

Her breakfast slammed against her esophagus. She took a moment to force it down. Then it struck her that she could exact a much more satisfying revenge if she could get the man to love her before she killed him. The sheer cruelty of it felt good.

That was when she first realized how truly deep her

hatred for Plainfield ran. It was an obsession. She would do anything.

She frightened herself. And did not like Moira very much. That was not the sort of person she wanted to be.

"What do you want me to do? I'll do it."

"Eh?"

"I'll do whatever you want me to do, as long as getting Plainfield is part of the deal."

Blake peered at her. "Don't let them turn you over to their women," he muttered. He seemed disappointed. "All right. Here's my thinking. It's still rough. We'll smooth it out as we go. First, we send you to Twilight Town. We're going to ticket you through to Old Earth. You can't get a through ship from any other port. We'll arrange a meet with our man there if we can. Then you'll take the first Earthbound ship out. You'll leave it at Weiderander's Station, cash in the rest of your ticket, and buy another for The Big Rock Candy Mountain under a different name. We're going to enroll you in the Modelmog. They've started taking rich kids in order to balance their books."

The Modelmog was the century's foremost study center for young artists, actors, and writers. As Blake suggested, the school had fallen on hard times. Rich no-talents were being admitted to carry the costs of subsidizing the talented but poor who made up the bulk of the student body. Substantial endowments were the price of the university's highly respected diplomas.

"What's this got to do with Plainfield?" Moira demanded. Her voice was plaintive. "It's awful complicated."

"Patience, child. Patience. I'm getting to it. At the Modelmog we want you to vamp a poet named Lucifer Storm. He's a talented young man, they say, and quite handsome. You shouldn't find him repulsive. Attach yourself. He'll be your passport into the Fortress of Iron. That's the headquarters of the mercenary Gneaus Storm. Dee is in and out of there all the time. You should have no trouble making contact. Become his consort."

"I see. Live with him and spy on him."

"Exactly."

"For how long?"

"There's more than Frog's paybacks to worry about, girl. There's Edgeward. I'm a big fish around here, but out there I'm just a minnow. I can't make enemies out of sharks."

Moira was intelligent. She recognized his problem, thought she found it emotionally unpalatable. "All right. But you're making it too complicated. I'll mess it up for sure."

Blake chuckled. "I've been studying Moira Eight, too, dear. She's no dummy. Her acquaintances say she's a very good actress, both on stage and in her personal life. Dramatist White thinks he's made a real find."

Moira shrugged. Secretly, she was pleased. Mr. White never said anything of the sort to her.

"My Dad, and my grandfather, they treated old Frog pretty bad. If I'd been in charge, I'd have done it different. Frog was important. He reminded us that we aren't gods. He reminded us that what was good for the Corporation wasn't always good for Edgeward's people. He didn't realize it, and my Dad only saw the edges of it, but your old man kept Edgeward from turning into something like Twilight. You'll see what I mean if we send you. Blake and Edgeward still have a human side—despite my Board of Directors. I digress. I'm sorry. It's my hobbyhorse."

"May you never dismount, sir," Korando said.

"Albin is my conscience. He came from Twilight."

"I know. He was an exile. Frog brought him in. He's sort of my brother. That was a long time ago."

"A long time ago," Korando agreed. "Had a habit of collecting strays, didn't he?"

Grimly, Blake said, "I wish he were here today. I've got to present this to the Board pretty soon. He's the kind who could have bullied them into line. They were afraid of him. Still are, in a way. As if he might come back to haunt them."

"He has, hasn't he?" Moira asked. "When do we start? What do we have to do?"

Thirty-Eight: 3031 AD

Going home did nothing to brighten anything. The Fortress of Iron was gravid with bad news.

Wulf and Helmut had put a prize crewman aboard the singleship Dee had stolen. She and her escort had been attacked while returning home. The guilty warships had been of Sangaree configuration. Only one of them had survived. Wulf and Helmut had been forced to let it escape. Its crew had managed to recapture the medicare cradles containing Benjamin and Homer. The High Seiners had tracked the fleeing ship. They said it had made planetfall on Helga's World.

"We're right back where we started," Storm groaned from his own cradle.

"Oh, no," Helmut told him. He wore a sickly grin. "We're way worse off. The Fishers say Michael and Fearchild Dee arrived on Blackworld this morning."

"That's impossible." Storm's heart hammered so hard his cradle fed him a mild sedative.

"Not quite," Wulf said. "His wife got him out. She was on Helga's World. He instelled her during the chase. She spaced and followed you to the prison. That's the story they're telling on Blackworld."

"He's got a new wife?"

"All we know is what we get in the reports," Helmut growled. "It's the old wife. I thought she was dead, too. But our man got into their pockets while they were explaining to Seth-Infinite. He even found out how she followed Dee."

"How?"

"Limited range, general broadcast instel. A little node of a thing he swallowed before he was captured. It didn't last long, but it got her into the area of the asteroid."

"We get an ultimatum?"

"The minute that raidship grounded," Wulf replied. "No signature, of course. We take the Blackworld contract or we never see Benjamin or Homer again. I guess they'll try to frame Blake Mining with the snatch."

Storm lay back, stared at a pale ceiling. He needed no signature to know who had sent that message. Helga Dee. And she would not bother trying to cover her tracks. He was tempted to ignore it. Benjamin and Homer were his flesh, but he could balance their lives against those of all the Legionnaires who would die in combat. "What's our movement status?"

"Go. We can start any time."

"Activate Trojan Hearse," Storm ordered.

Nobody protested. Nobody acted surprised. He was amazed. That had done everything but laugh when, years ago, he had presented the contingency plan. They had seen no need to be ready to break into Festung Todesangst.

"The operation went active the day Michael left," Wulf said. "We've already located one of Helga's ravens. Ceislak took the ship yesterday. He's on his way to Helga's World now."

Storm smiled his first smile in a long time. Hakes Ceislak was a fine, bloodthirsty youngster with a flair for commando operations. If anybody could slip a shipload of Legionnaires into Festung Todesangst as pretended corpses, he could.

"How many? All volunteers, weren't they? I don't think

she'd blow the scuttle bombs unless she thought she was dead anyway, but I don't like anybody taking risks if they don't want to."

"A full battalion. All volunteers. We turned another thousand away. They thought they might have to dig you out too. Ceislak picked the men he wanted."

"All right. We go to Blackworld. We stir it up there and get their attention till Ceislak can do his job. He's going to need a lot of stall time. If he takes the raven in off schedule she'll smell us out."

"He needs almost five months." Helmut shrugged apologetically. "It was the only raven we could find."

"We'll miss Ceislak on Blackworld," Wulf said. "I've been studying the layout. Blake's position is so much better than what Richard has to work from that he's got to have a whole bag of tricks up his sleeve."

"Of course he does," Storm said. "He's Richard Hawksblood. He wouldn't have taken the commission if he didn't think he could win. If it gets hairy, we'll miss Ceislak bad."

Cassius said, "My friend Beckhart might be persuaded to take that job off our hands. If we can deliver proof of a link between Helga and the Sangaree."

Mouse had begun to feel lost. He asked, "Why would that matter?"

"He'd have to have an excuse to nose around in a private war," his father told him. "Then he'd jump on it so he can grab Helga's World for Luna Command. Sangaree would make him a great *causus belli.*"

"I know they've done studies on the cost of taking her out," Cassius said. "Us, too, for that matter. The base plan was to saturate her defenses with missile fire. Go for overload and totalkill. They'd love to have us open the door and let them get their hands on all that sweet information."

"Arrange it," Storm ordered.

"You sure? He takes the place and the government gets a hammerlock on every corporation in this end of Confederation."

"I know," Storm said. "I know. No matter what way you go, it's no-win."

"What about Blake Mining?" Helmut asked. "They've been crying like babies for two weeks. I got a full-time guy in Communications giving them the stall."

"Keep him on the job. Meantime, start your preliminary movement. Surprise them. I'll be along as soon as Medical turns me loose."

"One more thing," Wulf said, as Mouse started to roll his father away.

"What?" Storm snapped. "What the hell other bad news can you hit me with?"

"Good, bad, who knows?" Wulf asked. "A message from Lucifer. He's a little embarrassed. Turns out his wife is an agent. For Blake, of all outfits."

"So? Does it matter anymore?"

"Maybe not. But answer me this, Colonel. Why was she planted on us? She hooked up with Lucifer before any of this broke. Which to me means she can't have anything to do with the Shadowline."

"Wheels within wheels," Cassius observed. He laid a gentle hand on Mouse's shoulder. "Some of us get born into the game. The wheels turn each other. Sometimes they never find out why."

"Ach!" Storm growled. "Take me down, Mouse."

The Fortress was a citadel of gloom. There wasn't a smile in the place. The Legion was a worm wriggling on a hook. A big fish was coming up to bite.

"It looks hopeless, doesn't it, Father?" Mouse asked.

"So it does, Mouse. So it does. But maybe we'll fool them all. It's always darkest before the Storm."

"Is that a pun?"

"Me? Make a joke of the family name? Horrors."

Moira strained to get used to the name she was supposed to assume at Weideranders. She tried even harder to become a genuinely creative artist. She failed abysmally. She had absolutely no talent for anything but acting.

Blake grumbled, "I guess that'll have to do."

"Do? What's wrong with it? It's legitimate. And dramatist White says Janos Kasafirek. . . ."

"I said all right." Blake smiled. "He's been at me harder than you have, pretty lady. He says it's your future."

She was thrilled. She would really get to do what she wanted. . . . She began cramming classical drama, the Old Earth classics, especially the Elizabethans. She was mad for Shakespeare. Dramatist White actually broke down and told her she played an inspired Ophelia.

She was floating. Her mission was going to give her a chance to realize her wildest dreams. She would get to study with the great Kasafirek.

"Slight change in plans," Blake said one day not long before she was due to leave. "They've tightened security in Twilight. You're going to leave here as Pollyanna, instead of waiting till you get to Weideranders."

She was to be billed as the touring daughter of Amantea Eight, an under-minister in Confederation's Ministry of Commercial Affairs. The lady actually existed and was obscure enough to cause local officials some concern. The obscure career people were the real powers in Luna Command. The identity of surnames was serendipitous.

Moira thought the going would be easy once she left Blackworld. The character was more nearly the real her than the one she portrayed for Edgeward. Her daydreams often revolved around an acting career. She never had given that serious consideration before because Edgeward had such little use for actresses. She had not thought of leaving home except to go stalking after Plainfield.

It came time to leave. She went to the crawler locks reluctantly. This would be the end of one life and the beginning of another. The doubts had begun to hem her in.

"Albin. What're you doing here?"

"Boss told me to go with you."

She spotted Blake, ran to his chair, gave him a quick little kiss. "Thank you. For Albin. I won't be nearly so scared."

"I thought not. And I thought we might learn something in Twilight. He knows the city. Be good, Moira. And be careful. You're going to be involved with some strange, dangerous men."

"I'll be all right."

She enjoyed the ride to Twilight. She had never been outdome before. She saw her world from an entirely new perspective.

Bleak ghosts of midnight landscapes slid by the crawler. Crewmen made garrulous by her beauty and exotic skin color provided her with a running commentary. This had happened here, that had happened there. Over yonder was a fantastic landmark mountain that stuck straight up a thousand meters, but you couldn't see it on account of it was dark. The crewmen were from The City of Night. They did not know her. She rehearsed her cover for them, as Pollyanna, telling outrageous lies about life in Luna Command.

She reached Twilight in a bright and cheerful mood.

It quickly soured.

At first glance Twilight Town appeared to be a clone of Edgeward City. She started to say so to Korando. The human factor intervened.

Two hard-faced policemen began checking papers as the passengers started shedding their hotsuits. They were especially nasty to Edgewarders, but only slightly more civil to the Nighter crew and the citizens of Darkside Landing. They were revelers in petty power, the sadists who gave police a bad image everywhere. Pollyanna lost her temper when they started in on Korando.

"You," she snapped, using words as gently as a torturer uses small knives. "You with the face like a pig's butt. Yes. You. The one with the nose like stepped-in dog shit. We *know* your mother made a mistake when she decided against the abortion. You don't have to prove it. Go beat your wife if you have to mistreat somebody in order to feel like a man."

Korando flashed a desperate "Shut up!" look. She just smiled.

The policemen were stunned. The other passengers made pained faces.

The man she had abused grinned malevolently. He had found himself a victim. "Papers, bitch!"

Malice turned to uncertainty. He looked at her, at her travel pass. White. Meant offworlder. Youth and sex might mean she was the brat of power.

"These better be good, bitch," he muttered to himself.

"Give them here, Humph," his partner said. "And calm down."

"Can you people read?" Pollyanna demanded. "You can? I'm amazed."

She expected more trouble than they gave her. The one officer became very solicitous once he saw the seals on her pass. "Be cool, Humph. This fluff's straight out of Luna Command."

Humph grabbed the pass, flipped through it. His eyes widened slightly. He thrust the booklet at Pollyanna. "I'll be watching you, smartass."

"I do believe you take after your father." She was a little frightened now. She had to concentrate to maintain her snottiness. "He never forgave your mother either."

And, before he could reply, in a gentler tone, she added, "A little courtesy doesn't hurt, officer. If you're nice to people, they'll usually be nice to you." She stalked away.

Korando came over while she was eating a snack at the station canteen. "That wasn't very smart, Polly. But I appreciate it. He forgot all about me."

For possible watching eyes they pretended to become acquainted. Korando told her he was going to stick a little tighter than he had planned. She needed keeping out of trouble.

And stick he did, like a limpet. So tight that he got no chance to interview Blake's agent. He stayed beside her until he had seen her enrolled in the Modelmog.

The trip thither was an adventure, Edgeward having been her whole universe and most of his. The space flies were like a visit to a dome devoted to happy times. The big Star Liners were space-going hotels.

Weideranders Station was different. That vast space-going roundhouse was too alien. Pollyanna and Korando spent most of their layover in their rooms.

Pollyanna remembered Weideranders. She had been there before, almost too long ago to recall anything but the fear she had known then. They had been running from men who had wanted to kill the people she was with. She could not face all those corridors and shops and eating places filled with outworlders, Toke, the Ulantonid, Star-fishers, and other strange people. Not without coming apart, without anticipating something dreadful.

She could not have endured it without Korando's help.

She was easing him into the role Frog had vacated by dying. He seemed to accept it.

The Mountain was terrifying too. Though it was the gentlest of worlds, it lacked that without which a Black-worlder never felt secure. It had no dome. Neither she nor Korando ever learned to face the open sky.

Lucifer Storm was almost too easy. She was sleeping

211

with him, loving him, and married to him almost before she herself knew what was happening.

Janos Kasafirek was impressed with her abilities. She was astounded and delighted. He had a reputation as a savage, unrestrained critic.

For a time she was thoroughly content. Life seemed perfect, except that she did not get to see Korando as often as she would have liked. Albin was her sole touchstone with her past and home.

Then, a year after their arrival on The Mountain, Albin announced that he was going home. She protested.

"There's been trouble," he told her. "A skirmish in the Shadowline."

"What can you do?"

"I don't know. Mr. Blake will need me, though. Be calm, Polly. You've got it under control. I'm nothing but excess baggage now."

She cried. She begged. But he went.

Looking back later, she chose that as the day when everything started going wrong.

During her tenure at the Modelmog, Lucifer's father and Richard Hawksblood fought a brief war on The Broken Wings. Lucifer followed the news uneasily. She tried to comfort him, and quickly became engrossed in the action herself, seizing every sketchy report from the Fortress of Iron, skipping from newscast to newscast to find out the latest. It was her first exposure to mercenary warfare. She was intrigued by the gamelike action and by the odd personalities involved. Once she did become enthralled, Lucifer lost interest. He expressed a virulent disapproval of her interest.

She was disappointed because the war ended so quickly.

A few months later Lucifer announced, "We have to go home. I got an instel from my brother Benjamin. Something bad is in the wind."

"To the Fortress?" She became excited. She would be a

212

step closer to Plainfield. And closer to the mercenaries she found so interesting. Lucifer's father had come to their wedding. What a strange, intriguing old man he had been. Two hundred years old! He was a living slice of history. And that Cassius, who was even older, and Lucifer's brothers. . . . They were like nothing Blackworld or The Mountain had ever seen.

What had begun as an ecstatic honeymoon was fading fast. She did not mind leaving a scene that promised to become unhappy—except that she would miss Janos Kasafirek and her studies.

"I don't want to go," Lucifer told her. "But I have to. And it's cruel to take you away from your studies when you're doing so well."

"I don't mind that much. Really. Janos is getting a little overbearing. I can't take much more. We both need to cool down."

Lucifer looked at her oddly.

He changed after they reached the Fortress. His joy, youth, and poetic romance fled him. He became surly and distant, and ignored her more and more as he tried to fit into the Legion. The Legion tried to adjust to him. He could not meld in.

Inadequate to the mercenary role, he would be little help during the grim passage he had returned to help weather. Pollyanna could see it. Everyone else saw it. Lucifer could not. He was a fingerling among sharks, trying to believe he was one of the big boys.

Pollyanna became his outlet for frustration.

Knowing why he was hurting her did not ease her pain. Understanding had its limits.

Loneliness, self-doubt, her own frustration, and spite drove her into the arms of another man. Then another, and another. It became easier each time. Her self-image slipped with each one. Then came Lucifer's father. A challenge at first, he began to remind her of Frog. He gave her

213

moments of real peace. He was gentle, considerate, and attentive, yet somehow remote. Sometimes she thought the body she clasped in their lovemaking was a projection from another plane, an avatar. The quality was even more pronounced in Storm's associates, spooky old Cassius and the Darkswords.

Plainfield, wearing the name Michael Dee, finally appeared. She met him with some trepidation, sure her hatred would shine through, or that he would remember her.

He did not remember, and did not sense her odium. Her scheme progressed with such ease that she lost herself in its pace. Before she knew it, she and Plainfield were aboard a ship bound for Old Earth and, eventually, Richard Hawksblood.

Her life seemed to become an ancient black and white movie. Jerky and depressing. Events followed Blake's script perfectly, yet she had a growing feeling that everything would fall apart.

She had lost a marriage that had meant a lot. She did not like the person she had become. Sometimes, lying beside Plainfield while he slept, she held discourse with Frog's ghost. Frog kept telling her nothing was worth the price she was paying.

It worsened. Storm forced her return to the Fortress. She would have killed Plainfield then had she not still felt an obligation to Blake, Korando, and her home city.

She became lonely in a way she had never known in Edgeward. She felt as if she had been dropped into the midst of an alien race. The men helped, for a few minutes each, but when a lover left her he took with him just a little more of her self-respect.

Then Plainfield was beyond her reach, running with the bodies of Storm's sons. She almost committed suicide.

Frog's ghost called her a little idiot. That stopped her.

She still had her duty to Edgeward. She had been living

with soldiers long enough, now, to see herself as a soldier for her city. She could persevere.

Forty: 3052 AD

How important is a place? A place is just a place, you say. And I tell you: Not so! You are either of a place, or you are not. If you are, then it is in your heart and flesh and bones; you know it without thought, and it knows you. You are comfortable together. You are partners. You know all the quirks and bad habits and how to sidestep them. If you are an outsider. . . .

It is the difference between new and old boots. You can wear both, but new boots can be trouble if you don't have time to break them in.

Blackworld was new boots for my father and the Iron Legion.

—Masato Igarashi Storm

Forty-One: 3031 AD

The spaceport crawler crested the pass through the White Mountains. Storm saw Edgeward City for the first time. "Looks like a full moon coming up," he murmured. "Or a bubble of jewels rising where a stone fell into dark water." Only half the city dome could be seen above the ringwall surrounding it. It glowed with internal light.

His aide studied him, puzzled. Storm sensed but ignored the scrutiny. He reached for his clarinet case, decided he could not play in this lurching, shaking, rolling rust heap.

He had to do something to ease the tension. It had been ages since his nerves had been this frazzled.

He returned to the reports in his lap. Each was in Cassius's terse, cool style. The data and statistics summed an impossible assignment. Meacham Corporation had gotten a long jump on Blake. Though they had the more fragile logistics, they had used their lead time well. They had put military crawlers into production years ago. Twenty-four of the monsters were laagered in the Shadowline a thousand kilometers west of Blake's shade station. They would be hard to root out.

Richard's supply lines, which also supported the Meacham mohole project at the Shadowline's end, could not be reached from Blake shade. They were too far into sunlight for even the hardiest charter to hit and run.

Cassius said there was a tacit agreement to avoid conflict Darkside. Blake would not hear the suggestion of direct strikes. He insisted that fighting be confined to the Shadowline.

"Idiots," Storm muttered in a moment of bloodthirst. "Ought to run straight to Twilight, kick a hole in their dome, give them something to breathe when they surrender, and have done." Then he laughed. No doubt Richard felt the same way.

Mercenary conflicts were seldom simple. Corporations, while willing to fight, seldom wanted to risk anything already in hand, only what they might someday possess.

The only positive he could see was that the Seiners were still out there somewhere, eager to ease his communications problem. It had been a lucky day when he had let emotion convince him that Prudie's people deserved his help. Those Fishers never forgot.

Darling Prudie. What had become of that sweet thing? She probably wouldn't let him see her now even if he could find her. Fishers didn't believe in fighting Nature. She would be an old woman. Storm shuffled reports, forced his thoughts back to the Shadowline.

He tinkered with Cassius's suggestion for cracking

Richard's laager till the crawler reached Edgeward's tractor depot. He was sure it was a workable solution, though they would have to run it past their employer's Brightside engineers to be sure. And past the Corporate Board. Those sons-of-bitches always had to have their say.

Blake met him personally. It was a small courtesy that impressed Storm because the man had to impose on his own handicap.

"Creighton Blake," the dark man said, offering a hand. "Glad you're here. You're recovered completely?"

"Like a new man. I've got good doctors." He glanced at the man behind Blake. He seemed vaguely familiar. "We've got the best facilities at the Fortress. You might want to try our regrowth lab."

"You know, I don't think so. I don't miss the legs anymore. And not having them gives me one hell of a psychological advantage over my Board of Directors. They get to feeling guilty, picking on a cripple." He grinned. "You have to use every angle on these pirates. Ah. My manners. I'm not used to dealing with outsiders. We all know each other here. The gentleman with me is Albin Korando. He's my legs. And my bodyguard, companion, conscience, and valet."

"Mr. Korando." Storm shook hands. "We met on The Big Rock Candy Mountain. At the wedding."

Korando looked startled. He glanced at Blake. Blake nodded slightly.

"Yes, sir."

Storm smiled. "I thought so. We walk from here? Which way?"

"You've got a good memory, Colonel," Blake said. "I believe you met Albin for just a few seconds."

"Why?"

"Excuse me?"

"Why did you plant Pollyanna on me?"

"Ah? You know?" Blake chuckled. "Actually, you weren't the target. I had no interest in you at the time. Ground-zero man was your brother Michael. We almost stuck her to him, too. But you tipped the cart over."

"Long as we're being frank, would you mind telling me why?"

Blake explained. Before he finished, Storm again found himself regretting his contract to protect his brother. Michael had outdone himself here on Blackworld.

"About the Shadowline," he said, trying to ignore the curious hundreds watching them pass, "how much interference am I going to have to put up with? Cassius tells me you've ruled out direct strikes at Twilight, as well as any other armed action this side of the Edge of the World."

"This is between Blake and Meacham, not Edgeward and Twiiight. We feel it's important to maintain the distinction. And we don't want civilians getting hurt."

Storm cast Blake a cynical glance, realized that the man meant what he said. The idea startled him. How long since he had worked for someone with a conscience? It seemed like forever.

Blake's humanitarian impulses could spell unreasonable casualties. "You didn't answer me."

"You won't have much trouble from me. I'm no general and I'm willing to admit it. But my Board won't make the same confession, as your Colonel Walters has discovered. They didn't want to release tractors for nonproductive employment. Maybe they thought you were going to fight on foot."

"How much voting stock do you control?"

"Thirty-eight percent. Why?"

"Any of the Directors your men?"

"I usually get my way."

"Will you assign me your proxy for the duration?"

"Excuse me?"

218

"One of my terms was five percent of the voting stock and a seat on the Board."

"That was rejected. Unanimously, I might add."

"Where's my headquarters?"

"Back at the depot. We set it up in an obsolete repair shed. Where're you going?"

"I'm going to pick up my toys and go home. I'm wasting my time here. I don't have a contract."

"Go home? Colonel Storm. . . . Are you serious? You'd dump us now?"

"Damned right I would. Things get done my way or they don't get done at all. I'm not Galahad or Robin Hood. I'm a businessman. My comptrollers will compute what you owe for transport and maintenance. I'll disregard penalty payments."

"But. . . ."

"Would you like to test your meteor screens against a heavy cruiser's main battery?"

"We thought that was a giveaway clause, Colonel."

"There were no giveaway clauses, Mr. Blake. You were presented a contract and *told* it was a take it or leave it. In a seller's market prices get steep. You're hiring an army, not buying one crazy Old Earth shooter. Do you have any idea what it costs to maintain a division even on a peacetime footing? Win, loose, or draw, the Legion gets five percent, twenty-year deferred payments, expenses, equipment guarantees. . . ."

"To be honest, Colonel Walters told us the same thing. We hoped. . . ."

"Get somebody else. Van Breda Kolff is looking for something. But he won't be much cheaper."

"Colonel, you have us. We've got to have you. They'll cry a lot, but the Board will give in. Their fussing has put us so far behind now that it's criminal."

"I don't have time for games, Mr. Blake."

"They'll come around. They see the Shadowline slipping

through their fingers like fine, dry sand. They want to get back what's been lost. You could hold us up for more and get it."

Storm saw that Blake was straining to control his temper. His Directors must have caused him a lot of grief.

He understood, once he was introduced to those select old armchair pirates. They were the sort who would buck a young whippersnapper like Blake simply because they resented his having come to power at such an early age.

Storm repeated his prima donna performance and stalked out. After what must have been a bitter hour of debate, Blake came to tell him they had acquiesced with the grace of virgins bowing to inevitable rape. Storm returned to the boardroom long enough to remind them of what happened to employers who defaulted contracts with the freecorps. Their bandit eyes became angry. He knew they had not surrendered completely.

He wondered why he bothered. The premonition could no longer be denied. Blackworld was the end. The last page of his story was going to be written on this hell of a world. What matter a contract?

The Fortress, that was what mattered. Even if the Legion entire encountered its death-without-resurrection, there were still the people of the Fortress. The dependents and retirees needed support. He hoped Mouse could handle the asteroid. Dumping the administration of the empire into the boy's lap as he had. . . .

His aide finished preparing his quarters. With Geri and Freki pacing him and the ravenshrikes watching with hooded eyes, he walked the floor and nursed "Stranger on the Shore" from his clarinet. He played it again and again, each time more mournfully than the last. He was exhausted, yet too keyed up to rest. His mind kept darting here and there like a fish trying to find a way out of its bowl.

Poor pretty Pollyanna. So young to be so driven. That Frog must have been something. He would have Mouse send her home. There was no point to her going on with her game.

Poor Lucifer. Played for a pawn. Pray it did not blind his sensitive poet's eyes. Maybe the boy would have sense enough to go with his talent now.

Poor Homer. Poor Benjamin. Gone to do hard time in the hell of Helga's World. Could Ceislak get them out? Hakes was the most perfect of commando leaders, but his chances were grim. The Festung in Festung Todesangst was an understatement.

Poor Frieda. She was about to lose a husband she never really had. He had not been much good for her.

Storm could not think of his wife without guilt, though she was a soldier's daughter and had known what she was getting into. Despite her peculiarities, she had been his best wife. In her way.

Poor everyone, Storm decided. There would be no winners this time. Not even the Sangaree Deeth. The shadow master was going to find the Shadowline a tool too hot to grasp. And poor Mouse was the dead-man's switch that would bring the Sangaree's folly home to him. . . .

Storm finally relaxed enough to fall into a troubled sleep. His dreams gave him little peace. Only death itself promised that.

Forty-Two: 3031 AD

Storm stayed clear of the tractor driver and asked no distracting questions. The briefing had made it clear that operators needed their full attention all the time. Storm's head and eye remained in constant motion as he both familiarized himself with the instruments and displays and observed the economy of motion with which the professional operator managed his crawler.

Storm gasped in awe when the convoy began its run to the Shadowline. He had never seen anything like this. Brightside in description was nothing compared to the hellish reality. He could not begin to imagine what it must be like beyond the interface of instruments and filters. A kilometer-long lake of molten metals slid past. He glanced at a rear-view screen and saw high-melting-point trace metals form a scum in the convoy's shadows.

This much heat was impossible to conceive.

The convoy consisted of fifty crawlers jury-rigged to transport troops and cargo. Ideally, they would have deposited their cargoes at the foot of the Shadowline and allowed the Legionnaires to proceed from the shade station under their own power. However, Storm and Cassius did not trust the vacuum-proofing of their equipment to withstand the punishment of the journey out to the Shadowline. They had elected to transport it all the way.

It would take months to move the legion that way. Every crawler outbound since Cassius's arrival had been ferrying, yet only half the Legion was in the Shadowline.

The force Storm was taking out to the point of confrontation consisted of a battalion each of engineers, artillery, armor, and infantry. Support troops would be distributed along the way. He had no intention of fighting immediately. The combat troops were along only to protect the engineers, who would prepare his move against Richard's roadblock.

Cassius had been laying logistical groundwork from the beginning. He had set up major depots each hundred kilometers, scattered secondary depots in between, had erected hospital domes, recreation domes, and had set out thousands of small inflatable emergency shelters so men working in spacesuits stood a chance if something went wrong. He had set out a galaxy of communications repeaters and transponders, had widened the extant road, and had charted the most defensible terrain.

The more constrained the battlefield, the more meticulous and extensive was the preliminary work. Cassius was a sound detail man. Given the help of the brothers Darksword, and time, he would prepare down to the last shell for the explosive-type artillery Storm had selected as his main heavy weaponry.

Already the Shadowline is cluttered, Storm thought as he studied the screens. Near its foot every square meter of shade was in use. And the work had scarcely begun. It would be a month before they were ready for even limited action.

How much more trouble was in it for Richard? His lines were tremendously more extensive.

Storm's scouts encountered hostile pickets twenty-five kilometers from Richard's laager. He stopped and dug in while the infantry went out as skirmishers. He distributed the artillery so it could hammer any enemy probe. The armor he tucked away well behind his front, as a reserve to be deployed against any breakthrough.

For the present only Richard would be doing the attacking. And Storm thought that unlikely. Hawksblood's mission was defensive. His task was to prevent interference with the Meacham project at Shadowline's end. All he needed to do was sit and let things happen.

After establishing his position, Storm concentrated on outflanking Hawksblood from the more difficult direction.

Hawksblood would anticipate a circling strike. He would have his heaviest weapons positioned to repulse anything coming out of the sun.

Fifty kilometers to his rear Storm's engineers exploded charges which demolished a hundred-meter-wide stretch of bluff, spilling megatons of rock into shadow. The engineers had estimated that it would take a month to clear the rubble, then five to ten days to grade a crawler road to the high side of the cliffline.

Storm was not sure taking the high ground would help.

It would be pure pissing into the wind if Richard figured out what was happening—and it could turn into disaster if Hawksblood anticipated the maneuver and was waiting for it.

It was more promising than the alternatives. Attacking out of sunlight would be expensive and dangerous. Attacking straight up the Shadowline would be suicidal.

The positional and equipment advantages were Hawksblood's. Nevertheless, Storm believed he could win. One way would be to go all out, attacking with the Legion's full might. That would force a war of competitive consumption, of attrition. The sheer magnitude of Richard's logistics would betray and defeat him.

That way meant a bloodbath. Storm did not want one. Neither did his opponent. Theirs were wars of maneuver, not of slaughter. They were in the business for financial gain, not for blood and glory, not for some shadowy concept of honor or duty or patriotism, nor even for the latest in ideological fads. Their men were good soldiers. They knew how and when to keep their heads down. They knew how to stay alive and that was their primary bet in the battlefield sweepstakes. They would do their jobs with a cool professionalism and weigh each risk against the importance of the goal they were being asked to achieve.

They were the best and worst, according to one's viewpoint. A man could hire them and get a nice, clean, efficient job done quietly and quickly. A politician could rant and rave at them, exhort them, cajole them, inundate them with all the magic catch-phrases and righteous lies, and not get them to look up from their card games.

The characteristics of the Shadowline battleground left very little room for traditional mercenary finesse.

Hawksblood's detection equipment proved sensitive enough to isolate the explosion tremors from ambient thermal gradient noise in the planet's crust. He pushed a reconnaissance-in-force westward. Storm's artillery and mine fields stopped it. Hawksblood left a wrecked military crawler's slave sections behind. Storm studied them, comparing them with the handful Blake's crawler factory had produced.

He did not find much difference. Both manufacturers had stuck with a basic pumper design, modifying the slaves to carry armor and extrudable weapons turrets. The Meacham variety revealed somewhat less designer concern for the safety and comfort of the fighting crew.

"He may try flanking us now," Storm told Helmut Darksword, who was in charge east of the rockfall. "Watch for him coming out of sunlight. Keep him from spotting the fall."

"I think we'll get enough warning on the ground-noise sensors."

The command setup had been arranged so that Storm and Cassius would take turns controlling the *schwerpunkt* while the brothers Darksword would take turns directing operations in the support zone. The off-duty commanders would return to Edgeward City, to oversee the Legion's interests there. Storm's son Thurston directed the permanent communications and liaison team stationed in the city.

Helmut's defenses were anchored upon a battery of heavy lasecannon unshipped from a Legion cruiser. They were the only weapons Storm had which could engage a vehicle in daylight. Explosive shells, so effective in the shade, exploded a few meters after entering sunlight. Lighter laser weapons did not have enough power to punch through a crawler's heat screens.

What would Richard do if he discovered the notch in the cliffs? Move his laager back? Storm did not think so. That would be an admission of defeat. The maneuver could be repeated indefinitely, forcing Hawksblood to withdraw again and again. It might take years, but Richard would eventually run out of room to back up.

Would he come from Brightside, in force, to isolate the

force screening the rockfall? That might work if he moved before the debris was cleared, so that units not inside crawlers could not retreat. But it would mean a bloody fight.

He might do nothing, hoping Storm would make a self-defeating mistake before his scheme came to fruition.

Storm favored the latter possibility. That was Richard. Hawksblood was a master of the art of doing nothing. He liked to wait till an opponent became committed before making a move himself.

Storm called the officer commanding the engineers. "Dahlgren, I hear you've got a problem back there. What's wrong?"

"Sorry, Colonel. It's bad news. We're going to take a lot longer than we figured."

"Damn! Why?"

"We didn't get a good enough picture of what was up top. We breached a metals lake up there. It's draining into the fall and hardening when it gets out of sunlight. We can't do anything till it stops."

Storm controlled his temper. "Very well." *I'm cursed,* he thought.

To someone at his end the engineer said, "Throw a spot up there, Henry, so we can show the Colonel what we're up against." His face vanished, was replaced by darkness.

In a moment the darkness gave way to a palely illuminated tumble of rock. Camera elevation climbed, revealing first a long rockslide, then an area where greyish material lay between the boulders, in places looking like leaden gobbets of hardened candle wax. Finally, the camera view rose to capture the dramatic, fiery frenzy of the liquid metal splashing and tumbling over the broken lip of the cliff.

"Awesome, Dahlgren," Storm said. "Do what you can while you're waiting." Storm secured comm, leaned back, stared at the wall of his specially-equipped command crawler.

Richard waited, as Storm had anticipated. Otherwise, that malicious, chortling little devil-god called Fate ragged the Legion with a special vengeance.

An attempt to run a line of shadow generators out to intercept Twilight's line collapsed when Blake's crews encountered a vast sea of heat erosion.

Heat erosion, which usually took the form of extremely fine powder, was not dangerous in and of itself. It was a mask hiding the real dangers over which it lay. It could conceal sudden drop-offs or spikes of hard rock that could open the belly of a crawler like a fish knife.

On Helga's World Hakes Ceislak failed in his initial attempt to penetrate Festung Todesangst. He did establish a surface bridgehead and seize control of her missile defenses. Cassius's friend in Luna Command, Admiral Beckhart, appeared to be in no hurry to commit his people.

Delays and delays. Obtaining vacuum-adapted equipment proved almost impossible. Confederation had a push on against the McGraw pirates. The Services were devouring everything being manufactured. And Richard was bidding in the same market.

There was no solace in knowing that Hawksblood faced as much trouble as did he. Richard had been born to trouble as smoke to a flame. Storm wished him a ton from the clutch of Dees he was letting camp in his back yard.

Storm still found it odd that the war did not carry over Darkside. Over there it was peace as usual. Intercourse between Edgeward and Twilight continued almost normally. They did not play psy-war games with one another's citizens. There was no trip-trip of spy over assassin. Neither city tried to whip its people into a war fever. Business followed its usual routines. Corporations controlled both cities, but only a small percentage of the population in each was involved in mining, and even of those each corporation was willing to risk but a minority. The war in the

Shadowline was a risk operation. Neither Blake nor Meacham wanted to hazard anything but money.

Well, Storm thought, *that's why they buy soldiers. To avoid wasting their own people.*

Forty-Three: 3031 AD

He returned to Edgeward after two grueling months Brightside. What had seemed a cramped, constricted city earlier now appeared so vast as to make him nervous. All a matter of viewpoint, he told himself as he tried to stretch and relax, free of the moment-to-moment survival worries of the Shadowline.

He discovered that he was a comparative unknown. Half the Edgewarders seemed unaware that the Legion was on Blackworld. The other half did not care. The war had not changed daily life.

Storm did not know whether to be pleased or dismayed. Blake had stirred up no hurrah at all. His employers usually went the reverse route.

He had a feeling Blake was a little ashamed of what he was doing.

His first day back he went through a rocky session with the Corporation's directors. They demanded action. Exasperated, Storm offered them weapons and transportation. "You know more about this business than I do," he told them. "I'm perfectly willing to run you out there and let you handle it yourselves."

After his initial aggravation, he enjoyed baiting them, delighting in their aghast expressions. He would love to have a chance to pull the same thing with the political pirates who ran Confederation. How many wars would there be if the warhawks themselves had to go put their fat asses on the firing line? The armchair warlord was one of the grotesqueries of post-feudal civilization. The Dark Ages were brutal, but then the ruling classes got out and whacked on one another. . . .

There were no takers when he offered an inspection tour of his Shadowline operations, either. Blake, he discovered, was the only one of them ever to have crossed the Edge of the World.

Typical of the breed, he thought. *Never been out of their plush chairs.*

A week after his return Blake invited him to a City Hall party for Edgeward's elite. Pretty spy Pollyanna was on hand, looking more comfortable and vivacious than he had seen her since her wedding day. She was a different creature in her home milieu.

"Gneaus!" She greeted him with a kiss and an unselfconscious hug. "I hope you haven't been too miserable out there."

"Miserable isn't a word that will touch it. It's too good. I can't think of one that's low enough."

"Come on. I'll introduce you around."

"I hit Blake up pretty good on the contract, but I'm beginning to wonder if he isn't getting off cheap anyway. My men don't get to come in for these R-and-R breaks." Helmut, who had traded jobs with his brother, trailed Storm, looking like a grumbling thunderhead seeking a target for its spears of lightning. He was followed by the Sirian warhounds. Helmut scowled fiercely at those Board members who had a habit of sticking their long noses into the new Legion offices downstairs. Cassius had moved them there to take advantage of the Corporation's superior communications facilities.

The first person Pollyanna introduced was Albin Korando.

"We've met," Storm said. "How are you, Mr. Korando?"

"Still kicking, Colonel."

"Albin's sort of my brother," Pollyanna said.

"Must be a pretty thin genetic relationship."

"Oh, no. Not by blood. We were both adopted by Frog. Albin's an exile from Twilight. Frog brought him in. Got him into hogging. You should swap lies with Albin someday. He's got some stories to tell about the old days."

Korando grinned. "Anything before last week is the old days to these kids."

"Uhm. Maybe we should slip off and swap a few over a bottle. After the amenities."

"Oh, no you don't," Pollyanna told Storm. "I've got plans for you."

He began to fear that he had misread her, that she had not changed after all. "Lucifer. . . ."

"The break is official. No hard feelings. It was good for a while, when we could both be ourselves. When we tried to be what we thought somebody else wanted, well. . . . No. I don't want to bore you. Just say I don't regret it. Most of it."

Storm doubted that there were no hard feelings. This would mark Lucifer for years. The boy would throw himself into soldiering, trying even harder to become what he would never be. He did not disabuse Pollyanna. He could sense that she would hurt for Lucifer, knowing she had hurt him.

Next was Blake's wife, Grace, whom he hadn't known existed. She was a short, slim, retiring, elfin woman, who was socially ill at ease. She looked much younger than her probable age.

"Mrs. Blake." He put on his courtly manners, bowed to kiss her hand. A bit of ancient chivalry might put her at ease.

A part of his mind watched cynically. *How we love to play at being paladins,* he thought. *Hired killers pretending to be knights of the Round Table. Dragons slain. Maidens rescued. Ogres dismantled. No, no, that's not really innocent blood taking the shine off the old armor. Just a spot of rust.*

"Is it? . . . Is it dangerous?" Mrs. Blake said, staring at the ravenshrike on Storm's shoulder.

"Only if he decides you're edible." He tried a boyish smile. "Nothing to fear. He's not fond of sweets."

She became flustered. He moved on to Blake, who gave him a frosty, "Good evening, Colonel." He seemed painfully aware of Storm's philandering reputation. His gaze darted to the warhounds. "I hear you're quite skilled with an ancient instrument called a clarinet. Would you favor us by playing?"

Storm became quietly reserved. He could not be comfortable playing for strangers. He seldom played to an audience at all.

Blake sensed his discomfort. "Oh, not for the mob. For Grace and myself, after dinner. And Pollyanna, of course. Grace's request. She's a musician herself. Favors classical strings."

"An honor, then. Perhaps the lady will join me in a piece or two?"

Grace Blake stared at the floor and nibbled her delicate lower lip. She really was a timid creature. Pollyanna squeezed his arm. She whispered, "You're overdoing it."

People were watching. Several faces betrayed the thinking behind them. A few women were eyeing him speculatively. Men turned up their noses at his menagerie or calculated their chances with Pollyanna. Both sexes envied his access to the throne.

He spotted a grim face behind the partiers. Thurston pushed through the crowd, trampling toes and egos alike. He was supposed to be on duty downstairs.

Storm murmured, "Dinner and music may have to wait."

"Father, Cassius needs you," Thurston boomed from ten meters away.

"What is it?"

Thurston shrugged. "Something's shaping up." Evidently, he did not want to talk in front of civilians.

"Mr. Blake. Mrs. Blake. If you'll excuse me?"

"Of course," Blake replied. "Wish I had an excuse to slip out myself."

"Creighton, Colonel Storm," Grace said, her tiny voice quavering, "could we go along?"

"Of course," Storm replied. "Your husband is the boss. I'd look silly keeping him away."

"Albin, make my apologies," Blake told Korando. "Then join us in Colonel Storm's war room."

The war room was lively when they arrived. The Legion had added a massive amount of specialized equipment to Blake Mining's Comm Center. The heartpiece was a gigantic display board on which was imposed a computer-mastered chart of the Shadowline. The long, dark river of the rift was alive with shoals of tiny moving lights. Each represented a particular unit. A susurrus of soft communications chatter filled the air as commtechs monitored Shadowline radio traffic. The theme of the moment was confusion on the firing line, questions racketing back and forth among "Foxbat," "Mirage I," and "Democles." The chatter was clear, but couched in jargon that Storm's companions could not interpret.

Cassius was on visual, and clearly impatient. "Command clear trunk, scrambled," the technician told Storm. Storm nodded.

"Gneaus," Cassius said the instant Storm moved in

front of the pickup, "they're starting something. We don't know what yet, but it looks big."

"What have you got? I don't see anything on the big board."

"They started probing with infantry and armor two hours ago. Pushed our observers back. We've had to withdraw past the limit of reliable sonic discrimination, so nothing's sure. The computer enhancements make it look like there's a lot of heavy stuff moving."

Storm glanced at the pictures from the sky-eye orbitals. The damned satellites were next to useless. The demon sun burned them out in a few days' time, and what pictures they did send down were no good. Too much contrast between the sunlighted plains and the darkness of the Shadowline. "You get anything from Intelligence?"

"There hasn't been a crackle from an open carrier since this morning. Looks like they've shut down communications completely. Yesterday we did get confirmation of your notion that Richard went back to Twilight."

"Who'd he leave in charge?"

"Doskal Mennike. The younger."

"Richard wouldn't set up a push and then leave."

"That's why I called. He's been gone awhile, near as we can tell. He wasn't here for their spoiling raids last week, either. Something strange is happening."

"Where are they up top?" Storm's own forces had begun moving to break the laager that morning, after the engineers, a month behind schedule, had completed the incline to the upward side of the Shadowline cliffs. Any attack by Hawksblood would catch the Legion overextended.

"About ready. They were getting into position the last report I had."

"You have comm with Wulf?"

"A bad link. The sun is distorting the relay beam."

"Patch me in on Tac Two." While he waited, Storm

asked, "Mr. Blake, is there any way we can find out what's going on in Twilight?"

"I have a man there, but I can't get in touch in a hurry. We have to wait till he finds some way to smuggle his microtapes out."

"That's no good. I need an idea of what's happening right now, today, not what was going on last month."

"Why?"

"I smell something rotten."

"Patched, Gneaus," Cassius said. "You won't get anything but snow on visual."

"I'll see if we can enhance. Switch it." He waited a few seconds. A 2 appeared momentarily. "Sky Writer, Sky Writer, this is Andiron, over." No response. "Sky Writer, Sky Writer, this is Andiron, do you read me, over."

"Andiron, Andiron, this is Blackwood. Sky Writer has lost lasecomm, over." The response was barely audible.

Storm whispered to a tech, "Who's Blackwood?"

The technician checked his charts. "Bill Allen, sir. In one of Colonel Darksword's crawlers."

"Blackwood, Blackwood, this is Andiron. Relay to Sky Writer. Query your position. Query can you relay visual of laager, over."

"Andiron, Andiron, this is Blackwood, relaying to Sky Writer. I read you loud. Am at point Romeo Tango X-Ray, engaged. Visual follows, over."

"Picture coming in," Storm said. "Enhance it."

A deep darkness, waxing and waning behind static snow, appeared before Storm. It wavered till the computer found how best to enhance it.

The darkness was broken occasionally by the fire-lances of lasecannon or the flash of explosives. The view was down from the rim of the Shadowline. Richard's laager was spread out like toys on a sand table. Here and there, jerkily in the flashes, movements suggested armor and

234

mobile artillery scuttling for better cover. The visible crawlers began to glow.

"Why are they lighting up?" Storm asked.

From behind him, Korando replied, "They're putting up their solar screens. That will stop the lighter lasecannon."

Storm leaned closer. "Those rigs look smaller than their military crawlers. Korando. What kind of units are they?"

"Pumpers and charters. Mostly old stuff. What I'd guess they'd be using for hauling supplies."

"Blackwood, Blackwood, this is Andiron. Query, Classes of defensive fire received, over."

"Andiron, Andiron, this is Blackwood. Receiving light projectile fire. Have silenced one lasecannon. Over."

"Wormdoom, Wormdoom, this is Andiron, do you read me? Over."

"Andiron, Andiron, this is Wormdoom," Cassius replied. "Switching to secure comm. Wormdoom out."

Shifting to the scrambled trunk, Storm said, "Cassius, they've replaced their heavy stuff with obsolete mining equipment. Watch for something coming out of sunlight. You might move up some artillery and armor. Go ahead with the blast. It's too late for Wulf to help you anyway. Try to get this lot to surrender. If you don't get hurt, and can push far enough past them, a sunlight sweep wouldn't be able to get back to friendly territory."

"I'm working along those lines already," Cassius replied. "Gneaus, if that's it, it's likely to be bloody. What's wrong over there? This isn't Richard's style. There's no need for an attack. And Mennike isn't any glory hound either."

Remembering what it had been like out there, penned in a suit most of the time and always surrounded by natural dangers as well as enemies, Storm posited, "Maybe he went around the bend."

"Maybe. But I can think of a more probable cause.

There are enough Dees over there to wreck a galaxy. I've got to get back and stay on top of this. Keep watching. I'll check in later."

"Later." Storm rose, surveyed the room. He moved a chair to its center, seated himself. From there he could hear all the monitors and see the big board. He completely forgot his guests. Thurston received a curt nod when he brought a tankard of coffee.

The razor's edge of Now swept forward, turning future into past. Hours groaned away, creaking on rusty hinges. Wulf took the laager under heavy fire. One of his crawlers ran on out along the cliff top, planted charges that would drop a rockfall behind Hawksblood's men. Wulf's fire wrecked several Meacham crawlers. The laager broke. The big units, manned by flighty civilians, fled into sunlight, abandoning everyone not already aboard. Cassius immediately applied pressure with his armor. Hawksblood's people withdrew till Wulf's rockfall barred farther retreat.

The Twilight fighting crawlers swept in from sunlight on a well-organized front two hundred kilometers wide, far behind Cassius.

"No doubt about it," Storm muttered as he watched the situation develop.

"Father?" Thurston asked.

"There's a crazy man running things out there."

The thirty Meacham crawlers attacked everything manmade, including hospitals, refuge stations, and recreation domes, all of which had been clearly marked for what they were. The crawlers maintained a grim comm silence throughout the action.

Albin Korando observed, "It looks like they don't want each other to know what they're doing. It doesn't take any military genius to know that our comm nets would let us watch every one of them."

"Curious, isn't it?" Storm said.

The Legion bent. Forewarned, it broke nowhere. The attack was still on when Storm said, "We've got them. They're going to be sorry they tried this. This might mean the whole war."

Before long the others began to see what he meant. One by one, Hawksblood's military crawlers were being disabled or forced back into sunlight. The specially designed military units were Richard's most potent tool. He was losing them fast, and would lose more when the retreating units tried to get back into the Shadowline.

A Lt. Col. Gunter Havik commanded the forces opposite Cassius. He had been Walters's student in Academy and had served with Storm in Confederation's Marines. He was the archetypal mercenary officer. He surrendered the moment it became clear that his position was untenable.

The modern freecorps would fight no heroic, doomed Stalingrads. Not when there was no known tactical or strategic justification. Glory was an epitaph for fools.

Cassius immediately started ferrying troops round the rockfall and digging them in for the return of Hawksblood's fighting crawlers. He did not expect to have much difficulty forcing their surrender. Most would be running near their limits of solar endurance and would be short of munitions. They would be eager to get into shade, and unable to shoot their way in.

Wulf's force withdrew to the Shadowline to recuperate from its extended exposure to the demon sun.

Storm glanced at a clock and realized that he had been in the war room, awake and intensely attentive, for twenty-two hours. Even iron man Thurston had taken a few hours to nap. Thurston started to suggest that he do the same.

"I was just thinking that," Storm told his son. "I can't do anything here anyway. It's all on Cassius right now. Get me up if it begins to go sour."

In the Shadowline, of course, the only sleep for the men involved was the big one. No one would rest till the issue was decided.

Blake was on hand when Storm returned. He did not seem pleased.

"What's his problem?" Storm asked Thurston.

"Casualty figures been coming in."

"Bad?"

"Not good."

Battle's confusion had begun to resolve itself into a grim statistical portrait, Storm saw when he checked the unit reports.

The first big battle in the Shadowline, still under way, would be a resounding victory for Edgeward. The laager had been broken. All but a handful of the attacking battle crawlers had been taken out. Cassius, with every available man and machine, facing light resistance, was racing toward the point where Twilight's supply line intercepted the Shadowline. He would reach it in four days if Hawksblood could not stop him. The war could be over before the end of the week.

And a thousand Legionnaires had died the death-without-resurrection. More were missing. The survivors were sifting the rubble. There were as many more injured and resurrectable dead.

Storm was appalled. He was dazed. He could not accept the figures. He had not encountered this much killing since the Ulantonid War. "Richard didn't do this," he murmured several times. "This's the work of a madman." Michael's face seemed to laugh silently from nowhere and everywhere.

Only a Dee stratagem could have spilled so much blood.

He circulated around the war room, trying to find some positive spark amid all the negatives. He found no promise anywhere but in Cassius's headlong sprint.

Suddenly, he caught one strained thread from amid the

constant babble being monitored. "...you read, Iron Legion? I've hit heat erosion fourteen kilometers off Point Nine Hundred. Main track in. Can't drop my slaves. I have thirty-two men aboard. Can you help? Mayday, Mayday. This is Twenty-ninth Brightside Main Battle Tractor, can you read, Iron Legion? I've hit heat erosion...."

"How's he sending?" Storm asked.

"Pulse-beam laser, sir. He's bouncing it off the cliff face."

Storm turned to the big display board. It portrayed incredible confusion. He wondered if even the computers were keeping track.

Point Nine Hundred would be nine hundred kilometers out the Shadowline, only about fifty kilometers east of the incline Wulf had used to scale the cliffs. "How long have we been getting this?"

The monitor checked the log for the previous watch. "Nearly four hours, Colonel. Colonel Darksword began rescue operations as soon as the message came in."

Storm turned to Blake. "What're the chances of bailing them out?"

Blake shook his head. "About zit. We haven't had a successful daylight rescue since Moira Jackson brought her father in. That was right after the Ulantonid War. And we get several chances a year. Finding them is the hard part. Point Nine Hundred and fourteen out don't mean that much. It's a dead-reckoning guess. DR gets pretty loose after a few hours in sunlight. If we ever develop the technology, we'll put out navigation beacons.... Anyway, you have to be right on top of another crawler to spot it. The charters have the best instruments, and even they can't see far. But we always try, if only because we hope we'll learn something."

The drama unfolded with painful slowness. Wulf had committed all his units to a computer-mapped search spiral around the trapped crawler's estimated position.

The tractor's commander grew more and more desperate as his screens drew nearer overload.

Suddenly, "Hey! Got him! Hey, over here!"

Storm chuckled nervously.

Soberly, the same voice said, "Intrepid, Intrepid, this is White Wing One. We have a contact bearing three four seven at six one zero meters. Over."

"White Wing One, White Wing One, this is Intrepid. Hold your position, over." Intrepid was Wulf on his own tactical net. "Storm King, Storm King, this is Intrepid. Assemble on White Wing One, immediate execute, over." Wulf shifted to command net. "Wormdoom, Wormdoom, this is Sky Writer. We have a positive contact. Request instructions, over."

There was no response from Cassius. Walters had outrun his communications engineers.

Storm bent to a pickup. "Sky Writer, Sky Writer, this is Andiron. Proceed with caution. Let one of the miners direct the rescue. Andiron out."

Storm stared at the big board again. He had a sudden bad feeling about this. Something told him he should let it go. Yet he could not overcome his feeling of moral obligation to a brother soldier. He could not make himself call Wulf off.

"Andiron, Andiron, this is Sky Writer. Acknowledge proceed with discretion under native direction. Sky Writer out."

Storm told the tech, "Keep a close monitor. Let me know if you smell anything funny."

The communications technician frowned questioningly. Storm did not expand.

The rescue attempt followed procedures which were little more than paper theory. It went smoothly, according to Korando and Blake, one or the other of whom was always present.

Charters moved into position sunward of the stricken

crawler. They set up portable shadow generators which were themselves protected by a series of disposable molybdenum-ceramic ablation sails. Pumpers, the leviathan crawlers which took liquid metals aboard and hauled them in for processing, ran their pump trunks to emergency locks designed to receive them. The inner diameter of the trunks was large enough to permit passage of a small man.

"Makes a hog more comfortable, knowing he has a theoretical chance," Korando observed. "Even if it's so slim it only pays off once a century. Knowing somebody will try means a lot when you're crawling Brightside."

"Andiron, Andiron, this is Sky Writer. We're getting no response from the crawler. We're sending a man from Main Battle One. Over."

Storm turned to Blake, frowning a question.

"The battle crawlers are modified pumpers," Blake told him. "The first few have converted pump slaves."

That was not the question Storm wanted answered. But Wulf was waiting. "Sky Writer, Sky Writer, this is Andiron. I read you, over."

Wulf had the man carry a hand comm and patched him into the comm net. There was a lot of back and forth about how to open the escape hatch from outside. Wulf had a lot to say about hurrying it up because the shadow generators would not last forever.

"What I wanted to know," Storm told Blake, "was why you couldn't have used this method to rescue that man Frog."

"Because his tractor was built on the other side of the hill where Noah was building the Ark. His only escape hatch was under his cabin. The high-hatch modification came about because of the trouble we had getting to him. Meacham picked up the idea the same time we did."

"I see."

"I don't see anything but dead men, Colonel," Wulf's

investigator reported once he had effected entry. "I'm starting forward to the control cabin."

There was a minute of silence. Storm waited tensely, something raising the hair at the back of his neck.

"Can't figure what happened here, Colonel. They're all bluish and puffy-faced. Their screens are still up and the oxy levels look good. ... "

"Wulf!" Storm thundered, ignoring the code rules. "Get the hell out of there! I mean now!" The bad feeling had bloomed into an intuition. "It's some kind of trap!"

His order came too late. It had been too late for an hour.

There was an instant of thunder on the net, then a silence punctuated only by static.

"Andiron, Andiron, this is Honeycomb," a tight voice said, breaking the silence. "We have a visual and lase-radar on a nuclear cloud at approximately Point Nine Twenty, fifteen kilometers out. Over."

And, "Andiron, Andiron, this is Charring Cross. I'm getting heavy richters epicentered at approximately point Nine Seventeen, fifteen kilometers out, accompanied by heavy gamma radiation. Over."

Similar and related reports came in from a dozen observers. Storm responded to none. The communications technician acknowledge in a dull voice.

Wulf. Dead. Along with hundreds of his men. Because of a humanitarian impulse. It *had* been a trap. Dee work for sure, predicated on a knowledge of mercenaries and miners.

Storm told Thurston, "That was Fearchild's doing."

Thurston nodded sadly. "It's his style. What are we going to do, Father?"

Storm paused a moment before answering. "You take over here." His stomach felt as though the great-granddaddy of all ulcers were trying to gnaw its way out. "I've got to tell Helmut. Try to get through to Cassius. He has to know."

242

He was surprised at himself. He should have been in an insane rage. Instead, he was emotionally numb, still trying to convince himself that it really had happened. Part of him kept thinking Wulf would call in and say it was all a bad joke.

He scanned his people once before going to Helmut. Their faces were all reflections of his own, he suspected. Each portrayed shock and an inability to believe.

Nuclears had not been used on-planet, against people, even during the most critical days of the Ulantonid War. They had joined the list of banned-by-gentleman's-agreement weapons ages ago. One would expect chemical and biological weapons to see use first. Their effects were less long-lasting. . . .

He had been right. The Shadowline war was the swan song of the freecorps. Confederation would move in and disarm them for sure, now. The public outcry would leave the government no choice.

He overlooked one small fact while thinking that. The media were completely indifferent to the Shadowline war. No one was covering it. Hardly anyone off Blackworld knew anything about it. He, the people in the war room, and perhaps a handful of men in Twilight, were the only folks Darkside who knew that proscribed weaponry had been employed.

Forty-Five: 2860-3023 AD

Only months after they had overcome the last Dharvon, Deeth growled, "I'm bored, Rhafu. I think I've figured out why my father was always so damned cranky. There's no real challenge in trying to boost a profit margin a tenth of a percent."

Rhafu looked at Deeth, perhaps thinking the young Head was fooling himself. "Your peers would argue the point."

"That's their life-style. The Haug and Gaab haven't ever done anything else. I might be happy if I'd had a normal childhood. But I didn't. The normal life makes me feel caged."

"We have a mission your father bequeathed us."

"We can't do anything about it. We're stuck with the tedious stuff here. By the time we clear it up, the animals will be warring with Ulant, and we'll have to wait them out. That could last twenty years. The Ulantonid are stubborn."

"I don't recall your father saying revenge had to be instantaneous. Even so, I have to admit to a certain restlessness myself."

"Any ideas?"

"Some."

"Let's hear them."

"I think we should divide ourselves into a greater and lesser House. One to go on being traditional Norbon, the other to exploit Osiris and pursue our vendetta with the animals. Creating a dual structure would isolate risks. If we fail, we wouldn't take the Family down with us."

Deeth eyed Rhafu uncertainly. They had built a very responsive, monolithic structure in order to destroy the Dharvon. He did not want to relinquish any of the power he had acquired.

"Your cousin Taake hasn't much imagination, but he's a competent administrator. Put him in charge of the Home-world arm of the Family. Collect up our more venture-some people and move to Osiris. You'll find plenty of excitement there. And all the work you want, too. We can build puppet empires. We can develop broader markets. Raise sithlac domes. Construct breeding stations. Hell, we could even get into ordinary commerce and industry.

It's a whole planet, and we don't have to share it with anyone."

A primitive, medieval world, Deeth thought. *We can play God, if we want. What more could I ask?* "I'll consider it. Any other suggestions?"

"We could exploit this war. We've collected a lot of new dependents since we came home. We have to employ them somehow."

"Build a raidfleet? Rhafu. . . . When I was little, when I first went to Prefactlas, that was all I ever thought about. Growing up to be a raidmaster."

"Don't think it's all adventure and romance, Deeth. Even piracy is plain hard work if you're going to be any good at it. Ships have to be bought or built. Arms have to be acquired. All that takes financing. You have to assemble reliable intelligence sources. You have to find men who'll work together without letting too much pride get in their way. Men without Family loyalties who would become loyal to you and one another. That's not easy with our people."

"Yes, yes. I see. More of the same old administrative hoohaw. But at least with an interesting end in sight." Deeth began to recover some of that awe and excitement he had felt when, as a child, he had studied the adventures of the great raiders.

If the Sangaree race had one outstanding weakness, it was a cultural bias against tight, devoted administration, a cultural aversion to administrative detail. They pictured themselves as a people of action and behaved accordingly. The sprawling, suffocating, ever-growing bureaucracies characteristic of human enterprises were unknown to them. They strayed to the extreme in the opposite direction, sometimes so far that the lack was as crippling to them as was the excess to humankind. Critical records might amount to nothing more than a few handwritten notes on scraps of paper soon lost. . . . What did not exist in the

245

minds of the Heads and their immediate assistants could be extremely ephemeral, and setbacks frequently came about simply through failure of communication or absence of administrative precision or reliable records.

A Family's most prized retainers were those few Sangaree capable of being clerkish and detail-conscious. The Families scrambled for them aggressively and traded them carefully.

Deeth's raiding and Osirian operations prospered. In time the Norbon were accepted, grudgingly, as one of the Sangaree First Families. Deeth and Rhafu earned a reputation as a team with a golden touch. Their projects usually sprang from Rhafu's fertile mind. Deeth's carefully recruited employees and agents put them into effect. The old man did his best to remain obscure and play his own role.

In a sense Rhafu was the power behind the throne, the real genius of the Family. Deeth simply manipulated hands.

Deeth did not want to be the brains. He dared not be. Despite all the lessons of Prefactlas, he remained impulsive. Rhafu usually softened the impact of his impetuosity, but there were times when the Family welfare suffered because of some ill-considered scheme Deeth launched without consulting the old man.

Though one of the First Families now, the nouveau riche Norbon were never fully accepted as such. They were a little too crude, too rough, too much involved in the more barbarous ways of garnering wealth. And Deeth employed outsiders.

He did not use them in the traditional way, as cat's-paws among their own peoples. He found good men and brought them into the Family operations on Osiris and, occasionally, Homeworld. Accountants. Economists. Data-processors. And soldiers, hard men who became the fist of the Family, led by trusted Sangaree retainers.

The more traditional Families were appalled. And not

a little jealous of the wealth-accumulating and fighting efficiencies of the Norbon.

Deeth received few social invitations, but even fewer slights that might be viewed as invitations to bad feelings. He did not miss the social life. He remained unregenerate in his distaste for parties and the people who frequented them.

During the war he saw occasions when he thought he could fulfill his father's charge on the cheap. He moved without consulting Rhafu, hoping, like a child eager to surprise a parent with an accomplishment. His enemies were cunning and slippery. They seemed to smell danger from light-years away. They evaded him every time, and so effectively that they remained unaware of the nature of the threat.

During the war, from a distance, he re-encountered his son, and could not shake the Sangaree sense of Family. He applied a few helpful nudges where the Norbon had the power, and helped create a rich man. And an instrument by which, Deeth hoped, Norbon influence might be intruded into the heart of human power structures.

Much later, long after he had revealed himself, Deeth began spiriting Michael off to Homeworld and Osiris for a belated Sangaree education.

There were grave deficiencies in Michael's character. Deeth was disappointed. He never let on. Michael was his only child.

Deeth did not marry. That he did not, and remained untempted by the prizes steered onto his path, caused quiet comment. There were ungrounded speculations about the nature of his relationship with Rhafu, and questions about Michael.

Only Rhafu suspected the truth, and even with his oldest friend Deeth refused to discuss the question.

Norbon w'Deeth was carrying a torch for an animal woman called Emily Storm.

For a bred pleasure slave.

That one dread secret could topple his empire. A physical relationship could be tolerated, could be winked at, but an emotional involvement could not. Not ever. Such weakness could not be accepted in a Head.

He dared not share his feelings for fear that it would, like a Frankenstein monster, get loose and destroy him. His own House would repudiate him.

He had won the loyalties of his relatives. They would go into hell for him if he ordered it, but for the sake of a perverted love they would not follow him to a new Wholar.

Yet he walked the edge. He dared bring Michael into Sangaree society. He formed an alliance with the Gaab by wedding his son to one of their daughters. He dodged all questions about Michael's mother by saying that she had perished on Prefactlas.

Rhafu, sensing the mild, unformed suspicion of the Heads, spread a tale of a companionship with a Sexon girl. He used the whole true story of Deeth's youth, merely changing Emily's name.

Time marched. Decades dwindled into the past. Deeth suffered severe and extended depressions whenever he withdrew from his work and realized that he had, again, become an administrator. Fulfillment of his great obligation to his father seemed to be ever more remote. There just was no time to plot against the Storms.

A sudden and unexpected opportunity arose on a world the humans called Amon-Ra.

Michael sent word that his brother, who had just assumed command of the Iron Legion had agreed to help the underground human government oust the Sangaree Families controlling the world.

The Amon-Ra Families were all small and weak. They would stand no chance against the Legion.

Deeth decided to help them. Over Rhafu's protests,

without adequate preparation, he threw in his raidships. Aboard them he sent the quasi-military forces he had developed on Osiris.

He lost everything. Every man, every ship, every weapon. It was a hard way to learn the truth about his officers. Landless, Houseless, Familyless Sangaree simply were not disciplined enough to make war in human terms.

Rhafu treated him to an extended lecture on those cultural biases which made it impossible to fight the Storms heads up. . . .

"All right!" Deeth finally snarled. "I can see that for myself. And I'm going to correct it. We'll build a real fleet and real army. And if our own people won't do, we'll use animals. All animals." They had used humans and Ulantonid from the beginning, but never in command positions.

Amon-Ra slipped away. The years and decades rolled on. Deeth buckled down, subjected himself to an intense self-discipline, did not let up till the Norbon had recovered from the Amon-Ra disaster.

When he did pause to look around he found himself blessed with an excuse for ulcers. Michael and his children. . . . They carried on as if they were alone and immune to anything. Time and again, one or another endangered his plans for the future of the Storms or threatened to scuttle one of his profitable intrusions into the human business sphere. The children were the despair of their mother, who was a stolid First-Family woman completely uninterested in bizarre adventures. She came to him, as the Norbon, again and again, pleading for his intercession.

What could he do? He dared not overcontrol them for fear of losing an invaluable bridgehead in human affairs.

With his financial backing they were pushing tentacles into every corner of Confederation, and those tentacles were channels along which Norbon influence flowed. And

249

when the Norbon prospered, all Sangaree eventually profited.

Following Amon-Ra, Deeth became an avid follower of the human wars, especially the Storm-Hawksblood contests, which contained so much genuine animosity at the command level. "Rhafu, I think this is what we need. We bend their own wishes and guide them into a to-the-death struggle. . . . "

"They're too intelligent to fall into that trap. They don't let personal feeling interfere with business."

"Nevertheless. . . . " Deeth tried putting agents into both mercenary forces. He failed. He had to rely on his son for inside information. And Michael was both unstable and the possessor of a strong streak of Sangaree self-centeredness.

The creation of Festung Todesangst strengthened the Norbon immeasurably. It freed the Family of the old Sangaree administrative bugaboo, and allowed Deeth to pirate invaluable commercial information. In a very few years the Norbon had as much power and wealth over the First Families as the First Families had over the average Sangaree Family.

Deeth's secret monitoring facility inside Festung Todesangst, existing outside the knowledge of his son and granddaughter, apprised him of Michael's discovery on Blackworld. It screamed a priority instel when Michael first ran his numbers.

Forty-Six: 3032 AD

It was not much of a New Year. The Legion did not celebrate. Edgeward City tried, but events in the Shadowline had killed any spirit of optimism. The various parties fell flat.

Storm spent New Year's Day and the following week alone, or, when he craved company at all, with Helmut Darksword. Helmut was taking Wulf's death badly.

Cassius was ripping Twilight into bloody chunks in the Shadowline. Hawksblood's leaderless troops were falling apart. Storm could not refresh his interest in the Legion's advances nor in the enemy's mysterious vulnerability. He played his clarinet, read his Bible, and sat and stared at his old .45, twirling the dark steel cylinder as he did so.

Cassius had cut off the Meacham crews at Shadowline's end. He was having no trouble repelling relief forces attacking from the shade of the Twilight shadow generators. His men, despite orders to the contrary, frequently refused to play the old mercenary games of fire and maneuver. While Walters remained cool and professional, they went and slugged it out with the enemy, determined to teach lessons that would remain forever unforgotten.

Thurston had been making a career of trying to suppress the news of the nuclear blast. He was, like the Dutch boy, trying to save a dike with a finger. His luck was worse. The whole Legion knew how Wulf and his men had died. That was why they were out for blood.

Storm did not interfere. He believed that the whole thing had gotten beyond any chance of control. Like a cold, it had to run its course.

He had won another war. Resoundingly. And, probably, had stumbled right into a Michael Dee trap.

He thought a lot about his brother, and about the promise he had given so lightly, so long ago. Michael was on his mind whenever that old revolver rested in his hand. . . . He often wished that, sometime, he had turned his head while Cassius or his sons had worked their will.

Keeping his word had cost too much. Far too much. And yet, even now, he knew he would shield Michael if Dee came begging for protection.

He returned to City Hall only when the first band of

prisoners came in. He wanted to talk to Lt. Col. Havik.

Havik spotted him first. He rushed over, face drained and worn. "Colonel Storm. I want to offer my apologies. I know they're not worth a fart in a whirlwind, but I've got to say something. That thing is eating us up. I want you to know that if any of us had known, we would've refused our orders."

Storm standing cold and silent, watched Havik's face. He knew the man was telling the truth, yet it was hard to separate the action from the enemy. . . .

"My men and I have had a lot of time to talk, Colonel. One of the corporals made a proposal. We've all agreed. The whole battalion wants to offer its services in bringing to justice whoever is responsible for the atrocity."

Storm inclined his head slightly in acknowledgment. Havik was professional to the core. Like so many Academy products, he was an attempt at a carbon of Cassius. "Thank you, Colonel. If there's any way you can help, believe me, I'll yet you know. And without trying to get you to compromise your commission. But if I can, I mean to handle this myself. It's become personal."

"Uhm." Havik nodded his head. Perhaps he had seen Dees floating around Twilight. Maybe he understood.

"What's happened to Colonel Hawksblood?" Storm asked. "I just don't understand how this could have happened in his organization."

Havik frowned, shrugged. "Colonel, nobody has heard from the Commandant since Colonel Mennike took over. We've started to wonder if he hasn't met with foul play. He'd been having a lot of trouble with the Twilighters. And now your men have found Colonel Mennike."

Storm sent a questioning glance Thurston's way.

"They found him the day before yesterday," his son told him. "In a one-man shelter near where the Twilight route enters the Shadowline. He'd been dead better than two weeks. Stabbed."

"Colonel Havik," Storm said, "I still won't ask you to compromise your commission, but if you'd volunteer a little information it might help."

"Sir?"

"What sort of communications did you have with your headquarters in Twilight?"

Havik did not think before replying. "We used microwave relay in the Shadowline, Colonel. Pulse-beam laser repeaters across Brightside. The system wasn't reliable. The laser's been down all month. The shadow generators are too far apart. The power you need to punch a beam through overloads the equipment. We've been using messengers between the down stations."

Storm eyed Havik. The Colonel's statement was a clearcut betrayal of his employer. The nuclear must have touched him where he lived. "Then Commandant Hawksblood could be perfectly healthy, crossing Brightside somewhere, completely ignorant of what's happened?" Storm hoped so. He did not want Richard taken out of his life by one of Michael's stratagems.

"Possibly. We were set up to be as independent of Twilight as possible. There wouldn't be much traffic. He'll eat heads when he gets back and finds out."

"Thanks, Colonel. We'll make you comfortable. I hope this won't last much longer."

"It shouldn't. You've won. Before the blast. That's what makes it so senseless. You lost a lot of men, but it didn't change anything."

Storm went to the war room to check the daily reports from Mouse and Hakes Ceislak. The Fortress was quiet. There was good news from Helga's World. Ceislak's engineers had sapped a tunnel into Festung Todesangst. His men were occupying the upper levels.

Where was this Beckhart, this friend of Cassius who had promised to land Marines as soon as the Legion established a bridgehead? He seemed to have vanished from the universe. And Storm wanted Ceislak on Blackworld.

He went on to Blake's penthouse. "Mr. Blake, I want to make a direct strike at Twilight."

"I've told you that's impossible, Colonel."

"Hear me out. That blast out there was a setup. That bomb had to come from their mining inventory. That means there was collusion by somebody up high in Meacham Corporation. And it means that Hawksblood has lost control. He wouldn't try anything like this. If he makes it back from Brightside, he'll end up dead or in a cell. They're not playing by the rules anymore. I'm telling you *we*'ve got to quit before they eat us up. The scenario I see is this: Richard will be the scapegoat. He'll probably get killed trying to escape after he 'orders' somebody to put a bomb in on Edgeward itself."

Blake looked baffled. "Colonel, I absolutely refuse to allow you to endanger civilians."

"I don't think you understood me. The civilians are in danger now."

Korando cleared his throat. "Mr. Blake, pardon me for butting in. I think you'd better give the Colonel's suggestion more thought. That nuclear was a storm warning. We can't ignore it. We'd better be ready for anything. Logically, the next step would be a move against Edgeward. They have to get rid of witnesses. And it's the only way they have left to get control of the Shadowline. You can't bet they won't do it. They've already gone further than any of us would have believed possible a month ago."

"Right!" Storm growled. "You people are going to be up to your ears in Confie snoops when this gets offworld. Personally, I want to keep you around to answer their questions. Mr. Blake, believe me, I know the man responsible for this. We slept in the same room for ten years. If you give him time, he'll not only destroy you, he'll get away with it. You know that. When you get down to it, it's not that much of a jump from Frog to Edge-ward."

"You think it's Dee?"

"Absolutely. And backing him is a Sangaree Head named Norbon w'Deeth. And the Norbon seem to be top dog among the Sangaree Families."

"Sangaree?" Blake was baffled. "What have they got to do with this?"

"It's too complicated to explain. Take my word. This confrontation was engineered from offworld. It started when Dee murdered your man Frog. If we don't scratch and claw, it'll end up with the Sangaree in complete control of Blackworld's mining industry. And they won't leave any witnesses to testify against them."

Blake slowly shook his head. "I'll consider what you've said, Colonel."

"Don't take too much time. They won't. By now they know their attack failed and they're being overrun. That bomb was probably meant to go off somewhere else, making the whole thing work. They'll do something, just to find out if it blew at all, then to cover it up. You'll find me in the war room."

Storm went back downstairs, settled into a chair facing the big board. The confusion of the previous week had begun to disappear. Unit lights had appeared throughout the territory Cassius had occupied. There was a big concentration a hundred kilometers west of the junction with the Twilight supply line. Cassius planned to sit there and wait for the Meacham people to come in and surrender.

Had this been a normal merc war it would have been all over but the prisoner exchange. Richard could do nothing to dislodge Cassius. His logistics were too precarious and there was no shade where he could assemble sufficient forces.

But if Michael had Meacham's ear, war would break out Darkside as soon as news of the Brightside defeat reached Twilight. Michael had cast the dice. He had no choice but to escalate his bets.

Storm issued orders. He wanted a new board set up to represent the Darkside territory between Edgeward and Twilight, and wanted all available personnel planting observation devices on likely approaches to the city.

How would Michael avoid the mutiny that was certain when Richard's men found out what had happened in the Shadowline?

Simple. He, or whichever of his sons it was who had taken Mennike's place, would destroy shadow generators while returning to Twilight, cutting communications with and abandoning Hawksblood's forces. It was a harsh move, but Dee-logical.

He had better warn Cassius to watch out for nuclear booby traps. The Dees would want to reduce the witness population fast.

"The Whitlandsund!" he growled. People turned to stare at him. "Of course!"

Edgeward's pass to Brightside was the key. Michael would want it bad. By capturing it, Dee could trap almost everyone who could damn him Brightside. In its tight, twisting confines he could play Thermopylae. If Edgeward were destroyed and he held the pass till everyone Brightside perished, who would be left to speak against him? Only his accomplices.

Storm had no one to send to defend the pass.

How long to travel from Twilight to Edgeward? How long from Helga's World to Blackworld? He calculated quickly. Not long enough, and too long. There was no point to having Ceislak abandon his mission.

"Thurston. Go find Havik. Bring him here. Then get Blake." He retreated into his speculations. The nuclear blast had to be part of a greater Dee plan. It could not have been an end in itself because it had not altered the field situation in the Shadowline. Was it a diversion?

Something to grab the attention while Michael snuck up on Edgeward and the Whitlandsund?

The idea deserved more thought. How had Michael arranged it? On timing? If so, then the southward movement toward Edgeward would be under way now. . . .

The fox. The fool fox, Storm thought. *I should have known he wouldn't be content to stay in the background while Richard and I tried to fake each other out with fancy footwork.*

Michael might be fated to win his game, but, damn it, there must be ways to make his winning expensive and painful.

Havik appeared. Storm said, "Colonel, I've got one hell of a problem." He retraced the path of his recent thoughts.

Havik suggested, "Put scouts out, of course. Fortify the pass. Hold a reserve to ambush them on their way down. Unless they've brought in someone from outside, there won't be many of them. We had almost everybody in the Shadowline. Meacham handled our logistics."

"The Legion is in the same position, Colonel," Storm said. "All I've got here are communications people and a liaison crew. And I expect Dee to use his own people. He won't want men who'll kick much about breaking the usual rules."

"I see." Havik remained thoughtful for more than a minute. Then, "The only help I could give you would be passive. I could go out and squat in the pass. If they attacked, I could consider that a move against my employer. I'd feel justified in resisting. But. . . . What would I use for weapons? We turned ours over out there."

Blake had arrived and had been listening during Storm's speculations. He still did not want to believe, but had begun to recognize the potential for disaster. "Colonel Storm, do you really think Dee is such a demon?"

Storm snapped, "I grew up with him, remember? I think I know what he's capable of, and that's just about any-

257

thing." He turned to Havik. "I don't know what we can do about arms. There're some personal weapons, but the only heavy stuff we have is what came back for maintenance work."

"We have our own weapons cache," Blake said. "It's obsolete stuff, though. It was used by the Devil's Guard during the war."

Storm made a face. He prided himself on keeping his men equipped better than Confederation's armed forces. "Any of it functional?"

"We've kept it up. We have a few men who play-act at being a militia."

"Colonel Havik?"

"I'll look it over." He did not sound excited. "But I want you to know, this is something I'll have to take to my men. I can't just order them to help the Iron Legion."

"I realize that, Colonel. Just ask them to hold the Whitlandsund till we can send someone to relieve them. They're your people caught out there, too. If you have doubters, send them to me. If I can't convince them, then I don't want them involved. It shouldn't be for more than a few days anyway. Mr. Blake. Do you have any people capable of managing the war room?"

"What're you planning now?"

"I'm going to do my job. I'm going to defend Edgeward City. I'm going to take my people out and ambush Michael Dee. I'll need somebody to keep track of things here."

"I have my communications people. You'd have to have somebody familiarize them with the equipment."

"I'll leave Helmut Darksword." Helmut was not yet ready for combat. "Thurston, how are your preparations coming?" His son had begun them immediately after contacting Blake and Havik.

"Half an hour, Father. They're loading the crawlers now."

258

Blake sighed, smiled a thin, worried smile. "I almost hope you've guessed right, Colonel."

Korando offered one of his rare observations. "Better a live fool than a dead skeptic, sir."

Storm smiled. He wished he had time to get to know Korando. The man interested him. "I'll keep in touch, Mr. Blake. I'm going to try to find Colonel Darksword."

It was a ragtag force he took out to meet the Dees. He had some three hundred men armed primarily with equipment that had been sent in for repairs. Their small arms were their only reliable weapons.

Still, if Michael did appear, the ambush should buy Havik a few more hours to get dug in in the Whitlandsund. Havik, in his turn, would stall Dee till the units Storm had recalled from the Shadowline arrived.

Forty-Seven: 3032 AD

Storm, wearing a standard infantry combat suit, stood on a hill overlooking the place where his men would fight. Silence and darkness surrounded him. To the west there was a hint of glow limning the Thunder Mountains, illuminated ions blowing on the solar wind. Before him, invisible to the eye, stretched a long, narrow plain flanked by the ringwalls of two immense meteor craters. The hill on which he stood was the wall of a third and smaller crater, which narrowed the nearer end of the plain to little more than road width. It was a nice tight place to defend.

The region had suffered intense meteoric bombardment over the ages. The plain, over which the customary Twilight-Edgeward route ran, was the only safe passage through the craters—unless Michael swung hundreds of kilometers eastward to come in along the route from The

City of Night. Storm was sure Michael would be too arrogantly self-certain to come in by the less obvious path.

And he would be too arrogantly sure of himself to charge south as fast as he should. While he was tootling along, smirking about having put one over on the best, his brother would have anticipated him and would have chosen their place of battle.

My brother, Storm thought. *That's what it comes down to out here. A fight between me and my brother.*

He now knew that Michael was coming. Dee's convoy had been detected by remotes an hour ago, ten kilometers to the north, rolling south at a steady eight kilometers per.

Storm smiled grimly when he saw the first running lights appear at the far end of the plain. The battle crawlers were leading. Michael had six of the monsters. If those could be wrecked. . . .

Though it was pointless, he turned to survey his dispositions. He could see nothing, of course, though he could vaguely sense the presence of the gun crew in front of him and Thurston there beside him.

Here I stand, he thought. *The Black Prince once stood like this on the hill at Poitiers. I know my soldiers are the best that ever were, but. . . .* He wondered how sure Edward had been. From the literature it seemed that he had *known* his Englishmen could handle ten times their weight in French, but those histories had been written after the fact, with the outcome no longer in doubt, and mainly by Englishmen. The Black Prince had stalled for days, trying to negotiate his way out of the mess.

There would be no negotiation today. And these enemies would be no gentlemen burdened by generations of chivalric tradition. If, as he had begun to suspect when he had learned the size of Michael's force, these were Sangaree troops spirited in through some city other than Twilight, he faced some rough fighters. They would not

260

be familiar with the terrain or their equipment, but they would be as case-hardened as his own people.

The fifteen-minute wait seemed endless. Storm caressed his lasegun. It felt cold and hard through his suit gloves. He hummed "Stranger on the Shore," and wondered why he had never learned to loaf through these final minutes. He had had a long life in which to grow calloused, yet he was as nervous today as he had been while waiting for the opening shot of his first battle.

"A time for living and a time for dying," he murmured. The leading Meacham crawler had entered the narrows between ringwalls.

His one lasecannon flashed blindingly, drilling a neat hole through the face of the lead tractor. It was a point-blank shot. In the second flash Storm saw frozen air spewing from the wound.

His artillery opened up. His armor, using radar and the enemy lights as guides, began scratching deadly graffiti on the crawlers' flanks. Their tracks were favored targets. His infantrymen, bouncing in on their jump packs, concentrated completely on tracks. Their guns and rocket launchers scrawled a thousand bright lines on the face of a startled night.

A secondary explosion ripped the guts out of a slave in the third crawler in line.

"A complete surprise!" Storm growled happily. He descended the hill in hundred-meter bounds, the compressed gas of his jump-pack rockets rippling the back of his suit stingingly. To his right Thurston was bouncing mightily despite the heavy load of satchel charges he carried. Thurston veered across Storm's path, heading for the stalled lead crawler. Storm followed him. The lead vehicle was the most important target. Properly wrecked, it would block Michael's advance for a long time.

The Twilighters started shooting back. Their fire was wild. Storm chuckled. They must have been riding along like tourists, bored, sleeping, completely indifferent to the world outside.

One of his tanks took a bad hit. The crew scrambled out before the ammunition blew. They joined the infantry, going to skirmish with bewildered enemy troops disembarking from the transports up the line.

The lasecannon disabled another battle crawler before dying of its own illnesses. That put the lead three out. The others put their solar screens up. The energy of the small arms could do nothing against those.

Storm stayed close to Thurston. Almost fifty men converged on the lead crawler. Though stalled, the machine was far from dead. Its weapons spit shells and coherent light. Storm's rocket men concentrated on suppressing that fire.

He and Thurston reached the tractor. His son cut his jump pack, tossed him a charge, then ran along the monster's flank, below its fire, limpeting charges to each slave. Storm attached his own over the hole drilled by the lasecannon, dove for cover.

He felt the explosion in his hands and feet. There was no sound and almost no concussion. He leaped up, yanked himself through the hole he had blown. He used his weapon like a firehose.

The cabin was an undefended shambles. Storm sabotaged the power controls. The men who followed him in moved to the hatch connecting with the first trailer. Storm began moving from chair to chair, peering into the faces of dead crewmen.

He could not tell. They looked human enough. He would have to take a few back for dissection.

Would Michael really take that risk? he wondered. The provable presence of Sangaree would bring Navy and the Corps whooping in here as if they were a day late for Armageddon. It probably would not be worth the trouble of lugging the bodies around.

Then he found the blue man.

"What the hell?"

He had seen blue men before, a long time ago. A lot more of them than he had wanted during the Ulantonid War. There were no Ulantonid in Richard's forces, nor did any reside on Blackworld. Cassius had said that the Sangaree Deeth employed men of several races.

The crawler rocked as Thurston's charges exploded in series. His men burst through into the first slave. There was a brief bit of gunplay. Storm ignored it. He pitched a corpse out of the cabin, broke radio silence long enough to call a crawler in to pick it up. He returned for another.

What would be going on in Michael's head right now? Would he be raging against the fates, the way he always did when things went bad? Or would he be wondering why resistance was so light?

He chose a half-dozen corpses all told. His men loaded them aboard the same crawler that had done passenger duty on the Edgeward-to-Twilight run. The operator became increasingly nervous as Dee's infantry pushed closer and closer, but held on even after spears of light began stabbing all around.

Storm's force got mauled, as he expected. But even his clerks and commtechs were Legionnaires. They delivered far more damage than they took. When Storm had his corpse collection and was satisfied that the lead battle crawlers were thoroughly disabled, he withdrew in good order.

The mass of armor and infantry that poured around the lead crawler, pursuing Storm, suddenly ceased to be, as a garden of mine explosions devoured them. Dee's caution afterward allowed Storm to finish disengaging.

"Now we'll see what Michael's made of," he told Thurston.

"Father?"

"We'll find out if he can control his temper. If he can,

he'll go after the Whitlandsund. If he can't, he'll come after Edgeward to get even."

"He wouldn't have much trouble taking the city."

"No. But he'd have to spend a week making sure it was pacified. And he doesn't have a day to waste. Go up and tell the driver to stop at the top of the crater wall. We'll sit up there and see what Michael decides."

Storm sat on that hill for a long, long time. He had done a superb job of blocking Dee's path.

Thurston wakened him. "He's coming, Father."

Storm went to the control cabin to watch the screens and displays. Crawler after crawler came from the north, lumbered past, and turned west. "Good. He had time to think it out."

"I feel sorry for Havik," Thurston said.

"So do I, Son. But he's got a better chance now than before. Driver, take us in to Edgeward."

An antsy Helmut awaited him at the depot. "Looks like trouble," Storm told Thurston.

"Gneaus, we've got trouble," Helmut said when Storm went to him.

"What now?"

"Ceislak has his ass in a bind. A Sangaree bind. They ran a big raidfleet in on him. Our ships had to haul out. He's holding them off with the captured batteries, but he says they can force a landing if they want to push it."

"Looks like Cassius got his wish, then. We've pulled the head spider into the game. Any word from Navy or Luna Command?"

"Not peep one. Cassius is on his way in."

"Eh? Why?"

"He said that if Dee means Richard's people to be trapped out there, he's cut the line to Twilight, so there's no need for us to hold on west of the shade station. They'll come to us. He's just leaving a few men to help them evacuate."

"I wonder. . . . You think Michael figured Cassius would think that way? That this Darkside thrust is just a feint to pull him in?"

"No. The nuclear. . . ."

"Of course. That changed everything. He's playing for all the marbles, not just the Shadowline."

They reached the war room in time to receive Ceislak's message that he was being attacked by Sangaree. Storm connected Cassius, brought him up to date on Helga's World, Havik, and his own recent action.

"Gneaus," Cassius burred, "I have a suggestion about those corpses. Send them over to Darkside Landing or The City of Night for the autopsy. The more you spread the proof around, the harder it'll be for Dee to eliminate all the witnesses. And they'll pressure Meacham to stop backing him."

"Good thinking. I'll do it. Got to go. Havik's in action now."

"Father," Thurston called across the room, "Instel from Helga's World. Ceislak has Sangaree on the ground now. Any special instructions?"

"Tell him to hold out as long as he can. Cassius's buddy will turn up one of these days. Helmut. Bring down the scale on the Whitlandsund there. Michael's dispositions look a little strange."

A half-hour later Thurston bellowed, "Yahoo! Hey, Father! Hakes says he's got ships in detection. They show Navy IFF, and there's a skillion of them."

Storm chuckled at his son's enthusiasm. "Calm down and keep an eye on it. Tell Ceislak to keep the comm open." He felt like whooping himself. "Helmut, this friend of Cassius's is as crafty as a Dee. He had me scared, but he knew what he was doing. Caught them with their pants down, making an assault. Bet none of them get away."

Darksword's face lit with grim pleasure.

Storm reveiwed the Whitlandsund situation again.

Michael's dispositions were not unusual after all, just unimaginative. Havik would not be in bad trouble for a while.

Thurston called, "Ceislak says he has contact with Navy. They brought in a full battle fleet. They've got them bastards nailed to the wall."

"Good. Good. Everything looks beautiful. I'm going to my quarters. Before I collapse."

He dreamed awful dreams. Something was nagging him. He had forgotten something. He had overlooked something, and one dared not do that when dealing with Sangaree and Dees.

Thurston shook his father. "Dad. Come on. Wake up."

Storm opened his eyes. "What is it? You look awful."

"They're attacking the Fortress. The Sangaree are. Another raidfleet. The Fishers just told me. They're watching and can't do anything to help. They've lost touch with Mouse."

Forty-Eight: 3032 AD

Mouse sat in his father's chair, behind his father's desk. His eyes were closed. He felt much as his father looked the day he had returned from Academy. How long ago? Just a few months. . . . It seemed like half a lifetime.

So much had happened. So much had changed. The Fortress had slipped quietly over some unseen boundary into a foreign universe, a hateful, actively hostile universe.

He had changed with his home. He had seen things. He had helped do things. None of them left him proud. He had turned a sharp corner on the yellow-brick road and had caught a corner-of-the-eye glimpse of a side of his family he had not known existed when he had gone off to Academy.

"I was a child then," he murmured. "This is just growing-up pain. Just reaction to a head-on with reality."

With reality. With a special reality unique to the family and Legion, with their bizarre array of problems and enemies.

He opened his father's comm drawer, punched for Combat. "Anything new?" he asked.

"Ah, negative, sir. Situations appear static."

"Keep me informed."

"Will do, sir."

"You're very good," Mouse whispered after breaking the connection. "If I were you I would've lost patience with me last week." He rose and began prowling the study.

He could not shake a subtle conviction that something dreadful was about to happen. He was restless all day. He had been unable to sleep well the past several nights.

"If there was just something to do around here."

He began strolling from cabinet to cabinet, looking into each, re-examining his father's collections. He did the rounds at least once a day. The circuit had a curiously calming effect.

He wondered if his father used them for the same talismanic purpose.

The coins, the dolls, the china, the books—they were all evidence of a past, of a connection with and a part in a vast, ongoing process. You could reach out and touch them and feel that you were touching part of something larger than yourself. You pulled in endless, invisible strands of humanity and spun yourself a chrysalis. . . . It was all very subjective and emotional.

Still restless, he quit the study and went up to Cassius's office. He met no one along the way.

The tiny, empty world of the Iron Legion made him think of still, abandoned cities, deserted for no reason history bothered to remember. Take twenty thousand people out of the Fortress and it became a self-contained desolation almost timidly murmuring to itself.

These days he heard sounds he had never noticed before, all the background noises of supportive machines that had been drowned in the chatter and clatter of human presence. The sounds left him with an eerie, spooky feeling. Sometimes, as he strolled the empty hallways of the office levels, he would freeze suddenly, for a fraction of a second completely convinced that he was alone, trapped in an empty structure seven light-years from the nearest human being.

In those instants he staggered with the impact of a very vacant, very hollow feeling, inevitably followed by an instant of panic. Alienation was not the same as being alone. The alienated man moved in a bubble, but could see other human beings outside. The soul of him knew they were there, accessible if he could find the enchanted key. The separation was emotional, not physical. The truly alone man was barred from human intercourse by insuperable physical barriers. . . .

Mouse would never forget the look on Fearchild's face when he had entered the torture chamber in that asteroid —such pathetic joy at the appearance of another being, an almost eager anticipation of torment that would reaffirm his membership in a fundamentally gregarious species.

Mouse decided that he had had an insight into the human animal. The bad marriages that went on, the cruel relationships that persevered beyond all logic—most people preferred pain to being alone. Even pain was an affirmation of belonging.

"The beast isn't really a solipsist," he muttered.

Cassius's toy purchases from The Mountain were still in their shipping packs. He considered unwrapping them, setting them up, abandoned the idea. They were Cassius's private pleasure. He had no right to interfere.

He spent an hour playing with an ancient electric train, just running it around and around its track, making switches, stopping at stations, restacking the boxcars,

268

wondering how the original owner had differed from people of his own age.

Beliefs and values made him think of his Academy classmates. Drawn from Confederation's farthest reaches, they had brought with them an incredible range of ideas and attitudes, some of which he had found wholly alien.

Tommy McClennon, with whom he had crewed and miraculously won in the Crab Nebula Sunjam Regatta two years ago. . . . Tommy was Old Earther and more alien than most of the racial aliens attending Academy. Those aliens were of the same caste, the warrior, as the Storms. Tommy's ancestors had been nonproductive wards of the state for centuries. Tommy's different ideas went right to the bone.

A *beep-beep-beep* sounded from a silver button on the breast of his tunic. An elf's voice repeated a number three times. Mouse opened Cassius's desk and punched it on Walters's comm. "Masato Storm."

"Sir, word from Ceislak. He's just had a Sangaree raidfleet drop hyper. . . ."

"I'll be right down." He ran to the nearest elevator, feeling foolish as he did. What could he do, really? Nothing but listen while this Helga's World disaster developed.

"I was right about something bad coming on," he told himself.

Frieda Storm stepped from another elevator as he left his. "You got the word?" she asked.

"The Sangaree? Yes."

"What the hell happened to that nitwit admiral who said he was going to help?"

Two big boards had been set up in Combat. One tried to follow operations on Blackworld, the other Ceislak's Helga's World action. They were not fully computerized, nor were they up-to-date. A mob of old folks and youngsters did their best with sketchy information.

"What's happened?" Mouse demanded.

"Donninger's trying to hold them off, but he's going to have to run. There's way too many of them."

Mouse glared at a newly activated display globe. At its heart lay a cue-ball-looking orb which represented Helga's World. Combat was receiving a data relay from Legion ships orbiting the planet. Mouse watched the blips a while.

"What's our real-time lag?"

"Five minutes and some seconds. Pretty good, considering. Your father's Fisher friends must be right in on top of it. Close enough to risk getting shot at."

Mouse considered the trend. "Tell Donninger to get the hell out. Ten more minutes and he won't be able to." A Legion ship winked out of existence while he spoke.

"They brought in some heavy stuff," someone said. "Bigger than anything on the ID lists."

Mouse tried to watch several screens at once as specs came through and the computers tried to build images of the enemy warships. "They are big," he told Frieda. "Something new in the way of raidships."

"I hear the Norbon are something new in the way of Sangaree."

"You think it's them?"

"Who else?"

"This's what Father and Cassius wanted, then. To draw that Deeth out of hiding."

Frieda sniffed. "He wasn't terribly cooperative about timing his appearance."

"Uhm." Mouse found himself a chair. He did not move, except to use the toilet, till the engagement reached its bloody conclusion.

"Astounding," he murmured, rising at last. "I wouldn't have believed it if I hadn't seen it. I'm going to get some sleep."

He awoke to the insistent scream of the general alarm.

For a moment he could not understand what it was. He had heard it only twice before, long ago, during drills.

A booming voice echoed through the hallways: "Action stations. All personnel to action stations. We are about to be attacked. All personnel to action stations. We are about to be attacked."

"Holy Christ!" He grabbed clothing and ran.

He burst into Combat. "What the hell is going on?"

The senior watchstander indicated a display globe. His face was pallid. He gasped, "We got about two minutes' warning from the Fishers. They snuck past them somehow."

Red blips surrounded the Fortress in the tank. Tiny wires of fire lanced across the globe. Little stars sparkled. Diminutive sub-blips swarmed and danced like clouds of gnats on a still spring day.

"Eighty-two of them, sir," someone said. "There were eighty-five to start. Mostly light stuff. Sangaree."

"But...." He did not understand. It made no sense at all.

"They range from singleships to light battle, sir. Computer's still trying to project their assault plan."

Somewhere else, a computer voice murmured, "Kill. Bogey Forty-Six. Five thousand tons."

Frieda arrived. She had been asleep too. She was groggy and disheveled.

Mouse kept trying to make sense of the ship movements in the display globe. He could detect no pattern but an inexorable inward pressure.

"Just a raid?" he asked. "Or are they serious?"

The senior watchstander gave him a funny look. "Damned serious. Suicidally serious. They said so." He punched up something on his comm screen. A face appeared. The man said he was going to do to the Fortress what had been done to Prefactlas.

Mouse asked Frieda, "You think that's him?"

"Probably. Nobody's ever seen him, as far as I know."

"I've seen him before," Mouse said, suddenly remembering a moment on The Mountain. "He was there when that old man tried to kill us. In the crowd."

"Sir," the senior watchstander said, "the computer says they're running a randomed assault pattern. Some sort of command battle computer is controlling their ships. It looks like the ships' commanders have free manueuver any direction but backward. They've got to come after us whether they want to or not."

"Then it's a kamikaze attack."

"Sir?"

"A suicide thing."

"Definitely. Until whoever controls the battle computer turns them loose."

Mouse glanced at the display. An additional two enemy ships had been neutralized. "Are they going to break through?"

The watchstander sighed. "I think so. Unless we get a little more efficiency out of the automatic defenses."

"How long before they touch down?"

"Too early to predict."

"Tell the Fishers to contact Ceislak. Tell them to pass the word to Navy. Then have them get ahold of my father."

He could take only two hours of watching the claws of doom creep closer. The enemy kept coming and coming, despite one of the most sophisticated and deadly automatic defense systems ever devised. A third of their number had been destroyed, and still they came on with a dreadful, almost machinelike determination. Plainly, a madman was in charge out there.

He walked the silent halls of the office level, in some way making tentative good-byes to the Legion and everything he had known. He visited his father's study again, thinking it would be a crime against history to destroy the collections gathered there. So many beautiful things. . . .

He returned to Combat. "What's it look like?"

"Still bad, sir."

"We going to hold till *Hittite* gets here?"

"Yes, sir. You think they'll commit her by herself?"

"I couldn't say. There's nothing out there that can stand up to her."

"Empire Class could take on any ten, sir. But there're fifty-some still."

"When you get signals from her, you give her everything we know. Especially about their combat lock. They'll have to break it to engage her, won't they? Maybe some of the individual ships' commanders will make a run for it."

"Will do, sir."

An elderly officer, retired from Legion service, said, "Some figures, sir."

Mouse scanned them. They predicted that the Sangaree would overwhelm the outer defenses and land at least fifteen vessels on the planetoid's surface. "Not good. This makes *Hittite* our only hope."

"Yes, sir."

"Sir," said the senior watchstander. "We've just picked up another group of them moving in."

"What?"

"Easy, sir. They aren't fighting ships. Here. Five of them. Four big ones that scan out as transports of some kind, and one medium one that might be the command ship."

"Transports. Of course. So they can send troops inside."

Frieda eased up on the senior watchstander's far side. She studied the data momentarily, then stalked out of Combat. It was the first she had moved in hours.

"Pass the word to the Armory to stand by to issue small arms," Mouse said. "And tell them to run a check on all internal defense systems. You computation people. I want some kind of parameters on best and worst times we can expect them to reach the surface." More to himself than anyone, he added, "Father thought the Fortress could stand up to anything. I guess he never considered being attacked by a madman."

"Uhm. Sir, there never has been a perfect defense against someone who doesn't care what happens to himself."

Next evening Mouse mustered the entire population of the Fortress in the gymnasium. He explained the situation. He asked for suggestions and received none. There was little that could be suggested. They could but try to hang on till Navy arrived. He bid them do what they could, and before he finished decided he had screwed up by bringing them together. It only rubbed everyone's nose in the fact that there were hundreds of children who would share the Fortress's fate.

Mouse's comm roused him from a troubled sleep. "Storm here."

"Contact with *Hittite,* sir. She's coming in."

"I'll be right down."

When he reached Combat, the senior watchstander told him, "We've fed them our data, sir. We've established a continuous instel link. She's got a couple of Provincials with her, for what they're worth. They're going to go for the command ship and transports first."

"How soon?"

The man checked the time. "They drop hyper in two hours and eight minutes, sir. They'll be coming in with a big inherent and only a couple degrees out of the slot to target."

"How much warning will our Sangaree friends have?" Mouse nodded at the red blips on the display.

"Depends on how good their detection gear is. Anywhere from five minutes to an hour."

274

It came up closer to an hour. "Damn!" Mouse spat. "Look. They're pulling back."

Within a half-hour it was obvious the raidships were being moved to protect the command ship and transports, and that they were still under that relentless outside control.

"I guess we'll see just how mean one of those big-assed Empire babies is," Mouse said.

"I suppose we will, sir."

Hittite dropped hyper and went into action in an awesome blaze of weaponry. She and her escort settled into a quiet, deadly routine of systematic destruction. The Sangaree seemed unable to touch her. But invincibility proved an illusion.

"Hello, Iron Legion. *Hittite* here. Boys, I don't want to tell you this, but I have to. We've taken some drive damage. We'll have to pull out or lose our screens. Sorry."

"Sorry?" Mouse snarled. "Sorry don't help nothing."

"At least we softened them up a little for you." *Hittite's* Communications Officer had not heard Mouse. "We make it eleven solid scratches and a whole lot of bloody noses. Good luck, guys. *Hittite* out."

"Run the numbers," Mouse snapped.

"They're still going to get through, sir. Unless those bloody noses are worse than they look."

"Bloody hell! I didn't want to hear that."

Frieda made her first appearance of the new day. "What's going on?"

Mouse explained.

"Damn it all, anyway!" She flew out of Combat.

Mouse was returning to his quarters when he saw the body lying on the stretcher in the corridor. A girl of about fifteen. He did not recognize her. She had to be a daughter of one of the enlisted men.

"What the hell?" He knelt, felt her pulse. She was alive. Just unconscious. Or sleeping.

275

A sound startled him. He glanced up, saw two old men go into a cross corridor carrying a youngster on a stretcher. The one to the rear gave him a furtive look.

He started to run after them, became distracted when he passed an open dormitory door. The lights were on. A half-dozen retirees were lifting children onto stretchers.

"What the hell is going on here?" he demanded.

They stared at him. Nobody said anything. Nobody smiled or frowned. Two hunkered down, lifted a stretcher, came toward him.

He grabbed an arm. "I asked a question, soldier."

"Mouse."

He turned. Frieda stood framed in the doorway, not a meter away. She held a weapon and it was aimed at him.

"What the hell are you up to, Mother?"

She half smiled. "We're loading you youngsters aboard the *Ehrhardt*. We're sending you to your father. The Fishers will give you covering fire."

His thoughts zigged and zagged. That was a good idea. It should have occurred to him. Gets the children out. It would be risky, but *Ehrhardt* was one of the fastest ships ever built. . . . But Frieda seemed to be including him in this Noah's Ark venture. He would not have any of that.

"I've got a job here."

She smiled weakly. "I relieve you of command, Mouse. Bring a stretcher, men."

"Don't try to pull anything on me. . . ."

"Take your father a kiss for me, Mouse." Her finger tightened on the trigger.

Mouse tried to jump aside. He was not quick enough. The stun bolt scrambled his thoughts. He was falling, falling, falling. . . . He never reached the floor.

Forty-Nine: 3032 AD

Storm flung himself out of bed. A real nightmare had closed in on him. An attack on his home. . . . That was it. That was what he had overlooked. This was a war against his Family. He had left a flank unguarded.

"Is that true?" he asked, able to think of nothing else.

Thurston looked baffled. "Why would I lie about that?"

"Don't mind me. I'm just confused. Let's go."

Mouse had reestablished a continuous instel relay by the time Storm reached the war room. "Mouse, what's it look like?" he demanded.

The burst went out. The response came back, it seemed, no swifter than the speed of light. "It doesn't look good, Father. They're coming at us like they've gone crazy. No maneuver or anything. And it looks like they know our weak spots. We're holding, but we're losing outstations faster than the program allows. I think we need outside help."

Helmut whispered in Storm's ear while Mouse was talking.

"Okay, Mouse. Just do what you can. Helmut says we've instelled Ceislak and asked the Fishers to pass the word to Beckhart." He listened to Helmut a moment more. "Oh. You've done that, too. Good. Look. The arrangements are made. You've got a heavy battle group on its way from Canaan, two squadrons headed there from Helga's World, and *Hittite* somewhere in your vicinity on shakedown cruise. The whole damned Navy is headed your way."

Navy would, anytime, anywhere, drop everything else for a dustup with Sangaree.

"Hang in there, Son. The Fortress will see you through. I designed it myself."

Mouse laughed. "Thanks, Father. Mother sends her love. I've got to get back to work now."

Mother? Storm thought. Who?... Ah. He meant Frieda. How was Frieda handling the crisis? He shrugged. She would cope. She was a soldier's daughter and a soldier's wife.

Time would tell the tale. If the Fortress cracked before Navy arrived, he would be a poor man again, in several senses. All his treasures would be gone, with most of the people he held dear. He would be left with nothing but the financial wealth of the Legion.... He forced his attention back to what was happening in the Whitlandsund.

Havik was taking a beating, but he was holding. An infantry battalion was assembling at the shade station. If Havik held till they crossed back to Darkside, Storm was sure he would win again.

He could do nothing but work up an ulcer here, he decided. "Thurston. Take over. I'm going for a walk."

"It's raining out, Father."

"I know."

After a while he realized he was no longer walking alone. Pollyanna, without intruding, was slouching along beside him. He had not seen her since the day Wulf died.

"Hello."

"Hi," she replied. "Is it bad?"

"They're attacking the Fortress."

"And nobody's there."

"Mouse is. And the families."

"But no one to fight."

"They'll fight. As well as any Legionnaire. It's mostly automated anyway."

"Couldn't you ask for help from Navy?"

"It's on its way. But it might take a week to get there. That's a long time to hold out if the raid-master is determined."

"And it's all because of Plainfield. Michael Dee."

278

"My brother is a pawn too. The shadow-master is a Sangaree named Deeth."

They walked a block in silence. Pollyanna said, "I like the rain. I missed that at the Fortress."

"Uhm."

"I couldn't go walking on The Mountain. The skies were too big."

"Uhm." Storm was not listening. His thoughts kept turning to the Fortress. "He must've gotten upset with the way things were going here. Or maybe because of Helga's World. I don't know. It doesn't make any tactical sense to move against the Fortress right now." He talked on, using a soft voice to describe how Helga's World had become a deathtrap for a major Sangaree raidfleet and how the Shadowline War might still go the Legion's way.

Pollyanna was not listening to him any more than he was listening to her. "Down here," she said, pausing at the head of a descending stairway. "I want to show you where my father lived. Where my heart still lives, I guess."

He followed her down to the tiny apartment she had shared with Frog. The dwarf's ghost was its only occupant now. Pollyanna now lived in quarters provided by Blake.

Storm felt right away that the place was a shrine. It made him uncomfortable. He remained carefully, neutrally attentive while Pollyanna told the story of each of her museum pieces. He felt like a voyeur peeping through the keyhole of her soul. The slightly dotty, obsessive monologue helped him understand Pollyanna Eight just a bit better.

From there they went to his rooms and made love, then lay curled together in the twilight afterglow and murmured of nightmares that had come true and dreams that had turned into smoke.

"I want to go back to the Modelmog, Gneaus," she said in her tiny, weary voice. "I was really happy there.

Lucifer.... I think we could have made it if it hadn't been for the rest of this."

"That's life, pretty thing. It won't leave you alone. It keeps hammering away till it finds the weak places, then it starts yanking everything apart."

"Does it have to be that way?"

"I don't know. Some people slide right through. They never have any bad times, never hit that tough piece of road. Or so it seems."

"Can you play something on that funny black thing? Whenever you do, you know, I get this image of this lonely old man way up on a mountain.... A hermit, I guess. He sits there looking down at this city wondering if maybe he missed something. But he can't figure out what it is because he used to live in the city and he did everything there was to do.... Aw, you're laughing at me."

"No. I'm just a little surprised."

"Anyway, hearing it always makes me sad. I guess I want to be sad now. Because I guess I'm feeling like that guy on the mountain. I was there but I missed something."

"You've still got a lot of years to find it."

"It wouldn't be the same. I'm not the same Pollyanna anymore. I've done a lot of things I don't like me very much for. I hurt people. Frog taught me never to hurt people."

Storm moistened the reed of his clarinet, startled Pollyanna with a couple of rollicking Hoagie Carmichael pieces.

She smiled when he finished. "I didn't know that thing could be happy. You never...."

"It could be happier. I didn't have my heart in it."

"That was really strange music. Kind of wild and primitive."

"It's very old. More than a thousand years."

"Thanks. I feel better. Come here."

They made love once more, and fell asleep lying side by side, reading Ecclesiastes.

His comm's shriek wakened him. An almost incoherent Helmut blurted, "They took the Fortress! It just came in, Gneaus. From Frieda. She sent a personal message. . . . You'd better come here. . . ."

Grimly, Storm began dressing.

"What is it?" Pollyanna asked, frightened by the sudden hardness of him.

"We lost the Fortress."

"Oh no! Not. . . . Your wife! And your children. . . ."

"Be quiet. Please." Feeling numb, he finished dressing. He did not remember the walk to the war room. Suddenly, he was there. Something within him would not allow him to react completely to the news. It felt like another in a parade of disasters that had happened to somebody else.

"Bring me Frieda's tape, Helmut," he said when he realized where he was.

"Gneaus?"

He looked up. Helmut was standing beside his chair, holding the microtape. Time had stolen away on him again.

He loaded the cartridge with the exaggeratedly careful motions of a drunk. It began with a continuous status report from Fortress Combat. He advanced it till Frieda's pale face formed on screen. Her thin, severe, colorless mouth writhed, but he did not hear anything.

What's happened to Mouse? he wondered. He had not been visible in the Combat views.

Don't take him, too, Storm prayed. *He's our only tomorrow.*

Frieda was saying something about there being fighting on Dock Level. He upped the sound.

". . . penetrate Residential. They're tough, Gneaus. Primitives, I think. Definitely human. I've put the kids into the *Ehrhardt.* She's set to boost whenever the computer decides she has her best shot at breaking through.

The Seiners say they'll try to cover her. We'll lose contact with them soon. The raiders are getting close to our wave guides. There it goes. The cruiser. Wish them luck getting through.

"Gneaus, I'm going to cut this short. I want you to remember me as a good soldier, but I'm so damned scared I might make a fool of myself. Forgive me now for whatever hurt I may have done you over the years. Remember my love, such as it was. And remember me to Father.

"We'll hold them as long as we can. Tell Navy to come get them."

She smiled weakly, pursed her lips in a last long-range kiss, then secured her screen. The instel relay continued. An old man calmly chanted ordnance data from the Fortress's Combat Information Center.

Storm sighed and closed his eyes. Getting the youngsters out was something, anyway. He shuffled around the dark places of his mind, collecting the old scraps of rage and hatred and hiding them in an out-of-the-way dust bin for nonproductive emotions. More than ever, now, he needed to keep a tight rein on his feelings.

"Helmut, give me an update on the situation here."

The news from the Whitlandsund was little better than that from home. Havik faced virtual human wave assaults. Michael appeared to be growing desperate.

The shade station was sending reinforcements, but only in driblets. Most of the functional crawlers were still far out the Shadowline.

Helga's World was the bright spot. The Fishers said the Sangaree raiders had been obliterated. Marines were taking over for Ceislak's commandos. The latter were taking ship for Blackworld. Already.

Storm sent Thurston to find Blake.

"Mr. Blake," he said when the man arrived, "I'm down

to my last gasp. The one option I have left is to scratch Dee's base of operations."

"Colonel. . . ."

"It's not open to debate this time. We're not going to argue about it. It's past that stage. I'm going to do it. I'm telling you so we can observe the proprieties. I'm going to do it even if you insist on a vote. Remember, I control the proxies. One of my ships will be here soon. When it shows, I'll use it to jump to Twilight."

"Colonel. . . ."

"Blake, it looks like we're going to lose the Whitlandsund. If Cassius is going to have any chance to break through and save your ass, I'm going to have to destroy Dee's logistics. Can't you understand that?"

"Won't he just grab Edgeward?"

"He might try. I can't guarantee that he won't. He'll have a lot of trouble doing it now. You're ready for him. And he's been outside a long time, without much coming down from Twilight to support him. Yet. He didn't count on heavy resistance."

"So?"

"So he's going to run low on munitions before he gets new stocks. I think he's going to take the Whitlandsund no matter what we do. But if we do hit Twilight, then we have him in the same position he has Cassius. In order to survive, he'll have to take Twilight or Edgeward. Either way, he'll have to pull me out of the pass. Enough, hopefully, so Cassius can break through. If we manage that, Dee is done for. Unless he uses nuclears again. Which I doubt he has with him, but which he'll have on tap up north. So from our viewpoint, taking Twilight has become an imperative."

Storm did not admit just how much he was guessing and hoping. Michael, even in predictable circumstances, could be unpredictable. There was a good chance he would go the easy way and spread nuclears around, if he had them. Or he might take a cue from Hawksblood and sit tight till his ammo was gone, hoping he could outlast Cassius. Walters's supply situation was just as iffy as Dee's.

Days groaned past. Men and arms trickled over from the Shadowline, but never enough to halt Dee's gradual conquest of the Whitlandsund.

There was a tremendous inertia in the westward flow of men and materiel in the Shadowline. It had to be overcome and turned around before a large and effective force could be mustered against Michael. . . .

"Father, Havik wants to talk to you," Thurston said one morning.

"Bring him up over here." Storm faced a screen. "Yes, Colonel?"

"Colonel Storm, I can't do the job. I'm sorry. I'm too bad shot up and this obsolete equipment. . . . Crying won't change it. Sorry, sir. What I'd like is permission to stop trying to be everywhere so I can concentrate on holding a bridgehead. We'll need some place to assemble a counterattack once you've brought enough equipment back."

Storm nodded. "I've been expecting it, Colonel. Go ahead and pull in your lines. And so you won't feel too bad, I want you to know I think you've done all you could. I'm sorry I couldn't give you more support."

"Thank you, Colonel."

"Thurston, where's Cassius now?" Storm asked.

"Still a long way to go, Father." Thurston indicated a light on the big board. "He's rolling around the clock, but those damned machines just don't move very fast. Do you want me to link you through?"

"Not now. It's too early in the morning for a squabble."

He and Cassius had been conferring regularly. Every conference degenerated into an argument. The loss of the Fortress had hit Walters harder than had anything else in the whole time Storm had known him. Finally, after ages, warfare had become a personal thing for Cassius. Storm anticipated a classic bloodletting when he came to grips with Dee.

He checked Ceislak's progress. It was a long fly from Helga's World. The Blackworld business might be over before Hakes arrived.

Storm spent much of his time alone, writing. He had a lot of thoughts he wanted committed to writing. He hoped Mouse would understand what he was trying to convey.

The *Ehrhardt* rumbled into Edgeward's crude little space port. Storm went out to greet her.

The pilot was one of his granddaughters. No one else aboard was conscious. He walked along the passenger aisles, looking down at Mouse, Lucifer, and others of his children and grandchildren, as well as the progeny of his men. He took a while, strolling along. This would be the last he saw them all.

Silly, lovely Frieda had surrendered her tomorrows on behalf of theirs. She was a soldier's daughter indeed.

"She tricked us, Grandpapa," his granddaughter told him. "We wanted to stay. Even the little ones. Grandmama drugged the water supply. I guess she cooked it up with the other old folks. They put us on the ship while we were out and sent us off on auto, with the Starfishers to cover us. It just isn't fair!"

"Did you want to die, Goldilocks?"

"No. But they needed us there. We should be there right now. . . ."

"You'd be dead if you were. We haven't been able to raise the Fortress for days. Even the automatic signals are out." He did not entertain the slightest illusion. The Fortress had been taken, all the way down to the computers at its heart. And Deeth would have taken no more prisoners than had Boris and Cassius on Prefactlas.

"Oh." His granddaughter started crying.

285

"Hey. Hey, Honey. No tears now. They chose. . . . We're the Iron Legion, remember?" He ground his teeth, afraid the tears would be infectious.

"I don't care!"

"Now, now, there're outsiders waiting out there."

She tried to stifle the flood.

"What about you, Goldilocks? Why were you awake?"

"They fixed me to wake up after it was too late to turn back. Somebody had to bring her in. I'm the best pilot. Mouse isn't rated on anything this big. What're we going to do, Grandpapa?"

Storm strained at being cheerful. "We won one, we lost one, Honey. Now we're going for best two out of three. We're going to settle with them here." His optimism fell flat. He could not force it through a very real despair. "They won't get away with it cheap, Honeycakes. We'll make them sorry they didn't leave us alone."

As with so many promises he had made lately, he did not see how he could make this one bear fruit.

The old shuttle crawler had to make three trips to carry all the youngsters into the city. Edgeward's people welcomed them warmly, not understanding that the city and its problems were not the real reason they found themselves orphaned and homeless.

The fourth trip out the crawler carried Storm's raiding party. Thurston. Lucifer. Helmut. Mouse. The best of the men who had survived the ambush of Michael's convoy. Pollyanna, whom no argument had been able to dissuade from going along in pursuit of a rapprochement with her ex-husband. And then there was Albin Korando, who wanted to go home, to help impose order and reason on the city that had sent him into exile.

Storm examined Korando before he started the liftoff checkdown. The man was a lean black eagle, grimly trying to familiarize himself with his weapons. He looked, Storm thought, much as Cassius might if ever Walters found himself a mission with special personal relevance. Much as Cassius must look right now, in fact.

They made a silent, grim band of commandos. There was no small talk, no nervous joking, no murmured rehearsals. On the edge of this action each preferred to be isolated with his or her thoughts.

Storm hit the go.

Fifty: 3032 AD

Storm took the cruiser in low and fast and put her down a hundred meters from Twilight's south lock. His weapons started talking while he was still aloft. Shafts of coherent light stabbed at everything outside the dome. Shellguns bit at the stressglass of the dome itself, chewing a hole through it two hundred meters west of the lock. Freezing atmosphere roared out, mixed with dust in violent clouds. His searchlights probed for enemies who never appeared.

The decompression was not explosive. The Twilighters would have time to get off the streets, into buildings that could be sealed. But time to insure personal survival was all Storm meant to allow them.

Helmut captured the lock before Storm finished cycling down. Darksword was moving the last of the raiders through it when Storm hit dirt himself. Accompanied by Korando, Pollyanna, Thurston, Lucifer, and Mouse, Gneaus set out for Twilight's equivalent of City Hall.

He had given orders to shoot anything that moved. He wanted these Twilighters cowed fast. The tininess of his force compelled him to hit hard and keep on hitting. He dared allow his enemies no time to regain their balance.

The only resistance he encountered was a lone sniper who surrendered the moment he received counterfire.

The entry to Twilight's City Hall, like Edgeward's, was

287

a massive airlock. The outer door was sealed. "Blow it," Storm told Thurston.

His son placed the charges. "Stand back, people," he shouted just before the *Boom!*

Storm clambered through the wreckage, checked the inner door. It was not secured. "Rig something over that outer doorway," he ordered.

Mouse and Lucifer scrounged plastic panels and pounded them into place. "They'll still leak, Father," Mouse said.

"They'll prevent complete decompression. That's all I'm worried about now."

He did not want to hurt civilians. The ordinary people of Twilight, like those of nations at war at any time, were simply victims of their leadership.

He was in a generous mood. In other times and places he had been heard to say that people were guilty of their leadership.

Storm and Thurston poised themselves, ready for the inner door. "Go!" Thurston growled. Storm kicked. Thurston went through on his jump pack, rocketing at an angle across a chamber twenty meters by thirty. Laseguns probed for him. Their beams went wide.

Thurston let go an antitank rocket. Before the debris settled, Storm, Lucifer, and Mouse moved in, firing, and spread out behind furniture. Pollyanna and Korando had enough sense to stay out of action for which they had no training. They indulged only in a little supportive sniping.

Thurston's second rocket, accompanied by grenades from the others, convinced the opposition. They surrendered. They wore no combat suits. Only four of fifteen had survived the exchange.

Korando sealed the inner door before more atmosphere escaped.

"Where're the big people?" Storm demanded of the

prisoners, after folding his faceplate back. "Where's Meacham?"

He received surly looks in reply.

"All right. Be that way. Lucifer. Shoot them one at a time till somebody answers me."

They looked into his one grim eye and believed him. He was not bluffing. He no longer cared, especially about Michael's men. The lives he valued most had been wasted already.

"Upstairs. Fourth level. Communications center. Yelling for help."

"Thank you. You're true gentlemen. Lead the way."

They balked.

A twitch of his trigger finger got them moving.

The elevators were dead. Storm shrugged, unsurprised. His guides led him to an emergency stairwell. Thurston blew the locked fire door. The big man could have achieved his end with a lasegun bolt, but he enjoyed the bangs.

A bolt poked through the smoke, stabbing a small, neat hole through Lucifer's right calf. The ambusher died before he could take a second shot.

"Pollyanna, take care of him," Storm ordered. "You four. Up the stairs. Smartly now."

Two went down before they reached the fourth floor. Three snipers joined them.

While Thurston prepared to blow the comm center door, Korando told Storm, "These men aren't Twilighters. They're not even Blackworlders."

"I didn't think they were. Blackworlders would be a little more careful about gunfighting in tight places. You spend your life worrying about vacuum, you don't go shooting where you might put holes in the walls."

"Exactly."

"Stand back. When that door goes we're going to get a lot of fire."

Thurston set off his charges. The counterfire came. Storm and his sons hurled grenades around the door frame, frags first, then tear gas, then smoke. After a brief pause they moved in.

Through the haze, using his infrared filters, Storm could see men trying to get out other exits. "Mouse. Stop those men over there. Korando, over there." He and Thurston bulled straight ahead, charging a group that looked like they could be troublesome. They were a tough-looking crew, and among them Storm saw his brother's son Seth-Infinite.

Thurston announced his approach with a rocket. Hands flew up. In all the smoke and tear gas the Twilighters could not determine the number of their attackers.

Seth-Infinite managed to slide away in the confusion.

Storm herded the gagging prisoners to the center of the room. He posted Mouse, Thurston, and Korando at doors. When Pollyanna, supporting Lucifer, arrived, he left the main door to her. He sat down and waited for the air to clear, for Helmut to report how it was going elsewhere.

The comm boards around him chattered wildly as people all across the city demanded instructions.

The air cleared enough. Storm opened his face plate. "Which one's Meacham?" he demanded.

A very sick old man, who fit Storm's notion of an elderly brigand, timorously raised a hand. The gases and smoke had left him puked out and aguey. From the corner of his eye Storm caught Korando's slight affirmative nod.

"Would you mind awfully, sir, explaining what the hell you've been trying to do? Would you kindly tell me why you broke your contract with Richard Hawksblood in favor of a deal with that bandit Michael Dee? Or Diebold Amelung, if you prefer? And, for the sake of heaven, why you've been using nuclears on my people in the Shadowline?"

Meacham's jaw dropped. He peered up at Storm in un-adulterated disbelief. Gradually, an air of cynicism crept over his tired old body.

"Ah. I see," Storm said. "He's done it to you, too. Believe it or not, old man. It's true. I wouldn't be here otherwise."

Briefly, he sketched what had happened to Wulf.

"I didn't know. . . ." Meacham mumbled. Then, "We lost communications with the Shadowline weeks ago. Equipment failure is what they told me. Amelung's son came back and said everything was going fine. He said our troops were holding you and work on the mohole was ahead of schedule."

"It isn't going fine at all. Not from your viewpoint. The fighting is over in the Shadowline. You lost. Because Hawksblood wasn't in charge. Because some nitwit Dee set it up that way. Now, tell me why the force that hit us Darkside? I thought that was outside the rules."

Meacham frowned. He was old, but obviously rugged. He was making a fast physical comeback. "What are you talking about?"

"About the convoy that's besieging Edgeward and the Whitlandsund. Somebody sent six armed crawlers with twenty-one mining units in support. Half of which are no longer with us, by the way."

Meacham stiffened. "Colonel Storm. . . . I assume you're Storm? Yes? I don't have the faintest idea what you're talking about. I specifically forbade any action Darkside." The old man's spirits were rising fast. "Establishing a tradition of Darkside warfare would be insane, Colonel. It would be bad for business."

"And what's become of Hawksblood, Meacham? Why is Dee fighting me, leading Sangaree troops?"

The old man glared. "That's not possible." Then his spirits collapsed again. He dropped into a chair so suddenly Storm was afraid that he had had a stroke.

"Sangaree?" he whispered. "Sangaree? No. That's just not possible."

There was a stir among the prisoners. The offworlders were getting nervous. They knew, whether or not they were Sangaree themselves.

"You don't have to take my word, Meacham. Call Walter Carrington at The City of Night. We sent him some of the corpses we took in after fighting near Edgeward. He had his people perform the autopsies. The word's out to all the domes now. Twilight is using Sangaree troops."

"My nephew," Meacham said in a barely audible voice. "Talk to him. He was in charge of military affairs. A little too anxious for the old man to die, I thought. Responsibility would settle him down, I thought. That's why I put him in charge. He was too weak, I suppose. The devils. The bloody devils."

How pleased Dee must have been, finding such an ideally usable man, Storm reflected. "Divide and conquer. The Dee way, Meacham. Get them by the greed. No doubt there was a plan to wrestle stock away from your directors. But their plans went sour. We attacked when they were overextended. Their bomb crawler got caught in heat erosion. Where is your nephew now?"

No one there would admit to being Charles Meacham. Storm glanced at Korando. Korando shrugged. The elder Meacham surveyed his fellow prisoners, shook his head. Then he rose and slowly walked to the tumble of bodies near the door Thurston guarded.

"Yes. Here he is. Caught up by his own sins." He shook his head wearily. "Children. They never quite turn out the way you want."

Storm sighed. It figured. The one prisoner who knew anything had been killed. Probably by Seth-Infinite's hand. He did not check to see if the nephew's wounds were in front or back. It was too late to matter.

What now? "Mr. Meacham, I'm going to draw up surrender terms. They'll be simple. You'll abandon your claim to the Shadowline. You'll agree to cooperate fully in bringing to justice members of the conspiracy to use nuclear weapons. You'll agree to help ferret out any Sangaree on Blackworld. You'll aid in the rescue and evacuation of personnel now trapped in the Shadowline. You'll free Richard Hawksblood and any of his men who might be imprisoned here. I expect Richard will have terms of his own to discuss. . . ."

"Gneaus?"

Storm turned. Someone was at the door guarded by Pollyanna and Lucifer. "Helmut?"

The old warrior came to him slowly, wearily, his helmet open, his face as pale and strained as it had become when he had learned of his brother's death.

"What is it, Helmut? You look awful."

"Won't be any more wars with Richard Hawksblood," Darksword muttered. He laughed. It was a soft cackle of madness. "We didn't get to him in time. They had him down in the service levels. Gneaus, it was the work of the Beast. It was like something from the Second Dark Age. Like the camps at Wladimir-Wolynsk."

"He's dead?"

"Yes. And all his staff. Beyond-the-resurrection. And death was a gift for them."

Storm stared into eternity, lost among disjointed memories of what Richard had been to him, of what Richard had meant. All their conflicts and hatreds . . . which had had their own formality and inflexible honor. . . . "We'll take care of them," Storm said. "An honorable funeral. Send them home for burial. I owe Richard that much."

One of the foundation stones of his universe had vanished. What would he do without his enemy? Who, or what, could replace a Richard Hawksblood?

He shook it off. Richard did not matter anymore. He

had his own plans. . . . He drew his ancient .45, slowly turned its cylinder.

"Father?" Mouse said softly. "Are you all right?"

"In a minute. I'll be okay, Mouse." Storm looked into his son's eyes. Today and tomorrow. . . . What seemed to be a depthless sadness stole into his soul. "I'll be okay."

"I evened scores a little," Helmut said. "Dee's wife. One shot. Through the brain. May the Lord have mercy on her soul."

"Gallant, chivalrous Helmut," Storm mused. "What happened to you?" The Helmut he had always known could not have slain a woman.

"I learned to hate, Gneaus."

There was no way of resurrecting a brain-destroyed corpse.

"Seth-Infinite's here in the city," Storm said. "We saw him."

"Fearchild, too. He did Richard in. He was there when we arrived. We're hunting him now. The citizens aren't giving us any trouble, by the bye."

"Good. Be kind to them. And watch all the exits from town. Dees always have a bolthole."

"We've accounted for most of their hired guns. We get an estimate of fifty on hand. What I didn't see anywhere else seem to be here, except for maybe five or ten and the Dees."

"Helmut, be careful. They'll be worse than any cornered rats if they think the game is completely up."

Worse than cornered rats. The Dees were intelligent, terrified, conscienceless rats who went straight for the throats of those who threatened them.

They attacked through the door where Thurston stood guard, coming hard behind a barrage of rockets that slaughtered the prisoners without harming Storm's people. They came in screened by a handful of Sangaree gunmen.

Thurston killed one attacker by smashing his skull with

a rocket launcher. Seth-Infinite shot Thurston point-blank, through the faceplate.

Beams stabbed around the room. People scrambled for cover. A rocket killed Albin Korando. Frog's orphan had returned home only to die.

Storm's old .45 spoke. A Sangaree died. Beside Gneaus, Helmut gasped and collapsed. Storm fired again, dropped another Sangaree. He got down and tried to drag Helmut to cover.

He was too late. Beams had punched fatal holes through Darksword's helmet and chest.

Storm crouched and, unable to do anything, watched Pollyanna try to pull Lucifer out her door. Beams found them both. Hers was a minor wound. She got off a killing shot herself before fainting from pain.

Me and Mouse, Storm thought. *So it's finally here. The last battle. It's almost laughable. It's so much smaller than I thought it would be. Two of us against. . . . How many?*

He peeped cautiously around the end of the console that concealed him. Seth-Infinite, casually, was killing the last of Storm's prisoners. Getting rid of witnesses, Storm supposed. Leaving no one who could repeat the name Dee. Startled, he realized they might nuke the city if they escaped.

"Mouse. . . ." he moaned softly. His favorite son lay on the floor before his door, his suit badly discolored along one side. He looked dead.

"Uhn . . ." Storm gasped. Mouse's head was turning slowly, toward Seth-Infinite. Mouse's suit had withstood the bolt. He was playing possum.

"I should've left him behind," Storm muttered. He smiled grimly.

Where was Fearchild? Storm assumed the men who had come in with the Dees were dead, killed by their employers if not during the attack. None were in evidence, and no Sangaree would have stood by while Seth-Infinite slaughtered his captured comrades.

An explosion slammed the console against him, tumbled him backward.

He had seen the grenade arcing through the air, could judge whence it had come. He seized Helmut's fallen weapon, rolled, bounced up, fired with both hands. He narrowly missed ending Fearchild's tale. Dee scrambled for better cover.

Storm's .45 roared at Seth-Infinite. He plunged back behind the console. The cabinet crackled as a lasebolt spent its energy inside.

Storm moved to his left, to get near a wall that would make flanking him difficult, and to make them turn their backs on Mouse. He fired as he went, to hold their attention.

The .45 stopped thundering, cylinder spent.

Storm reached the last cover available. He paused to catch his breath.

Now what? They would be crafty-aggressive. They would be sure they had him. He would have to do more than stall. . . . Was this the time for it?

He had decided there was a thing that had to be done before Michael's game could be beaten. The act would ruin all Michael's calculations, and blacken his heart with terror.

Now *was* the time to do it.

He was afraid.

Faceplate open, laughing at Michael's spawn, he rose and hosed lasegun fire over the area where they were hidden.

A bolt pierced his lung two centimeters from his heart. It did not hurt as much as he had anticipated. His weapon tumbled from his hand.

Fearchild and Seth-Infinite rose slowly, their faces alive with malicious pleasure.

Storm smiled at them. He croaked, "You lose, you fools!"

Mouse shot with preternatural accuracy, a single bolt stabbing through the back of each Dee skull. They did not have time to look surprised.

Storm smiled as they fell. And smiled. And smiled.

"Father?" Mouse had come to his side. The boy's hands were on his arm, urging him to sit.

"A time for reaping and a time for sowing," Storm whispered. "My season had fled, Mouse. The season of the Legion is gone. But the rivers still run to the seas. . . ." He coughed. Funny. It still did not hurt. "It's time for the young." He forced a broader smile.

"I'll take you to the ship, Father. I'll get you into a cradle." Mouse's cheeks were wet.

"No. Don't. This is something I have to do, Son. In my quarters in Edgeward. A letter. You'll understand. Go on now. Take command. You're the last Storm. I give you Cassius and the Legion. Complete the cycle. Close the circle."

"But. . . ."

"Don't argue with orders, Mouse. You know better. Go help Pollyanna." Storm leaned against the console, turned his back on his son. "Don't rob me of this victory. Go on." Then, to himself, "Vanity of vanities, all is vanity. What does a man profit? . . ."

Death descended on quiet, silken wings and enfolded him in gentle, peaceful arms.

Fifty-One: 3023-3032 AD

One of the Osirian commtechs called out, "Lord Rhafu, I've got a red light on something from Todesangst."

The old man limped across the huge communications center whence the Norbon empire was directed. "Get me a printout."

A machine whirled and rattled. Paper spewed forth. Rhafu caught the end and read as it appeared. "Uhm!" he grunted. He balled the whole thing up and carried it into a seldom-used office where he studied and researched it for several hours. He came to a decision. He picked up a phone. "Number One." A moment later, "Deeth, I've got a critical here from Todesangst. I'm bringing it up."

Deeth looked up from the printout. Rhafu was *old.* Probably older than any Sangaree alive, and near the time when rejuvenation would no longer take. The shakiness of massive nerve degeneration had set in.

Deeth frowned. He would not have Rhafu much longer. How would he manage without the man?

He scanned the report again. "I must be missing the point. I don't see anything remarkable here."

"It came red-tagged. I wondered what Michael is up to, that's all."

"Send someone to check."

"I already have. Deeth, if I may?"

Deeth smiled a soft smile. That was Rhafu's bad news tone. "Yes?"

"It looks to me like he's trying to bail out on us."

"What makes you say that?"

"The figures. What they add up to. A hell of a lot of wealth if this thing can be tamed. That and the risks he took."

"I don't see. . . ."

"Sir, your son is Sangaree by your will only. If the truth were known, I expect, he wishes you weren't his father. He grew up a Storm. Inside he still wants to be a Storm. Or, second-best, some anonymous human. We're a closet skeleton he'd rather forget. He could disappear if he wanted, but he's hooked on money and power. If he could be somebody else and still have those. . . ."

"He's got all the money and power anybody could want, Rhafu."

"Sangaree money. Sangaree power. Tainted. And shared. We can control him. We can destroy him by exposing him. With the wealth of this Blackworld thing he could assume any one of several identities we don't yet know and leave us standing around with our fingers in our noses wondering what happened. Except that he was stupid enough to use his own computation capacity to run this feasibility study."

Deeth leaned back, closed his eyes, tried to banish the pain. Rhafu was probably right. . . .

"Deeth, there are indications he tried this once before. Nothing concrete, but he apparently went after a Starfisher harvestfleet years ago. He's never told us about it."

"And he might have achieved the ends you're arguing?"

"Yes. I hear it was an eight-ship harvestfleet. That's a lot of wealth, and a damned good place to hide."

How could Michael prefer anything else to being heir of the leading Sangaree house? That was not logical. What more could a man want? He put the question to Rhafu.

"Respectability. Acceptability in Luna Command. Rehabilitation from the sin of youth that got him rusticated in the first place. You can smell on him how badly he wants to get into the humans' elite club. He'll do anything, including selling us down the proverbial river if the payoff is big enough."

"Rhafu. . . . I can't accept that. I refuse to accept that."

"I have the same emotional responses you do. Intellectually, I see how his emotions are driving him, but I don't understand." Rhafu stared over Deeth's shoulder, out a vast window, at Osiris. Deeth turned, also considering that slice of world.

"He wants to be loved. By the species which rejected him. Is that what it boils down to, Rhafu?"

"Perhaps. And does anybody love Michael Dee? Not really. Not unless it's Gneaus Storm. To everyone else he's a tool. Even us. And he knows it."

Deeth nibbled his lower lip. Put that way, he could feel some empathy. . . . "Let me see that printout again." After a glance he said, "He won't evade his Family responsibilities."

Rhafu stared out the window while Deeth examined the numbers for the third time. After a time, he said, "Deeth, this Blackworld thing may be what we've been looking for. I checked it out before I came here." He dropped a chart onto Deeth's desk.

"It has some peculiar physical characteristics. Look how it lays out. A pot of gold here. In this Twilight Town's territory, but it's accessible only from this Edge-ward City's territory. The pot's big enough to fight over. I would if I were in their shoes. And engineered right, we might end up controlling it. Here's my thinking. We en-gineer a war. We manipulate it so these cities hire Storm and Hawksblood. If the fighting is confined here on the dayside, we might trap both gangs. Suddenly, no Storms, no Thaddeus Immanuel Walters. And no Hawksblood, which would be Michael's payoff for running the show. That's just rough thinking, of course. It would take a long time and a lot of money and research to set it up right."

Deeth smiled. "I see it. I think you're right." He scrawled his name across a piece of paper, wrote a few words. "Take this to Finance and get whatever you need to do your own feasibility study. I'll cut loose whichever people you want. But don't get carried away. Just map it out and see how it looks. If it'll go, then we'll set up a special organization."

"All right."

"Rhafu? Go as carefully with this as you did with the Dharvon. For the same reasons. If there's that much pow-er metal there, let's come out on the far end not only finished with the Storms but controlling that mine."

Rhafu smiled, apparently considering the Homeworld

impact of yet another quantum jump in Norbon wealth. "Don't overreach, Deeth."

Deeth was not listening. The possibilities had revivified his childhood dream of restructuring Sangaree society to suit himself. "Call Michael in before you do anything. It's time for face-to-face. And you'll want his first-hand impressions."

If there had been any doubt that Dee was up to something, it vanished when Rhafu tried to summon him to Osiris. Michael dodged messengers the way lesser men dodged process servers. Rhafu had to collect him in person.

Deeth was appalled by the sullen creature Rhafu brought in. Michael snarled, "I've had enough. I didn't want to get involved with you in the first place."

"You're part of the Family."

"I don't give a *damn* about your Family. All I want is for it to stay out of my life."

"Michael. . . . Look at all we've done. We've made you one of the richest men alive."

"Yes. Look what you've done to me. My children . . . belong in asylums. My people hate me. They think I'm a monster. And they're probably right. . . ."

Deeth snapped, "We're you're people."

The usually evasive, cowardly Michael looked him straight in the eye. He did not speak.

He did not have to. Deeth recognized his failure. He did not have a son. He had an unwilling accomplice. "All right, Michael. What do you want?"

"I want out. OUT. Nothing to do with you, and you nothing to do with me or mine, now or ever."

"It's not that simple. I still haven't settled with the Storms. That's why I brought you here. This thing on Blackworld. . . ."

"Not that simple. Forget it. They're not that simple. Your buttboy here explained on the way. The scheme won't work. You're not dealing with some First Expansion primitives or tenth-generation pleasure slaves. You're talking about people even tougher and nastier than you. And smarter."

Deeth bolted up from behind his desk, face puffing with anger. He swung hard. Dee leaned out of the way. "You see? You can't control your temper."

"Rhafu!"

"Sir?"

"Explain it to him again. I'll come back when I calm down."

When Deeth returned he found Dee no more receptive. "Michael, I've considered everything. Here's my offer. Help us put this thing through and we're quits. We'll divvy up the organizations and go our own ways."

"Sure," Michael replied, voice dripping sarcasm. "Till the next time I'm a handy tool."

"Quits, I said. My word. The word of the Norbon, Michael. I even keep it with animals."

Dee gave him an odd look. Deeth realized that by tone or expression he had betrayed his secret pain. He massaged his face and forehead. Michael wanted to break all ties. He wanted a son. They could not both have their way.

"That's the deal, Michael. You're either with me or against me. No in between. Help me destroy the people who destroyed Prefactlas, or be destroyed with them."

Michael stared at him with that defiant, fearless look once more. Very, very slowly, he nodded. Then he turned and started toward the door.

He paused, took a priceless piece of Homeworld carved jade off a shelf, examined it. It was better than two thousand years old, and so finely carved that in places it was paper thin. He held it at arm's length and let it fall. Fragments scattered across the tile floor. "Damn. Am I clumsy."

Deeth sealed his eyes, fought his anger.

"That's going to be a very difficult tool to control," Rhafu observed.

"Very. Answer this. Was that bit of vandalism a message, or just the spite of the moment?"

"I don't think we'll know till the dust settles. And that's probably why he did it."

"Watch him. Every minute. Every damned minute."

"As you will."

Rhafu put the operation together with his usual genius. It rolled along with such perfection, for so many years, piling and building like the growing crescendo of a great orchestra, that Deeth became convinced of the inevitability of a Norbon success. The little setbacks were there, but carefully accounted for in a program put together with all the information and computation capacity of Helga's World. An absolute and unavoidable doom loomed darker and darker above the murderers of Prefactlas.

Then word came to the hidden headquarters chalet on The Big Rock Candy Mountain. A puzzled Rhafu announced, "The man called Cassius is here. Asking questions about Michael."

"I don't understand. How could they have gotten wind of us?"

"I don't know. Unless. . . ."

"Michael?"

"Does anyone else know we're directing it from here?"

"Not a soul." Deeth considered. He had monitored Dee's dealings with Storm. Michael had kept his mouth shut. "Maybe we left tracks without knowing it."

"Possibly."

"Cut off his sources of information. We'll tend to friend Cassius ourselves."

"Deeth. . . . Never mind."

Deeth studied the old man. Rhafu's nervous degeneration was so advanced he had trouble managing a drinking glass.

"I want this one, Rhafu. We'll hit them and move somewhere else."

"As you wish."

They entered the hotel by separate doors. Unfortunately Rhafu had the only clear shot.

The old man's nerves betrayed him. He missed.

Cassius did not.

Deeth's nerve betrayed him. He froze. He never touched his weapon.

Deeth found himself aboard his escape vessel without remembering how he had gotten there. Just one image remained clear in his mind. Meeting the eyes of Cassius's companion in the street, over Rhafu's body.

It went sour after that. He did not have Rhafu's enchanted touch.

Storm stunned Deeth by attacking Helga's World. He gathered the Norbon forces. His raidships blundered into a trap more disasterous than that at Amon-Ra.

Blackworld was becoming a debacle. Michael just could not handle his half of the chore.

Deeth remembered a shattered piece of jade and wondered.

He lost his temper. He ordered the attack on the Fortress of Iron. "I may not get them all," he told himself, "but they'll know they paid the price of Prefactlas."

He had abandoned hope of profiting from Blackworld. And he had abandoned Michael Dee.

"My son, if you've done your best, you deserve an apology. But I suspect you've subtly sabotaged the whole thing. Enjoy the trap you've built yourself."

His last few fighting ships reached the Fortress's surface. His troopships went in. His men forced the entry locks.

The fighting continued for days, cubicle to cubicle, corridor to corridor, level to level. His soldiers encountered only women and old people, but they too were Legionnaires.

Near the end one of his people told him. "Lord Deeth, enemy scoutships have been detected. . . ."

"Damn!" The Fortress was almost clear. Only a handful of defenders remained, holding out in the old Combat Information Center. "Very well." He could not run now. He had to finish. For Rhafu. For his father. For his mother and the Prefactlas dead.

"All right. I want everyone out but the crew of Lota's raidship. Take space like you're in a panic. Let them intercept messages that will convince them that there's no one left alive here."

"Yes sir."

Deeth joined the one raidship crew in the final attack. His participation brought him face to face with Storm's wife, Frieda.

Book Three
GALLOWS

**What are the carpenter's thoughts as
he constructs the gallows?**

Fifty-Two: 3052 AD

Never be amazed by me. My teachers were classics.
Strategy and Tactics: Professor Colonel Thaddeus Immanuel Walters. Command and Administration: Professor Colonel Gneaus Julius Storm. Hatred, Vengeance,
and Puppet-Mastery: Professor Sangaree Head Norbon
w'Deeth. Cute Tricks, Cunning, Duplicity, and Artful
Self-Justification: Professor Entrepreneur, Adventurer,
and Financier Michael Dee. Between them they provided
me a very solid background. Cuss the Admiral if you
want. The most he did was give me an opportunity to do
post-graduate work.

I was a stinker when he recruited me.

—Masato Igarashi Storm

Fifty-Three: 3032 AD

Mouse crouched over his father for a long time, holding
Storm's hand, fighting back tears. Someone came and
rested gentle fingers on his shoulder. He looked up. Pollyanna had come over, using a laserifle as a crutch.

"He's dead," Mouse said. Disbelief distorted his face.
"My father is dead."

"They're all dead. Everybody's dead but us." Her
voice was as dull as his.

He rose slowly, mumbling, "Everybody. Helmut and
Thurston. And Lucifer. And everybody." The magnitude
of it slowly sank in. His father and two brothers. His
father's friend. And all the people and family who had
died already. . . .

"I'll kill them," he whispered Then, screaming, "All
of them!" He started smashing consoles with his rifle. But
it was a delicate weapon. Soon he held nothing but a
shard.

"We've got things to do, Mouse," Pollyanna reminded,
indicating the corpses and wreckage. Her voice held no
real interest. She was in such a state that getting on with
the job was the only glue holding her together.

"I suppose." The dull voice again. "Will you be all
right while I hunt up some of our people?"

"Who's left to hurt me?"

Mouse shrugged. "Yes. Who's left?"

He went hunting Legionnaires, using business like a
sword with which he could fend off the madness clawing
at his mind "All of them," he kept muttering. "Someday.
Every Dee. Every Sangaree."

Withdrawing from Twilight took a day. Too many
people, including Hawksblood and the brothers Dee,

could not make it to the *Ehrhardt* under their own power. And the dome had to be patched, and someone had to be found who would take charge in Twilight, someone whose loathing for Sangaree was insurance that Michael would have nowhere to run, insurance that Twilight would not come under the worldwide sanctions being threatened by her Blackworld sister cities. Mouse found his candidate after a long search. Most Twilighters wanted shut of any identification with the seat of power. They seemed afraid the Sangaree disease was contagious.

Time to leave arrived. And a new problem raised its Scylla-like head.

"Polly," Mouse said, "I don't know if we're going to make it back "

"What? Why not?"

"I'm the only pilot left, and I'm not rated on anything like the *Ehrhardt*."

"Call for somebody to come up here."

"Can't waste time waiting for somebody to come overland. I'll just give it my best go myself."

"Don't be stupid."

"It can't be that much harder than piloting Cassius's corvette. I managed that fine."

"With him there to help if you got in any trouble."

"Yeah." He truly believed he could handle the cruiser. And he was determined to try. "Strap in, lady."

"Mouse. . . ."

"Then get out and walk."

She grinned. "You're as stubborn as your father."

He grinned back. "I'm his son."

His liftoff was a little rocky.

"Gah!" Pollyanna grunted, nearly throwing up

"We're off!"

"That was the part that had me worried. Anybody can come down. It's just how fast you're going when you get there. . . ."

"A man does what he has to," Mouse told her.

For a few hours the pain and hatred did not touch him. The cruiser demanded all his sweat and guts and concentration.

He managed to get the *Ehrhardt* to and down on Edgeward's landing field without any irreparable damage.

Getting down required some careful maneuvering. A bank of ships had arrived during their absence. They were the battered bones of the Legion's once-powerful little fleet. They had brought Hakes Ceislak in from Helga's World. They were still off-loading the commando battalion.

Mouse had not informed anyone that he was returning, but the word was out by the time he entered Edgeward. Blake was waiting for him.

"Where's Colonel Storm?" Blake asked. His face was drawn. He feared the worst.

"My father was killed in action against Sangaree...." Mouse stopped to look inside himself. Somehow, for the outside world, he was removing himself from his feelings. He was reporting it as if it had happened to a stranger.

"And Albin Korando?"

"Killed in action, Mr. Blake. I'm sorry."

"No. That's terrible. I'd hoped.... What about Colonel Darksword?"

"Dead, sir. If you don't see someone with me, he's dead. The cruiser is full of bodies. It was rough up there."

"Your brother Thurston, too?"

Mouse nodded.

"Who's going to take charge? Colonel Walters is cut off in the Shadowline...."

"I speak for the Legion, Mr. Blake. We have a new commander. Nothing else changes. If you'll excuse me?"

Blake struggled to roll along with Mouse. "What *happened?*" There was an almost whining, pleading note in his voice. The Shadowline War was tearing him to pieces.

For a moment Mouse could sense the man's feelings. Blake was thinking, What have I wrought? What have I unleashed? What did I do that reduced Blackworld to this state?

Mouse shut everything out. He strode toward City Hall, unconsciously imitating the walk of Gneaus Julius Storm. Knifing through his pain was a driving need to demonstrate his competence, to show everyone that he could step into his father's role.

Heads turned when he entered the war room. He checked the boards. Dee now held the Whitlandsund. Cassius's marker had reached the shade station. The unit markers were dense there. Only a handful lay more than five hundred kilometers west of the station. Those were all small units meant to aid the Twilighters in their withdrawal from the Shadowline's end.

The situation was in balance, in tension. Cassius was ready to jump off. It was discussion time.

"Get Colonel Walters on the scrambled clear trunk," Mouse ordered.

The man responsible, who seemed on the edge of exhaustion, gave him a brief who-in-the-hell-are-you? look before turning to his equipment.

Cassius came on quickly.

"Masato, Colonel."

"Mouse. How are you?" Then Walters got a better look at his face. "What happened?"

"Father's dead. And Helmut. And Thurston and Lucifer. Both younger Dees. And Richard Hawksblood. They murdered him and his staff."

Cassius frowned.

"All beyond-the-resurrection."

Cassius's features grew taut, grim.

"Cassius, we're the only ones left."

"It's ending, then. But first there's Michael Dee. And his Sangaree."

313

"Dee is trapped. We cleaned out Twilight. He can't go back."

"He doesn't know? Don't let him find out."

"Ceislak's here now. I'm taking over at this end. I can squeeze him. . . ."

"Keep Ceislak at Edgeward. Protect the city. Don't let Dee hold it hostage. And get your ships off the ground. Don't give Dee any way out. Make him stand and fight. But let me take care of that part. I'll make the wasting of the Legion useful."

Mouse had never seen Cassius's face so expressive. His grief and hatred were primal.

"As you wish. I'll make my dispositions right away."

"Did your father . . . say anything?"

"Not much. He did it on purpose, Cassius. To give me a chance to get the Dees from behind. He left a letter. He wrote it before he went up. I haven't had a chance to read it yet. I have a feeling he knew he wasn't coming back."

"Let me know what he had to say. Soon. We'll be jumping off in a few hours."

"Right."

Blake, with his wife's help, arrived. The head of the Corporation seemed to have shrunk into a tiny old cripple. Before he could begin condolences that would only aggravate, despite their sincerity. Mouse told him, "It'll be over soon, Mr. Blake. We'll start clearing the Whitlandsund in a few hours. I'll be holding Ceislak's battalion in reserve in case Dee turns on Edgeward."

Blake started to say something. Grace touched his hand lightly.

"Pollyanna's in the hospital, Mr. Blake. I expect she'd appreciate a friendly face. I think her heart has been hurt worse than her body. She lost Lucifer and Korando both, and she was very fond of my father." He turned away from Blake. "Ceislak. I want a screen of pickets around the crater. I want all the listening devices out there double-checked. If Dee turns on us, we'll need all the warning we can get. Donnerman. Where's Donnerman? Donnerman, I want your ships off planet as soon as possible. Gentlemen, I'll be in my father's apartment if I'm needed." He pushed out of the war room and went to Storm's quarters.

Geri and Freki whined pathetically. They rushed into the hall, ran back and forth anxiously, searching for their master. Finally, they turned on him with sorrowful eyes.

"He won't be coming back," Mouse whispered. "I'm sorry."

They seemed to understand. The whining grew louder. One let out what sounded like a low moan.

Mouse looked at the ravenshrikes. They had retreated into their little nest, into a tight, intertwined tangle from which they refused to be drawn. They knew. He tried coaxing them with canned meat from the store of delicacies his father had kept. They would not open their devil eyes.

He sighed, looked for the letter.

It lay on his father's desk, page after page of hasty scrawl beneath a plain sheet bearing nothing but the name Masato. Storm's Bible and clarinet weighted them down. The Bible lay open at Ecclesiastes, the clarinet bookmarking.

"I should've guessed when he didn't take them with him," he whispered.

The letter, though addressed to him, sounded like an ecclesiastical missive from Gneaus Storm. It began: "Today I hazard the Plain of Armageddon, the blood-drenched field of Ragnarok, to play my part in a destined *Götterdämerung. . . .*"

Mouse read it three times before he returned to the war room, the Sirian warhounds tagging his heels apathetically. Their tails were between their legs and their noses were down, and they made strange snuffling sounds in their throats, but they stayed with him.

A whisper ran around the room. Technicians turned

to watch his entrance. The Legionnaires took the behavior of the dogs as somehow symbolic, as a seal on the transfer of the mantle of power.

"Cassius," Mouse said, "he knew he was going to die. He planned it. So there wouldn't be any reason for the rest of us to coddle Michael Dee anymore. It was the only way he could keep from breaking his word."

Cassius's laugh was both harsh and sad. "He always found a way to slide around that promise. Too bad he couldn't find it in him to go back on it." Walters's mad humor faded. "Don't let Michael find out. That's got to be our most important secret." Walters's face became dreadful, something inhuman, something demigodly. Something archetypal. "It's time to jump off. Take care, Mouse." He switched off before Mouse could question him as to his intentions.

What is he going to do? Mouse wondered. He knew Cassius. It would be something unusual, something nobody would expect. Quite possibly something impossible. ... He settled into the chair his father had been wont to occupy. His gaze seldom strayed from the situation boards.

At times one or another of the technicians would glance his way and shudder. A slim, oriental youth of small stature filled the Colonel's chair, yet. ... Yet there was an aura about him, as if a ghost sat in the chair with him. The body of Gneaus Julius Storm had perished, but the spirit lived on in his youngest son.

Fifty-Four: 3032 AD

The man called Cassius, through holonet exposure in Michael Dee's merc war documentaries, was more widely known than Confederation's Premier. Yet he was a figure of mystery, an unknown even to his intimates. What made

316

him tick? What made him laugh or cry? No one really knew.

He surveyed the Legion. He considered his public image, and reflected that he probably knew Cassius less well than did all those billions who watched the holocasts. They had an image of Thaddeus Immanuel Walters, and the tape editors maintained its consistency. But the Walters self-image rambled around—centuries, and he had not had time to discover who and what he was.

The massed crawlers showed up well on infrared. There were thirty-five of them, in two long lines, idling, awaiting his commands. The longer line of twenty-five, led by eight captured battle crawlers, would run for the Whitlandsund. They would do so without benefit of shade, which would warn Dee that they were coming.

The remaining ten units would follow Cassius himself.

No point in delaying any longer, Walters thought. He picked up a mike, said, "White Knight, White Knight, this is Charlemagne. Go. I say again, go. Over."

"Charlemagne, Charlemagne, this is White Knight. Acknowledge go. Out."

"Charlemagne, out."

The larger force began rolling.

Cassius's group consisted of six long-range charters, three pumpers, and his own command combat crawler. The charters, carrying minimum crews, were expendable. They would find the way. The four big rigs were crammed with men and equipment.

Cassius shifted comm nets. "Babylon, Babylon, this is Starfire. Signals follow. Stray Dog One, go. Stray Dog One, go. Over."

A charter rumbled into sunlight.

The formations Cassius used crossing uncharted territory, once he entered it a few hours north-northeast of the Shadowline, he adapted from those of ancient surface navies. The charters ran in a broad screen ahead of the four important crawlers, ready to relay warning of any danger.

They ran far faster than was customary for explorers. The run Cassius was making was dangerously long. If the crawlers escaped sunlight at all, it would be with screens severely weakened.

He kept the crawlers rolling, knowing his chances were grim.

Maximum computation capacity and power in each vehicle was devoted to keeping in touch with Walters. He wanted to know what was happening every instant, hoping he could keep up speed and still not lose two crawlers to the same trap. Like a spider in hiding, waiting for something to disturb her web, he sat amid his comm gear, listening. Hour upon hour passed. He said not a word. His crewmen began checking to see if he was all right.

The bad part of warmaking, he thought, is the 'tween-battles. There's too much time to think, to remember.

He could do nothing but endure the pain, the care, the fear. He tried to banish the ghosts that came to haunt him, and could not. He discovered that he had acquired a new squad. His wife and daughter. The Fortress of Iron. Gneaus. Wulf. Helmut. Big, dull Thurston, who may have been the only happy man in the Legion. Richard Hawksblood, the ancient enemy, with whom he had felt a bond of spirit. He had not seen Hawksblood in so long he could not remember the man's face. Homer. Benjamin. Lucifer. The younger Dees, long might they burn in torment. Doskal Mennike, who had been his protégé at Academy. Someday he would have to explain to Mennike's father. What could he tell the old man? Only that, one and all, they had been played for pawns and fools by Sangaree. It was not an admission that would come easily.

A long-ago ghost came. Tamara Walters, a favorite niece whose ship had vanished without trace during the Ulantonid War. Why was he remembering that far back?

318

Hadn't he made his peace with the elder terrors? Were all his losses, injuries, and sins going to return and parade?

"Starfire, Starfire, this is Stray Dog Four. I've hit heat erosion. Can't back free." The voice was tight and rigid. The man talking knew there would be no rescue attempt. There was not enough time. To try would seal the fate of everyone else. But he had accepted the risks when he had volunteered. "My instruments show a streak running zero five seven relative, eighty meters wide at least six meters deep. Good luck, Starfire. Stray Dog Four, out."

Cassius did not respond to the signal, merely passed the warning to the other crawlers, each of which slowed to skirt the danger. What could he say to a man he was leaving to die? He could do nothing but add a face and name to the list of men he had, through his own doing, outlived.

The media and his colleagues called him the ultimate commander. None but he realized that the ultimate commander was a pose, an image behind which Thaddeus Immanuel Walters concealed himself. Sometimes he managed to delude himself with the illusion.

Life, it would seem on remote observation, was something Cassius held no more holy than did the universe itself. Yet, like certain forgotten gods, he noted the fall of every sparrow, and put himself through silent, private purgatories for each. And still he went on, from battle to battle, without thought of becoming anything but what he was. Like Gneaus Storm, like so many mercenaries, he was a fatalist, moved by convictions of personal predestination. Unlike Storm, he did not fight and mock Fate, merely accepted it and sailed dispiritedly toward his final encounter with it.

At least a touch of solipsist madness was a must at every level of the freecorps.

Once past the heat erosion he redistributed his screen to fill the gap left by the lost crawler.

He lost another charter before he reached the Thunder Mountains three hundred kilometers north of the Whitlandsund, and yet another, through screen failure, while searching for a shadowed valley where the unit could hide from the demon sun. The crucial four heavy crawlers remained unharmed.

As soon as the charters had cooled down and loaded some gas snow, he sent them out again. Somewhere up here, according to the surveys done before the orbitals burned out, there was a possibility of slipping over the Edge of the World. A way to sweep around and beat Michael's game of Thermopylae. The pass had shown as a small, dark trace on a few photo printouts. . . .

It was a long shot. The darkness might not be a pass at all. . . .

While he waited on the charters Cassius played with the command nets, hoping to intercept something from the war zone. He got nothing but static, which was all he really expected in that cove of darkness on the shores of the sea of fire.

He thought Brightside was what the old Christians had had in mind for Hell. With the Legion here Blackworld certainly was a planet of the damned.

The charters returned two days later. They had found the way across the mountains, but did not know if the larger units could manage it.

"We'll give it a try," Cassius said. He had spent too much time with his thoughts and away from his command. He had to be moving, to be involved, soon, or he would go mad reliving his losses.

The pass was a tight, tortuous canyon, and the going was slow, but there were few real problems till they had crossed the Edge of the World. Then, after they had passed the limit of the original survey, they encountered a crack in the mountain which crossed and blocked the way. The crevasse threatened Cassius's entire scheme.

He refused to turn back. "We're going over these mountains here," he growled, "or we'll die here. One or the other. Let's find out how deep the son-of-a-bitch is."

His driver idled down. Cassius clambered out his escape hatch, approached the obstacle. The lead crawler had put lights on it, but they did nothing to illuminate its depths. He stared down into darkness. After a minute he fired his lasegun downward. The flash revealed a bottom much nearer than he expected.

He returned to his crawler. "Stray Dog One, this is Starfire. Maneuver your unit around parallel to the crevasse. Over."

It took two hours for the charter to wriggle into a position that suited him. "Stray Dog One, abandon your unit. Stray Dog Three, Stray Dog Six, push it over. Over."

The two surviving charters groaned and strained. The vibration of their effort shook the stone of the Thunder Mountains, made the big crawlers shudder. Their engines growled and whined, their tracks ripped at the earth. They injured themselves badly, but managed to topple the crawler into the crevasse.

Cassius offloaded his troops and had them gather loose rock. They dumped the detritus around the fallen charter. Hours crept away. The bridge grew, became level. Cassius sent a charter over to test and tamp, then an empty pumper. The fill held both times. One by one, the remaining units rolled.

That crevasse was the last serious obstacle. Abandoning the surviving charters because they could no longer keep pace, Cassius swung the big units onto the route between Twilight and Edgeward. He sped southward, maintaining radio silence. Near Edgeward he swung west, toward Michael Dee and the Whitlandsund.

His troops were exhausted. They had been cramped in their crawlers for days, racked by tension, constantly haunted by the fear that the next minute would be the one when a track went into heat erosion, or the mountain slid away beneath them. Even so, Cassius offloaded them at the eastern mouth of the Whitlandsund and sent them in. They made contact quickly.

Walters broke radio silence at last. "Andiron, Andiron, this is Wormdoom, do you read, over."

Mouse came on net only minutes later. "Wormdoom, this is Andiron. Shift to the scrambled trunk, over."

Cassius shifted. Mouse squeaked, "Cassius, where the hell are you? We've been trying to get ahold of you for six days."

"I'm right outside your door, Mouse. Moving into the Whitlandsund. I need Ceislak's men."

"You're on this side of the Edge of the World?"

"That's right. How soon can you get those men here?"

"How did you manage that?"

"Never mind. I did it. Send me those men. We can talk after we finish Dee."

"All right. They're on their way. I don't know how you did it. . . ."

Cassius cut him off, turned to listen to the tactical nets once more.

He had been listening in since returning to Darkside, trying to assess the siutation back in the Shadowline. It did not look good for those he had left behind.

Fifty-Five: 3032 AD

It was a very grim, very sour Masato Storm who watched the big board in the war room. It looked terrible.

Someone moved a chair into place beside him. He glanced up at at a commtech. He was holding the chair for Pollyanna.

Mouse smiled weakly. "How are you? Any better?"

"Ready for anything. Except I limp a little. They say it'll go away. How is it going?"

"Not good. I haven't heard from Cassius for days. I'm scared for him. And up there...." He indicated the board showing the Whitlandsund. "We made some gains when the first wave came over, but it's slowed down. Way down. We're still pushing them back, but not fast enough."

"But you outnumber them."

"We've lost too many tractors. We can't bring our people over fast enough. It looks like we've only got two chances. Either Cassius turns up or my uncle runs out of ammunition."

"Sir!" one of the commtechs yelled. "Sir, I've got Colonel Walters on Tac One."

"Put him on over here. Pollyanna, you're a good-luck charm. Maybe I'll strap you into that chair."

She smiled wanly. "I wasn't too lucky for Frog. Or Lucifer. Or...."

"Can it." Cassius's grim face came on screen. They argued back and forth about Ceislak's battalion, and Mouse tried to discover how Walters had gotten to Darkside. Cassius broke off.

"He's in a foul mood, isn't he?" Pollyanna asked.

"That he is. And he can be just as nasty as he wants as long as he does his job. I feel a thousand percent better now."

"Sir," commtech said a few minutes later, "I have Colonel Walters again."

"Put him over here."

"Mouse?" Cassius said, "Sorry about snapping. It's the nerves, I guess. It's grim out here. As your father would put it, the Oriflamme is up."

Pollyanna frowned a question. Mouse whispered, "No quarter given or asked."

Cassius continued, "We're in a bad spot. Nobody can

back down. It's all or nothing, and the losers die the death-without-resurrection."

"I understand, Cassius. We're all under pressure."

"Your uncle has got what he wanted. His battle to the death." A nasty smile crossed Walters's mouth. "I don't think the fool counted on being part of it, though."

"No. One thing. He doesn't know about Father yet. I want to save that as a special surprise. Let him count on that last-minute protection till it's too late."

"But of course! That's why I wanted to keep it quiet."

"The Legion never fought this bitterly," Mouse said.

"Never before. We've got an emotional stake in this one, Mouse."

Had it not been for the topographical advantages, Michael's crew would have been obliterated long since. Dee's men were good fighters, but they were not soldiers, not in the sense that the Legionnaires were. They were unaccustomed to extensive teamwork and the complexities of large, enduring operations. Though largely of human origin, they were tainted with the Sangaree raid-and-run philosophy.

"Michael's people aren't doing bad."

"They're cornered. I've got to get back to it. I just wanted to say sorry for growling."

"It's all right."

Cassius's battalions shoved Dee deeper and deeper into the Whitlandsund. The lines facing Edgeward had been thin and unprepared for a heavy stroke.

The hours cranked along. Mouse sat that chair till his behind began to ache. Pollyanna remained beside him, partly because she was interested in events, partly because she sensed his need for a bridge to the Mouse that used to be.

Dee's resistance stiffened.

"He's figured it out," Mouse said. "He's shifting men now."

Cassius kept the pressure on. At the far end of the pass Legionnaires from the Shadowline began to make headway against defenses weakened by the removal of men shifted to halt Cassius.

Pollyanna touched his hand lightly. "You think we're going to do it?"

"Uhm? What?"

"Win."

"I don't know. Yet. I think the odds are shifting." He caught fragments of tactical chatter. Cassius was moving Ceislak's commando battalion into position.

Hours dragged on. Finally, Pollyanna whispered, "You've got to rest before you collapse."

"But. . . ."

"Your being here or not won't change anything, Mouse. They can tell you if they need you."

"You're right. I won't be any good to anybody if I pass out from exhaustion. I'll stagger over to the apartment. . . ."

Pollyanna went with him.

When he returned to the war room he carried a raven-shrike on his shoulder. The commtechs' eyes widened. A secret understanding seemed to pass among them. Mouse surveyed the boards as the warhounds began their fruitless search for enemies.

He sensed the change in the men. They had accepted the shift in power. It was not a matter of humoring the Old Man's kid anymore. He had become the Old Man.

The boards did not look good. Things had gone static.

"Sir," one of the commtechs said, "Colonel Walters would like to speak with you at your convenience."

"Okay. Get hold of him."

Cassius was on the scrambled trunk in minutes. "Coming up with a few problems, Mouse. We've pushed them from both sides till we've got them surrounded in a big crater. They've dug in on the outside of the ringwalls, where they can fire down into the pass. They've pulled back into a small enough circle so that they can run men from one place to another faster than I can make surprise attacks. I was going to cut them up one place at a time. Slice off a little group and take them prisoner. They've managed to keep me from doing it. Looks like it could turn into an old-fashioned siege."

"There're thirty thousand people in the Shadowline who don't have time for that, Cassius. They're running out of air."

"I've heard the reports."

The breathables situation was becoming dangerous. Food and water were good for weeks yet, with rationing, but there was no way to cut back on a fighting man's air. Recycling was never completely efficient, and lately the equipment had begun to deteriorate.

Mouse said, "I got the medical people started putting the wounded into cryo storage yesterday. We can resurrect them when we open the pass. They suggested we do the same to Meacham's people."

"They have the cryo storage facilities?"

"No. Not enough."

"I may start using some of Hawksblood's people. If I can get them over to this side."

"Why?"

"Sometimes you run out of ways to finesse. Then the only thing left is the hammer. Hit hard, with everything you got, and grit your teeth about the casualties."

"Your munitions picture don't look good for something like that."

"That doesn't bother me as much as the air situation. It looks like Michael will run dry first. His fire patterns show he's trying to conserve ammunition."

"That's a plus."

"I don't know. What I'm afraid of is having to offer

terms so we can save the people across the way. I think that's what he's doing now. Trying to hold on till we're ready to trade his outfit for ours."

Mouse glanced at a depressing visual from Blake's shade station. The station was surrounded by a tide of emergency domes occupied by men waiting to be evacuated or sent into action. The encampment grew steadily as Hawksblood's men and Twilight's miners filtered in. Dee could lose his war and still win a Pyrrhic victory.

Mouse looked over at charts listing the various crawlers and their status. "Cassius, we're going to be in trouble no matter what. We don't have enough crawlers to get everybody out."

"So don't be proud. Ask your neighbors for help. Have Blake call the City of Night and Darkside Landing and beg for help if he has to."

"We've tried once. They say they won't risk their equipment if there's fighting going on."

"Keep trying, boy. I'm looking it over here. I'm going to try one more big push, then see what Michael is willing to dicker about."

"Don't deal. Not unless there's no choice."

"Of course not. I saw the trap that got your father into."

Mouse summoned one of the techs. "See if you can find Mr. Blake. Ask him to come down."

Blake joined him a half-hour later. Pollyanna accompanied him.

"Mr. Blake, could you try Darkside Landing and City of Night again? You can tell them the fighting will be over before they can get their equipment here."

The worn wreck of a man in the wheelchair showed a sudden interest in life. "Really? You've finally got them?"

"Not exactly. We're going to try one more push, then negotiate if it fails."

327

Blake protested. Boiling anger resurrected the man who had ruled the Corporation till the impact of the Shadowline War had driven him into hiding.

"My feelings exactly," Mouse agreed. "I don't want any of them getting away. But we may have no choice. It could be negotiate or let the men in the Shadowline die."

"Damn! All this slaughter for nothing."

"Almost. We could console ourselves with the thought that my uncle isn't getting what he wants, either. In a way, even if he negotiates his way out of the Whitelandsund, he'll have lost more than we have. He'll be on the run for the rest of his life. He used nuclears. He served the Sangaree. Navy won't forgive that. They'll confiscate his property. . . ."

Pollyanna had been rubbing Mouse's shoulders. Now her fingers tightened in a surprisingly strong grip. "You negotiate if you want. You make a deal for the Legion. You make a deal for Blake and Edgeward. But don't count me in, Mouse. Don't make any deal for me. August Plainfield got away once. He won't again."

Mouse leaned back, looked up. Her face betrayed pure hatred.

"You been drinking snake venom again?"

She squeezed so hard his shoulders ached. "Yes. I drink a liter with every meal."

"Wait." Mouse indicated the boards.

Cassius was starting his attack.

"Sir, he's sending in everybody this time," one of the techs reported. "He's even stripped the crawlers of their crews."

Mouse stood up. "Mr. Blake, find me a crawler. Anything that will run. I'm going out there."

Fifty-Six: 3032 AD

Cassius found himself a laserifle and climbed the crater ringwall.

The fighting was close, grim, and positional. Rock by rock, bunker by foxhole, his men flushed Dee's and drove them back. Man by man, they broke the Sangaree defense. The Legionnaires invested all their skill and fury. Dee nearly fought them to a standstill.

What had Michael said to make his people so damned stubborn? Cassius wondered.

"Wormdoom, this is Welterweight. I've got my hands on a prime chunk of ringwall rim real estate. Give me some big guns."

"You've got them, Welterweight."

Finally, Cassius thought. A break. He ordered all the artillery possible into the position Ceislak had seized.

The nets resounded with chatter about furious counterattacks and dwindling ammunition stocks. Cassius decided to join Ceislak. The man's position had to be held. It provided a platform from which the interior of the crater could be brought under fire.

He studied the fighting from the rim. It took time to fall into patterns. He had nothing but weapons flashes by which to judge.

"I think that last one was their last counterattack," Ceislak told him. "We're ready to finish them." Gesturing, he indicated the far rimwall. Heavy weapons flashes had begun to appear there. Legionnaires were coming over from the Shadowline side. Ceislak's bombardment had broken the stubborn defense of the ringwall.

A dwindling number of enemy weapons flashes indicated failing powerpacks and munitions supplies on the other side.

"Looks like we might manage it," someone said.

Walters turned slowly, wondering who had broken radio silence. One of a pair of figures, just joining the crowd and barely visible in the backflash of Ceislak's weapons, raised a hand in greeting.

"It's me. Masato. I said it looks like we've finally got them."

"That's Michael Dee down there," Cassius growled. "He'll still have three tricks up his sleeve. What the hell are you doing here? You're the last Storm."

"It isn't a private war," was all Mouse said by way of defending his presence.

Cassius turned back to the crater. The boy was his father's son. There would be no talking him out of staying.

A flash illuminated the face of Mouse's companion. "Damn it, Mouse! What the hell's the matter with you, bringing a girl out here?"

Pollyanna reminded him of that niece he had lost during the Ulantonid War. He felt strangely avuncular and protective. He was startled by an insight into his own ambivalent feelings toward Pollyanna. Tamra had meant a great deal to him.

The flashes on the far rim showed the Brightside troops making good headway. Michael's people seemed to be running out of ammo fast. Good. "Looks like we won't have to offer terms."

Mouse stuck with his previous contention. "She has as much right to be here as anybody. Her father. . . ."

"Was I arguing? I've heard all about it." He caught a ghost of something in the timbre of Mouse's voice. The little slut had gotten her hooks into another Storm. "Let's stick to business. It's time to find out if Michael's ready to give up."

Michael contacted him first.

One of Cassius's officers called on Command One. "Sir, I've got Dee on a public frequency asking to parlay with Colonel Storm. What should I do?"

"I'm on the rimwall right now. Tell him he'll be contacted as soon as possible. And don't let on about the Colonel. Understand?"

"Yes sir."

With Mouse and Pollyanna tagging along, Walters descended to his crawler. He ran through the command nets, ordering his officers to keep the pressure on hard. Several units reported the surrender of individual human, Toke, and Ulantonid soldiers.

One commander reported, "Their munitions situation is so desperate they're taking small arms ammo from their troops and saving it for Sangaree officers."

"Good old Michael," Cassius said. "Really knows how to make and keep friends."

He started to signal Dee, suddenly stopped. "I just had a nasty idea." He went across the command net again. "Wormdoom. Gentlemen. I want a radiation scan on that crater. These guys used a nuke on us once before."

In two minutes he knew. There were two radiation sources not identifiable as tractor piles. They were nowhere near any of Dee's heavy units.

"Looks like my dear old uncle was going to close the pass after he made terms with Father."

Cassius smiled. "He's in for a surprise."

"He'll be asking merc terms, won't he?" Mouse asked.

"Of course. But he's not going to get them. If I end up dealing at all. I'm going to be against the wall hard before I let Sangaree get out."

"Better get hold of him before he panics."

Cassius found the band on which Michael was waiting. "Dee?"

"Gneaus? Where the hell have you been?" Only Dee's

331

word choices betrayed his anxiety. His voice was cheerful. "I've been waiting half an hour."

Cassius silently mouthed, "He hasn't caught on about Twilight yet. That gives us the angle on him."

"Set the hook and reel him in," Mouse suggested.

"Been out directing artillery," Cassius said into the pickup. He kept the visual off so he would not correct Dee's presumption that he was speaking with Gneaus Storm. "What you want?"

"Keep it on the edge of the band or he'll recognize your voice," Mouse whispered. Cassius nodded, made a fine adjustment.

"Terms. We're beaten. I admit it. It's time to stop the bloodshed."

Cassius controlled a snort. "What reason do I have for giving them? We're winning. We'll have you wiped out in a couple hours."

"You promised. . . ."

"I didn't promise your people anything. They aren't covered by any of the usual conventions anyway. They're not merc. They're Sangaree hired guns."

"But. . . ."

"If you want to talk, come to my crawler. We'll sit down face to face."

Dee crawfished. He wriggled. He squirmed. But Legionnaires now held all the heights. Their artillery made an ever more convincing argument.

"You think he'll come in?" Mouse asked.

"Yep." Cassius nodded. "He isn't finished, though. He's got a trick or two up his sleeve yet. Besides the bombs. If he wants to have any men left to help pull whatever it is off, he's got to get them out. He'll come trotting over like a bad little boy expecting to get his hand slapped."

"I'm going to call Blake." Mouse cleared another channel, spoke with the city. "Cassius, he did it. City of Night and Darkside Landing are sending crawlers."

Cassius felt a century younger, knowing there was a chance.

"What about those nuclears?"

"I've got a plan. Stand back and be quiet. I'm going to call him again. Michael? You coming over here or not?"

"All right. But you make sure nobody shoots me on the way."

"You're clear. I'll leave the carrier on as a homer." Walters gave orders for one crawler to be allowed to leave the crater.

"Better watch him close," Mouse said. "He could have those bombs rigged to blow on signal. He won't give a damn if he loses his army."

"Maybe not. But he'll parlay first. Now listen close. Here's what I want. You two just be hanging around here when he comes in. I'll be back in the next section. You cover him and make him get out of his suit. Make him get out of everything, just in case. You don't know what he might be carrying."

Which was exactly what Mouse and Pollyanna did while Walters watched through the cracked door to the slave section. Stripping with a great show of wounded dignity, Dee kept demanding, "Where's your father?"

Michael had grown gaunt during his sojourn on Blackworld. He had spent so long in-suit that he was emaciated and pale. He shook noticeably. His nerves seemed to have been stretched to their limits.

Cassius watched, and searched his soul. He could find no sympathy for Michael Dee. Dee had made this bed of thorns himself.

He stepped into the command cabin. "Michael, you've got one chance to live out the day."

"Cassius!" Dee was startled and frightened. "How the hell did you get over here? You're supposed to be in the Shadowline." He whirled to face Mouse. "And you're sup-

333

posed to be at the Fortress. What's going on? Where's your father?"

"Tell us about the nuclears you've got planted up there," Cassius suggested. "And I might give you your life."

And immediately Walters found himself fighting an intense desire to kill Dee. Wulf. Helmut. Gneaus. All the others who had died because of this fool. . . . But Storm's ghost whispered to him of his duty to his men, to the thousands still trapped in the Shadowline.

He did not often run on his own emotions. He almost always ran on the feelings and ideals of his dead commander. His own inclination, at that instant, was to let the bombs blow and send the Legion off in one huge, dramatic stroke. It would be like the ancients sending their dead out to sea in a burning ship.

He had very little purpose left in life, he thought. Since leaving the Shadowline he had not looked ahead, beyond surviving long enough to exact revenge. He was no longer a man with tomorrows.

"Tell me about those bombs, Michael. Or I'll kill you now, here."

"You can't." Sly smile. Gneaus wouldn't permit it."

"Oh, my poor foolish friend," Cassius said, wearing his cruelest, most self-satisfied smile. "Have I got news for you. Gneaus Julius Storm died leading a successful assault on Twilight Town. You and yours are all mine now."

Dee became more aguey and pallid. "No! You're lying."

"Sorry, boy. He died at Twilight, along with Helmut, Thurston, Lucifer, and your wife and sons." Metallic chuckle. "It was a classic bloodletting. And now you've got no exits."

Dee fainted.

"The circle closes, Michael," Cassius said when Dee recovered. "The cycle completes itself. The last revenges are in the wind. Then it begins anew." Wearily, Cassius drew the back of his handless wrist across his forehead. "Those were some of your brother's last thoughts."

Mouse picked it up. "A revenge raid on Prefactlas to even scores with the Sangaree, and from the ruins a survivor returned like a phoenix to exact a revenge of his own. Now Cassius is the only survivor of the Prefactlas raiders. And of Deeth's people there's only you."

The word had come, while Michael was unconscious, that Navy had caught up with the remnants of the fleet that had attacked the Fortress. No quarter had been given. None ever was.

Though there was no physical proof, Cassius wanted to believe that the Sangaree Deeth had died there. But there was no justice in this universe. His hope might prove mere wishful thinking.

"You and me, Michael," Cassius said. He laid a gentle hand on Mouse's shoulder. "Then it begins anew, with Gneaus's phoenix."

He was sad for Mouse. The boy was filled with hatred for his father's killers. He had done some tall and frightful promising during Michael's unconsciousness. "Mouse, I wish you wouldn't. I wish you'd just let it be," he said.

A stubborn, angry expression fixed itself on Mouse's face. He shook his head.

"Michael? About the bombs?"

Fifty-Seven: 3032 AD

Deeth waited till the woman was a step away, swinging her knife. He blocked the blow, stepped inside, sank his own blade into her chest. She clawed at his face as she went down.

He stood over her, watching her die. His stroke had been the only one he had struck himself. This was the first death he had dealt personally since he had killed the old man in the cave.

He felt no special satisfaction or joy. He felt almost nothing. The lack surprised him for only an instant. He never had been enthusiastic about fulfilling his father's plans.

What now? The Norbon revenge was nearly complete. The debt was almost paid. The final act, under Michael's direction, was beyond his participation. There was nothing left but to evade the fleet now passing the Fortress, pursuing his raidships.

Nothing remained but the mundanity of Norbon directorship. A huge loathing welled up within him. He never had wanted to be Head. He no longer needed the position's power. And without Rhafu, feeling the way he felt now, he might not be able to hold on.

He stalked through the Fortress of Iron, a thoughtful specter silently prowling a tomb. He paused in Storm's study, slowly poked through his enemy's effects. He began to feel a sense of spiritual kinship, to scent out a kindred loneliness. The man was not entirely alien. He was as much out of tune with humanity as his enemy was with his own people.

He found several undamaged, space-ready singleships on the shiplock level. He considered them. They were slow, but could travel almost indefinitely, seizing their power from the binding energy of the universe itself. A man who had the time could ride one forever.

Deeth summoned his remaining raidmaster, gave him a letter for his cousin Taake. It assigned Taake the duties of Head till his own return. The raidmaster glanced at it. "Where will you be, sir?"

"I'm going to make a pilgrimage."

"Sir?"

Deeth waved him away. "Go. Go on. Get out before they send someone back to check this place out."

Still not sure what he would do, Deeth boarded the ship he had chosen. It was a fat, slow vessel that had done small-time raven work. It carried both medicare cradles and cryobiological storage units. But no instel. Even the Legion had been unable to afford instel for all its ships.

The raidmaster spaced. Deeth spent more hours wandering the ruins of his enemy's home, wondering, at times, if Boris Storm and Thaddeus Walters had done the same after silencing the Norbon station. He finally took space himself, cutting a hyper arc for the center of the galaxy. He had no intention of going that far, only of running along till he had come to some understanding with and of himself.

His course sloped through the Centerward March of Ulant. He dropped hyper long enough to gather news of what had happened on Blackworld.

He could not be sure. It sounded like he had failed.

Without Rhafu there to push him he could not care. It no longer seemed to matter.

He apologized to his father's ghost, set his drives on auto, sealed himself into a cryo storage unit.

Someday the drive would fail and he would fall into normspace. Then he would waken and look out at a whole new universe. . . . Or the ship might plow through the heart of a sun, where the field stresses were so great they would yank the vessel out of hyper. Or. . . .

He did not care.

Staying alive did not much matter either.

Fifty-Eight: 3032 AD

Mouse sat in the crawler operator's seat, watching Cassius and Pollyanna. Polly kept zigging round, unable to stand still. She kept looking at Cassius strangely. And Cassius kept smiling that funny, boyish, embarrassed smile.

Mouse was a little surprised at Walters too. Cassius never thought out loud. Not about the way he felt.

Walters asked Pollyanna, "You know the character in *The Merchant of Venice,* the Jew, who does the soliloquy about his right to hurt like anybody else?"

"Shylock."

"Yeah. Shylock. That's me. I'm like him. I've got a right to be human too. It's just that I'm so old and been in this business so long that I don't show it anymore."

"But that wasn't what Shylock was really talking about. He was just trying to rationalize the revenge he was taking on. . . ." She shut up.

Mouse did not know Shakespeare, but he got the feeling Pollyanna had reached the sudden conclusion that Cassius and this Shylock were alike after all. He lifted a leg onto the control panel, leaned back, chewed the corner of a fingernail. "You're not going to start singing your death song, are you?" he asked Cassius.

"Me? Never. I may not be completely happy with my life, but I sure as hell plan to stick around as long as I can. No, I've been thinking about getting out of the mainstream. If this kind of life has been in it. I might become a crazy old hermit on a mountain somewhere, coming down to prophesy at the villagers once a year. Or run off to the Starfishers. Or become a McGraw or a Freehauler. Anything to get away from the past. I'd just as soon do my fade before Confederation starts investigating the Shadowline, too. I don't have the patience to deal with those people. That's why I left the Corps."

"Somehow," Mouse said, "I can't picture you being anything but what you are. What about those bombs? Wouldn't you say Michael's had enough time to decide?"

Dee, still standing in the middle of the cabin, had not spoken for a long time. Only his eyes had moved, watching every muscle in Cassius, Mouse, and Pollyanna. And the weapon hanging with such apparent negligence in Cassius's hand. "What're you going to do?" he whimpered.

"Now, if it was up to me and I could do what I want," Cassius replied, "I'd kill you. But I won't. Unless you don't start talking about those damned bombs. You've had your time. Talk. And talk straight, because you're going to be out there beside me when we disarm them. How are they armed? How did you plan to set them off?"

The tractor's comm buzzed, demanding attention. "Mouse, get that. Michael, start talking."

"Guarantees, Cassius. I want guarantees," Dee countered. "You don't know what he's like. You don't know what he'll do if I don't set them off."

"Who?" Mouse asked.

Dee ignored him. "He'd destroy the whole universe to get you and the Storms. He's been a raving madman since you killed Rhafu."

"All right, damn it. I'll keep you in my closet if I have to. Just tell me how to get rid of those bombs."

"Your word?"

"What do you want? Me to cut my wrist and write it in blood? You're getting too good a deal now, and you know it."

"They're radio-controlled. My driver has the trigger."

"How long before he pushes the button?"

"He won't. He doesn't know he has it. I screwed up. I was too sure I'd find Gneaus here."

"Ah." Cassius chuckled evilly. "Fooled you."

"You promised."

"Cassius," Mouse said, "here's a little something to brighten your day. Helga's surrendered Festung Todesangst."

"What?" Michael demanded.

"That's the word from Naval Intelligence."

"For God's sake, why?" Dee demanded. "I don't believe it. She would have blown her scuttles. . . ."

"I don't know why," Mouse said. "The report came

from the Corps, filtered through Intelligence. They didn't explain. They just said it was a standoff, with Helga threatening to blow the scuttles and the Marines hanging on but not pushing her so hard she'd really do it. Maybe she got wind of what happened at Twilight and decided it wasn't worth it anymore. She suddenly just gave up."

Michael frowned and shook his head. "What the hell's the matter with her?" he muttered to himself. "The spoiled, self-centered twit. Just because she got what she wanted. We needed. . . ."

Cassius was frowning, too. "It's got to be a trick. She put the bombs on timer or something. Dees are always up to tricks."

"Cassius, they got Benjamin and Homer out. They look like they'll be all right. We'll be able to resurrect them."

"Uhm? Good. Maybe. If she didn't have them programmed, or something. What kind of deal did she make? It can't be anything good for us."

Michael turned on Mouse. The Dee cunning took control of his face. He shook with anticipation, sure his daughter would have made a worthy trade.

Mouse smiled at him. "Nothing. No deal. Just plain surrender. Like she didn't have anything to live for anymore, so she quit."

"But? . . ." Cassius started to ask.

Mouse glanced at Michael, who seemed appalled. "They killed her, Cassius. Beckhart himself shut her support systems down."

"Dead?" Dee asked in an incredibly tiny voice. "My little girl? All my children? You've killed all my babies?" Mouse sat up as a mad light caught fire in his uncle's eyes. "You murderers. My wife. My children. . . ."

"They all got a clean death," Mouse snapped. "Which was damned well better than they deserved. They brought it on themselves."

Cassius took a step toward Dee, staring into his eyes.

340

He spoke slowly, twisting the knife. "He's right. They should have died a thousand deaths each, in fire. And even then they wouldn't have hurt enough to suit me."

Pollyanna screamed. "Mouse!"

Dee plunged forward.

Cassius was not expecting it. He suffered from the life-long misconception that a coward could not act in circumstances where he did not hold the upper hand.

Michael Dee was a coward, but not incapable of acting.

Cassius's instant of delay cost him his life.

Dee knocked the pistol from his hand, caught it in the air, fired one lucky, nose-destroying shot before Mouse slammed into him from the side and sent the weapon skittering across the cabin. Cassius fell disjointedly, slowly, like an empire, almost in pieces, as if different parts of his body were being acted upon by varying gravities. His mechanical voice box made skritching, clacking noises, but no sound that could be interpreted as anger or a cry of agony. He piled up in a heap, twitching, voice box still making those strange noises.

Mouse and Dee thrashed about on the deck, the youth cursing incoherently and weeping while he tried to strangle his uncle.

At first Dee fought in pure panic. He scratched, kicked, bit. Then reason set in. He broke the stranglehold, writhed away, unleashed a kick that hit Mouse over the heart.

Mouse got onto hands and knees. He put all his strength into attaining his feet. The deck rushed toward him instead.

Dee poised for a killing kick to his throat.

"No."

He turned slowly.

Pollyanna held the weapon that had killed Cassius. Her hands shook. The weapon's muzzle waggled uncertainly, but threatened.

"Pollyanna, dear, put it down. I won't hurt you. I don't

want to. Promise. This's between them and me. You're not part of it."

He used his silkiest voice. And he may have meant what he said. He had no real reason to harm her. Not then.

"Stand still," she said as he started toward her, hand reaching for the weapon. She was terrified. This was the moment for which she had been living. This was the instant for which she had put herself through a personal hell. "I am part of it. I owe you, August Plainfield."

Dee's whole face seemed to pucker with consternation.

"You don't even remember, do you? You bloody, cold-hearted snake. You don't even remember the name you used when you murdered my father."

"What on earth are you talking about, child? I've never murdered anyone."

"Liar! You damned liar. I saw you, Mr. August Plainfield of *Stimpson-Hrabosky News*. I was there. You gave him drugs and made him tell you about the Shadowline, and then you murdered him."

Dee went pale. "The little girl at the hospital."

"Yes. The little girl. And now it's your turn."

Dee attacked, diving first to one side, then bearing in.

Had he remained where he was, waiting, Pollyanna might never have pulled the trigger. In the crux, when it came time to take a life in cold blood, she was not as ready as she had thought.

Dee's sudden movement panicked her. She shot wildly, repeatedly. Her first bolt hit the control console. The second pierced Dee's leg. He pitched past her with a shriek of pain and despair. She fired again, wounding him again. Then again. And again.

Groggily, not even quite sure where he was, feeling like someone had tied an anvil to his chest, Mouse again forced himself up off the deck. He shook his head sharply, to clear the water from his eyes and get them into focus.

He saw Pollyanna pounding Dee's ragged, almost unrecognizable corpse with the butt of the spent weapon while babbling incoherencies about Frog. He dragged himself over, took the weapon away, folded her up in his arms and held her head against his chest.

"It's over now, Polly," he murmured. "It's over. It's all over. He's dead now. They're all dead but us." She cried for almost an hour, the hysteria-sobs gradually becoming the great, deep, soul-wrenching grief-sobs, and those eventually diminishing to sniffles, and finally, to nothing but the occasional whimper of an injured animal.

"You just stay here," he whispered when she finished. "I've got work to do. Then we can go away." He rose, went to the comm panel, found a frequency which worked, and resumed command of the Legion.

Fifty-Nine: 3032 AD

In the deep black gulf great engines throbbed. A ship more vast than many planet-bound cities began to move. Her commander ordered maximum tolerable acceleration. She had fallen months behind her sisters.

Clouds of smaller vessels gathered to her. They had finished their part in the Shadowline War. There were no more debts to pay.

The Starfisher decision-makers were saddened because the results had not been more positive. But history, like everything else, is seldom fair. The balance had been rectified, and that was enough.

The great ship fled ever farther into the deep.

Who am I? What am I?

I am the bastard child of the Shadowline. That jagged rift of sun-broiled stone was my third parent. Understand what happened there and you understand me. Stir that hard, infertile soil and you expose the roots of my hatreds.

The Shadowline and four men. Gneaus Julius Storm. Thaddeus Immanuel Walter. Michael Dee. Norbon w'Deeth. Stand me trial for what I am and you had better indict them too.

And that, my friend, is fact.

—Masato Igarashi Storm

Epilogue

HANGED MAN

The Hanged Man represents sacrifice or ordeal. Afterward, though, he may feel his card is really The Fool.

Epilogue: 3052 AD

"That's it?" McClennon asked. Captain McClennon now. Midshipmen Storm and McClennon crewed the winning sunjammer in that long-ago Regatta.

Captain Masato Storm, Confederation Navy (Intelligence), replied, "You asked about the Shadowline and why I hate Sangaree. I told you." The ghosts of earlier days haunted his eyes as he studied the night sky thirty degrees off galactic center. There, in a few thousand years, if anyone were around to see from this vantage point, a bright new star would bloom.

McClennon freshened his drink. "Want to finish this game before Jupp gets here?" He moved to the chess table. Their game had been deadlocked for hours.

"I suppose." Mouse kept staring at the sky. "I can't believe it. I know it happened, but I still can't believe it."

Seldom had McClennon seen Mouse so disconnected. "Cassius and Dee dying might look like the end of it to you. Because they were the last principals. But you weren't

347

really talking about the Legion. Or the Shadowline War. You were explaining the survivors. Especially Mouse."

"Maybe. You're right. Okay. We had to round up Michael's men and defuse those bombs and get our people out of the Shadowline. We did it, with the help from Darkside Landing and The City of Night. . . . Wait a minute. What do you mean, explaining the survivors?"

"Seemed to me you were really explaining Masato Storm."

Mouse's gaze shifted to a section of sky where a new war raged. Humankind and its allies were locked in a ferocious struggle with a nasty enemy.

"You know, my uncle really blew it. He could've gotten away if he'd kept his cool."

"How so?"

"He always had that one more trick up his sleeve. The last one surprised everybody. We never had a hint till we found out we had to storm Edgeward."

"What do you mean?" McClennon asked, just trying to keep Mouse talking. He had worked for the commission investigating the Shadowline war. He knew most of the answers. But his friend needed herding out of the depthless morass of depression.

"That trick of Michael's. He had some minority board members in his pocket. They pulled a coup. It wasn't hard to change their minds, but Michael could've changed his face and disappeared in the confusion."

"Then the commission descended on you."

"Like vultures. Lucky for me, my father, Cassius, and Richard had heavy drag in Luna Command. They didn't hurt us too bad. The holding corporation is still in business."

"What about the girl?"

"Polly? She went back to the Modelmog. Found out she couldn't stand the Shakespeare thing anymore. Changed her name again and went into holodrama. You'd recognize her if you saw her. She's completely different now. Getting something you want bad does that, I guess."

"And the Sangaree? Deeth?"

"Who knows?" Storm left the window long enough to fix himself a drink. "Maybe he died at Helga's World. Maybe during the Fortress attack. Maybe during the chase afterward. Or maybe he got away. Sometimes I think he did."

McClennon finally selected a move. He offered a pawn trade. "Your move. Why's that?"

"The Sangaree fleet the Starfishers engaged at Stars' End. That wasn't just a Family raidfleet. A dozen Families must have gone in on the operation. Which should have meant chaos in the fleet's command structure. But they were damned near as efficient as any human fleet."

"So?"

"So Deeth had a thing about organization and discipline. And he had the willpower and stubbornness and sheer insane vendetta spirit to put a thing like that together. I'm not saying it was him the Fishers fought. I'm just saying that fleet had his feel."

"Then you think you're going around the circle again? That now it's their turn to get revenge?"

"Maybe. There's plenty of them left. If they could find a way to mate off Homeworld. . . ."

"They've always had that, Mouse. Your move." Mouse accepted the pawn trade. "Your uncle Michael was conceived on Prefactlas. And he was no mule. They just need to overcome their prejudices."

Mouse dropped his drink. "Breeding slaves. Why didn't I think of that? I wonder if Beckhart knows?"

"He knows everything. That's his job. Drop him a reminder anyway, if it'll make you feel better."

Mouse snickered wickedly. "For a minute I thought I was unemployed."

"For a while I'd hoped you'd quit. What now?"

"Polly is going to be here next week. Some kind of tour. She's got our kid with her. Maybe we'll skip over to the Fortress and see my brothers."

"You said . . ."

"He didn't destroy it. He just killed everybody. Ben and Homer live there now. Couple of crazy old hermits. They keep the family business rolling. When's Jupp going to get here?"

"Tonight, I hope. What do you think? Should I accept that offer from Ubichi?"

"Resign? Beckhart wouldn't let you. There's a war on, you know."

"Suppose he did?"

"Then walk carefully. Luna Command is watching them. The merc forces are gone. Now they're looking for excuses to break up the company police forces."

"At least the companies are run by honest crooks, not sanctimonious bandits like Admiral Beckhart."

Mouse looked angry. He growled, "We'd better let the game slide. Call me if Jupp turns up." He stalked out of the room.

McClennon turned to stare at the night sky. Mouse conspired in the destruction of an entire Sangaree star system? That was a lot of revenge.

Norbon w'Deeth, are you out there somewhere? Are you polishing your guns, getting ready to come to town? Will the cycle continue round, and never mind the greater, more desperate struggle down toward the galactic core?

"Hate is the worst poison," McClennon muttered. "Mouse, your father was right when he told you to go back to Academy. You should have listened."

MORE GREAT READING FROM WARNER BOOKS

THONGOR AGAINST THE GODS
by Lin Carter (E94-178, $1.75)
At first Thongor's goal seemed simple—to rescue his princess. Soon Thongor finds his mighty sword pitted against the sinister magic of those who serve the Black Gods of Chaos. And the survival of mankind depends upon the outcome.

THONGOR IN THE CITY OF MAGICIANS
by Lin Carter (E94-208, $1.75)
The magician's eyes gleamed as he charged the Council of Nine: "Let us enact upon Thongor the eternal slavery of his soul to Chaos." If the curse is carried out, Thongor's body and soul will suffer throughout eternity. The Magicians of Zaar also plan to conquer Lemuria—and only Thongor and his mighty sword can keep that world free.

THONGOR AT THE END OF TIME
by Lin Carter (E94-332, $1.75)
The stranger throws back his cloak—Mardanax! The Black Magician of Zaar has survived Thongor's destruction of the dread City of Magicians. With a hellish gleam in his emerald eyes, Mardanax strikes Thongor dead, drugs his beautiful Queen into mindless obedience, and kidnaps his son.

BLOODSTONE
by Karl Edward Wagner (E90-139, $1.95)
Kane, the Mystic Swordsman, unearths a dreadful relic of an ancient civilization that will give him dominion over the world.

NIGHT WINDS
by Karl Edward Wagner (E89-597, $1.95)
Kane travels to the ruins of a devastated city peopled only by half-men and the waif they call their queen; to the half-burnt tavern where a woman Kane wronged long ago holds his child in keeping for the Devil.

GREAT SCIENCE FICTION
FROM WARNER...